Simon Raven was born in London in 1927. He was educated at Charterhouse and King's College, Cambridge where he read Classics. After university, he joined the army as a regular officer in the King's Shropshire Light Infantry and saw service in Germany and Kenya where he commanded a Rifle Company. In 1957 he resigned his commission and took up book reviewing. His first novel, *The Feathers of Death*, was published in 1959. Since then he has written many reviews, general essays, plays for radio and television as well as the scripts for a number of successful television series including *Edward and Mrs Simpson* and *Love in a Cold Climate* plus a host of novels. The highly acclaimed ALMS FOR OBLIVION sequence is published by Panther Books in chronological order. The sequence takes its title from a passage in Shakespeare's *Troilus and Cressida*, has been referred to as 'a latter-day Waugh report on another generation of Bright Young Things', and has been compared favourably with the *romans fleuves* of Anthony Powell and C. P. Snow. With the publication in 1984 of *Morning Star* he began a new novel series under the title THE FIRST-BORN OF EGYPT. It is a sequel to ALMS FOR OBLIVION. Simon Raven lives and works in Deal, Kent.

By the same author

Novels

The Feathers of Death
Brother Cain
Doctors Wear Scarlet
The Roses of Picardie
Close of Play
An Inch of Fortune

The ALMS FOR OBLIVION sequence,
in chronological order:

Fielding Gray
Sound the Retreat
The Sabre Squadron
The Rich Pay Late
Friends in Low Places
The Judas Boy
Places Where They Sing
Come Like Shadows
Bring Forth the Body
The Survivors

THE FIRST-BORN OF EGYPT

Morning Star

Belles-Lettres

The English Gentleman
Boys Will Be Boys
The Fortunes of Fingel

Plays

Royal Foundation and Other Plays

Autobiography

Shadows on the Grass

SIMON RAVEN

The Face of
the Waters

The First-born of Egypt: Volume 2

PANTHER
Granada Publishing

Panther Books
Collins Publishing Ltd
8 Grafton Street, London W1X 3LA

Published by Panther Books 1986

First published in Great Britain by
Anthony Blond 1985

Copyright © Simon Raven 1985

ISBN 0-586-06352-8

Printed and bound in Great Britain by
Collins, Glasgow

Set in Times

List of Characters in Order of Appearance

Fielding Gray, a novelist

Jeremy Morrison, an undergraduate of Lancaster College, Cambridge

Brother Piero, a Franciscan Friar

Captain the Most Honourable Marquess Canteloupe of the Aestuary of the Severn

Leonard Percival, his secretary, a Jermy Street man

Balbo Blakeney, art historian, of Lancaster College

The Marchioness Canteloupe (Baby), *née* Llewyllyn; niece to Isobel Stern

Jo-Jo Guiscard, her friend

Gregory Stern, a publisher

Marius Stern, his son

'Glinter' Parkes, headmaster of Oudenarde House

Palairet, a school boy

'Mrs' Maisie Malcolm, Proprietress (with Fielding Gray) of Buttock's Hotel

Teresa (Tessa) Malcolm, her 'niece'

Max de Freville, a sick man

Doctor La Soeur, of La Soeur's Nursing Home

Sir Thomas Llewyllyn, Provost of Lancaster College, father to 'Baby' Canteloupe

Len, his secretary

Ptolemaeos Tunne, an amateur scholar, uncle to Jo-Jo Guiscard

Peter Morrison, MP, Squire of Luffham by Whereham, father to Jeremy

Nicos Pandouros, an undergraduate of Lancaster College, and page to Greco Barraclough after the Maniot custom

Jean-Marie Guiscard, an antiquarian, husband to Jo-Jo

Matron, Sister and Staff Nurse, of La Soeur's Nursing Home

Carmilla Salinger, an undergraduate of Lancaster College

Theodosia Salinger (Thea), an undergraduate of Lancaster College, Carmilla's twin

Rosie Stern, school friend of Tessa Malcolm, and daughter to

Isobel Stern, wife of Gregory Stern, and sister-in-law to Sir Thomas Llewyllyn

Mrs Gurt and Mrs Statch, servants to Ptolemaeos Tunne

Colonel Ivan Blessington, a stockbroker and honest soldier

Ivor Winstanley, Fellow of Lancaster College, a Ciceronian

Ivan 'Greco' Barraclough, Fellow of Lancaster College, an anthropologist

Shamshuddin ⎫
'Artemis'   ⎬ Conspirators
'Pontos'   ⎭

Sir Jacquiz Helmutt, an art baron

Lady Helmutt (Marigold), his wife

Mungo Avallon, Bishop of Glastonbury

PART ONE
Laguna Morta

Dreams out of the ivory gate, and
visions before midnight.

SIR THOMAS BROWNE: *On Dreams*

'Massorbo,' said Fielding Gray: 'a corruption of *Maxima Urbs*, i.e. The Greatest City. You will hardly credit it, but there was a time when this hamlet on an islet was the most powerful and populous community in the whole archipelago.'

The vaporetto throbbed out of the grey lagoon and into a greasy canal. On the left a rank of small, crimson villas straggled along an embankment of mud and yellow reeds, which stood fragile but rigid in the September stillness. On the right a café and a sub-sub-post office stood sponsors, as it were, to a public landing-stage which, agitated by the approach of the vaporetto, seemed to clutch at the jagged quayside for reassurance. The vaporetto closed on and clamped the landing-stage, emitted six passengers and accepted three.

'Massorbo, Massorbo,' shouted a vaguely nautical personage who handled the gang-plank; 'Massorbo e Burano.'

'If you walked down the quay to that church,' said Fielding Gray, 'and walked across a mournful meadow and a crooked bridge, you'd come to Burano.'

'And what,' said Jeremy Morrison, 'would you find there?'

'Some fishermen, closely related, and a kind of dotty, maternal church – once of cathedral status, I rather think – with an Asolano over one of the side altars: a group of succulent juveniles, showing the plague buboes in their groins to a neurotic and gesticulating Virgin.'

Jeremy's large, smooth, round face puckered in annoyance.

'You know how fascinated I am by Asolano,' he said. 'Why didn't we get off and go to see the bloody thing?'

'Patience, sweetheart. The church in Burano closes at noon and won't be open again till four P.M.' Fielding Gray's tight little mouth twisted in anticipation of his next announcement. 'On Torcello the cathedral is open now, exhibiting a very different kind of virgin. A colossal mosaic, universally and icily compassionate. So let us have pain before pleasure, and leave Asolano for the journey home . . . on which, incidentally, the boat stops actually at Burano itself, not two minutes from the masterpiece which you yearn to visit.'

The boat edged past the last of the blind crimson villas and turned left, out of the canal and into a channel, for Torcello.

'*When* was Masorbo so important?' Jeremy asked.

'After Torcello was stripped by ague and malaria. Torcello was the first stop for the fugitives from the mainland. The Roman Empire of the West had collapsed, the Roman Empire of the East had not yet established itself in this area. Along the coast were only the Huns, and anything was better than the Huns, even an island of mud in a sea-marsh.' Fielding Gray paused. The young, he knew, disliked being lectured; but on the whole Jeremy Morrison had shown himself amenable to instruction during their journey, and since this was nearly done, he (Fielding) might surely risk one more brief discourse. After all, his friendship with Jeremy had begun (last summer) at Jeremy's suggestion and on Jeremy's request for information. Worldly information he had wanted then: let him have it (in the form of history) now. 'So they built a cathedral on their mud-bank,' said Fielding, pointing at a bleak, lurching campanile which was now visible over the water, 'to the glory of the God who had saved them from the Huns, and then found, to their gratification, that it was a great attraction to passing ships, the masters of which deduced that where there was such an edifice there might also be harbourage, shelter – and trade. The God of the Cathedral was angry at the consequent shift in priorities, and plagued the people of Torcello with all the fevers of the marsh. So they left his dismal island and went in search of others – Massorbo, Murano, the Rialto – where they prospered, or at least survived in great luxury, for the next thousand years. What is to happen now,' said Fielding, as he crossed the gang-plank on to the territory of Torcello with hesitant middle-aged dread, 'is anybody's guess. Will Venice continue to subsist as a despoiler of tourists who are still so dazzled by her whorish paraphernalia that they empty their whole purses to enjoy a bare pretence of her favours? Or will the old courtesan lose her cunning and pass into the Lazar House . . . like Corinth or Monemvasia?'

'I liked Monemvasia,' Jeremy said. 'It reminded me of those ruined gun-emplacements near your house on the Norfolk coast. Power, crumbling into a heap of nostalgia and broken masonry.'

'You liked Monemvasia,' said Fielding grouchily, 'because Nicos Pandouros was there, showing himself off in his Y-fronts.'

As they walked along the canal that wound through the reeds to the cathedral, Fielding recalled the scene, first silently, to remind himself of the details, then orally, hoping to provoke reaction or comment from Jeremy.

'It was near the first church on the way up to the Castle, in the little courtyard just beyond and above the

11

apse. There was Greco Barraclough poking about and looking silly, when he saw us, because he hadn't kept his promise to meet us at Gythaion – why not, one wonders now? – '

' – *That* I can tell you,' said Jeremy. 'He thinks you're a bad influence, at least potentially, on Nicos.'

'That *I'm* a bad influence on Nicos?'

'Yes. You see, he's quite sharp, is Greco Barraclough. For all that ponderous, prosy talk, he is very quick. And so he has noticed, even though he has seen us together only once before we came out here, that you have, not just a very strong and subtle appeal for me – the charm of the indulgent Mr Worldly Wiseman, who dispenses shrewd advice and pleasurable suggestions – , but also an ability, Fielding, when you are at your best, to bind and persuade and draw me after you, down paths which I should not, of myself, be man enough to tread.

'Now, if you have that effect on me, he tells himself, you may well have it on other young men of my age – and among them his boy, Nicos Pandouros.'

'How do you know all this?'

'Nicos told me, told me on the very occasion which we are now discussing.'

'I see. Or rather, I am beginning to. Let me go back to my reconstruction. There we were in the courtyard, you and I; and the Greco, embarrassed at our appearance, seemed very anxious to send us on our way. "The view from the Castle Platform is magnificent," he said; "but you want to get up there before the charabanc party which is now going round Hagios Andreas." Instead of taking the hint, I asked him why he'd cut our rendezvous in Gythaion; and he said, sorry, they'd had a puncture that day, and if we wanted to look at the view from the Castle Platform without being jostled by prolix tourists we should go *now*. At that very second, just as we were about to move off, Nicos appeared in the doorway of one of those ruined houses, wearing nothing but a pair of brief purple Y-Front pants – hardly even pants, more like a *cache-sex*. At this stage, while you gauped at Nicos as though you would like to lick him all over – '

' – Very lickable he was. Straight, strong and smooth with that organic sheen that poor Greek boys have – and middeclass English boys don't, because they've been given too many baths as children – '

' – While you eyed and ogled – '

' – I did nothing of the kind, Fielding. Nicos is not the sort of chap that allows himself to be eyed and ogled. One look of admiration, then just a friendly "hullo", appropriate on meeting a fellow undergraduate of my College.'

'Your "one look of admiration" was positively operatic. I expected the Greco to hustle Nicos away to safety at once, but all he did was hustle *me* away, right up to that confounded Castle Platform, leaving you alone with the quasi-naked Nicos.'

'He's not afraid of me, you see. First, because he knows that Nicos wouldn't let me touch him, secondly because it wouldn't matter even if he did. That sort of thing is no menace. The Greco wouldn't mind Nicos having a little fun on the side (though on this occasion, I do assure you, there was none); what the Greco fears is that Nicos might be piped away over the hills by somebody of long experience who can play the oldest and most enticing tunes – somebody like you.'

'Why would I want to entice Nicos?'

'Ah. Barraclough is afraid that intentionally or otherwise you might give Nicos a few hints about *how to make himself free*.'

'Make himself free? Is he a slave or something? Jeremy, what can you mean?'

They passed a small bridge with no balustrades. It led across the canal and into a copse of holm-oak. Under the bridge a barge was moored, brown, empty, about ten feet long.

'Il Ponte del Diavolo,' read Jeremy from a notice on the side of the bridge: 'The Devil's Bridge, Fielding. Which leads to the only trees on this beastly island. Perhaps we should cross it?'

'The way to the cathedral is along this path. What do you mean . . . about Barraclough's being afraid I might entice Nicos . . . might give him hints about how to make himself free?'

'He explained it all to me that afternoon in Monemvasia, after Greco Barraclough had marched you off up the hill. He'd had a row with Greco about the kit he was wearing – a light blue sleeveless vest and boxer's shorts. The row had gone drizzling on the whole morning, with Greco saying such a costume was unsuitable for his attendant – '

' – *Attendant?* – '

' – Listen with patience, and all will be made plain. There was the Greco complaining about Nicos' shorts and vest, and there was Nicos saying that they were, after all, on holiday, and there was the Greco saying that was no reason for his attendant to make an exhibition of himself, and the end of it was that Nicos stopped the car – he was driving – while they were on their way through the modern town of Monemvasia, and went into some store, and bought a white shirt and some grey trousers . . . into which he intended to change, in order to put an end to the Greco's grizzling, as soon as opportunity offered. Which it did when they had crossed the causeway

14

into the old town and walked up as far as the little court of ruined houses near the first church. So while the Greco kept "cave" Nicos went into one of the shells of houses to change – and just then we appeared. Nicos saw us through a window, heard the Greco trying to move us on, and being anxious for a spot of company other than the Greco's he came rushing out in his knickers, in order to greet us before we left and make sure of keeping us there. In the event, as you know, he only kept me, and it was then that he did the explaining. First, about how he came to be in his knickers and nothing else, and secondly how it was that the Greco was entitled to boss him about in this annoying fashion.'

They came to a second bridge, and this time crossed the canal, on the other side of which many people were lunching vociferously under trellised vines. Their accents were not of the prettiest.

'Lunch now, or after we've seen the cathedral?' Fielding asked.

'After. Perhaps this appalling crew will be gone by then.'

'Come, come, Jeremy. They're only harmless tourists who've come here on the Harry's Bar boat.'

'Why couldn't the bloody thing sink? I tell you, Fielding, the more I see of the human race the more I loathe it.'

'This is hardly,' said Fielding, peering with his single eye, 'a typical cross-section.'

'Typically loathsome.'

'I dare say they don't much care for you and me either. Go on about Nicos and Greco.'

As they began to cross a tiny meadow, Jeremy said:

'Nicos was an orphan in the Mani. When he was sixteen he was taken on by Greco Barraclough, who was at that time living and researching in Vatheia, not far from Areopolis, where Nicos had been brought up by a set of poor cousins who shared him round between them. Barraclough liked the idea of an attendant and had heard of Nicos as a prospect – his parents had been educated people, far superior to the cousins – , so he went to see him and found him only too eager to get quit of his life in Areopolis. After a lot of Greek chin-thrusting, it was eventually agreed that the Greco should adopt Nicos in the local manner . . . which meant paying off the cousins, who were just beginning to get a bit of value out of Nicos as a labourer on their wretched bits of land, and swearing an oath to protect, educate and support him until he was twenty-five years of age. Nicos, for his part, had to swear to serve, honour and obey Barraclough for the same period. He became, in effect, his "squire-cum-body-servant".'

They walked along a dank and gritty narthex and came to a man who was selling tickets by the south door of the cathedral.

'Five hundred lire . . . to enter a sacred building?' Jeremy said.

'I'm not sure it hasn't been de-consecrated. Worth every penny in any case. I suppose all went well with Nicos and Greco until they came to England. Then Nicos found out that "serve, honour and obey" weren't fashionable words any more?'

'Right. When the Greco was made Fellow of Lancaster, he brought Nicos with him and persuaded Sir Thomas Llewyllyn, as Provost, to give Nicos a place as an undergraduate.'

'The more fool Tom.'

'So it turned out. The Greco's demands on Nicos' time and energy prevented Nicos from doing his work properly or making friends of his own age. His existence was barely known about – outside a small circle of dons who were friends of the Greco. Nicos began to make noises, he said: couldn't the *Kyrios* Barraclough moderate his requirements and give Nicos more time to himself? No, the *Kyrios* Barraclough could not. He reminded Nicos very sharply of the oath he had sworn – a serious matter in the Mani – and also reminded him that it was only because of his influence with Tom that Nicos had a place at Lancaster at all, a place in which he was maintained by Barraclough's money.'

They walked past the slender columns of the roodscreen and stood under the Bishop's crude throne, looking at the Virgin above it, who wept her one huge tear.

'So far,' said Jeremy, 'Barraclough is winning on points. But he thinks that you are just the sort of person who might interest yourself in the matter and pipe a ditty to lead Nicos a dance away from his master.'

'Then he's wrong. What should I have to do with penniless foreigners?'

'Major Gray,' said a small voice. 'Fielding Gray, Fielding.'

Jeremy and Fielding turned sharply. A slight figure in the Franciscan habit stood between them and the roodscreen. Below the skirt of his habit his legs were bare; one foot was sandalled, the other encased in a bulky surgical boot.

'Major Gray. Fielding.'

A small voice from the past. It entreated him to know its owner and his name. Come now . . . A tower in a Venetian garden and a pretty Sicilian face, with a smile like Lazarus risen.

'Oh, Piero,' he said. And then, stupidly, 'What are you doing here?'

'I am still living where you last saw me, at our Convent on the Island of San Francesco del Deserto. I have come to Torcello to collect a wounded sea-gull, and take it back for my brothers' care. I have only minutes to spare, Major Gray, for if the tide is too low I cannot reach our landing-stage, and if I wait for the next tide they will punish me. So come with me, please, to my barge: I have so much to ask you. And perhaps you will introduce me to your friend?'

'This is Jeremy Morrison. And his, Jeremy, is Brother Piero . . . or have they given you another name?'

'Piero still serves.'

He turned his face up to look at Jeremy's, placed his hands together, and bowed.

'You are so pale, Piero,' Fielding said.

'The air in the Lagoon is not healthy. The food is sparse. Come.'

Outside the south door Piero picked up a cage in which was a small yellow sea-gull. It flapped its left wing against the bars. The right wing hung limp, at an evil angle. A squeal came from a broken beak.

'It is horrible,' Piero said. 'Follow, please. My barge is by the Devil's Bridge. Tell me, tell me first of Lykiado-poulos. I dreamed that he was dead, here in Venice.'

'Your dream did not lie.'

'A good, kind man, for all his jealousy. And Miss Baby, Miss Baby Llewyllyn?'

'Married. To Lord Canteloupe, whom you will also remember. They have,' said Fielding grimly, 'a son.'

'And you, Fielding?'

'I do not complain.'

'And Tom Llewyllyn?'

'Tom is distinguished. Provost of his College.'

18

'Ah. The Lancaster College of Cambridge. I remember.' Piero nodded in confirmation of his own remark and hobbled faster in front of them. The monk's tonsure was absurd, obscene, in his curly black hair.

'Tom did not like me,' Piero said. 'He suffered me for Daniel's sake.'

'Tom came to know your worth.'

Piero turned interrogatively.

'We all did.'

'Piero the whore,' said Piero: 'Lykiadopoulos' whore. Piero the monk, watching the grave of his friend on an island drowned in fog. And yet there are good days, Fielding, Jeremy, days when I can see the mountains with their snow, blue days and clear, and the birds chatter in the cages which my brothers have made for them.'

They all came to the Devil's Bridge.

'For nearly five years I have watched by Daniel's grave . . . when they find no other task for me. They are not hard men, you understand, but there is a discipline to be followed. And the food is so wretched. And the days, especially in the fog, the days are so long, Fielding, Jeremy. I must not call you "Jeremy". I have hardly met you. I am not of your world.'

'Piero,' Jeremy said.

'Nor of yours and more,' Piero said to Fielding. 'I must go now.' He lowered the cage into the brown barge under the bridge and prepared to follow it.

'Piero,' Fielding said.

'Stay,' said Jeremy. 'A gift for the good brothers.'

From where Fielding stood it seemed a very large gift: a thick wodge of 10,000 lire notes. As Piero took it, Jeremy leaned forward and whispered into Piero's ear, so close that he might have been kissing it. For a short while Piero listened; then he shook his head and moved it bleakly away from Jeremy's and then, deliberately keeping his face turned away from both Jeremy and Fielding, he climbed down into the barge, his surgical boot hitting the bottom with a bang that echoed under the Devil's Bridge.

'Piero,' said Jeremy. 'Say something, if only goodbye.'

But Piero huddled over the engine and pulled the starting cord.

'Piero,' said Fielding.

For the second time the engine failed to start. And the third. Piero picked up an oar from the bottom of the barge, and stood.

'Piero,' called Jeremy and Fielding.

'Please. Go now,' said Piero, keeping his back to them. He began to row in the style of a gondolier. 'You see,' he called, still without turning, 'there are useful things which my brothers have taught me, they have taught me to row in the old manner. Besides,' he called, 'I have made a promise, when I first came to them. A promise to Daniel too.'

Jeremy and Fielding started to walk along the path by the canal, behind Piero's barge and towards the Lagoon.

'Do not follow me,' called Piero, sensing though not seeing what they did. 'Please do not follow me, Fielding, Jeremy, as I call you for the last time. Go to your luncheon under the vine trellises with good people from Harry's Bar.'

Under the vine trellises Fielding, at Jeremy's request, told him about Piero.

'Venice,' he said: 'autumn, 1973. A very odd season. Some of us were here for a PEN Conference. There was also a Greek called Lykiadopoulos . . . *not* here for the PEN Conference, but to run a Baccarat Bank at the Winter Casino. Somewhere or other he had picked up Piero, a lame Sicilian boy, who at that time, though he was officially supposed to be seventeen and occasionally looked it, can hardly have seen his fifteenth summer.'

'Younger and younger these pick-ups are getting. Was Piero born lame?'

'No. There'd been a street accident when he was a child in Syracuse. Of course his foot had been badly treated and often gave him great pain . . . which I suppose was what made him look much older some of the time. You saw how . . . shrivelled . . . he looked today.'

'But not aged. A bit peaky but still . . . fetching. And how did you and your friends get in on all this back in 1973?'

'Lykiadopoulos had a business partner called Max de Freville – '

' – Ah. The skeleton at the feast. The one who stood as godfather, with you, to Canteloupe's son, Sarum.'

'Right. Max was an old and very close friend of Canteloupe, who, being then as now a publisher, was attending the PEN jamboree as an interested spectator. Someone spotted Max and Lyki and Piero getting out of a gondola at the water entrance of a potty Palazzo which they'd hired, and we were all introduced there by Canteloupe.'

'And then you all started lusting after pretty Piero, who fled for his life to a monastery?'

'No one did any lusting. Lykiadopoulos would not allow lust, not even between Piero and himself. The name of the game that autumn was strictly chastity. All round.'

'Something must have been afoot, or you wouldn't be putting that special dramatic face on.'

'Have you ever heard,' said Fielding with reluctance, 'of Daniel Mond?'

'I've heard him mentioned. Dim mathematician. Fellow of Lancaster. Now dead.'

'He died in Venice. That autumn. That winter. Tom Llewyllyn was with him to take care of him. They lived in a little casino, a specially furnished summer-house, in the garden of Lyki's and Max's Palazzo. Canteloupe arranged that. Piero used to come from the Palazzo to see them, though Lykiadopoulos didn't like his going and Tom Llewyllyn didn't like his coming.'

'Yes. Piero said as much just now.'

'But Daniel Mond liked it. He and Piero went on little trips . . . as long as Danny was strong enough. When Danny died Piero arranged for him to be buried on the Island of San Francesco del Deserto, and entered himself as a Friar in the Convent there.'

'There has to be more to it than that.'

'There was. I can't explain it all . . . beyond saying that Piero loved Daniel in some extraordinary way. And vice versa.'

Fielding appeared to think that that was now that and

22

all was one for it, but Jeremy tried a little marginal persistence.

'I noticed,' Jeremy said, 'that Piero asked after Miss Baby Llewyllyn.'

'Yes. At the beginning Baby was there with Tom for a holiday before going back to school. Canteloupe escorted her home, as I remember.'

'So,' said Jeremy, 'some went home and others stayed: one died and another entered a convent where the body was buried. There must have been, I repeat, a great deal more to it.'

Fielding shrugged, put his hand through his hair and sighed from his twisted mouth.

'I'm not one,' said Jeremy, 'to stick my nose in where it isn't wanted. Let the dead bury their dead. But an inoffensive question about the living suggests itself: surely, Fielding, the Franciscans are a mendicant order? They're meant to move about, not hang around on islands, as Piero has for the last five years.'

'I dare say that's all changed. Anyhow, that convent is for training novices and housing the old and ill.'

'And just which is Piero? If he joined in 1973 he can hardly still be a novice.'

'Perhaps . . . they keep him there because of his poor foot. In any case, he joined on special terms – Lykiadopoulos put up some money. Perhaps they respect his wish to stay near Daniel's grave.'

'He seems to think that he's now done a long enough stint, to judge from his remarks this morning. He seemed altogether restless, wouldn't you say?'

'I really didn't notice,' said Fielding, who had in fact been deeply moved by the encounter but now wished, once and for all, to forget it. 'As I told you in the cathedral just before he made himself known, it is not my habit to concern myself with penniless foreigners.'

As the boat carried them from the landing-stage on Torcello to the little harbour in Burano, Jeremy Morrison thought about two things. First of all he thought about Piero; but this thought he speedily dismissed, telling himself, with the plain good sense of his kind, that he had done what he had done and that the result would be what it would be. Since what he had done was to give Piero nearly £100-worth of lire, his mind, forbidden to dwell uselessly on Piero, at once turned to money.

Of this he had plenty, if he cashed the sterling which he had brought as a reserve, to see him back to England, even though Fielding planned to take a good week in crossing France and was not attracted to cheap hotels. Since car, petrol and meals taken outside hotels (in practice almost all meals) were paid for by Fielding under the heading of travelling expenses, Jeremy would not be strapped for cash to pay for his nightly beds, however luxurious these might turn out to be. The trouble, he told himself, would come when he arrived home. True, he could spend the few remaining days of his vacation in some comfort in the family house at Luffham by Whereham, and true again that by the time he returned to Lancaster College his quarterly allowance of £750 would have been paid into his banking account and would be, for once in a way, unencumbered. The fact remained that all other resources, in June still very substantial, had now been dissipated, and that £750 was not going to support him, in the manner to which he was beginning to become accustomed, until the end of December. Even if he stayed in his rooms and minded his books during the Term, there would come a problem of how to amuse himself, after the obligatory Christmas at home with his father, over the New Year. Plans were already making, among his acquaintance, for ski-ing parties or cultural excursions at that time, and the one thing about which all such arrangements were exigent (particularly the cultural ones, it seemed) was the absolute need for grim deposits in ready money . . . 'Pretty soon, Jeremy dear, like November one latest. And don't forget you'll need a nice fat packet in your pocket – there are several interesting restaurants with two and three rosettes in Michelin which we all want to try . . .'

All in all, thought Jeremy, a studious but civilized term, followed by a suitable and reviving holiday, would require (even if the holiday were followed in its turn by a period of Lenten meanness) a good £1,000 over and above what he was going to get. So where to apply for *that*? His father? 'Dread Sire, today at Ascot I' – no, never, not on that pretext or any other. Fielding? Too early in their friendship; besides, for all Fielding's apparently effortless expenditure on this present tour, he had begun to exhibit, when getting out his Credit Cards, a sort of arithmetical expression about the mouth which indicated that he too was going home to problems, was not looking forward to the day on which the American Express account would come in. No: not Fielding; not yet. Well then: his friends at Lancaster, the two Salinger girls? They must be vastly rich now that their father had croaked. The trouble was, he, Jeremy, had tapped Theodosia for a pretty shrewd sum in April and had much offended Carmilla a few weeks later. So his stock in that quarter was low. Perhaps he could pay back the one (in *very* small part, as a gesture) and make it up with the other, and then marry whichever would have him? A bore, being married, of course, so the thing to do was to goad his bride into divorce as quickly as possible, and then claim half the loot. That was the way of it, he'd heard these days. Fantasy, idle fantasy, first things first, and the first thing was to raise £1,000, so that there need be no more worry or annoyance for the time being, by (say) the twenty-fifth of October. What about Len? Len would half die of laughter while refusing . . . though at the same time he might have some useful suggestions, one of which would almost certainly be Ptolemaeos Tunne. *Yes*: Ptolemaeos Tunne in his house in the fens; Jeremy might well be able, as indeed he had been able before, to make himself very useful in that region . . . in which case, a modest request, tactfully preferred . . .

'Just over there,' said Fielding's voice.

They disembarked, walked across a small campo, and entered the church of San Martino by the west door.

'Third altar on the right,' Fielding said.

Jeremy, who had been looking forward to a collection of fresh young thighs (plague buboes and all) was annoyed to find a blank frame in the middle of which an ill written notice proclaimed that Asolano's Ragazzi della Peste was 'In Restauro'.

'Which means,' said Fielding savagely, 'that the brutes will keep it about ten years.'

'Ten years?'

'Yes. They put them in a special warehouse to await restoration, then run out of money and can't employ any restorers or even heat the warehouse, so that when they do get money again (ours or the Americans'), the pictures have deteriorated still more and cost three times what they should to repair – if, that is, the cash hasn't been embezzled by some big-mouthed blue chin in the Belli Arti or the Government, and so good night.'

'In short,' said Jeremy with relish, 'the Italians aren't fit to have care of their own inheritance.'

'Nor are the Greeks. Look at that stupid bitch of an actress who's agitating for the return of the Elgin Marbles. If they go back to Athens, they'll simply be allowed to rot to pieces in the polluted air like the Acropolis they first came from.'

Both of them felt better after this bout of misoxeny and better still when they found the boat hadn't yet left the harbour and they need not wait there an hour for the next. As they cruised up the channel from Burano, the clouds to the north cleared and gave them sight of the ranks of white-helmed Dolomites; and a light breeze rose and flickered in the reeds along the mud-banks.

'Dinner at the Antico Martini,' Fielding said, and at once wished to retract the offer: too late.

The Antico Martini provided delicious food and a suggestive cabaret. The evening would cost Fielding not far off a hundred pounds, adding grievously to his Diners' Club Account (for Diners, he had decided, should bear the evening's cost) on which he already owed over £2,000. To pay this account and all the others on which he had drawn during this gyro with Jeremy, he must sell shares worth up to £5,000, when he got home, not indeed the last he had but not so very far from it. For months, as disappointment succeeded disappointment (film deals cancelled at the eleventh hour, options taken out and never paid for) he had been living off fat, telling himself that *something* must sooner or later go right, as always in the past something had. Most things went wrong; one

27

accepted that: something, just occasionally, went right; one depended on that, depended, lately, in vain. Five thousand pounds' worth of bank shares must go, which left seven (at best) in property and oils. The house at Broughton Staithe, never much more than a sea-side shack, had been so neglected (since Harriet left) that it was almost worthless . . . as, in practice, was Buttock's Hotel.

Fielding owned half of this establishment, his friend, 'Mrs' Maisie Malcolm, the other half. Unless Maisie agreed to sell, the thing was unsellable; and Maisie would not agree to sell as long as the place was 'home' to fourteen year old Teresa (Tessa) Malcolm, officially Maisie's niece and ward but in truth, as Fielding knew, her daughter. Even if Maisie agreed to sell, they were forbidden, by the terms of the will of the late owner, Mrs Buttock, from selling to property developers who might pull the place down, and if they could not sell to them, then to whom?

No; it was not a time to be taking people to the Antico Martini; but then how could one stop? If one was used to the Antico Martini, then one continued, as a matter of course, to go there; one could not economize, or not in this area; it made one feel silly.

Years ago, Fielding remembered, on finding that he would have to stay in Venice for longer than he had expected, he had moved out of the Gritti to a marginally humbler establishment, remarking as he did so that his middle-class sense of propriety made him feel uncomfortable in the Gritti (as he would in the Ritz in Paris or the Connaught in London) except for very short visits: it was simply not fitting that he, being who and what he was, should live there for weeks on end, even when he could afford it. He still felt this: he could still very easily eschew the Gritti Palace because it was intended for someone else, it was intended for a certain set of people which did not include Fielding Gray. But the Antico Martini was another matter. *This* was intended to provide food and drink and diversion of the kind to which he had been accustomed for the last thirty years and more, ever since he was first commissioned as Cornet in Hamilton's Regiment of Horse. He could not give up the Antico Martini when in Venice any more than he could give up, when in England, his Club or his annual badge at Goodwood or his seat in the Pavilion at Lord's; occasional evenings at the Antico Martini and places comparable were part of the package which he had earned for himself and proposed to keep. The Antico Martini was something . . . well . . . something to which he was entitled. Of course he had been right to tell Jeremy that they were going there that evening for dinner, and go they would. There was plenty of money to settle the Diners' Club Account and the rest . . . this time, at any rate, and something must surely go right before the next.

'Success?' said Lord Canteloupe to his private secretary, Leonard Percival.

'Success,' said Percival, lowering the tip of his convex nose as if he intended to insert it in the cleft of his chin. 'They like the one which I showed them. They are waiting for your good self to bring the rest and strike the price.'

Lord Canteloupe paced with military demeanour to the window of his study and looked out, over a meadow with a copse of lady-birch at its centre, past a river which wound through a parade of bat-willows, and on to the damp flats which marched from Wiltshire into Somerset.

'I'm not a good salesman,' he said at last, swivelling the top half of his gangling body towards Percival, then executing an elegant about turn with his feet and legs – Cavalry fashion, as though wearing spurs. 'Can't you go again?'

'When these kind of goods are in question, they like to deal with the owner in person, particularly if he is entitled. They like to talk on and in their own terms to an aristocrat, and to observe his well-bred embarrassment at the questionable nature of the commodity for sale.'

'A real aristocrat,' said Canteloupe, 'shows embarrassment at nothing.'

'That might amuse them even more.'

'I am not a real aristocrat, only a very weedy imitation. I should just flop about and giggle and make a muddle of the whole thing. Please go for me, Leonard.'

'They have absolutely asked for you. If you dislike the notion, Detterling, I suggest you simply abandon the whole thing.'

Leonard Percival always called Canteloupe 'Detterling', the name by which he and everyone else had known him before he inherited his Marquessate.

'I very much want to go ahead.'

'Why? You can't need the money.'

'I do. For private purposes. You forget, Leonard: although my house is one of the most successful "stately homes" in the tourist business, I cannot touch the income – or only a tiny fraction – for my personal use. I have a private scheme on hand, for which I need to sell the Canzonis.'

Leonard Percival, close as he was to his employer, sensed that further enquiry would be unwelcome.

'Very well, Detterling. If you want to go ahead you must go to California. Here is the number which you must telephone when you reach Los Angeles. You will then be told what to do. I will reserve a first class passage for you by TWA tomorrow.'

'The day after. I have to go to Sandwich tomorrow, and then pay a visit in London.'

'The day after tomorrow, then. I shall meet you at the airport. My presence there to see you off will ensure that you will be untroubled by Customs men on your way out.'

'Useful, knowing an ex-Secret Service man.'

'A Jermyn Street man is the proper expression. No "ex" about it. Once a Jermyn Street man always a Jermyn Street man, even when retired with ulcers.'

'Anyhow, useful. Thank you, Leonard.'

'My pleasure, Detterling. As for your entry into the United States, I cannot, of course, give a one hundred per cent guarantee. But I think you will find that your hosts – though they will not make themselves personally apparent to you until you have telephoned that number – will have arranged that everything should be as comfortable as possible.'

'Anything I should know about the pictures? Useful patter? Balbo, you speak.'

A bald, bent, shabby little gnome of a man scuffled out of a corner where he had been examining a set of twelve watercolours, unframed but handsomely mounted and protected by transparent covers, all of them fifteen inches by nine.

'Set of thirteen,' said the gnome in a gentle tenor, 'twelve here and one which Percival took to California as

31

a sample. Just to remind you: the inspiration of the series was a picture by Asolano in the church of San Martino in Burano – a crowd of boys showing their plague buboes to the Virgin. The eldest son of the first Lord Canteloupe, while on his travels incognito, saw the possibilities here and commissioned the Venetian Canzoni to paint some watercolours, the first of which should be a copy of Asolano's original, while the rest should develop the full physical and emotional potentialities of the situation, stage by stage, with Mary Magdalene, Martha and others effectively intervening as the affair rises to a climax. The paintings were sent home in the diplomatic bag from the British Chancery in Venice only a matter of weeks before Napoleon got there and the young nobleman who commissioned them was murdered, in the general confusion, by unidentified enemies.'

'Thank you, Balbo. All very clear.'

'One more thing, Canteloupe. I am told, by Jacquiz Helmutt and other friends in the art world, that the original Asolano has recently been removed from its place in the church at Burano, the official reason given being "restoration". But since some that have seen it during the last year vouch for its near perfect condition, there must be something suspicious in its removal. It is at least possible that somebody – God knows who, perhaps the parish authorities in Burano or some ecclesiastical fund-raiser from Venice or even Rome – anyhow that *somebody*, Canteloupe, may be selling the thing under cover, possibly to America, possibly to the very Americans with whom you are to deal. This, of course, would add considerably to the value of your paintings, for a number of obvious reasons. So let *them* know, in a friendly way, that *you* know of the Asolano's removal from Burano and of the possibility that there is more behind this than needless restorations. Then they'll deduce that you are well up in such matters and not to be trifled with.'

'I very much doubt whether I shall carry it off,' said Canteloupe, 'but thank you, old friend, for the hint. I'm away to London this evening as tomorrow is a long day out, but do stay here as long as you'd like to. Leonard will see that you are entertained.'

'Thank you, Canteloupe, but I'll go back to Lancaster tomorrow, I think. Leonard's entertainments, excellent as they are, cannot disguise or mitigate the fact that there is a very pregnant young woman in your house. As you know, I dislike any notion of fertility in animal species. So revolting. Not aesthetically, of course, for many artists have presented the condition very attractively in terms of line and draperies, but *biologically*. As a former biochemist, you see I know all too clearly the horrors that are hidden by those draperies. If only mammals could be as seemly in reproduction as plants or the lesser invertebrates.'

'Point taken, Balbo,' said Canteloupe with a shift of his eye towards the window. 'I suggest that you and Leonard dine à deux in this evening, away from the females.'

'So Balbo Blakeney will be off tomorrow,' said Canteloupe to his wife, Baby.

'Good. Horrible old thing.' Baby stretched her long, strong thighs in their green corduroy, pouted at them with wet lips, then grinned complacently at Canteloupe. 'Horrible old thing,' she repeated.

'Time was,' said Canteloupe, with something of the Private Tutor in his voice, 'when the girls – *a* girl anyway – very much liked him. And he's been very useful, in one way and another – to me and my cousin before me. So wave him a nice good-bye as he goes. That's all I ask.'

'I'll do my best, my lord,' said Baby meekly, curling the fingers of her right hand into her groin.

'That's my girl. Now: I shall be gone anything up to a fortnight. Will Jo-Jo have had that baby of hers by the time I get back? And what are she and Jean-Marie going to do about a house? As far as I'm concerned they can stay here for ever – one remembers the huge contribution Jo-Jo makes to household expenses – but don't you think they might prefer a place of their own? After all, Jean Marie has finished revising his book, and Jo-Jo has finished translating it into English, so really they've not got so much else on that they couldn't start house-hunting.'

'Except, Canty, that Jo-Jo has still to have the baby?'

'Of course. I meant, after that.'

'We'd better see how it goes, sweetheart. There is one rather alarming thing, you see.'

'Surely it's the right way up and all that?'

'Oh yes. But there is a problem. Don't you worry, darling. You leave it to me and Jean-Marie, and go happily off on your jaunt to America.'

'Sandwich first. Marius.'

'Oh yes?' said Baby Canteloupe vaguely. 'Give him my love, of course.'

'Then La Soeur's Nursing Home tomorrow evening. Max.'

'What shall you find?'

'I shall see, shan't I?'

'And then this mysterious trip to Hollywood. Oh Canty you haven't fallen in love with a film star?'

She beckoned him to sit beside her in the double armchair which she had had built especially for her boudoir, and started to stroke the creditable remnants of his grey hair.

'No film stars, thank you. Just a spot of business over there. Money. If you're a good Baby, Canty may bring you back a nice presy.'

'Oh, Canty darling, whatever will it be?'

'I can't tell you now,' said Canteloupe, 'in case it all falls through. But I rather think it will surprise you.'

'Oh goodie, goodie. Baby does love a surprise,' she said, as she placed her head against his waistcoat and began their customary ritual of farewell.

Late in the afternoon, after her husband had left, Baby Canteloupe went to find her friend, Jo-Jo Guiscard, who was resting in a deck-chair by a small pool in the middle of a grove of lady-birch, which they kept private to themselves, in a meadow in the home park.

'This September feels particularly autumnal,' Jo-Jo said. 'Sometimes the summer lingers till October . . . but not this year.'

'It's not cold,' said Baby: 'there's still plenty of sun. It's nice enough for you to sit here.'

'Only because I'm kept warm by memories of these last months,' said Jo-Jo, 'all our talks and backgammon and you reading to me from Mrs Gaskell and Rosamond Lehmann. All over now. "Farewell, summer; summer, farewell."'

Jo-Jo sat up on the edge of her chair and straddled in her shorts like an ill conditioned boy on a circus bench.

'You shouldn't sing that song,' Baby said. 'They say it's unlucky.'

'Who's singing? I am just regretting the end of a season, the season of my pregnancy. Because I have a feeling,' Jo-Jo said, framing her butch little face with her palms, 'that Alexandre will be on his way very soon now. So have we anything to discuss first?'

'Yes,' said Baby: 'suppose Alexandre turns out to have a slit?'

Jo-Jo gave Baby a sharp, street Arab's grin, and said nothing.

'Suppose,' Baby insisted, 'that Alexandre turns out to be a girl?'

'Why bring that up now? You've gone along with me all through the summer. It will be a boy, we've said: to be called Alexandre, after Paris of Troy.'

'Does it matter so much? You can always have more. Jean-Marie will be happy either way.'

'I shan't. I want a boy, a red-faced, bawling, imperious boy, with a cute little prick that goes stiff when I play with it. That makes them love you. That's why Italian boys all adore their mothers – because they play with their little prickles to keep 'em happy.'

'And just look at the results.'

'Don't you ever play with Sarum? In his bath?'

'I don't often see him in his bath. That's what I pay his nurse for.'

'Then what about when you feed him?'

'I can't say it's occurred to me. Anyway, you're generally there.'

'I shouldn't mind. I'd like it. I might even masturbate.'

'What a very peculiar mood you're in.'

'Why don't you play with Sarum? Someone's got to wash him and dry him there anyway, so what's the difference? That's the excuse all mothers make: "I was only washing him." I'm just being honest when I say I shall do it deliberately.'

'And how long shall you go on?' said Baby in a sympathetic tone, knowing that one must humour pre-natal fantasies or obsessions. 'I mean, till he's five . . . eight . . . eleven?'

'For as long as he seems to enjoy it. I'll tell you another thing,' Jo-Jo said. 'Uncle Ptoly told me. Most healthy boys, he said, when they get to be about fourteen or fifteen, they want to fuck their mothers.'

'Jésu-Maria,' Baby said, but just managed to hang on to her aplomb. 'And are you going to let Alexandre fuck you?'

'Oh, good. At last I've shocked you. Despite that carefully patronizing tone of yours, I know I've shocked you. Am I going to let Alexandre fuck me? Well, I might. If he's attractive and shows that he'd like to . . . in a nice kind of way. They say that all boys should be taught to do it by an older woman, at about that age, so why not by their mothers? Who could be better qualified? Common sense, darling; plain common sense. I can't see what all the fuss is about.'

Gregory Stern, his son, Marius, and Lord Canteloupe stood together by Canteloupe's magenta Mercedes in the drive of Oudenarde House Preparatory School in Sandwich. Glinter Parkes, the Headmaster, had told them to stand there for at least forty minutes in order that parents coming to deliver their sons for the Michaelmas Term that autumn afternoon should see that Marius Stern, who had been under a huge cloud and might have had to leave the school for ever, even now enjoyed the company and glad countenance of Captain the Most Honourable Marquess Canteloupe of the Aestuary of the Severn, and was therefore fit to be received back into any society whatever, no matter how he might have erred heretofore.

'I think that's a bit much, Glinter,' Canteloupe had complained, 'sticking us on a dreary piquet.' And then, taking Glinter on one side, 'That boy's been keeping an absolutely straight bat since they had him circumcised. You've nothing to worry about now.'

'That's all very well,' said Glinter, 'but the parents don't know that.'

'*You* agreed that Marius could come back for his last year here if Gregory paid for your new indoor rifle range. That ought to be enough. You can't go imposing extra conditions now.'

'Indulge me, Canteloupe,' Glinter had said: 'just hang about with Marius and his father for forty minutes or so in this very agreeable sun. After all, Marius did nearly kill young Palairet last term, and the parents and the boys need reassuring. *They* don't know about his operation, nor, if they did, would they understand what difference it can have made. I'm not sure I do myself. But everything will be as right as the Royal Enclosure if they see *you* standing there with your arm round his neck.'

And of course Glinter, who was not in the prepper game for winkles, was absolutely right. One rather common mother got so over-excited that she curtsied. Walter (Wally) St George, an assistant master at Oudenarde, nearly bust his gut with pride when Canteloupe (having met him before, at the time of Marius's deepest disgrace) shook hands with him and called him 'St George' without prefixing the middle class 'Mister'. A number of old cricketing acquaintances, who had come with their grandsons, rumbled with pleasure when Canteloupe waved to them and wheeled Marius up for a word.

'This is Marius Stern,' Canteloupe would say, 'my old friend Gregory's boy.' And to Marius, 'This is "Gin-Sling" Carhart-Harris, who downed ten Tom Collins in five minutes and then hit the ball clean over the Pavilion at Bangalore – and won a bet for a monkey.'

'How do you do, sir,' Marius would say, giving a smile at once manly and flirtatious. 'Where did you keep the monkey afterwards?'

'Haw, haw, young 'un. A monkey means five hundred quid.'

And Marius, who knew this perfectly well as his mother used that kind of slang, would be led on to 'Whiffy' Cave-Browne, while 'Gin-Sling' Carhart-Harris said to his daughter, his son-in-law and his three grandsons, 'By Jove, what a fine little chap'; and the son-in-law said, 'But isn't his father a Jew?'; and Gin-Sling riposted, 'Eton and the Brigade. Poor chap can't help the other thing. Anyway if Canteloupe likes the boy, the boy's all right. I remember when Canteloupe – "Detterling" we called him then – used to cut the ball later than any man in England.' And the daughter might say, greatly daring, 'But didn't that little boy hit another little boy very nastily last summer?' Whereupon all the males present, from Gin-Sling down to the tiniest grandson, said, 'Of course there's going to be some scraps at a proper school with proper fellows in it' and laughed at the poor silly bitch until she retired to the car in tears, and from that day to this has never presumed to open her mouth at a school function.

All ways round, then, Canteloupe's tour of duty in the drive was a huge success. Indeed, by the end of it almost everyone present had agreed that Palairet was privileged ever to have been struck by such a one as Marius, nor would Palairet himself have dissented.

'Stern,' he called across the drive as soon as he was out of his parents' car, 'Marius Stern', and ran across and stood with him, side by side. 'I'm glad you came back,' he said, moving his head just enough to see Marius's face. 'I'll say good-bye to my people and then we can have a game of pingers.'

So Palairet said good-bye to his people and Marius to his – Canteloupe having tipped him a gold sovereign (which Leonard Percival had dug up), largesse which was lordly without being offensive, as the equivalent in paper money would have been – and the two boys went off to play pingers.

'Cut,' said Glinter, coming up to Gregory and Canteloupe, who climbed into the magenta Mercedes and were driven away within seconds.

'So,' said Fielding Gray at Liverpool Street Station, 'I'll come and see you at Lancaster next term.'

Their journey together was over and Fielding was seeing Jeremy off home.

'Early next term, Fielding.'

'If you like. Good. More trips, like we've just had, later on . . . do you think?'

'I do think,'

'Right. So now . . . go well, Jeremy Morrison, go well to Luffham.'

'Stay well, Fielding Gray; and stay with God.'

When they were tired of playing ping-pong, Marius and Palairet went for a walk round the cricket ground in the last of the autumn evening.

'No cricket for eight months now. Pity,' said Palairet, a slight frown on his plain, amiable, rather crumpled face. 'Soccer's a rotten game. I wish we played Rugger this term as well as next.'

'There'll be Fives and Squash. I wish we had a Racquets Court,' Marius said. 'Someone took me to watch Racquets last hols. At the Queen's Club. Super game. Fast.'

'Who took you?' asked Palairet, suddenly jealous that

41

he himself had not been of the party, though he had spent an entirely happy holiday in Somerset and Biarritz.

'My father's friend, Major Gray. As a treat after my operation.'

'Your . . . oh, I see,' said Palairet, who did see quite a lot, in a very general way, and also, being a boy of rare courtesy, realized that the fact of Marius' operation, though not its nature (whatever that might have been), required recognition. 'A bit of a celebration,' Palairet said, 'because they'd let you out okay.'

'That's it.'

'Major Gray. Fielding Gray. My mother says his books are "pure filth", but I know my father reads them. He has them in a drawer in his desk. What's he like to go out with – Major Gray?'

'Quite interesting. On the way to Queen's he told me all about a journey he was going to go on – in Italy and Greece. I thought he would probably be fun to go with, except that he does . . . well . . . look you up and down a bit.'

'Lots of them do that when they get old. They don't often mean any harm. They just . . . like looking . . . that's all. You see that seat up there, Stern?'

Palairet pointed to a wooden bench at the top of the bank which surrounded most of the cricket ground.

'It's funny about that,' Palairet went on. 'It only came last term, just before – just before you went away. Things like that usually come in the holidays, not in the middle of term.'

'Well, let's go and look at it.'

The bench was facing away from the cricket ground and over a canal which was on the other side of the bank.

'I say,' said Marius; 'look who gave it. Jeremy Morrison, it says.'

'Who's he?'

'Old Boy of Oudenarde. A . . . a friend of mine. During the hols.'

'Last hols?' said Palairet, jealous, once more, at his own exclusion.

Marius nodded. 'We had great fun,' he said, 'games of cricket in the garden and a marvellous afternoon at Newmarket Races. I won nearly ten pounds.' He grinned, then shook his head. 'But I don't care about him so much now,' he said, 'not now that I'm back here.'

'You mustn't just drop him, you know,' said Palairet anxiously, jealousy assuaged and decency aroused, 'even if the hols are over now.'

'Oh, I know that. But I don't suppose,' said Marius, 'that I shall be seeing him much any more.'

'What I want to know,' said Canteloupe as the Mercedes cruised towards London up the M2, 'both as your friend and your partner, Gregory, is how long you are going to keep up your anti-Jewish campaign . . . how long you are going to go on writing those inflammatory anti-Jewish articles which only a Jew could get away with?'

'I am anti-Israel, not anti-Jewish,' said Gregory, fingering the buttons all down the front of his Guards' Blazer and then along the sleeves.

'Forgive me, my dear Gregory, but it would take something of an expert to tell the difference.'

'So what is this to you, Canteloupe?'

'There is beginning to be what Lady Bracknell called

43

"comment on the platform". One such article as you have written for the *Scrutator* might proceed from whim or irritation, and a second might have been mere carelessness – an almost unconscious repetition of the first – ; but a third and a fourth, Gregory, require explanation.'

'Very well. You remember that Isobel and I went astray on our travels last summer?'

'I remember vividly, as I was landed with the problem of your son.'

'And very sensibly you handled it,' said Gregory reluctantly. 'But the point is . . . that Isobel and I were detained by certain people, somewhere in what used to be called the Levant, until I gave my promise that I would write such essays as I am writing now – and then follow them up with a whole book on the subject. If I break my word, something similar will happen again – something similar to, but much nastier than, what happened last June. Even as it is, I must submit, later this autumn, to meeting these people and being taken somewhere secret while they examine my notes and hear about my preparations for the book.'

'Which will be saying . . . what?'

'That the Jews have no moral or historical right to Israel; and that their behaviour, both before and since they re-occupied the country, has been greedy, treacherous and cruel – to say the very least of it.'

'Will your heart be in this book?'

'It must be. The safety of my wife and children may depend on it.'

'But can you contemplate your thesis with pleasure?'

'If not with pleasure, then with less distaste than you might think. The Jews' claim to Israel has always been questionable: unfortunately, at the very time when it should have been most closely questioned, the whole world was blinded by pity and guilt because of the way the Jews had suffered in the thirties and forties.'

'And the other accusations – greed and treachery and the rest?'

'My dear Canteloupe, the human race, taken as a whole, is ignorant, arrogant and envious; overseeing and vengeful in victory, snivelling, deceitful and whorish in defeat. The Jews are part of the human race, therefore the Jews share these characteristics. A simple syllogism.'

'I can see that you can make a convincing case, and very possibly a best-selling case, in general terms. But what happens when you come, as come you must being a just and intelligent man, to the individual exceptions to this rule? They are, after all, many and honourable, be they gentile or Jew.'

'The people with whom I have to deal, Canteloupe, do not think in such terms. To them, their side is noble and righteous, while the Jews are in every way vile and hideous – with no exceptions. They will hear of no just men in Sodom. Their intention is to procure from a Jew – from me – a one hundred per cent excoriation of Jewry.'

'Silly of them. They would have a much better case if only they would not be extreme. As it is, Gregory, if you write this book to their exact specification as you have just described it, then it will not be, cannot be, the sort of book that a respectable firm, like our own Stern & Detterling, could even begin to consider publishing. Is that not so, my dear?'

Gregory's head sank between his shoulders.

'Not if the author himself paid for publication?'

'Not even then. It is a question, as you well know, Gregory, of decency. Such a book would not be *decent*.'

'I, as senior partner, must determine that.

'You know as well as I do that it is improper for a publisher to publish himself.'

'You know as well as I do that it has been done,' said Gregory. '*And* by a senior partner.'

'You would not, I think, wish to find yourself the only partner?'

Silently and without moving a muscle of his face, Gregory began to weep. Tears welled from unblinking eyes, rolled down fleshy cheeks, and plunged, from his still elegant chin, on to the collar and lapels of his Guards' Blazer.

At last:

'Help me, Detterling,' he said.

'I cannot. But I know someone who might be able to. For some years I have had a personal Secretary – and a friend – called Leonard Percival.'

'I have met him with you.'

'He is formerly of Jermyn Street, or just "of Jermyn Street", as he prefers to put it. Is the phrase familiar to you?'

Gregory shook his head. Canteloupe began to explain.

When Fielding Gray had driven himself from Liverpool Street to his London quarters in Buttock's Hotel, he examined the mail which had come in during his month of absence. Although some letters might have gone to his sea-side house in Broughton Staithe on the Norfolk coast, almost all interesting or urgent items would have come to Buttock's.

An envelope from his agent, of the kind used when advising that he had received money on Fielding's behalf and passed it on to his bank (less ten per cent), looked quite promising. It contained the news that the VAT due on his earnings, for the quarter June/August, 1978, had been duly paid into his account: all £17.83 of it.

A letter from his accountant looked as disagreeable as such letters always did, the address having been typed in Stygian black and the envelope having the texture of burnt, soggy toast. However, he told himself, he must grasp the nettle – and for all the determination with which he did so, he was staggered by the sting. His accountant informed him that the Inland Revenue, having called for figures from his agent and his publisher (both being Stern & Detterling, though in different departments, as the firm both published and represented him), had calculated that during the last three years he had under-declared his gross earned income in the sums (respectively) of £8,146.32, £13,045.1, and £517.24. His comment was invited.

A knock on the door. Maisie Malcolm came in.

'They said you was back when I came in, dear. Glad to be home? Tessa and I have got up a special little welcome home dinner.'

'Home', he thought, that word twice in the same speech: of course she'll never agree to sell the place.

'How kind,' he said, and meant it.

'You don't look very well, dear. I said you should never have gone off with that Jeremy Morrison.'

'It's the Tax people, Maisie. They've suddenly said that I've been short-changing them for the last three years, that I've been concealing thousands of pounds of my income.'

'Don't worry about them, dear. Just take nine months

47

to answer, then pretend you've gone to Tibet. I had a client once who used to send all Government envelopes back where they came from with "MISSING, BELIEVED DEAD" written by his name.'

'What happened to him?'

'He set fire to himself smoking in bed. He was only twenty-six.'

'There you are, you see. God is not mocked, Maisie, neither is the Tax Man. Besides, if I tried anything on like that my accountant would refuse to act for me.'

'Sod him, lovey.'

'It'd be sod me. The Inland Revenue always do you down in the end, unless you have an accountant, and often even then.'

'So tell this dozy bugger of yours to pull his knickers up and start earning his living. And for God's sake take that dismal look off your face. Tessa's friend Rosie is coming to the welcome-home dinner, and I don't want my girls sitting down to table with a gargoyle.'

'I thought it was just you and me and Tessa. Family. Why's Rosie coming?'

'Rosie Stern's pretty well family too, these days. All that business about Rosie's brother, Marius – it's just made Tessa and Rosie closer than ever . . . Besides, duck, it's not just a welcome-home dinner, it's an end of holidays dinner. The girls go back on Monday.'

'But since they are both day girls, I can't think that it makes much difference.'

'Oh, it's not so much that they're going back to school. How shall I say it? It's all to do with something I read in one of Tessa's poetry books – how did it go? – "Goodbye, summer; summer, goodbye . . ."'

'*Farewell*, summer, Maisie, if I'm not mistaken. Either

48

way, I now recognize the nature of the occasion and shall try to honour it.'

'That's my good boy.'

The telephone rang on the table by Fielding's bed. He crossed from his desk to answer it.

'Fielding?' said Tom Llewyllyn's voice.

'Yes, Tom?'

'I've got a Franciscan here with a club foot. He says he's Piero – you remember, Venice in seventy-three . . . ?'

'I remember.'

'He says he's hitch-hiked from that island he went to – how does one hitch-hike from an island?'

'By boat, I presume – the first stage anyhow.'

'He says that Daniel is at peace but he isn't, and he wants to be with Daniel's friends. What shall I do?'

'Cherish him.'

'What?'

'Be kind to him, Tom. He's come a very long way. I'll come down tomorrow, and we'll discuss it all with him.' So much, he thought, for his policy of ignoring 'penniless foreigners'. 'Did he say that he'd met Jeremy Morrison and me on Torcello?'

'No.'

'That's because he thinks you're unsympathetic. You're not fully in his confidence.'

'Thank you very much. Then why did he come here?'

'Because yours is the only address he knows – the Lancaster College of Cambridge, as he calls it. What does Len say?'

'Len says he's adorable,' said Tom crossly, 'and means nothing but trouble. Out with him, Len says: out with him tomorrow, or we'll have another Nicos Pandouros on our hands.'

'Come to that, I should think Piero would make an altogether admirable undergraduate . . . once you gave him something decent to wear instead of that pitiful habit. He's only about twenty even now, you know.'

'I do know,' said Tom. There was a brief pause, then, 'Beware of pity,' Tom said. 'See you tomorrow about noon.'

Canteloupe looked down at Max de Freville, who lay on his back, rigidly at attention, under coverings that might have been the carved draperies on a tomb.

'Max,' said Canteloupe. 'Max. It's Canteloupe. Detterling.'

He was totally ignored.

'Since his eyes are open,' said Canteloupe to Doctor La Soeur, 'he must be awake.'

'That doesn't necessarily follow. Or again, he could be awake, but not to you.'

'Then to what?'

'Despair,' said Doctor La Soeur. 'I've tried several treatments to snap him out of this, drugs and shocks of one kind and another. Sometimes I've got him muttering. It seems that he had just one thing left that he believed in, that made him want to go on breathing. His mistress is dead, his partner is dead, but he had just this one thing going for him – or rather two: an old friend, and the friend's son. You want me to go on?'

'If you please.'

'Something he has seen or imagined he has seen in the

50

son has made him mad. First it made him violent, then reduced him to total inertia, as you see. Despair.'

'My son,' said Canteloupe. 'Sarum, I mean. That is, Tullius.'

'I know.'

'He seemed to like him when he first saw him, at his Christening. Then he came to see him down in Wiltshire a couple of months later, and said . . . said that he had funny eyes. He ran straight out of my place and got a lift in the dairy truck to the station at Warminster. Apparently he kept babbling about Sarum . . . that is, Tullius . . . the whole way, so the dairyman put two and two together and told me about it later. We had to send his luggage on. And then, a few days afterwards, they rang me up from his club – also one of mine – and said he was breaking the place up. The rest you know.'

'What sort of things did he say when he was babbling in the dairy truck?'

'He was still on about Tully's eyes. He said they were a whore's eyes – as if one could possibly tell in a child of that age. He said they were the eyes of a boy we all once knew, in Venice years ago, called Piero, who was the kept boy of Max's partner, one Lykiadopoulos. Oddly enough my wife says that Tullius' eyes *are* like Piero's, though I can't see it myself. Anyway, what difference would it make? Piero was a perfectly decent lad who was making his way as best he could . . . very polite, as I remember, and highly intelligent. Or perhaps "quick" would be a better word. He did have rather a creepy smile – perhaps that was what Max was thinking of in some curious way. But what had any of that to do with little Tullius? Do you suppose he's listening to all this?' asked Canteloupe, nodding down at Max de Freville.

'No. He's ceased to care.'

51

'But why?'

'Some people do. It simply means they've gone on long enough. They just can't be bothered any more; they can't see any possible point. That could be what we have here – a terminal sense of futility apparently brought on by disappointment in your son – '

' – Tullius. But that's ridiculous. How could anyone be disappointed in a child of that age . . . unless it were a monster?'

'Perhaps, Canteloupe, Max saw something in – or near – your son – '

' – Tullius – '

' – Which reminded him, in a purely subjective way, nothing to do with the boy himself, that is, but by some obscure process of association . . . reminded him of some person or occurrence the memory of which reduced him to despair . . . something or somebody of which he hadn't thought of for many years, perhaps, but which now rose up to make him wish he were dead. If he were predisposed for that kind of thing to happen, then almost anything could have set him off – the shape or colour of the pram, the tilt of the nurse's nose, or a chance smell in the room – '

' – It happened in the rose garden – '

' – A chance smell of roses . . . or grass. Anything.'

'Then why, if it was really something else that upset him, was he carrying on about Sarum – Tullius – all the way to the station – *and*, they say, when he went berserk in the Club?'

'I simply don't know, Canteloupe,' said Doctor La Soeur; 'and if he keeps it up like this, none of us ever will.'

'Now let's get this straight,' said Fielding Gray to Piero:
'I saw Jeremy Morrison give you a lot of money on
Torcello; did you use it to come to England?'

Fielding Gray, Brother Piero (still in his habit, sandal
and surgical boot), Sir Thomas Llewyllyn (Provost of
Lancaster College, Cambridge), and the Secretary to the
Provost, commonly called Len, were all in the morning
room of the Provost's Lodging.

'No,' said Piero. "A gift for the good brothers," Mr
Morrison said. My brothers. So that's where his money
went – into our communal chest.'

'But he whispered to you, after he gave you the money.'

'Yes. He asked me to smile. I hadn't yet smiled, not
since we met, he said: please would I smile as I said
goodbye.'

'And as both Tom and I remember,' said Fielding,
'you prefer not to smile?'

'I used to smile all day long when I was a child in
Syracuse. A beggar's smile. Then one day somebody
pushed me aside, and I was still smiling as my foot went
under the iron wheel of the refuse cart. You understand?'

'So you turned away from us – on Torcello, I mean –
to excuse yourself from smiling and in the pretence that
you must attend urgently to the boat.'

'I suppose so. I should have smiled for Jeremy – for
both of you – if I could.'

'But in none of this,' said Tom Llewyllyn, 'was there

53

any indication that Morrison was hoping or suggesting that you should come to England?'

'No. But I think, all the same, that he may be pleased to see me. Others too. Anyhow, I could stay no longer with my brothers. Some of them stink. Others bully me . . . sometimes try to touch me with their grey hands. They are good men, really, who will cure the sea-bird I was collecting for them from Torcello, if it is to be cured. But they are old and bored and they have seen through God. Men say that to lead the religious life one should be free from the distractions of the world. But if there are no distractions, if one is left alone with God all day long, as we were on that island, then one very soon realizes how cruel and monstrous he is, how much misery and horror he has to answer for. Which of us has asked – would ever have asked – to live this life of pain? How *dare* God make such a life possible – and threaten to damn us if we seek solace from it in sin? That is the sort of thing which one asks if one is long alone with Him. So either one comes to hate Him, or, better perhaps, one ceases to believe in Him. Either way that island is a bad place to be and my brothers, though good men in themselves, are bad men to be with.'

'Yet you left Jeremy's money with them?' said Len.

'My honour told me so.'

'Then how did you manage the journey?'

Piero looked at Len, then at Tom and Fielding, then back to Len, then once more at Tom and Fielding.

'Both of you I know,' he said to Tom and Fielding, 'but this man, not. Is he your friend?'

'Yes.'

'Then I shall tell you how I managed the journey. Once a whore,' said Piero, 'always a whore. This habit

54

helped, and in some cases my foot. There are people who hanker for such things.'

The door opened without a knock. Eighteen stones' worth of Ptolemaeos Tunne moved in.

'My word,' he said to Piero: 'what a little beauty you are. That tonsure has made my day.' And to Tom: 'I came to ask your permission to take Chromios Iason's *De Animis Animalium* from the special section of the college library. I will leave Hermes Chrysorrapis' *De Aquis Reducendi* as a hostage. A fair exchange, I think. Chrysorrapis will teach you how to distil liquors to revive the dead, while the volume which I shall be taking is merely an elementary dissertation on the psychology of brute beasts.'

'And very misleading,' Piero added. 'We had it in my monastery to help us treat the animals. Chromios Iason, though an observant man, was without love. Therefore he totally misunderstood the sounds and movements with which animals seek to indicate their needs to us and to each other. The whimpering of a hungry dog he interprets as adoration of its master, and so on and so forth.'

'Ah,' said Ptolemaeos, 'a man of learning, come from one cloister to visit fellow scholars in another.' He bowed to Piero. '*Salve, eruditissime doctor*,' he said: 'what is the news from our brothers in Palermo?'

'My cloister is in Venezia, *egregi domine*.'

'But you yourself – you are from Sicilia – *non è vero*?'

'*Si. Ma da Siracusa.*'

'Ah. I should have realized. A boy of your age from Palermo would long since have gone right off – hairy legs, blue chin, a sort of distortion between the nostrils and the corners of the mouth, to say nothing of other indigenous deformities, result of a low strain, much inter-married. But you . . . you are a typical open-bred Syracusan – product of strong and various outside strains which came early and lingered long. Achaean, Dorian, Vandal, Jute, Norman . . . they all flocked through Syracuse . . . to say nothing of the German and later the British occupation during the second World War. You owe your looks to the brutal and licentious soldiery down the millennia, you cute little mongrel, you. What are you doing here – in that ridiculous outfit?'

'I have left my convent in the Laguna Morta to come back to my friends.'

'But you went into that convent to get away from us,' said Tom: 'you wanted to leave the world and all that therein is.'

'I have explained,' said Piero patiently: 'it is not possible to live in isolation with God. Had I stayed, I should have become like those whom I left behind – a skilful maker of splints and special cages for maimed birds, growing old at thirty on a diet of muttered liturgy and rank vegetables.'

'So you've come to knock on the gilded gate of Lancaster College,' said Ptolemaeos, looking at Tom and Len, 'and to ask for admission to the enchanted garden. House and garden full, dear boy. These aren't the old days, when only gentlemen or scholars were allowed in and there'd be plenty of room left over for a promising number like you on sheer curiosity value: these days they pack the place with any old rubbish years in advance in case the equality artists at Westminster go into a tantrum and confiscate all their lovely lolly.'

'At least, Ptoly,' said Tom, 'I found room for Nicos Pandouros. It wasn't easy – and the less easy as he was sponsored by a Fellow of the College. You know the sort of Council I have to deal with. If they had their way they'd fill the College with Borstal boys.'

'The fact remains,' said Ptolemaeos, 'that you, as

56

Provost, retain an absolute right to nominate whom you please to places in this College.'

'In theory,' Tom shuddered. 'If I exercise my right,' he said, 'the left wing of the Council nearly tears my cassock off . . . particularly if my nominee has had a relative in Lancaster or a public school education.'

'Our friend here has had neither.'

'I am not asking to be nominated to anything,' Piero said, 'but merely to meet some old friends again – the only friends I ever really had since I was first taken from Sicily – and find out if there is any place for me among them. And there is one new friend, or may be – '

' – If you mean Jeremy Morrison,' said Fielding, 'remember that Cambridge is a very long way from Torcello. Now he's back here again, Jeremy will have other things to do than pursue a chance acquaintance with you.'

'Ah, take heed,' said Ptolemaeos Tunne to Piero. 'Fielding Gray thinks you're just a common gate-crasher, another bloody time-wasting nuisance.'

'I've come all the way from London – '

'To keep your conscience in good nick. You'll sail smoothly with Tom and Len through all the arguments for turning this little wretch into the street, and then glide off home, congratulating yourself on having played a compassionate but practical part in the dialogue – and never caring that the answer was a small, sour lemon for Brother – Brother what's your name?' he barked at Piero.

'Piero.'

'That can't be all.' Piero shrugged. 'What does it say on your passport?' Ptolemaeos asked.

'They took that from me when I came to the Convent. With my watch and my fountain pen.'

'Well then, Piero . . . how did you get into France and England?'

'There was a bus load of English pilgrims who were coming home from Monte Gargano. One of them was ill and had been left behind in a hospital, and the priest in charge had forgotten to leave his passport behind with him. On condition that I made myself useful, he let me take the sick man's place in the charabanc and ride in it to England. With parties like that the men at the borders just count the heads then the passports to make sure there is the same number of both, and the same at Dover. Or so it happened this time. So there was no difficulty.'

Ptolemaeos chuckled.

'I suppose not. One dear little Friar in the Padré Pio party – what could be more natural? But tell me did the nice kind priest let you keep the extra passport?'

'No. It had to be sent back to Italy, for the man that was ill.'

'So it will be an interesting problem fitting you up with an identity,' Ptolemaeos said: 'it's always been an ambition of mine – to find an officially non-existing person and construct a new identity for him; so if you've got nothing better to do – and you haven't – you'll come along with me. My name is Ptolemaeos Tunne,' he said: 'I am an old member of this College and a most respectable person, as all the gentlemen present will vouch. I live in an ample house in the middle of the Fens. Although they are not far from here, they sometimes seem lonely to the uninitiated; but since we both know Jeremy Morrison we can ask him to come and see us – at the risk of incurring Major Gray's displeasure – and as time goes on we can invite all the rest of your English friends . . . who will be rather proud when they hear,' said Ptolemaeos, taking Piero's left hand in his, 'what you have been through in order to see them again. And so now, Provost Llewyllyn,' he said to Sir Thomas, 'you may care to consider this young gentleman's future while I take care of his present. Here is Hermes Chrysorrapis: Piero and I will collect Chromios Iason on our way out, if you will have the goodness to telephone the Librarian and warn him that we shall be passing.'

'I'm glad to have this chance to talk to you,' Peter Morrison said to his son, Jeremy. 'In fact I came here with that in mind. It occurred to me that you might find it convenient to spend a few days here before returning to Cambridge, after your costly foreign travels.'

They were sitting in the dining room in the Manor House at Luffham by Whereham. Peter Morrison was at the head of the table, under a portrait of his father: Jeremy was sitting some way down on his father's right, opposite a portrait of his dead mother, Helen. The Chamberlain of the Household (as he liked to be called) took post, when not actually serving, beneath the portrait of Helen, as neither Peter nor Jeremy was comfortable with a servant at his back.

'It wasn't all that expensive,' said Jeremy defensively; 'Major Gray paid for the car and so on.'

'You know, of all my friends,' said Peter Morrison, 'I think the very last one I should have chosen as a companion for you would have been Fielding Gray.'

'He speaks of you with great affection, father.'

'And I think of him with great affection. Nevertheless,

he is the last man whom I would wish you to have as a friend. Why not someone of your own age?'

'So insipid, most of them.'

'I thought you had two particular girl friends at Lancaster – Donald Salinger's daughters.'

Jeremy did not say that when his father had last seen him with the Salinger twins, on an occasion in Lancaster, he had shown clear signs, not of approval, but of being bitterly peeved and jealous at the favour which Jeremy enjoyed in that quarter. He merely remarked:

'I saw a lot of them at the beginning of the vacation. One needs a rest from people, you know. Anyway, they had to accompany their father to America – and then take care of everything when he died.'

'They must be immensely rich.'

'Where did the money come from?' Jeremy asked, very much wanting to know.

'Donald inherited a lot from his parents, a little in land, most of it money in the funds. He used it well. He made a fortune by providing an accurate printing service, which started with commercial rubbish (as his partner at that time was a cheapjack) but ultimately included almost every language and script in the civilized world, as well as all major mathematical and scientific notations . . . and this at a time when the printing trade was rapidly going downhill. He then founded several technical magazines which, because of the reliability of their matter and presentation, were in heavy demand all over the world, particularly behind the Iron Curtain, and so attracted a large volume of highly paid advertising. In the end, he could afford to distribute the magazines without charge, so high were his revenues from advertisements . . . which, in consequence of the free and thus ever wider distribution, became even higher.'

'And when did the bubble burst?'

'When many of the products advertised proved worthless and went unpaid for. If you sell a large quantity of tractors to China, you're going to find it hard enough to get paid, in any currency worth having, at the best of times. If the tractors start falling apart and you have neglected to ensure a proper supply of spare parts, then you are not going to get paid at all . . . or certainly not more than once. Donald, being the man he was, had foreseen all that. He sold up his magazines at their peak period, in 1964, just before the introduction of Capital Gains Tax. The printing firm he kept – and gave sound and honourable service to the new owners of the magazines which he had sold, until one by one they went bankrupt, Donald having carefully discounted the money they owed him in all his calculations. He was left with a printing firm of huge prestige – which from then on handled works of science and learning only, Donald's hobby, you might say, and still a very profitable one; and he was also left with an enormous sum in ready money which was most prudently laid out and invested.'

'After which,' said Jeremy with zest, 'he had a series of ulcers and allergies and mental breakdowns, and got no joy of any of it. And now he is dead. Carmilla once told me that for the last ten years or so the only pleasure he ever had was from occasional days at Lord's . . . the only place, she said, in which he was at peace. I asked why he didn't go there more often – after all, he must have been his own boss – and do you know what she said?'

'No,' said Peter, rather huffily, for this had started as his story, not Jeremy's.

'She said, father, that he had an old fashioned Yorkshire conscience about attendance at his place of business, he liked to keep the same hours as his employees . . .

61

and when, eventually, his doctor *ordered* him to take more time off and go to Lord's, his wife, knowing how much he loved it, spoilt it all for him by ringing up every half hour with fake messages about her own health, and having him called to the telephone over the loud-speaker.'

'I'm told,' said Peter, 'that they're very reluctant to page anyone on that loud-speaker – that they soon spot trouble-makers and ignore them.'

'That's what I said to Carmilla. She said that her mother – adoptive mother – was the most poisonous and persistent woman in England, more than a match for the officials at Lord's. It's a wonder, if you come to think of it, father, how jolly those two girls have grown up.'

'And prodigiously rich with it,' his father said. 'Why don't you marry one of them?'

'A very good idea, gentlemen,' said the Chamberlain. 'There is nothing like pounds sterling, Master Jeremy, to enhance and support strawberry leaves.'

'Strawberry leaves, Chamberlain?'

'I have been advising your father for some time, Master Jeremy, that he should procure entrance to the Upper House by accepting a peerage as Earl or Marquess.'

'Oh, I see . . .'

'I think, Chamberlain,' said Peter, 'that you may place the decanters and withdraw. I wish to discuss your advice with my son.'

'Indeed, sir . . . So good-night to you, gentlemen both, and God bless you.'

'God bless you, Chamberlain . . .'

'When he came from Canteloupe,' said Peter after the Chamberlain had gone, 'Canteloupe swore that he had never touched a drop of drink from the day he had first known him as a recruit in Hamilton's Horse. He became

Canteloupe's servant at some stage in Egypt; went every-where with him – you could still arrange that kind of thing in those days, at any rate in a proper regiment – came out of the Army when Canteloupe sent his papers in, still being, if we're to believe Canteloupe, an absolute teetotaller and never left Canteloupe, not even for a holiday, until the day he came here to take care of your brother. It was thought, you see, that since they were both going mad and knew each other well from Canteloupe's frequent visits down here, they might provide good com-pany for each other.'

'And so they did, father.'

'Yes. Only of course Nicholas was being destroyed by some virus in the brain, whereas the Chamberlain was merely going mildly potty. Why did I start all this? Ah, I know; potty the Chamberlain may be, Jeremy; but this idea of his that I could be ennobled at will sometimes makes me think, despite all Canteloupe's oaths about his abstinence, that he must be drunk as well. He gets oddly *unctuous* when he talks of it, and unctuousness is the brand of drunken servants.'

'His idea isn't all that odd, father: you could have a Life Barony for the asking tomorrow – whichever party were in power.'

'Possibly. But not the Earldom or the Marquessate which the Chamberlain suggests.'

'Pure affection on his part. Affection for the family and a mistaken idea of its grandeur.'

'Ah,' said Peter, passing the port; 'but in one respect he is not mistaken. Never mind that rubbish about straw-berry leaves; what he was quick to see was that a fortune like that which would come with one of the Salinger girls could do great things for the estate. Modernization, enlargement, security – '

'I see, sir,' said Jeremy, who often called his father 'sir' in bad moments, being off and on a reader of Trollope: 'you would like me to marry one of those girls and devote her money and my energies to improving and increasing the estate?'

'Yes. I can think of few more satisfactory occupations.'

Jeremy downed his glass for strength and poured another.

'I can, sir,' Jeremy said.

'What, for example?'

'Almost anything. Why should I sit here in the Norfolk mud for the rest of my life, doing what bores me stiff? What bores you stiff too, father, and don't try to deny it. Fielding Gray says you loved this land when you were a boy, but gradually politics and power and the rest took over, and so now you want to sling the whole bloody albatross round my neck, to leave yourself free for your nasty game in Westminster.'

'The estate would descend to you at my death in any case,' Peter said. 'Sooner or later you will be responsible for it. Best accept that with a good grace.'

'That's what Fielding Gray says.'

'I'm much obliged to Major Gray. It's only common sense; accept the responsibility, then make proper arrangements, a process which some Salinger money would certainly facilitate. That done, you need not trouble to spend too much time here . . . three months a year would probably be enough.'

'Oh no, they wouldn't be,' said Jeremy fiercely. 'If a man once takes on this sort of thing, then he must do it with his might – Chamberlains, tenants, turnips, cows and curates, milkmaids seduced and made pregnant by the factor, the village idiot and the village cricket team, the whole ridiculous rural lot. He has to care, sir. You have got away with not caring, first because people remember that once you did care, and secondly because since then you have been in Parliament – have even been in the Government – which just makes your position respectable . . . that of the landed magnate who is slightly negligent because he has higher duties. But if I am to do this thing, I must do it fully and honourably; and I'm telling you flat, sir, I don't want to do it at all. Surely . . . there are some cousins somewhere who could have it – cousins on my mother's side.'

'Oh yes,' said Peter; 'but they'd have to have all the money too, wouldn't they? They might even start asking for some sort of guarantee immediately, which would mean that there'd be none for you, not even enough to keep you at Cambridge.' He stood up and came to attention. Jeremy did the same. 'Good-night, my dear boy,' Peter said. 'Tomorrow I leave for London, very early, so I shall not see you. Enjoy yourself here until you go back to Cambridge, where you should make my best compliments to my old friend, your Provost. As for this evening's discussion, we shall talk of these matters again at our meeting here for Christmas, when I shall hope to find you more inclined to make the very easy compromises which must be effected to ensure the future welfare of the estate . . . and of yourself. Good-night to you: make free with the decanter: and tomorrow, Jeremy, when I am gone, stay well and stay with God.'

It was just as well that Jeremy Morrison, despite his father's encouragement, contemplated no immediate courtship of the Salinger girls, either one. On the day he returned to Lancaster he saw them as they were walking together in the Great Court; he waved and hurried to meet them, only to find that as he came near to them they simply moved apart from each other by a couple of yards and marched firmly past on either side while he went lurching through the gap.

'What on earth can I have done to them?' he later and rather disingenuously said to Len, who combined his rôle as Provost's Secretary with that of College confessor, know-all and fix-it.

'You've upset them both by sleeping with that little Marius Stern.'

'But there was nothing wrong in that, Len. Ptoly Tunne as good as ordered me to. It was to stop his being frightened in the night.'

'Nevertheless, the Salinger sisters don't think men of twenty ought to share their beds with boys of twelve. Silly, isn't it? And then I suspect, Jeremy baby, though I can't actually prove, that you've been putting your hot little handies in their money box.'

'In Theodosia's money box.'

'In Theodosia's money box – and in Carmilla's honey pot. So now, I dare say, they've swopped confidences, and you've been consigned to the kennels.'

'How do I get back into the house . . . and into the bedroom?'

'Start looking miserable about something. Women love misery; it never fails to excite them.'

'How very odd.'

'Not at all odd. It's serious, you see – or so they think. If there's one thing gets a woman into bed, it's thinking the man is serious. Which means marriage or misery. On the very lowest level, you could say that the man's unhappiness literally bores the knickers off her. Let's have a good healthy whoop of lust, she tells herself, anything instead of these squeals of self-pity.'

'I might have something to squeal about at that. My father's coming it heavy about my taking over the estate. He really is a most cynical man, Len. When I said it would bore me, he suggested that I needn't bother about the place very much, just go through the occasional motions. He can't understand that if one takes on people in that way one must do the thing one hundred per cent.'

'Nor can I, baby. Those peasants will be as right as the rum ration without you, don't you kid yourself. Just take the thing as it comes.'

'I can't, Len. Either I must be – well – the Squire, ready to help all my people every minute of the year . . . or I don't want to touch it. Since I don't see myself as Squire in the full and demanding sense, I *don't* want to touch it. So I suggested there might be a cousin somewhere who could fill the part.'

'And what did Daddy say to that?'

'That if it went to someone else, the someone else would have to have the family money – the lot, Len – to keep it going.'

'Leaving little Jeremy in rags and bare tootsies? Now since we're thinking feudal, darling, wouldn't it be just as disloyal to your villeins to refuse the job – thus leaving them in the care of someone who may be a real turd for all you know – as to take it on and be a bit floppy about it? After all, you're the one they look to see succeed your father, and even if you were a bit slack and away most of the winter, at least they've watched you growing up for twenty years and remember when you wet your velvet knickers at the village concert . . . and when you sang Drake's Drum a few years later.'

'How funny of you to have guessed that.'

Len sighed.

'Anyway, wet knickers and Drake's Drum is all they want, darling – to know your heart's in the right place. They don't need you telling them about manure or birth control or Granny's arthritis – you pay other people to do that with your taxes.'

'Perhaps you're right, but I feel very wretched about it all.'

'No, you don't,' said Len: 'you're just trying to draw attention to yourself. It's all so bloody *got up*, Jeremy doll, so fucking *voulu* as the Frogs say, that it wouldn't get a self-respecting nymphomaniac into bed with you, let alone Miss Carmilla. Now, if you just stop being the Week's Man of Sorrows, I've got two things to tell you. First, if you're a good boy and work hard, Tom will deal with your old man – that's if he shows any sign of landing you with that estate too early and messing up your career in this College.'

'Thank you, Len – but how can I be sure?'

'Because I tell you, and I'm not talking just to give myself a nice feeling in the throat. And second, listen good to this: if you want to be in everybody's good books, darling, ride your bike out to the Milton Road and climb into that Morris 1000 which both University and College regulations forbid you to keep there – don't worry, sweetheart, Uncle Len won't sneak so long as you toe his line – and drive your lovely carcass cautiously to Ptolemaeos Tunne's house in the Fens, where you will find little Master Lonelyheart longing to see you again.'

'You can't mean . . . Marius Stern?'

'No, darling. He's gone back to his school, we hear, after Gregory has promised to present them with a new stadium or something, and is sitting there as pie as Tom Brown himself, not playing with his nice new circumcised penis.'

'Then who?'

'Brother Pixie.'

'PIERO. How did he get here?'

'Ask him. You should enjoy listening to the answer. Now look, lover boy. Piero means problems. While those problems are being sorted out by your elders and betters, Ptoly will have him in the Fens, reconstructing him and his *data* so that he can take some sort of place over here. Everyone seems to reckon, you see, that Piero is somehow *owed*. Now, you're being appointed to keep him amused – and to keep him strictly inside the Parish, because he's got no passport or anything and we don't want any Nosy Parkers asking questions. You can bring him into the College for the odd day – the poor little bugger must have a change from time to time – but he is *not* to be taken round other Colleges or into public restaurants or *anywhere* outside the precincts of Tunne Hall in the Fens or those of this College.'

'Can I introduce him to anyone here?'

'Yes. I think he might have a fellow feeling for Nicos Pandouros, who's a decent boy and knows how to keep his mouth shut.'

'Good. I like Nicos.'

69

'That old ninny, Barraclough, won't like it when you take Nicos out to the Fens, but Nicos and you can fix him between you. Incidentally, if we can only get Ptoly interested in Nicos as well as Piero, there might be an end of Greco Barraclough's hold over Nicos, and high time too.'

'Nicos says he's sworn an oath to the Greco. He doesn't take such things lightly.'

'Well, we'll see about all that later. Your real baby right now is Piero. The trouble is, you'll find, that he's hoping to see more of his *old* friends – like Canteloupe and Baby, and even Max de Freville, all of whom knew him in Venice. Well, Max is in a state of autistic retreat, and Canteloupe is in Los Angeles, and as for Baby – tush, tush – '

' – Tush, tush what, for Christ's sake?'

'Tom doesn't want her to see anything of Piero. He's scared lest she regress into her childhood – into the less wholesome regions of it at that. You see, Baby was only fourteen when she last knew Piero, and their relations were curious and even weird. It seems he showed her some very unsavoury things which she should not have seen in the Palazzo he lived in, and that they later corresponded about the ghosts in the place. So all ways round, the Provost doesn't want Piero hanging round Baby, and since we aim to keep the Provost happy, we say Amen to that. But it does mean that for the time being you're the one who'll have to do all the Piero-sitting.'

'Fielding Gray might help.'

'Fielding Gray doesn't live within ten miles of Ptoly.'

'Point taken. I'll do my best, Len. There's something very strange about Piero. On that one time I met him in Torcello he enormously excited me. Not in the obvious way. I don't really know how to describe it. I felt almost as if I were talking with an angel or a devil, with some totally unfamiliar kind of being who might change shape at any moment, might humble or exalt me, might present me with untold gifts or bewitch me with – '

' – Just stop right there, honey,' said Len. 'Piero's a Sicilian tart with quick wits and a club foot. That'll do to be going on with.'

Early in October, Baby Canteloupe came to Cambridge to see her father, Tom Llewyllyn.

'Jo-Jo,' she said to Tom as they strolled back and forth on the rear lawn of Lancaster, 'is getting bigger and bigger and more and more peculiar. It's almost like one of those Greek legends – you know, when the girl has been cursed by a goddess and the baby just can't get out.'

'You came all the way from Wiltshire to tell me this?' –

'She made me promise to come to you – not just telephone but come to you –˙and persuade you to agree that Alexandre – that's the son she thinks she's going to have – that Alexandre can be christened in Lancaster College, just like Sarum. It's her latest craze – and less embarrassing, I must say, than some of the others she's been having lately.'

'I shouldn't have thought that either she or that French husband of hers would have been in the least bit bothered about christening.'

'Nor should I. But she's not exactly herself, as I've explained to you, blown up like a Zeppelin, with all this

71

waiting. Anyhow, that's what she's made me promise: to obtain your permission, from you in person, for Alexandre to be christened in your Chapel. She keeps saying that he must be christened in the same place as Sarum was.'

'That's all very well, Tullia,' said Tom Llewyllyn, surveying his daughter with some disquiet. 'I think you're running to fat,' he said.

'If so, it's in sympathy with poor Jo. Now, poppa, can she have Alexandre done here?'

'I was about to say . . . that the College Chapel is only available, for purposes of this kind, to connections of the College. You, my daughter, were Sarum's mother: that's the only reason he ever got in here.'

'I shall be Alexandre's godmother, if that's any help. Oh please, poppa. Please do this for Baby and Baby's friend Jo-Jo, or Baby and Jo will blub.'

'The Michaelmas Term,' said Tom, 'started on October the first. Full Term starts on the fifteenth. If this child is born soon enough to be christened before the fifteenth, then I'll arrange it. Although the Dean and the Chaplain and all the rest of them will hate it, I can fix them. Len has got all *their* numbers, you see, and a very little pressure will do the trick. But I'm not having any christenings during Full Term – it's not what my College is here for.'

'Sarum was christened in Full Term.'

'Sarum,' said Tom, at once serene and ironic, 'is the Heir Apparent to a Marquessate.'

'Suppose Jo still hasn't let him drop by the fifteenth?'

'Then she'll have to leave the christening until after the end of Full Term. Any day after December the sixth – Founder's Day.'

'Then that's all right. She won't mind waiting – unless

72

Alexandre is one of those ghastly babies that may die on you at any second, and then I don't think she'll care. It's nothing to do with religion, you see, to judge from some of her other plans for Alexandre, but sheer love for me. She likes us,' said Baby, who was now looking intently at the far corner of the lawn by the West Gate of the Chapel, 'she . . . likes . . . us . . . to have everything possible . . . in common. I know those boys,' she said.

'Never mind them,' said Tom.

'I do mind them, very much. The one with the round face is Jeremy Morrison, son of that odious MP whom Canteloupe likes for some reason. And the other one . . . the little one . . . the one with the limp . . . it can't be but it is . . . it *is* . . . *PIERO*,' she called, 'PIERO.'

'Miss Baby,' came a distant voice. 'Oh, Miss Baby.'

And much to the annoyance of Jeremy Morrison at the North East corner of the lawn and of Tom Llewyllyn at the South West, Piero and Baby made towards each other straight along the diagonal, Baby running with long strides and kicking her heels up behind her, Piero hobbling as fast as his poor foot would permit.

Jeremy Morrison, obedient to instructions, had visited Piero at Ptolemaeos' house in the Fens on the day after his conversation with Len. Although Jeremy was a little uneasy about meeting Piero again, he was also very excited; and at the same time he was glad of a good excuse for frequenting Ptolemaeos' house, as the insights gained might help him to contrive methods of encouraging

Ptoly to contribute, in the not too distant future, to the Jeremy Morrison Benevolent Fund for Jeremy Morrison. For one thing, he thought, it was quite possible that if he made himself useful with Piero (whatever 'useful' might turn out to mean in the present context) this in itself might nudge Ptoly into at least a preliminary stage of gratitude.

When Jeremy had reached Ptolemaeos' house, the door had been opened to him by one of the abominable old women whom he remembered from his visit in the summer (Mrs Spatch or Mrs Grind, he thought she might be called, but could not remember). Whatever her name, the crone emitted a very mean sniff when Jeremy asked, on being told that Ptolemaeos was out, for the 'young gentleman who was staying'. Since Mrs Gramp or Mrs Crutch (he must remember her bloody name and use it) must be used to the comings and goings of peculiar people in this household, Jeremy was at a loss to understand why Piero was held in such evident disfavour . . . until Mrs Frodge (could that be it?) started cackling about the Scarlet Woman and the Great Beast. Clearly, it was Piero's habit which had got him into hot water with the lady, who had smelt the devilish vapours of Rome. She condescended, nevertheless, to bring Jeremy to Piero in the summer-house at the end of the garden.

'Those jeans you're wearing – they're a woman's – no fly,' was all Jeremy could think of to say when Mrs Grunt (surely not) had left them.

'They belong to Mr Tunne's niece,' Piero had said. 'It was essential I should change into something, if only to lessen the distaste of Mr Tunne's good ladies, Mrs Gurt and Mrs Statch,' (Ah, thought Jeremy, and don't forget them this time). 'Since his own clothes were much too big, I was accommodated with a pullover and some trousers of the niece called Jo-Jo, who used to live here with her uncle. It appears that she is now married.'

'Where is Ptolemaeos?' asked Jeremy.

'He has gone into Ely to buy me other, more suitable, clothes. I am to be passed off as a distant cousin while it is decided what to do with me. "Details later," as Mr Tunne puts it. I think,' said Piero, looking along a dyke which proceeded from the end of Ptolemaeos' garden, between two endless expanses of yellow sludge, and so on into nowhere, 'that this place is nearly as sad and unhealthy as the Laguna Morta.'

'They'll have to keep you hidden for a while, Piero. You did enter the United Kingdom illegally, you see. You'll find Ptolemaeos great fun to be with, and I'll be over a lot, and I'll drive you to Lancaster to meet my friend, Nicos Pandouros.'

These treats were breathlessly catalogued, as if to give the impression that there were so many of them that there was a danger of the whole day's being consumed in their rehearsal: but in truth, thought Jeremy, the list was pretty thin.

'Do you like reading?' he asked. 'Ptoly has an enormous library.'

'All these things will be very well,' said Piero.

His face belied his words.

'I think you're rather low, my friend,' Jeremy had said. Funny, he thought: when I saw this boy on Torcello I could have taken him into my arms and wept over him – that silly tonsure, those grimy bare legs, that pathetic surgical boot – but now all I feel is indifference. And yet I know that this too will pass; and something tells me that if I drop Piero now I shall not only be failing him in faith and love but also failing – and deeply depriving – myself.

But the minutes ticked on and there seemed little to say.

'I have something to show you,' Jeremy had said in desperation.

Then he had taken Piero back up the garden, into the house and into the library. In an alcove, under the presiding bust of Socrates, was a massive sarcophagus of marble, curiously carven on the outside with both Christian and Pagan motives, and fitted with taps, drain and plug, like a bath.

'Ptolemaeos used this for experiments last summer,' said Jeremy. 'I'll show you.' He plugged the bath, turned on the taps, and began to take his clothes off. When the sarcophagus was three-quarters full, he removed the last of what he was wearing and climbed in.

'There are two inflated rubber rings somewhere,' he said to Piero, who found them where they had last been discarded, on an empty shelf under the Pathagoreans and early Eleatics. Jeremy raised his huge round calves so that Piero might slip one ring over them and up to his knees.

'You look mightiful,' said Piero; 'tender but mightiful.'

The other ring he pushed down over Jeremy's raised arms, until it rested just under his armpits.

'Now I am floating,' said Jeremy. 'Now you may ask me . . . anything you wish to ask me . . . and since I am floating in limbo, in nowhere, all at ease and without weight of body or distraction of mind, I shall tell you the truth. Later on, you will lie in here, and I shall ask. But as you are a guest, you may ask the first question.'

As Ptolemaeos, back from Ely, opened the door of the library, he heard Piero say, in his gentle lilt:

'Do you believe, Girolamo mio, do you believe in the Love of God?'

After Jeremy and Piero had questioned each other for some hours, four times refilling the sarcophagus with warm water, Jeremy, not wanting to leave his friend, suggested to Ptolemaeos that he might stay the night. But Ptolemaeos said that he did not wish to be involved in a breach of the regulations of Lancaster College (which even in these days required Jeremy to sleep there) and that in any case there was such a thing as overdoing it.

'Go back to Lancaster,' Ptolemaeos had said to Jeremy, 'and come back here in two days. Meanwhile, I too have questions to ask of Piero. So come back here on the second day from now, fairly early in the morning, and take Piero for the day to Lancaster, where he will see new sights and faces. But only Lancaster,' he added, echoing Len, 'and only let him talk to people you really trust.'

And so it happened that Jeremy and Piero had been standing at the West End of the Chapel (looking at the carvings above the gate) near the North East corner of the rear lawn, while Tom and Baby had turned, in their walk, at the South West corner of the lawn, and Baby had seen Piero. If this had not happened, she might long have been ignorant of his presence in England, as her father would not have told her and there was no particular reason why anyone else should, though it was at least possible that Fielding Gray might have, if only in order to make trouble. But as it was, Baby had turned when she turned, and had seen Piero and roused him by her shout, and they had hastened to each other across the lawn; and now Baby was standing close to Piero, holding both of his hands in both of hers, and talking fluently. Tom, who was troubled and annoyed by the meeting but realized that no one was to blame and that he must now put a good face on it, moved past Baby and Piero, pausing very slightly to nod civilly at the latter, and on towards Jeremy at the end of the diagonal line across the lawn. As he reached him Nicos Pandouros, who had had luncheon with Jeremy and Piero in the former's rooms (thus arousing Greco Barraclough's violent displeasure, as he had wanted Nicos to serve him in his own), came out from behind a buttress which he had been examining and joined the group.

'Mr Morrison. Mr Pandouros,' Tom said.

'Mr Provost,' said Nicos and Jeremy.

'You will kindly tell our Italian friend . . . that in normal circumstances no one except a Fellow of the College and those with him may walk upon the grass.'

'We have already told him, sir,' said Jeremy. 'I think something has occurred to over-excite him.'

'My daughter,' said Tom evenly, 'they were close friends years ago, when they were children. So of course it is all right this time: but he must not walk upon the grass again.'

Piero and Baby, side by side, no longer holding any part of each other but unassailably united, Baby tempering her imperious stride to accord with Piero's limp, came galumphing dot-and-carry-one towards the three Lancastrians. Jeremy politely introduced Nicos to Baby, and Baby graciously remembered having seen Nicos on the edge of a party in her father's Lodging some months ago. After this they were all silent for some moments, until Baby coolly said:

'I should like to take Piero to Wiltshire, poppa. The country there is very sweet in the autumn. Canteloupe will be back from California soon. He will be interested to see Piero once more.'

Jeremy exchanged a respectful glance with the Provost. Nicos, not minding his own business but keen to contradict a Peeress (being inimical to her order) remarked that as he understood the matter Piero might sit tight in the Fens.

'Wiltshire will be equally suitable,' said Baby, her mouth tightening.

'I think,' said Tom, 'that Ptolemaeos Tunne has certain arrangements to make before Piero can be set at large.'

'No reason why he shouldn't make them while Piero stays quietly in Wiltshire,' Baby said.

'The fact is,' said Jeremy, 'that there is a lot to be done on behalf of Piero which can only be done if he stays with Mr Tunne in the Fens.'

Baby Canteloupe, who disdained to quarrel with a mere Greek boy and would not, in courtesy, do more than quietly confute her own father, now turned and struck.

'Who asked you?' she said. 'Who do you think you are?'

'I think,' said Jeremy, 'that I am Piero's friend. Any further information which Lady Canteloupe may require is to be had from the Registrar of this College and Burke's *Landed Gentry*.'

Nicos grinned. *Landed Gentry* did not stand very high in his democratic scheme of how things ought to be, but Ladyships stood even lower. Anyhow, he liked Jeremy.

Piero frowned. He was not quite sure of the distribution of power among the group assembled, but he was anxious to stand well with Baby, first because she had always fascinated him, and secondly because he reckoned (not altogether wrongly) that as Tom's daughter she would have some influence with the Provost, should she care to exert it, when it came to deciding the question of Piero's admission to Lancaster College . . . where he now wished to be admitted.

Baby scowled like a spurned trollop.

'You had better decide, poppa,' she said.

'I think,' said Tom, 'that Piero himself must decide. It's his life, and I think he appreciates the factors involved.'

Baby looked at Piero, Eve offering the apple, and not only the apple but a softer landscape ('the country there is very sweet in the autumn'), a great nobleman's establishment, expensive styles and amusing toys.

Jeremy looked at Piero, his round face damp with sweat and shining like a moon.

'I think,' said Piero, 'that Jeremy had better drive me back to the Fens now.' Jeremy winced at the mention of his forbidden motor, but Tom shook this off with a slight toss of his curly grey hair, indicating that he was not the man to take advantage of Piero's chance and unintended delation. 'You see,' said Piero turning to Baby, 'Mr Tunne has taken me in. It would be ungrateful to leave him quite so suddenly.'

Baby nodded. Face had been well saved and an implied promise made for the not very distant future. As for Big Mouth Morrison, Esquire, she could attend to him later.

'Quite right, Piero,' she said. 'You always had jolly decent manners. I'd almost forgotten how thoughtful you were.' And then, turning her back on Nicos and Jeremy, 'Please take me back to your Lodging, poppa. I must telephone Jo-Jo in Wiltshire and check that she's all right.'

'Good afternoon, gentlemen,' said Tom, as he turned to follow her.

'Good afternoon, Mr Provost,' said Nicos and Jeremy.

'Ciao, Tom,' said Piero, remembering that he had addressed him in this fashion in the tower in the garden, for although Tom had not liked him they used to keep up an appearance of friendliness for Daniel's sake.

And now, hearing the voice from the tower and recalling how Piero had borne himself in the presence of the Angel of Death, Tom turned again, looked back at Piero, and waved a greeting between old allies, a greeting which excluded all the world but them.

When Baby rang up Wiltshire from the Provost's Lodging, she asked for Jo-Jo but was answered (eventually) by Jo-Jo's husband, Jean-Marie Guiscard.

'It's just happened,' he said: 'in your special grove, by the pool.'

'You mean . . . they didn't move her?'

'There wasn't time. One minute she was sitting there reading with your little Sarum and his Nanny; and the next she was having it. It seems that Nanny had advised syrup of figs, and this did the trick. Luckily Nanny was quite competent to deliver the child, as she's a fully trained nurse.'

'Do you suppose Sarum saw it happen? All of it?'

'I don't know. I imagine not if he was lying in his pram.'

'Suppose he was sitting up?' said Baby, accusing. 'But

obviously it's too late to worry about that. How are they both – Jo-Jo and Alexandre?'

'Jo-Jo's fine. So's the baby. The only thing is,' said Jean-Marie in a matter of fact voice, 'it is a girl.'

'Oh,' said Baby; and after a long pause, 'What does Jo say about that?'

'"How bloody boring," she said at first: "I hope it dies instantly."'

'But it didn't?'

'No.'

'So what will you do?'

'I have decided to call the child "Oenone." You know, the nymph on the Mountain of Ida, who was betrayed by Prince Paris of Troy – also called "Alexander", for whom Alexandre was to have been named. Something about this idea has amused Jo-Jo. "Alexandre has betrayed us both," she says, "Oenone and me both." So for the time being she has a fellow feeling for the child.'

'So everything is all right after all, Jean-Marie. Will she feed Oenone herself?'

'She would,' said Jean-Marie in the same matter of fact voice as that in which he had announced the birth of a girl, 'and she could; but Oenone will not take her breast. Jo has plenty of milk, but Oenone refuses it.'

'Does she refuse all food?'

'No,' said Jean-Marie; 'she is very contented with your English Cow & Gate.'

At about the same time as Baby was talking to Jean-Marie on the telephone, Doctor La Soeur made an afternoon round of the patients at his Nursing Home. When he came to Max de Freville's room, he found Max, who had been lying absolutely still for days except when 'turned' or otherwise attended to by the nurses, was heaving and thrashing under his blankets.

'How long has this been going on?' he asked the Matron.

'Sister?' said Matron.

'Staff?' said Sister.

'Nurse?' said Staff.

'He was absolutely quiet when I looked in on him five minutes ago,' said the Nurse.

'Angie,' said Max de Freville, 'listen to this, Angie. That child of Canteloupe's. I made a horrible mistake when I decided to give him some money. I went to see him – did I tell you? Are you listening, Angie?'

La Soeur nodded to Matron.

'I'm listening, Max,' Matron said. 'Lie still and tell me.'

' – I went to see him when he was christened, I was one of the godfathers, you know, and he was a good healthy baby, bawled the roof off. Then that little wife of Canteloupe's asked me down to Wiltshire about two months later. The child looked well enough at a distance but when I came close to him – ' Max started thrashing again. Doctor La Soeur bent over him. 'Calm yourself, de Freville,' he said. 'I examined that child myself a few weeks ago. Lady Canteloupe asked me to go down and advise on whether or not the boy should be circumcised. The answer was "no", because in that department and all others he's as normal a child as ever I saw.'

'You didn't see him when he was christened,' Max said, 'so you can't know how he's changed since.' He arched his back and spat, then seemed to relax. 'He was normal enough when he was christened, you see; but two months after, it was as though a changeling had been put in the pram, a little gnome, with slit eyes, whore's eyes, like Lyki's whore Piero in Venice. I intended to love that child and give him a fortune, but you can't give your gold to a changeling, a gnome, something which the fairies have put in the pram. I wonder that nobody has noticed, Angie. Neither Canteloupe nor that girl-wife of his nor that brute Fielding Gray – though he's the other god-father – nobody but me has noticed that the real Sarum has been taken away and a changeling put in his place. There's nothing really left now – there would have been Canteloupe as well as the boy, but what do you make of a father who doesn't know his own son from a shrivelled little gnome? So there's nothing left now, and I'm through.'

He rose from the bed, fought off La Soeur and the four attendant females, made for the window (which wasn't barred, being on the ground floor), flung it open, and then, after powerfully resisting further attempts from La Soeur and the women, at last kicked them off, scrabbled his way under the sash (still kicking) and fell forward, screaming 'Angie'.

'Never mind,' said La Soeur. 'He'll simply land on the flower bed. Staff-Nurse, Nurse, go and get help and have him brought back.'

'He's in a very funny position, doctor,' said Sister, who was looking through the window.'

'I dare say. I've just had the results of some tests from the laboratories. I had a hunch about Mr Max de Freville,' La Soeur said to Matron, 'and it's come up *en plein*.'

'*En plein,* doctor?'

'Straight win on a single number. You know what he's got? What we used to call GPI – General Paralysis of the Insane. He must have caught the pox many years ago – long before penicillin – , then been skilfully but, as was inevitable in those days, incompletely cured, and now the dormant disease has come back to fetch him away. Despair, violence, delusions – all part of the pattern. A classic instance, this perverted vision of little Lord Sarum. Flawed sight and a brain part eaten by spirochaetes has caused him to see a nightmare in place of a child who is suffering from nothing worse than rather close-set eyes and a snub nose. As I said, I've examined him myself. Socrates or Silenus, if you like, but not the Faery Fellow's work.'

Socrates or Silenus, it was all one to Matron and Sister, who now started browbeating the Staff Nurse as she re-appeared, looking rather woozy, in the doorway, for not attending her charge while he was carried back to his room by the porters.

'Not my fault,' said Staff, disrespectful and truculent, waving away rebuke with a weird circular movement of both hands: 'he won't be coming back in here. That notice saying DON'T PICK THE FLOWERS – he swallowed the stake as he fell.'

'It seems,' said Canteloupe to Baby shortly after his return from California, 'that Max had prepared considerable sums as gifts for me and Sarum, to be made over on his death or whenever ordered by him. Obviously he hadn't the time to change anything – or simply didn't get round to it – between that day he took against Sarum – Tullius – down here and actually going off his rocker in the Club. And after that, of course, it was too late.'

'You've no hesitation in accepting the money?' Baby said.

'None. I contributed quite generously some years back to a fund which Max got up to save parts of the Jewish Ghetto in Venice. So you might say that Max owed me . . . and I'm happy to tell you that the sums he'd got together for me and Tully were substantially larger than anything I ever sent to his fund. Anyway, he's got no one else to will it to: why not us?'

'Sarum's will go into trust, I suppose?'

'Tully's will go into trust. All of it's in America, so we should be able to keep it quiet and not pay any gift tax or whatever they have the impertinence to call it. So what with the dollars I was paid for the Canzoni watercolours while I was in California, we've got a nice little pile on the safe side of the water. I'd better put some in Ptoly Tunne's account over there – you remember he lent me a bit when my pocket money ran low a few years back. As for the rest – at least some of it – I thought it was time I gave you a present. Come to think of it, I promised you one before I left for America. Celebration of Tully's first birthday, which isn't very far off.'

'How sweet, Canty. Whatever will it be?'

'Wait and see, girl,' Canteloupe said.

'Well, I'll be needing something to cheer me up. Jo-Jo and Jean-Marie will be off any minute, now she's had Oenone.'

'Where shall they go?'

'She's being a bit mysterious about that. Sly. In fact I don't at all like the look of things, Canty. When Oenone first came, Jean-Marie somehow persuaded her that it was really all right – that Oenone was a girl, I mean. But it didn't help that Oenone wouldn't take Jo's milk . . . and in one way and the other there's been a lot of back-sliding. Jo keeps looking at Oenone . . . you know . . . *there* . . . as if she was hoping for a miraculous change.'

'But she hasn't done anything frightful?'

'No. But I'm worried. And so is Jean-Marie. And now all this . . . obscurity . . . about where they're going . . .'

'Surely Jean-Marie will decide that?'

'It's her money. She's always said it's his as much as hers, but when one really gets down to brass tacks, Canty, I don't think she quite means it.'

Jeremy Morrison fell into a beneficial and agreeable routine whereby he would work hard one day and drive over to the Fens the next. It was just as well he had good reason to do this, as otherwise he would have been lonely. The Salinger girls, formerly his greatest friends in

Lancaster, continued to ignore him utterly; and most of his other friends, who had heard of his long journey with Fielding Gray during the vacation, seemed to shun him slightly, to sidle away from him at parties, and when they spoke with him to manipulate the conversation through a series of spiteful references to young men who battened on older and more distinguished ones. The only people who were not thoroughly unpleasant on the topic were Len and Nicos.

'You stick to senior men,' Len said. 'They're ten times as interesting and a hundred times as rich. If it came to a showdown, Ptoly Tunne would be better value than Fielding Gray, but I see no reason why you shouldn't have 'em both.'

As for Nicos Pandouros, 'I know how one becomes attached,' he said. 'The great thing is to make sure they don't have a rope to haul you in. By all means come to them when they call politely, but don't let them keep a leash on you.'

Greco Barraclough had a leash on Nicos, he said, because (leave money out of it) he had sworn on oath when the Greco adopted him. Now, Barraclough did not mind Nicos' friendship for Jeremy, but he did object to the visits which Nicos made to the Fens in Jeremy's company.

'He's worried about Mr Tunne,' said Nicos. 'Although they're old friends, he thinks Mr Tunne may tell me that my oath, made in the Mani, need not bind me here. I think he mistrusts your friend, Major Gray, for the same reason.'

'A lot of people are going to say that about your oath before very long,' said Jeremy; 'not just Ptoly Tunne and Fielding.'

They were driving out to the Fens. Jeremy decided he

had had enough of Nicos' oath for the time being, and started to talk of the Truth Game in the marble sarcophagus, to which Nicos was now to be introduced.

'It is obligatory to tell the truth?' Nicos enquired.

'In the circumstances,' said Jeremy, 'if you really lie back and relax, it is almost impossible not to.'

'I do not relax easily. Is it essential to be entirely nude in the sarcophagus?'

'It is much more convenient.'

'I am shy . . . just about the one thing. Poor Greek boys often are, as they are very strictly brought up . . . over certain matters.'

'So are poor Italian boys. Piero seems to have got over it.'

'We are not the same,' said Nicos sharply. 'I like him, but I despise him. No, not despise, disapprove of him. I could not behave the same as he. If I lay in the water nude, what would the *Kyrios* Barraclough think?'

'No one's going to tell him.'

'If you swear on oath, you behave as the person to whom you have sworn would wish you to behave – whether he will know or not.'

'But why should the *Kyrios* Barraclough object to your bathing naked in the presence of two other men? In many schools in this country all the boys bathe naked together.'

'In this country. Not in Greece, *not* in the Mani. The *Kyrios* Barraclough wishes me to behave as I was brought up there. If I once break loose from the customs of the Mani, I may break loose, he thinks, from the oath.'

'That oath. Your albatross. I have mine too, you know.'

'You have said something of this. The estate which must come to you?'

'Yes. The difference between you and me is that your albatross will fall from your neck when you are twenty-five, whereas that, on present form, is just about when mine will finally be secured . . . under my nose for ever.'

'Mission accomplished,' said Lord Canteloupe to Leonard Percival. 'No difficulties in getting the Canzonis there, thanks to you: no trouble with the sale: and here, for our most private records, is one copy of the credit note given to me by the Bank of Southern California, where I deposited the cheque.'

'I may presume, Detterling,' said Percival, 'that you hung about long enough to make sure the cheque was cleared?'

'You may. I know as well as you do that some people change their minds at the last minute.'

'Very satisfactory,' said Percival, looking along the curve of his nose and past its point to the credit note. 'Had they heard any news of the original Asolano from Burano?'

'Indeed they had. They told me that even if it were up for sale through the most dependable official channel, they wouldn't touch it. The word is – has been for some years – that it's a forgery. Its colours, its condition, its whole appearance is altogether wrong, too glossy, Leonard, for a picture painted when Asolano is supposed to have painted this one. That's why it's been taken away for "restoration" – not because it needs it but because it doesn't. It has now been examined, inch by inch, by experts of the Belli Arti, whose conclusion is that the painting is a copy by Canzoni, the same Canzoni who did my water-colours, and that it was made between 1790 and 1820.'

'Canzoni seems to have had a penchant for copying Asolanos. I thought he was an easel man, not one for large canvases.'

'Correct. But my chums in Los Angeles said he could make pretty good shift to turn out a full scale oil-painting if the money was right. Canzoni had made a very skilful copy, it seems, though of course there were differences of technique and material which enabled the experts very easily to detect what had happened, once they'd had a proper chance to go over it.'

'I see,' said Leonard Percival. 'So at some stage after 1790, which is the earliest date ascribed to the copy, the Asolano vanished from the church on Burano and the Canzoni appeared in its place . . . unnoticed, it appears, by anyone at the time.'

'I dare say that a few sweeteners were handed out to key personnel. As for the fisher-folk – who cared about them? And what did they care about Asolano?'

'New lamps for old?'

'Precisely. But as in the legend the old lamp – the Asolano – was worth a thousand times the new. Although Asolano never quite got his 1st XI colours as a Venetian painter, he was a reckonable member of the 2nd . . . whereas Canzoni, besides being of a much later period, when standards had sunk through the floor, was only a giggler and a flouncer selling lewd pictures behind the pavilion.'

'But a very competent copyist? Competent enough to run up an Asolano that has been prominently placed over a side altar and has subsequently passed muster there for nobody knows just how long.'

'The early days must have been the trickiest. Provided the swop wasn't noticed, or at least nothing was said, for the first few months, then all might be well . . . indeed all *was* well, as you have just observed, Leonard, until the busybodies started sniffing at that side altar only a comparatively short time ago. So let us consider a possibility. What better time to effect a swop of this kind than when things were breaking up . . . when the enemy was at the gate, the barbarians were coming, and nobody had much time for pictures over side altars – '

' – Except those with plans to steal them – '

' – Steal them under cover of the fear and confusion that must have swept the Lagoon in – say – 1796, when Bonaparte the Bogeyman was coming.'

'1796. Some six years after the earliest date at which the experts think the copy could have been painted. 1796,' said Percival warily, 'when your ancestor, son of the first Lord Canteloupe, was there, engaging Canzoni to make a pornographic series which stemmed from the original painting – '

' – *Not* my ancestor, as he died a few months later and the line was continued, his father having remarried, through his half-brother. But let that pass. He was at that time – 1796 – the first son of the reigning peer of our house, and had been sent on his travels, on a trumped up mission to His Majesty's Resident Minister in Venice, in order to get him out of England, where he was in deep disgrace. He had set Canzoni to making a small, watercolour copy of that Asolano, to be the first of the pornographic sequence, so why not set him – he may have told himself – to paint a full size copy in oils as well, now that he'd got his hand in? Then exchange the two oil paintings, at a time of panic and locked churches (though not locked to our man, of course, with his diplomatic status), new lamps for old, as you put it, and despatch the old lamp, the valuable if not immediately marketable work of an acknowledged but not inconveniently famous Master, under diplomatic seal in a British Man o' War, putting out from the Serene Republic just before it finally tottered, back to England, Home and Beauty – and so, ultimately, to this address in Wiltshire. How do you like that tune, Leonard?'

'Have you seen an Asolano around the place lately, Detterling?'

'No. But I shall have a good look.'

'And what shall you do with it if you find it?'

'My friends in California did indicate that the *real* Asolano of the "Ragazzi della Peste" would be of considerable interest.'

'A stolen painting?' Percival said.

'A reward to the finder?'

'A member of the family by which it was received and concealed?'

'Apparently without their knowledge, as there's been no sight nor sound of it. Anyway, if the Asolano doesn't belong to us, the Canzoni does. We commissioned and paid for it. Quite a nice consolation prize. The two might be put on exhibition together. CAN YOU TELL THE REAL OLD MASTER FROM THE FAKE? WIN A FREE HULA HOOP. There's a large supply of those round the place, as my predecessor was caught when the craze crashed. Perhaps we could revive it.'

'Leave all that to the Cant-Fun Corporation men,' said Percival, who deprecated any mention, by his employer, of the Stately Home charade which kept them both. 'Leave it to the professionals. Which reminds me. Your friend and partner, Gregory Stern has been in touch with me – at your suggestion, I gathered – wanting my "professional" advice, as he was civil enough to call it, about those people who kidnapped him last summer. He is disposed, he says, to do what he promised them, and it is difficult to see that he has any way out.'

'Is that what you told him?'

'I advised him at any rate to keep the rendezvous which they have appointed for later this month. In Trieste.' –

'That fits. He reckons that last time he was taken to an island off the coast of Dalmatia . . . not so far down from Trieste. Obviously their area.'

'Perhaps. He says they want a three-day meeting to discuss his arrangements for the forthcoming book – his Bumper anti-Jewboy Annual for Kiddies of All Ages.'

'It's going to be a horror, that book, Leonard. Stern & Detterling can't publish it. Nobody could.'

'He knows that. But he says that his persecutors particularly want it done by Stern & Detterling – or under some similarly reputable imprint. This would be possible only if the book were moderate and responsible in tone, and here is his problem: these people refuse to be moderate, he says; they won't let him urge a sensible and temperately argued anti-Israeli case, although there is an excellent one, as we all know, to be made. They want hate and ridicule and obscenity. At one time he thought he could just manage this – for his family's sake – and he still thinks he could – had it not been brought home to him, by you, that the kind of book which would result simply could not be published.'

'He could have it printed at his own expense and under his own name, with no actual publisher designated – if he could find a printer for it.'

'Will he be able to?'

94

'I imagine so. Somewhere.'

'Some sweat-shop or other, you imply,' said Leonard Percival. 'The people he is dealing with have ruled that out. They want respectability. More, they want distinction.'

Canteloupe walked to the corner of his study, took up a bat which he kept there (the one with which he had once made a double century for his School) and faced up to an imagined bowler.

'It was always my ambition,' he said to Leonard, executing his famous late cut, 'to put the ball between the wicket-keeper and first slip. Impossible, you say; impossible to play it so fine. But is it, Leonard?'

Percival offered no comment.

'Suppose . . . just a touch when it is already past the wicket, just a touch on a ball going straight through . . . I wonder, Leonard. Too late now. But I think,' he said, playing a leg glance off the front foot by way of a change, 'I think, after all, that I can persuade a firm of sufficient distinction to print Gregory's book. Not to distribute it or to publish it, he'll have to manage all that himself. Privately. But at least we may be able to find him a high quality printer. Please lift the telephone receiver, Leonard, and get the Provost's Secretary at Lancaster College, Cambridge.'

'Question one,' said Jeremy Morrison to Nicos Pandouros, who was floating in the sarcophagus wearing only a pair of tiny purple Y-Fronts: 'have you ever had a woman?'

'No,' said Nicos so flatly that there seemed no point whatever in pursuing or qualifying the question.

'Your turn,' said Jeremy to Piero.

'Tell me, Nicos,' Piero began: 'you have sworn this oath to the Professor Barraclough – '

' – He is not a Professor,' said Jeremy pedantically.

'In Italy,' said Piero, 'we call any man of learning a *Professore* from respect. Please do not interrupt.' And to Nicos in the sarcophagus: 'You have sworn an oath to honour and obey him. In what case would you break this oath?'

There was the sound of a car, an ebullient changing down of gears and a scrunching of gravel.

'I should cease to honour him,' said Nicos, 'if ever I found he was no longer honourable.'

'And at the same time would you cease to obey him?'

'Yes,' said Nicos after some time. 'One need not – must not – obey a man who has forfeited his honour.'

After Canteloupe had spoken on the telephone to Len, the Provost's Secretary, Len paced through Lancaster in his pearl grey suede brogues in search of Carmilla Salinger, who had rooms in Sitwell's Building which overlooked the Great Court of the College and the South wall of the Chapel. With Carmilla was her twin sister, Theodosia: they were seated at a round table, examining a pile of letters. When Len had knocked and entered, the sisters rose together, placed Len (literally) in an armchair,

96

and set refreshment in the form of a bowl of fruit before him on a shining stool.

'"Thou art an honourable guest and a welcome",' Carmilla said. '"Speak what is in thy mind; our heart bids us fulfil it, if fulfil it we can, and if it is a thing that hath fulfilment."'

Both girls smoothed the velvet trousers over their fine shanks and smiled down at Len. 'Calypso speaking to Hermes, the Messenger of the Gods,' said Theodosia, 'so you at least are appropriately cast.'

'Well then,' said Len. He loosened the knot of his mauve knitted tie and gave a twirl to his eyebrows, bringing them both to resemble tiny pointed horns. 'Are you two in a lenient mood?' he said.

'Not,' said Carmilla, 'if you're talking of Jeremy Morrison.'

'I'm talking,' said Len, 'of Gregory Stern.'

'The publisher?' said Theodosia. 'The one who's been writing those ugly anti-Jew pieces in *Strix* and the *Scrutator*?'

'Right,' said Len. 'He's about to write an even uglier anti-Jew book. Lord Canteloupe rang up just now to tell me he badly needs a publisher.'

'What's wrong with himself?'

'Canteloupe, as his partner, won't have it. But Canteloupe is anxious that he should find *somebody* to help him.'

'Let us hope not,' Theodosia said.

'If he doesn't, he'll be in trouble.' Len gave a brief account of the pressures that had already been brought to bear on Gregory Stern, and of the graver ones that would follow his default.

'I'm sorry for that little Marius Stern,' Carmilla said. 'He's getting it rotten, one way and the other.'

97

'Marius will be all right,' said Len, 'and so will the rest of them, if I can get your agreement to one very simple request.'

The twins looked puzzled.

'Salinger & Holbrook,' said Len. 'The printing firm. Your father's printing firm, Holbrook having long since retired. The one thing which your father kept when he sold out in the sixties. I suppose you two now own it.'

Carmilla looked down at the letters on the table.

'I suppose we do,' she said.

'Can I tell Canteloupe to tell Gregory that your firm will print, with the utmost care and for generous payment, Gregory's anti-Israel book? That you will make of it what they call in the trade a "quality job"?'

'There'll be plenty of firms that will do this if the money's big enough,' Carmilla said. 'Why should *we* publish the kind of filth which this is going to be?'

'He needs your sort of presentation and prestige. And I said "print" not "publish",' Len said.

'You also said, earlier, that he badly needs a *publisher*.'

'So he does, but he won't get one. I'm trying, Canteloupe is trying, to fix the next best thing. A decent piece of printing for him to set his name to. That's all. You would in no way be responsible for or giving countenance to what he's written. You would not even undertake to deliver the volumes when they were bound. You – your firm – would simply see to it that Gregory's words were correctly and elegantly printed, so that those who wished might read them, as is their right.'

'You'll have to do better than that, Len,' Carmilla said.

'All right. Although the need is Gregory's, remember that the request is Canteloupe's.'

'So what do we owe Canteloupe?'

'He was your father's friend. He played cricket with him. He dined and drank with him afterwards.'

Carmilla shook her head. But Theodosia remembered a day when she was about fourteen and had been taken by her father to the last big match of the season at Lord's. Carmilla was abroad learning French, she remembered, as their adoptive mother was having one of her bouts of "keeping those girls separate", and her father had promised to take her to this match, a festival match which was to be between an XI of England and an XI from the Rest of the World. Her mother had opposed the expedition, because she knew that happiness would come of it, but had suddenly been invited to a grand garden party and had forgotten, during her hysterical preparations, to interfere further with Theodosia and her father . . . who had left the house that morning while her mother was in the hands of a visiting hairdresser. Shortly after they had sat down in the Warner Stand, her father and she, at the end of the third or fourth over, a high grey flannel figure under a huge Panama hat had come flickering along the row towards them. 'Hullo, Donald,' the figure had said, removing the hat: 'can you budge up a bit and let me sit with you?' Then her father had flushed with pleasure, and said, 'Yes, oh yes, this is my daughter, Theodosia – Thea, this is Captain Detterling.' And although Theodosia was nearly squashed to a pap, she had never forgotten how happy she had been . . . how happy her father had been . . . as they all sat there during the next hour and Captain Detterling had commented lightly on the play (rather bad and boring, as she remembered) and occasionally told her about some match he had played in with her father, when her father had done rather well. Captain Detterling: Captain Lord Canteloupe.

'Oh yes,' she said now, and nodded. 'If Captain Detterling asks, we shall do this thing for Mr Stern.'

Carmilla, very surprised at first, looked Theodosia in the face, saw what she saw there, and then nodded also.

'Oh yes,' she said; 'if Captain Detterling asks, we shall.'

When Jeremy, Nicos and Piero went to join Ptolemaeos in the kitchen for a late lunch, they found that the car which they had heard earlier had contained Jo-Jo and Jean-Marie Guiscard, and Oenone in a carry-cot. Although both Jeremy and Nicos had met the Guiscards when they had visited Lancaster College (for Sarum's christening) during the previous Spring, neither they nor Piero were acquainted with recent events in that gallery, and all three were rather put out by this unscheduled irruption into what they were beginning to regard as their own territory.

The situation became gradually more comprehensible, though not much more agreeable, as curious dishes, concocted from Fenland produce by Mrs Gurt and Mrs Statch, were distributed round the table.

'Those women have fucked up the tench mousse,' Jo-Jo said: 'it's just as well you're going to have me in charge of the cooking for a while.'

A wail came from the carry-cot.

'Shut up,' said Jo-Jo, with indifference rather than unkindness; 'Cow & Gate later.'

The wail persisted. Jean-Marie took the child up and comforted it. The wail turned to a bubbly grizzle.

'Better make the best of Dadda while he's here,' Jo-Jo said.

What had happened, it appeared, was that Jean-Marie's mother, who had been ill for some time in her home in Clermont-Ferrand, had now been moved into hospital, where it was thought she would stay about another month before catching Charon's ferry. Meanwhile, Jean-Marie's father was uncared for and, being himself not many miles from Acheron, quite unable to cope; and Jean-Marie, the only child, had been summoned to take charge of him by a nonagenarian Great Aunt, who was Abbess of a Convent outside Grasse.

Quite what solutions Jean-Marie would contrive and impose must be uncertain, to say the least; what was certain was that he was obliged, by every rule in the book, to go at once to Clermond-Ferrand. This, Jeremy inferred from gestures and parentheses, Jean-Marie was not eager to do, as he would not yet wish to leave Jo-Jo alone with Oenone, to whom her attitude was ironic when not contemptuous. Jo-Jo, it seemed, regarded Oenone at best as a bad joke and at worst as a tedious parasite . . . who must, however, be nourished, cleaned and suffered. None of this was pleasing to Jean-Marie, who, furthermore, remembered Jo-Jo's once telling him that Fen air was unhealthy. Why then, he now enquired, was Jo-Jo so keen to bring Oenone here while he was absent in France? Why could she not stay with their good friends in Wiltshire?

They had been in Wiltshire long enough, responded Jo-Jo, apparently objecting no more than her husband to having three (more or less) strange boys privy to all this (perhaps, thought Jeremy, they were being regarded as a kind of Greek chorus and would be expected, at some suitable crisis, to stand in line on the table and moralize on the affair). They had been in Wiltshire long enough, Jo-Jo repeated: Wiltshire had been fine until the baby was actually born, but now they must move elsewhere, and since no definite decision could be taken until Jean-Marie had settled what to do with his aged parent, she might just as well stay here . . . where she would have her darling Uncle Ptoly to love and care for her (as he had done so copiously before her marriage), to say nothing of his advice on young motherhood – and Jesus Christ, she could use it.

Jean-Marie, too polite to impugn Ptolemaeos' qualifications as a pediatrician, repeated his fear that Fen air was bad for babies. Had not Jo-Jo herself once said this when they were discussing the possibility of coming to live near her Uncle Ptoly?

Yes, she had, but she had really meant during the winter, not during the autumn, which would still be with them for some time; and anyway, look how she herself had thrived while living there – obviously the Fens were in Oenone's blood, so to speak.

Ptolemaeos, appealed to by Jean-Marie in the matter, said there was nothing wrong with the Fens once you understood them, and that Mrs Gurt and Mrs Statch knew effective remedies for every Fenland ailment that Oenone could conceivably contract. Jean-Marie, knowing when he was beaten, looking at his watch and saying that he must be at the airport by six-thirty, gently replacing his daughter in her carry-cot, courteously saying good-bye to Jeremy, Nicos and Piero, largely unheeded by Jo-Jo, who was banging about the kitchen complaining of 'those two filthy old sluts, they're not fit to sweep out a cat house, Ptoly only employs them because he thinks they're witches' – Jean-Marie, having given a last sad little look into the carry-cot and having been granted a lascivious kiss by Jo-Jo to make up for her recent neglect, faded away into an unconvincing taxi which had been conjured up from somewhere, and set off through the gathering fen mist, bound (one assumed) for Heathrow.

'Thank God he's gone,' Jo-Jo announced. 'I dote on my husband but since Oenone came he's been a nightmare . . . behaving as if he were Joseph of Nazareth, Doctor Spock and Madame Curie all rolled into one. Let's hope that old woman in Clermont-Ferrand goes the full distance, because as long as she's above ground Jean-Marie's stuck there.'

'What will you do about Jean-Marie's father when the old lady dies?' said Ptolemaeos.

'A very pertinent question, good Uncle, but one of which, with your permission, we shall postpone discussion. There are, there just are, more immediate questions,' she said, tipping a tin of Cow & Gate over a seething saucepan: 'like what does one do with a perfectly amiable infant whom one simply finds supererogatory? Is there any hope – after all – that the Fen air may help?'

'I know I'm vulgar and insensitive,' said Len to the Provost of Lancaster, 'but this I must declare: if I had the sort of money Jo-Jo Guiscard has, or even the sort of money I myself have, I'd not be marking this event – happy or unhappy – by crouching in the Fens.'

Ptolemaeos had just rung up Tom to report on the situation.

'The boys have gone back to playing games in the

bath,' Ptoly had said, 'and Jo-Jo is giving Oenone her bottle in the kitchen, and I thought you might be amused to hear about it all.'

'Though why I should want to hear about that ill-conditioned minx,' said Tom to Len a little later, 'I cannot imagine. Thank God she's had a girl – at least we'll hear no more of a christening in the Chapel.'

'There might be more spectacular disruptions,' said Len, 'than christenings in the Chapel.'

'Expand.'

'Jo-Jo Guiscard is your daughter Tullia's best friend, the one Baby loves more than anyone at all, and probably vice versa. Now, Ptoly Tunne is telling you, in his own cool way, that Jo-Jo is ripe for heap big trouble, and we needn't expect that Baby will be left out of it. Ptoly is giving out a gale warning.'

'But *what* trouble?' said Tom. 'Madame Guiscard will be perfectly contented in the Fens with her Uncle, as she has been in the past. The Fenland effluvia will *not* kill that child, nor does she think they will: she clearly made that remark about Fen air as a bad taste joke. And again, Len, if anyone *can* give her good advice in the circumstances, it probably *is* Ptolemaeos. So what is all this about gale warnings?'

'You are being obtuse, Provost,' said Len. 'You are reckoning without our little chum, Piero.'

'It has a fascination, that game in the sarcophagus,' said Nicos to Jeremy as they drove through the mist and out of the Fens towards Cambridge; 'but I don't think I wish to play again for a while.'

'We'll miss you,' said Jeremy, and meant it. He had enjoyed the sight of Nicos' hard limbs in the bath: he had been intrigued by Nicos' strained attempts to play the game in the spirit intended and yet to conceal anything of real importance to him.

'Funny,' said Nicos: 'Lady Canteloupe arriving like that.'

Baby had arrived, rather breathless, while Jeremy, Nicos, Piero and Ptolemaeos were having tea with Jo-Jo and Oenone in the kitchen.

'I knew you'd come here,' Baby had said to Jo-Jo, 'and I knew you'd only left Wiltshire because you thought I'd had enough of you. So I'm here to prove that I haven't. I think you want me,' she said, and kissed Jo-Jo softly on the lips. Jo-Jo did not demur. Baby gave a slanting look towards Piero.

'Madame Guiscard and her child are the excuse,' Nicos said now in Jeremy's car: 'Piero is the reason.'

'Yes. She knew Piero when she was a little girl, on a holiday in Venice. You saw and heard,' said Jeremy, 'what an effort she made to hi-jack him the other day in Lancaster.'

'She could hi-jack me and welcome,' Nicos said. 'A little too fat, but who cares? I bet . . . plenty of juice.'

'I see what you mean. I don't like her . . . but as a lust object she has plenty to be said for her. Jo-Jo too. She must absolutely crackle when her tail's up.'

'It is not up just now,' Nicos said. 'I'll tell you something, Jeremy: although Lady Canteloupe is seething for Piero, and although Piero is doing his best to appear enthusiastic, I do not think his heart is in it.'

'He could have fooled me. He evidently fooled her. Do you think that he doesn't like girls – prefers men?'

'I think he is fairly easy as to that. I think he fancies Lady Canteloupe quite a lot, and he will acquit himself with credit: but though his prick is in it, Yeramy *mou*, his heart is not.'

'He will also be worried about our good Provost, whether he will give him a place in the College. On the one hand, a happy Baby might make good interest for him with her Daddy.'

'And on the other,' said Nicos, 'an unhappy Daddy, not liking his Baby to be naughty with dirty street boys when she has a lovely lord for a husband, might bar the gate of Lancaster to Piero for ever.'

'Well, Piero is never tired of telling us he is a whore – every other answer he gave in the sarcophagus seemed to turn on that – and these are pre-eminently whorish calculations. We had best leave them to him.'

'I should like to see them together,' said Nicos greedily, more relaxed alone with Jeremy in the dark, moving car than ever in the soothing waters of the sarcophagus: 'dainty Piero and the hot little Canteloupe.'

'I'm sure that Piero would arrange it if the price was right.'

Both boys laughed, grating and coarse.

'Come and have dinner at Malvolio's,' said Jeremy: 'my treat.'

'I am sorry. I cannot accept this invitation.'

'If we are to be friends, Nicos, you must learn to accept my hospitality without worrying about returning it.'

'Oh, it is not that. The *Kyrios* Barraclough dines on High Table tonight. He will be curious if he does not see me in Hall. He will wonder where I am, and question me, and be angry.'

'Then let's sit together in Hall. I'll order some Burgundy.'

'No Burgundy for me, Yeramy. The *Kyrios* quite likes you and thinks you are a suitable friend for me . . . but he is always suspicious, and expensive restaurants and bottles of Burgundy he does not approve. Such things are not for orphans from the Mani unless generously bestowed by himself. It is not good that you are a friend of Major Gray; and if *Kyrios* Barraclough should see that we had . . . the high life with one another, he would forbid our friendship.'

'That would be unfair and dishonourable of him. And so then, as you said in the sarcophagus, you need no longer obey him.'

'Disobedience is difficult on an empty stomach,' Nicos said.

'Do you remember, Piero, when I was a little girl, that dinner at the Palazzo in Venice, and I couldn't find *the place*, and I went right upstairs and out on to the roof and piddled on the balustrade?'

'Yes, Miss Baby.'

'Why do you call me that?'

'Because that is how I remember you. And I remember how shocked and excited I was, when I came on to the roof and you told me what you had done.'

'Are you excited now?'

'Very excited, Miss Baby.'

'Show me.'

'And you show me . . . yourself as you were on that roof . . . Why, Miss Baby, what are you doing, squatting there like that?'

'Piero, oh Piero – don't look, Piero, I've nearly finished – but you *are* looking, aren't you, so you must let me watch you to make up.'

'Do you think it would have been like that, if I'd come up to the roof a little earlier?'

'I don't know. I'd like to think so. We were both so delicious then.'

'You are delicious now, Miss Baby. I must taste you, everywhere. That is what I would have done on the roof, if I had arrived a little earlier and not been afraid lest Mr Lykiadopoulos should follow us and catch us. I should have respected the little girl, the virgin, but I should have tasted her all over . . . until at last her tight young thighs were quivering along my cheeks.'

'So that was for starters?' Jo-Jo said the next morning, as she and Baby walked up and down outside Ptolemaeos' summer-house, in which they had parked Oenone and her carry-cot.

'Another instalment this afternoon.'

'No guilt about Canty?'

'No. It's not happening to me, you see, but to that little girl in Venice. We are playing a game of what might have been.'

'Very ingenious. But limiting, if Piero must continue to respect your "virginity".'

'All that means is no fucking. And just as well too. No fucking, no trouble, as Poppa once said to me when he was drunk. And after all, there are about a million other things you can do.'

'I wish I wanted to do some of them,' said Jo-Jo. There was a small burst of weeping from the summer-house. 'Although I haven't had it for literally months,' she said as they started towards the weeping, 'and although you'd think I'd be ready to go off like a Catherine Wheel, I just am not in the tiniest bit interested.'

She peered down at Oenone.

'Don't be boring,' she said.

'I hope *I'm* not being boring,' said Baby, picking up Oenone and stroking her bald little head, 'talking about me and Piero when you're right off the whole thing.'

'Not so far. It's all quite interesting in a theoretical way, like the latest discovery about sub-atomic particles. Better put her back before she gets a fixation or something ghastly. You see,' said Jo-Jo, 'I just cannot feel any keenness in the idea of doing anything myself. It's all Oenone's fault,' she said, as Baby replaced the offender in the carry-cot. 'I can't explain but I know I shan't want to do a single bloody sex-thing until I've settled what to do about her. As long as she's there she'll be like a duenna, watching, always watching.'

'Such rubbish. She's asleep most of the time.'

'I *feel* she's watching. I've already said I can't explain,

109

darling, and I know it makes no sense at all, but to me Oenone is just nine pounds solid of highly concentrated anti-aphrodisiac.'

'Poor Jo. What on earth can you do? I mean . . . she's here now.'

'I'm hoping that Ptoly will work something out before Jean-Marie gets back. Perhaps . . . some sort of wet-nurse, you know, some country woman who takes her in with her own family, and Jean-Marie can see her when-ever he wants. The fact that she won't take my milk might make an excuse.'

'That sort of thing hasn't happened for a hundred years, darling. I shouldn't think it's allowed, these days. Anyway, Jean-Marie won't allow it.'

'Something else, then,' said Jo-Jo, taut and peevish. 'I can't have that child with me much longer. Before she was born, I used to say that if I had a girl I'd expose her, like the Greeks used to. These days that's not allowed either.'

'You wouldn't have done it.'

'I sometimes wonder. If it could be done painlessly, without the cold and the creatures with claws coming closer over the mountains . . . I don't hate her you see. I want her to have a nice time.'

'Being exposed, darling?'

'Painlessly, I said. What could be nicer than being painlessly exposed and then dead? But since this can't happen, I'd like her to have a nice time while she's here, and every now and then I'd like to go and watch her having it. But I can't keep her with me.'

'You have a nice long talk with Ptoly. He'll help you if anyone can. I'm sorry you're off sex, darling, because I wanted you to distract Jeremy Morrison from Piero, give him a good healthy interest elsewhere.'

'You think they – '

' – No. But even so, Master Jeremy might get jealous and that would upset Piero and take his mind off his job. Now, he's a hulking brute, that Morrison, but all the same he's quite dishy, don't you think, or perhaps *scrummy* is a better adjective in his case, but something he certainly has got, and I do wish you would amuse him if he comes, as he might, this afternoon.'

'Uncle Ptoly says he usually comes every other day, which would mean he won't be coming till tomorrow.'

'Yes, but when he was here yesterday he may have smelt something between me and Piero . . . which could just bring him back today. If so, darling, I rely on you to *divert* him.'

'I can certainly put up a little light conversation, if that will be any good.'

'You're sure you can't manage anything . . . more riveting than that?'

'I have told you, darling. Not while Oenone is here or anywhere near.'

'If that Greek boy comes with him,' Baby went on, obsessed, 'all will be well. They can entertain each other in that sarcophagus you've told me about. But if Morrison comes alone, he will want Piero.'

'He will want Piero anyhow. Why can't you wait until tonight?'

'Because I can't. I can hardly wait till this afternoon.'

'Then *why* wait till this afternoon?'

'Because Piero is with your Uncle Ptolemaeos. There are problems which will very soon have to be settled about his passport and so on.'

'All right,' said Jo-Jo; 'if Jeremy Morrison turns up here and asks for Piero, I'll do my best to turn him round and send him back to Cambridge.'

'You *promise*?'

'I shall do my best. Whatever excuse I make, Mr Morrison will almost certainly guess the truth. Yet it's quite possible that he *won't* be tiresome or jealous,' said Jo-Jo, who was by now viciously irritated by the whole affair and was deliberately seeking to anger or injure, 'but will go away quietly, looking forward to a blow by blow description, if you will excuse the pun, next time he sees Piero. Men are often like that: not jealous, just prurient; and Piero will probably give an hilarious imitation of you while you're coming; and both of them will howl with laughter. But whatever happens,' said Jo-Jo, 'I won't go on acting as door-keeper for ever. It's a fucking imposition. You'll have to work something out for yourselves, you and Piero, and the sooner the better, because Loppylugs Morrison and Nick the Greek are not going to vanish from the earth just for your convenience.'

'All right, darling. No need to be a shrew just because you've dried up between the legs. We'll manage fine without your help,' Baby said.

'You see,' said Ptolemaeos to Piero, 'although this is an easygoing country, no identity cards required or anything like that, you must be able to explain, at a need, who you are and where you come from. Now then: you say that the Franciscans took your passport when you joined their order: and obviously you were not able to get it back before absconding?'

'It was in any case out of date by then.'

112

'If,' said Ptolemaeos carefully, 'we went to the Italian Embassy in London, we could almost certainly, with careful persuasion and explanation, re-establish you in the identity which you had before you went into that convent. You are, of course, an illegal immigrant as far as the British authorities are concerned; but I have friends who have friends who would take care of that. But something tells me,' said Ptolemaeos, 'that you are no longer much in love with the boy who went into the convent . . . with Piero of Venice . . . and that you would like to be somebody else.'

'I should like to be an English gentleman.'

'Yes,' said Ptolemaeos complacently; 'a lot of people would like to be that. Jean-Marie Guiscard, whom you met yesterday, would give one eye to be taken for a member of the English Upper Class.'

'Just an English gentleman will be enough for me,' said Piero: 'it is not, I think, quite the same thing?'

'I'm afraid not. Many of the Upper Class in this country are not gentlemen. This is sometimes embarrassing.'

'Jeremy Morrison, however . . . he is both, *non è vero*?'

'Not *really*. He is a plausible and well mannered boy, as they go, but he is not chivalrous, unless he finds it strictly convenient, and so not quite a gentleman. The lands he will inherit are ample, but they have not always been, and even now they make a large farm rather than a feoff or estate. All this means that the Morrisons were, until recently, yeomen rather than esquires, making their claim to be Upper Class definitely dubious. No title – but then that, as it happens, doesn't matter. Family old, which does matter, but frankly . . . rather too loamy. However,' said Ptolemaeos, 'if one is prepared to stretch a point or two, Jeremy Morrison can be taken as a fair working model of an English gentleman of the Upper Class . . . *pour nos jours.*'

'And I would wish to be . . . a fair working model simply of an English gentleman . . . *pour nos jours*. Can this be done?'

'What price are you offering, Piero? You have no money and no influence. I dare say you would offer your body, which I do not want – nothing personal, you understand, it is just that these days I am too large and lazy. So how can you pay me?'

'Jeremy tells me . . . that you employ people over very wide areas to find out things which you wish to know . . . rather like Max de Freville in the old days, when I knew him with Lykiadopoulos in Venice.'

'Yes, one heard a good deal about that at one time. Max lost interest some time before he died, of course, was indeed already losing it when you knew him in Venice, and switching his resources to restoring Venetian buildings.'

'You know why? It was on instructions which he kept receiving from his dead mistress. In her shrine on the roof of the Palazzo.'

'Ah. So you are offering that little tit-bit on approval, so to speak?'

'Yes; you see . . . I could perhaps serve you.'

'You certainly deserve to be tried. Let us say for the sake of argument,' Ptolemaeos said, 'that from now on you are my personal secretary – probationary and in training. Part of your training, we hope, will be undergone at Lancaster College, which will do something, though regrettably little these days, towards turning you into a gentleman. The rest I shall have to do . . . during the vacations, when you will be working for me.

'As for your identity,' Ptolemaeos continued, 'I have

114

already given thought to the matter, and I see you as the son of a British Army Officer, a distant cousin of mine, who served for a time in Cyprus, came to like the place, and retired to live in the hills near Kyrenia . . . with his Italian wife, your mother, whose nationality explains the foreign components (which we shall do our best to lessen but cannot obscure entirely) in your own charming appearance. During the Turkish invasion of Cyprus your parents were murdered by Turkish soldiers – '

– One of the brightly coloured telephones on the desk in front of Ptolemaeos began to ring. Ptolemaeos lifted the receiver, uttered a minatory greeting, listened, then said:

'By all means, Jeremy, come this afternoon if you wish. Your parents were murdered by Turkish soldiers,' he said to Piero without hiatus, 'who ransacked and then fired your home. But you, who had been sent down to friends in Kyrenia harbour – whither your parents intended, in vain, to follow you with important papers and portable objects of value – *you* got away in an open dinghy, drifting without food or water, like the shipwrecked Don Juan, and in much the same part of the Mediterranean Sea. You were eventually rescued by the Italian Air Force, taken on by the International Red Cross . . . by whom, on my intervention – for by that time I had heard of my cousins' fate and managed to trace you – were placed in the care of a certain Doctor La Soeur, who runs a private nursing home in the outskirts of London.

'After some years of acute nervous and physical suffering, you have now recovered and come to live with me, for I, as a distant relation and a rich philanthropist, am to oversee your present welfare and future employment. When we have drilled you long and hard enough in your history, we shall apply for documents – Birth Certificate, Passport, National Insurance (if applicable in your case), etcetera, etcetera – to replace those which were either burnt in your parents' house before they could get them out, or mislaid by Government Officials in Kyrenia during the war.'

'Surely, copies of such documents – of my Birth Certificate at least – would be in England already?'

'I am glad you are joining in the spirit of the thing. If we assume you were born out of England, a copy of your Birth Certificate would have been sent to Somerset House in London, from whatever place your father was serving in at the time of your birth, by the Military or Consular Officials responsible for issuing the original Certificate. How, for a start, shall we explain *that* omission? Whatever the solution,' said Ptolemaeos, 'the place of your birth will have to be very carefully chosen to accord with my cousin's career, which itself must be submitted to painstaking research. You see the kind of problems which lie before us?'

Piero nodded. 'My arrival in England, after the rescue,' he said. 'I was without name, papers, money – with only you to vouch for me. Surely my arrival should have been reported – by somebody – to many different authorities?'

'Indeed,' said Ptolemaeos, looking at his pupil with ironic appreciation. 'With the aptitude which you evidently have for this kind of operation, you will not be surprised to hear that these very serious gaps and cracks have to be plugged and papered with ready money. The dead Officer and his wife will be no trouble – I did in truth have such cousins – and will not require payment: but a very large number of people will – from the supposed owner of the supposed dinghy which took you out of Kyrenia; all the way along the line to Doctor La

116

Soeur, who received you in his nursing home in England, but did not report your presence because he understood that this had already been done by me; who, in my turn, thought it had been done by the Red Cross . . . which must somehow have neglected this duty, and so, and so, and so. You are going, *caro mio*, to be a very expensive item.'

'I shall try to give good value. I am well accustomed to doing that.'

'Precisely. So I have a notion that you will prove a very efficient confidential servant. It is your métier. As I grow older, I feel the need of having someone close at hand. I envy Tom Llewyllyn that Secretary, Len. Indeed it's from there I got the idea.'

'How do you know that I shall stay with you, after I am fully explained, equipped and trained . . . so to speak?'

'I cannot be sure of that. But then, if you lose interest and wish to go, you will have ceased to be of use to me anyway. So go you would – though just where is another question, which you would find more difficult to answer, once I had washed my hands of you than you might think. But I am hoping . . . and supposing . . . not without ample reason . . . that life in my employment will continue to have appeal for you. You will, incidentally, be required to do a number of things, later on, which you will find a fascinating challenge to your talents; and even during your apprenticeship you will be faced by intermittent and quite demanding tests. In fact I have one for you even so early as this.'

'Indeed, Mr Tunne?'

'You will address me as "Sir" or "Ptolemaeos", which-ever you prefer. "Mister" these days, is for banausics. And what might they be?'

117

'Mechanics. A class just above peasants or menials.'

'Very good. Any deficiencies in your education can always be explained by irregular tuition, consequent on following the drum with your parents; but I am not well disposed to ignorance any more than I am to folly.'

'I fear . . . sir . . . that a childhood in the streets of Syracuse affords severely specialized instruction, though I have tried to make up for it since.'

'Continue. There is my library here . . . and all the resources of Lancaster should you be admitted there.'

'And meanwhile, sir, you say there is a test?'

'Yes. One in which the specialized instruction of Syracuse may assist you.' Ptolemaeos gave a passable imitation of a Sicilian street sign which meant 'Trespasser on our Pitch'. Piero corrected him, making the same gesture, but with his thumb (which was inserted between the third and the little finger, the fist being reversed) protruding further and tilted backwards.

'Get rid of *la piccola marchesa*,' said Ptolemaeos. 'She's no good to my niece, just now, and I want her pert little ladyship out of this house – and preferably out of your life as well – in twenty-four hours at most. Baby Canteloupe is a superfluity, my dear Piero – Piero, by the way, will continue to be your Christian name, whatever else must change – and I shall be very interested to see how you dispose of her.'

When Jeremy reached Ptolemaeos' house that afternoon, he rang the clinking rust-red bell outside the front door, but was not answered. He should have remembered, he told himself, that Wednesday was Mrs Gurt's and Mrs Statch's half day off. He opened the front door, peered into the Library, into the office with the multi-coloured telephones, into the dowdy drawing room: no one. He walked through the drawing room and through a door into the garden. Down the garden he went, to the summer-house: empty.

But at last the sound of gentle sobbing guided him to a place which he had not come across before, though he had spent many days in the house and garden during the summer; one reached it, he discovered now, by a concealed path that started at the rear of the summer-house, ran back towards the big house through a thick clump of small fir-trees, and at length came to a pond, little more than a puddle, which was covered by water lilies and surrounded by a narrow margin of rough grass. On this grass, on a camp stool, sat Jo-Jo, snarling, while beside her Oenone sobbed in the carry-cot.

'To think,' said Jo-Jo with venom, 'that Ptoly gave that boy my clothes to wear. My jeans, my shirt, my socks.'

'You surely had no more use for them,' Jeremy said. 'He arrived in a Friar's habit, you know. He had to change into something, and anyhow Mr Tunne very soon bought him his own stuff to wear. Where is everybody?'

'He was wearing *my* shirt, jeans *and* socks – on that

119

horrible foot – at lunch. I think it's some joke he's having with Baby.'

'And you're jealous at being left out of it?'

'That's the sort of thing a man would say, particularly a conceited know-all like you. But of course I should have expected something nasty. *You* were *rude* to me when we last met – '

' – Yesterday? Surely not? – '

' – Last April, smart arse, in the Provost's Lodging, at Sarum's christening.'

'You were pretty gruesome yourself. All those questions you kept asking, like the Grand Inquisitor. Let's forgive and forget. We have other things to worry about now.'

Oenone started glugging. Jo-Jo looked into the carry-cot as though it were a box of chocolates from which she knew that all the soft-centres had been taken.

'Forgive and forget,' repeated Jeremy, 'at least forgive?'

'I'll try. I am not in my giving – or forgiving – mood to-day.'

'Richard the Third. He came to a horrid end.'

'All right. You're forgiven.'

'And so are you. Now then: where is everybody?'

'Oenone and I, as you see, are sitting by this pool. Uncle Ptoly has gone racing at Newmarket – something which he has not done for some time, so I imagine it is a mere excuse to get away from us all. We are,' said Jo-Jo, 'a tolerably unattractive crew – all of us totally absorbed in our own squalid preoccupations.'

'Where is Piero? At Newmarket too?'

'No. He is upstairs with Baby. They know you are coming and are waiting for you.'

'Can you mean that?'

'Piero told me,' said Jo-Jo, 'that you had telephoned Ptoly this morning and would be coming this afternoon. "Tell him when he arrives," Piero said, "to come upstairs to me and Baby." I assume that he spoke for Baby as well as himself, though she was not actually present when he said this. Being in a thoroughly disobliging frame of mind, as I have just informed you, I determined that I was not going to be used as a kind of receptionist to pass on other people's messages, so I hid from you. However, since you have found me out, you deserve to be told. First floor landing, fifth door on the left.'

'Ah. The room with the four-poster. I was in there last summer.' He lingered. 'Suppose,' he said, 'that my friend Nicos had been with me, what would have happened then?'

'He and I would have gone blackberrying, or something of the kind. With Oenone. I did not look forward to it – another boring task to suit someone else's convenience – so that was one reason the more for me to hide. Where shall I go? I thought. And then I remembered this pond. When I lived here with Uncle Ptoly, I used to come out here, with the same stool, to read.'

'Why didn't you bring a book this time?'

'I did.' She reached down to the carry-cot and extracted a thin book from behind Oenone's pillow. 'Potted Tennyson,' she said. 'I'm going to read "Oenone" aloud to Oenone; I'm going to read her her own lament.'

'I'll be off then.' He shuffled about.

'Yes, you be off.'

'You're sure they're expecting me?'

'I can be sure of nothing,' said Jo-Jo, 'except that Piero told me to tell you to come to them when you arrived. I wasn't going to, as I told you, but now I have. First floor landing – but we've been through all that.'

'Yes, we have. Thank you . . . er . . . Mrs Guiscard
. . . that is – Madame Guiscard. I'm very much obl – '
'For Christ's sake, bugger off.'
. . . that is – Madame Guiscard. I'm very much obl – '
' – For Christ's sake bugger off.'

PART TWO
Traghetto

Come d'autunno si levan le foglie
l'una appresso del l'altra, infin che il ramo
vede al la terra tutte le sue spoglie,
similemente il mal seme d'Adamo:
gittansi di quel lito ad una ad una
per cenni, come augel per suo richiamo.
Così sen vanno su per l'onda bruna,
ed avanti che sian di là discese
anche di qua nova schiera s'aduna.

As in the autumn the leaves drop off and fall,
one and then another, until the bough sees
all its finery strewn upon the earth, so on the
shore wait the ill-born heirs of Adam. One and
the other they fling themselves thence, at signals,
as a hawk flies to its lure. Then they depart
over the grey waters; and before they arrive on
the other bank, there is a new company growing
dense on this.

DANTE: *Inferno,* Canto iii,
ll. 112 to 120

On the morning after Baby's first night away in the Fens, Canteloupe came up to London, entertained his solicitor to a quiet luncheon at his Club, and then, by previous arrangement, waited on Fielding Gray at Buttock's Hotel.

'Piero,' said Canteloupe, as he sat down on the one armchair in Fielding's bed-sitting room. 'Baby has gone to the Fens to get him out of her system.'

'Did she say so before she left?'

'As good as. She *said* she must go to take care of Jo-Jo, but she made it very plain how much she was looking forward to seeing Piero. She knew I wouldn't mind, you see. But there is a problem. Tullius. Although that nice little ginger Nanny is coping very well, she can't be left alone with him for too long: so either Baby must come back pretty soon, or Tullius and the Nurse must go to the Fens – and *that* would not be a suitable thing at all. Tully's place is in his own home in Wiltshire.'

'Did Baby say anything about that before she left?'

'No. Tullius has now been weaned, and she may think she deserves a holiday from him. Which is all right with everybody, as Tully is quite happy with the nurse – almost prefers her, I sometimes think – provided it doesn't go on too long.'

'How can I help?'

'You've seen Piero, I understand . . . since he came to England, I mean, I haven't. What is he after, in your view?'

'He's not after Baby – or not for keepers. Mind you, I

125

haven't seen them together, but I do know of one thing which Piero wants, and that thing rules out protracted dalliance, with Baby or anyone else. Piero wants to make a place for himself as his own man. In his time he's been a beggar, a tart and a Franciscan messenger boy. Now he wants something *sérieux*, as the French say.'

'How do you know this?'

'The day after he arrived, I went down to see him in Tom's Lodging in Lancaster. Piero was liking what he found there – and I don't just mean the handsome furniture or the Corots on the wall; I mean the sense of achievement. He saw a successful and respected man – the Provost of Lancaster College – slowly beginning to approach the last stages of a long and interesting career. Repeat, Canteloupe, career. That's for Piero. At the moment his money is on Ptoly Tunne to get him started, and the signs are – so Jerry Morrison writes to me from Cambridge – that Ptoly's getting ready to keep Piero exceedingly busy.'

'And what's in all this for Baby?'

'Very little indeed, I'd say.'

'So we just let the thing go on, and hope he lets her down lightly?'

'That's about it. I'd be very surprised if she's not back with you in Wiltshire within a week.'

'Without Piero, I hope. At one stage she was talking of having him to stay.'

'Should you mind that?'

'Who was it who said that the decline of upper class families begins when "they start bringing vice into the house instead of going out for it"?'

'Nigel Dennis. *Cards of Identity*. I had to review it in the bad old days, when I was doing a novel column. He goes on to add that when "the lower orders are admitted into the better bedrooms the vertical structure of society begins to totter." It's a very nice point, Canteloupe. But I shouldn't worry. If Piero's instincts are as sound as I think they are, he'll stay put with Ptoly Tunne.'

'Gregory Stern has written,' said Carmilla Salinger to Theodosia, 'to thank us for our offer to print his book. He wants to know how we would wish him to proceed. Apparently the typescript will be ready before very long – soon after some trip he's going on to consult what he calls "his principals".'

'P, A, L, S or P, L, E, S?'

'Former.'

'Pity,' said Theodosia. 'If only it were the latter, they might tell him to give the whole stinking thing up.'

'You got us into this, Thea – because of your childhood pash on Lord Canteloupe.'

'On Captain Detterling. I know I did. And believe me, I'm sorry. Shall we back out after all?'

'No,' said Carmilla. 'You've given your word, which means that we have given our word. It's too late to go back now.'

'Right you be, Carm. So we'd better tell Gregory Stern to get in touch with Ashley Dexterside at the firm as soon as the stuff's ready.'

'And that's that settled,' said Carmilla, scribbling a note on a pad. 'One more nasty problem out of the way – at least for the time being. But there are plenty more, even nastier in some ways and certainly more boring.

Oh, so many, Thea: look, look, look, girl, at all of this horrible cag.' She waved both hands in circles over the piles of opened and unopened correspondence which covered the round table, and looked through the window at the Lawn and the South Wall of the Chapel. 'Sheer disruption,' she said, bringing her eyes back to the table. 'How can a girl concentrate on Stubbs or Motley when she has this sort of muck to deal with every day?'

'It's not helping my badminton either,' Theodosia said.

'We need someone to handle all this for us until we are finished here at Lancaster. Salinger & Holbrook will be always with us, Thea: Lancaster not much longer. We mustn't waste it.'

'I expect *you'll* get a Fellowship and stay on.'

'Very tricky work – writing a thesis for a Fellowship. Whichever way we look at it, we must be rid of this, for the time being at least.'

Again Carmilla waved her hands over the piles of envelopes.

'We need an honest man,' said Theodosia, 'or one whose margin of dishonesty is moderate and constant. There's a character in Trollope who says he doesn't mind if his lawyer robs him of ten shillings in every sovereign provided he himself can be sure of the other ten. Whom shall we approach?'

'Ashley Dexterside? An old chum of Da's. He's been with the firm for ever.'

'His thing is lay-out. That's what he knows and that's what he loves. He doesn't want to be buggered up,' said Theodosia, 'with endless niggling correspondence. What about John Groves, the lawyer?'

'Unsympathetic,' Carmilla said.

'Len? Would he take it on? *Our* Secretary as well as the Provost's?'

'We can always ask.'

128

After Canteloupe had left him to return to Wiltshire, Fielding reviewed his accounts. In the days since his return from his expedition with Jeremy he had sorted things out pretty thoroughly, and the upshot was that if he sold most (not, as he had feared, all) of the bank stock which was one of his two major holdings, he could pay up and look big all round – though some months of economy and the rapid completion of his next novel would also be required of him before his affairs were tidy.

So far, so bad; but it could have been a lot worse. His real worry was the accusation, by the Inland Revenue, that he had been under-declaring his income. The figures which Stern & Detterling had sent to the Inspector of Taxes were now being investigated by his accountant, whose interim report indicated that the Inspector's charge appeared to be well founded. But it cannot be, Fielding thought now; I simply did not try – would not have dreamt of trying – to get away with such a thing; there would have been no point; I *know* I transcribed the figures accurately, that all the monies received by me were included in my returns over the last three years – over the last twenty, for the matter of that.

But what if the thing went against him? If they claimed tax on the money which they alleged he had not declared – and that was the very least they would do if he were proven to have made false returns, whatever the explanation – what could he then do? To whom could he apply? Even if he cashed the last of his reserves it would not be enough to meet the bill of at least £12,000 which would then be facing him. Would Canteloupe help him? But Canteloupe had comparatively little ready money (or so he always used to say) under his own control; and in any case, would it not seem like blackmail? Give me twelve, thirteen, fifteen thousand pounds, or I shall tell the world how you and Baby asked me to father on her the son whom you could not. That was how it might sound in Canteloupe's ears. So what, some would have said, provided the tactic were successful? Desperate situations called for, and justified, desperate remedies. But to Fielding it would be unbearably horrible should his old friend and publisher think that he was using him in this way. Or yet again, suppose Canteloupe did not think this (for after all, Canteloupe trusted Fielding, otherwise he would not have been at Buttock's that afternoon, seeking his advice), suppose he realized that Fielding was asking out of need and not demanding with implied threat, suppose he took the request in good part and acceded to it with all promptness and kindness, suppose all this – and what, what then, of Fielding's ghastly loss of face? I, Fielding Gray (he would in effect be saying), have so far lost control of my affairs that unless I am given many thousands of pounds I shall be a ruined man.

Wait and see, wait and see, Fielding told himself: the accountant might yet find the simple explanation which might, which must, lie behind this apparent error in his returns; or perhaps a fresh supply of money might come in from somewhere (there was renewed interest, it seemed, in the possibility of making a film of his early novel, *Love's Jest Book*); or perhaps, great shades of Mr Micawber, perhaps even both.

'Sorry, girls,' said Len to Carmilla and Theodosia, 'I'm not sure that I'd want to take it on – even with the generous honorarium which you're offering – but in any case I can't. My contract as Secretary to the Provost rules it right out. But I think I have a good candidate for you. Do you remember a large, grinning man, with what foreigners call "the English sun tan", at Sarum's christening in April?'

'Hung about on the edge of things,' said Theodosia; 'not a friend of Da's or Max's – '

' – But a friend of Canteloupe,' said Len: 'Colonel Blessington. An honest soldier. Retired.'

'Dreary, sensible wife,' said Carmilla remembering, 'and two jolly little girls. So perhaps the wife isn't as dreary as she looks.'

'That's them. Blessington is a stockbroker these days. He gets by but doesn't get rich. Too slow, and in any case rather bored by it, even disgusted. Not the kind of thing which an ex-A.D.C. and ex-Military Attaché much cares for.'

'Intelligent, then,' said Theodosia, 'if he was once an Attaché, and well mannered. Slow, you say, but intelligent and well mannered . . . and very possibly in need of extra income. What about it, Carm?'

'I think we should have a word with Colonel Blessington,' Carmilla said. 'I don't like to think of those two little girls on short commons.'

'So Lord Canteloupe was here this afternoon,' said Maisie, when she paid her tea-time visit to Fielding's room to ask what he'd like for dinner. 'Steak and kidney pudding,' she said, writing it down: 'more a lunch-time thing, dear, but I don't see why not. Tessa's out at Rosie's, so there's just the two of us. So Canteloupe was here?' she said.

'Trouble with Baby. He wanted my opinion.'

'Pity it's not his cousin, old Loopy, having the trouble. He'd have settled that little madam in ten seconds flat.'

'You liked the late Lord Canteloupe very much, didn't you?'

'Yes, and I know what you're thinking, and you're wrong. He's not Tessa's father, and neither are you.'

'When are you going to tell me who?'

'What's the matter with now?' Maisie said. 'I promised I'd tell you sometime, and I reckon you need your mind taking off that Tax man.'

'Cheering up?'

'This isn't a story to cheer anybody up, Fielding Gray – '

' – Sorry, love – '

' – But it may take you out of your dismal self for a bit. So . . . where shall I begin? Rosie's mother, Isobel Stern. It was a long time before she had Marius and Rosie. It kept going wrong, right?'

'Yes. It went wrong so often that she began to think of herself as permanently barren. She still used to talk as if

132

she was childless years after Marius and Rosie were born – she couldn't really believe she'd had them.'

'Well . . . one of the times it went wrong she actually got as far as having the child. Did you know that?'

'Yes. It was in 1964.'

'While she was in hospital, her husband . . . Gregory . . . came to see me.'

'Gregory Stern came to see you? In your professional capacity?'

'Yes. He'd heard of me from you. Once, when you were drunk, you'd told him . . . that I'd been kind to you.'

'You had.'

'So, being drunk, you pressed my address and telephone number on him. And since he wanted to humour you he'd taken them down in his book. Months later, years later, Isobel went to hospital to have this baby. Now, although he'd never had eyes for a girl in the world but Isobel, he began to be tempted – after weeks of not doing it because she was pregnant – when his secretary made advances in the office. A sheer animal thing. But he knew he mustn't come on his own doorstep, so to speak; he'd better off-load temptation somewhere – almost anywhere – else. So he looked in his book, remembering that time you'd been drunk, and came to confidential, ever-so-understanding me. You'd told him so much about me, he said, that he regarded me as a friend already. Then he put an envelope under the pillow. Then he told me he was so happy, his wife had had their first baby that afternoon, he'd always heard that made a man feel sexy, but anyway he must do it with someone, otherwise he was afraid he'd make an ass of himself over his prick-tease of a secretary and then there'd be a row and his wife Isobel would be so hurt and unhappy for him, and he loved her so much that he couldn't bear that. I used to hear a lot of nonsense in that line, but somehow I believed Gregory; I liked him, I liked him a lot, Fielding, and so when he asked, could he just ring up the hospital, he should have done an hour ago but he'd been stuck in a traffic jam and forgotten, so could he use my 'phone and of course he'd pay, I told him to help himself and have it on the house.

'So he rang up and they said his baby had died. They didn't know why. It was big and strong and doing well. It had just died.

'I saw from his face. And I thought . . . what did I think? . . . I was so sad, it seemed so unfair, and he just kept saying, "Oh dear, poor Isobel, she's tried so hard, Maisie, so often, it'll break her heart." And yours too, I thought. God giveth and God taketh away, and perhaps tonight God will give back what he has taken away, give back to me what he has taken away from you and Isobel, it won't do you any good but it may settle some accounts somewhere, so come to me, Gregory, I said, come to me, what a funny little lump on your shoulder, nice, though, nice, that's it, my darling, you be happy while you can, you're making me so happy too . . . yes, darling, come if you want to, oh warm, warm, I can feel it, come, Gregory, come, you come warm in Maisie's womb.

'Just that once,' Maisie said to Fielding, 'the only time ever, I didn't take any precautions and I didn't make him either. I left it to God, to see if he would settle the account, to see if he would give as well as taking away. And God gave me Tessa.'

'But why . . . darling Maisie . . . why do you pretend to be her aunt?'

'Just in case Gregory ever guessed, and it upset or

embarrassed him. I think, if he'd never had children of his own, I might one day have gone to him and said, "Here's your daughter", I might have said, "complete down to that little lump on her back, here's your daughter, love her if you will." But as it is, he has his own by the wife he loves. So let Tessa be just mine, my orphan niece, and the world none the wiser.'

'He may have guessed. He must know about Tessa's little hump. And he must realize that you are the same Maisie.'

'Oh, he realizes that all right. And very kind to me he is when we meet. Rather as if . . . I had been his nanny when he was a little boy. He never refers to that time with me, of course, but I know he remembers, and that's why it's so important that I insist on Tessa being my niece, so that he need feel no worry, no responsibility. Luckily she doesn't seem to favour him in the least, except for that little lump, there's no hiding that.'

'So . . . she really is Rosie's sister. How happy they would both be if they knew.'

'Much happier just imagining it,' Maisie said. 'A fantasy that turns out to be real loses its charm.'

'Shall you tell Teresa? Oughtn't she to know?'

'I nearly told her when I thought she might start fancying Marius. "No games of doctors with your brother," I nearly said. And then I thought, would it really matter? And then it turned out, anyway, that she only loved him like a brother, even if she may once have got a bit carried away, and there seemed no point in complicating things. As things are, Fielding, and as they may well be for some considerable time to come, it will be better, believe me, for Tessa to remain my niece. Do you remember, last Spring, when suddenly nobody came

135

to the hotel for weeks and weeks, and we couldn't think why?'

'I remember.'

'That was God, I think now, warning me not to tell Tessa, saying that it would be a wicked thing to tell her how she came to be born and what sort of woman I'd been – for she would have had to be told that if told anything at all. God, who gave me Tessa, was warning me to keep quiet, showing me that my punishment for snatching her from Him, almost by stealth as I had done, was that I could never let her know I was her mother. As soon as I began to think that I had better tell Tessa who she really was, now Marius and she were growing up, just in case – as soon as I began to think that, the guests ceased to come here, and they only came again when I had at last given up all idea of speaking out.'

'Maisie . . . it can't have been that.'

'What else?'

Fielding went to his one window and beckoned her over.

'What do you see, Maisie?'

'A very pretty Garden of Rest, love, with a quaint Victorian Church on one side of it and the Underground cutting on the other.'

'Precisely. A Garden of Rest which was an ordinary graveyard until February, when they widened the Underground cutting. Half the graveyard had to go, so they decided to take the stones out of the rest as well, and put all of them along the wall . . . work which took until June. Of course nobody was going to come here, Maisie, when the word began to go round that dead bodies were being dug up under the bedroom windows – and that even in that half of the cemetery which wasn't actually being destroyed the stones were being moved . . . the graves, in a sense, desecrated. Our lack of guests was caused in part by superstition, Maisie, and in part by distaste for charnel engineering.'

'Why didn't we realize at the time that that was the explanation?'

'Because once the work had been going on a very few days we simply ceased to notice it.'

'No guests and a gaping graveyard,' said Maisie: 'a message from God, whichever way you look at it.'

The telephone rang. Fielding lifted the receiver, listened, muttered, rang off, and began to sweat.

'Another message from God,' he said, slowly closing his one eye as if to rest it.

Tessa Malcolm and Rosie Stern were having tea in Rosie's house in Chelsea. Tessa was to stay on to dine as a special treat for Rosie, to make up for her parents' having gone down to Sandwich to see Marius.

'Though quite why I deserve a special treat because of that, I don't know,' Rosie said to Tessa.

'They're worried,' said Tessa, 'because Thursday is the wrong sort of day to be going to see anyone at a boarding school. They'll only interrupt things. So to make up for upsetting Marius they're being extra kind to you.'

'But they've got a very good reason for going to see him. Daddy has got to go to Trieste soon, and so he'll miss Marius's first exeat and wants to see him before he leaves instead. Today is the only free day he's got before then, even counting the week-end, so that's why they've gone to Sandwich.'

'Marius's first exeat,' said Tessa scornfully: 'it's quite ridiculous, all the exeats and half-terms and days off they have at schools these days. No sooner has anyone learnt anything than they come home for a week and forget it.'

'Well, this I will say,' said Rosie; 'in Marius's case he certainly seems to be learning a lot to forget. He wrote me a very interesting letter about doing Greek for his scholarship exam next summer. He says he's playing a lot of Eton Fives, whatever they may be, and sends you his love. So it looks as if everything is turning out all right . . . which is rather surprising, really, when you remember how horrid it all was only a few months ago.'

Marius would certainly have agreed with Tessa's strictures on the ease and frequency with which pupils were let out of schools, even schools as well disciplined and conservative as Oudenarde House. In Marius' view term was term and hols were hols, and while it was term he did not in the least want to go home or see his parents or be taken out on Sunday – which was one of the best days of the week for playing Squash or Fives. Although he could just endure official breaks in the term, because they affected everyone, he really did draw the line at unofficial visits, on a normal school day, such as his father and mother were paying him now. He knew just why they had come – because his father would be abroad during the first exeat – and very absurd he considered it:

as if his father and he couldn't go without seeing each other from mid-September to Half Term, which came only three weeks after the exeat. Not only was it absurd, it was downright annoying, as he was going to miss an important 1st XI pracker game and his favourite period with Wally St George – Latin Verse, which even these days could carry high marks, at the particular school for which he was entered, in his Scholarship Examination in June. And quite apart from that, what could be more pleasing than to be employed in an occupation which only .001 per cent of the population (so Wally had calculated) could begin to understand, let alone to emulate? What could be more superior, more absolutely and superly élite (the favourite word at Oudenarde that term) than writing poetry in a foreign language and a dead one at that?

So it was a deprived and unhappy Marius that walked the streets of Sandwich with his parents, killing the time before tea – until suddenly his mother saved the afternoon by saying,

'How silly of us to forget. Green Oxley Laris – it's only a few miles away.'

'What's there?' said Marius.

'You'll see,' said his mother, and propelled him into the windy back seat of her Lagonda, while Gregory, delighted as always at the prospect of motion, scampered round the bonnet (all six foot of him) and into the near-side front.

'Isn't there some story about Green Oxley Laris?' Gregory said. 'Something to do with someone we know?'

'There's a legend,' said Isobel, 'but since it dates from the twelfth century it can hardly concern our friends or relations.'

Isobel drove South, by-passed Deal, and continued

South along the Dover Road. After about two miles they came to a steep dip; they passed some kennnels in a meadow on their left; they entered a forest at the bottom of the dip; Isobel stopped the car under a bank by the mouth of a rough drive which led up into the forest; all of them disembarked.

'Through here,' Isobel said.

They scrambled over the bank above the drive, through some fifty yards of trees and malevolent undergrowth, and down into a bowl where a little chapel sagged and rotted and dripped.

'Now,' said Isobel. 'Notice those vouzoirs over the West Door, both of you: three orders of them. I don't think much of the tympanum – a pretty crummy Christ. It used to be the private chapel of the manor house up on the hill.'

How élite, thought Marius, to have a private chapel with a tympanum (however crummy the Christ) and three orders of vouzoirs. He accompanied his mother through the doorway (the door itself had vanished) and into the half-roofed chapel. 'Lancet windows,' said Isobel. (Goodness, how élite.) 'Thirteenth century sedilia over there, to the South of the sanctuary. An aumbry to one side of them.'

'An aumbry, Mummy?'

'Where the priest kept things. Bread and wine. Do you see the point of this place, my darling?'

'I think so. It is beautiful. And it is sad.'

'And it is wicked. An abbess used to meet the Lord of the Manor here . . . to make love with him.'

'Inside this chapel, Mummy?'

'I dare say . . . if it were cold or wet. He repented and went on a crusade.'

'What did the abbess do?'

140

'Waited for him to come back, I suppose.'

'And did he?'

'I don't know, darling.'

'Perhaps he died fighting in the Holy Land, under the Cross . . . and she put up that tablet in his memory . . . How silly of me,' said Marius, ashamed of his gushing; 'she wouldn't have been allowed to. An abbess. Anyway, it's quite modern, the tablet. It's for someone who died les than twenty years ago.'

'I believe the family were still in the house on the hill for some years after the war. Come on: this place has given me an appetite. Do you know somewhere that will give us poached eggs for tea . . . crumpets . . . anchovy toast?'

'Yes,' said Marius as they came out under the tympanum, 'I know just the place.'

'Good. There aren't many left these days. Not enough money in teas. They all want to sell you a filthy dinner with corked wine.' Thirty yards away, above the rim of the bowl, a shadow moved into the trees. 'Daddy,' called Marius.

'I expect he's back in the car. He doesn't like the cold.'

'But it's beastly cold in that car of yours, Mummy. I thought I saw him by those trees over there.'

'Why are you so nasty about my beautiful Lagonda?'

'Oh, it's very élite. But it *is* cold, Mummy . . . Daddy, why didn't you come in with us? It was lovely . . . superly weird. Sedilia and aumbries. Mummy knew all about them.'

'I know a little too, my dear. I know that the people who sat in those sedilia eight hundred years ago spent much of their time murdering and torturing our ancestors, yours and mine.'

141

'Who richly deserved it,' said Isobel, 'as they lent out their money at eighty per cent.'

Gregory chortled.

'There was someone else hanging about without going in,' he said. Isobel started the Lagonda. 'Woman in a sort of cape,' Gregory said. 'I passed her on my way back. She looked upset about something . . . as if she resented our being there. That must be her car.'

A Rover 2000 was now parked at the side of the drive, beyond the Lagonda. Isobel executed a neat three-point turn, missing it by inches . . . which was just as well, as a surly man in gaiters and breeches had come down the drive and was watching her.

'More resentment,' said Gregory, as Isobel inched forward again and the man in breeches climbed into the Rover.

'Anchovy toast and crumpets,' said Isobel; 'which way?'

'Mr Brown's in Deal is best,' said Marius. Isobel turned right and accelerated. 'That man with the Rover hasn't waited for the lady,' Marius said.

'She looked so disagreeable,' said Gregory, 'that I am not at all surprised.'

When Isobel and Gregory arrived at Oudenarde House to deposit Marius, Glinter Parkes in person, wearing the gown of a Master of Arts, met them in the drive.

'Your brother-in-law,' he said to Isobel, 'Sir Thomas Llewyllyn. He telephoned from Cambridge.'

'How did he know I was here?'

'He tried your London number about half an hour ago, and got your daughter, Rosie. She told him.'

'What on earth does he want?'

Palairet ran across the drive and stood with Marius.

'Off you go, you two,' said Glinter, anxious to clear the ground.

'Good-bye, Mummy; good-bye, Daddy.'

'Not so much as a kiss,' said Isobel as the two boys faded into the shadows.

'Better that way,' said Glinter. 'Quick.'

'What did Tom want?'

'You, Mrs Stern. To go at once to Cambridge.'

'What nonsense is this of Tom's, sending for people in the middle of the night?'

'It is only five-forty-five,' said the literal-minded Gregory. 'Tom does not play jokes. We must go.'

'*You* must get back to dine with the girls in London,' said Isobel. '*I* must go to Cambridge. You are right,' she said, as she moved towards the Lagonda: 'Tom does not play jokes.'

She drove away before there could be any argument.

'Better that way. Quick,' said Gregory, wryly quoting Glinter. 'I'd better telephone Rosie and say I may be a little late.'

'We'll put you on a train as soon as possible, Stern. But by all means come in and use the telephone first.'

'That was Daddy,' said Rosie to Tessa in Chelsea. 'He may be just a little late for dinner. Too many telephone calls.'

'What else did your father say?'

'Mummy has to go to Cambridge – something to do with that call we had just after tea, the one from the Provost of Lancaster. Daddy is coming from Sandwich by train because Mummy has taken the car. Marius is very well. They went to see an old chapel this afternoon which Mummy and Marius liked and Daddy didn't. They all had poached eggs and hot buttered crumpets for tea, and Mummy was cross because she couldn't have anchovy toast as well. The café was so famous for it that it had all run out, which made Mummy even crosser than if there hadn't been any in the first place. She hates things to run out.'

Tessa bowed her head slightly and crossed her wrists in front of her, touching both her little breasts, left breast with right hand, right with left.

'I wonder what Sir Thomas Llewyllyn wants her for in such a hurry?' Tessa said.

'A very pertinent question,' said Rosie, whose father had recently adopted the expression.

Glinter Parkes, MA, having first removed his gown, took Gregory to Dover Station in his car.

'You've missed the five-forty-three from Sandwich,' he explained, 'but we'll easily catch it up before it gets to Dover.'

On the way they drove through the forest at Green Oxley Laris. Gregory wondered whether the lady in the cape was still watching the chapel.

'Don't think I'm not grateful,' Glinter was saying. 'We need that indoor range, and it'll give a lot of pleasure and instruction. But frankly I think we'd better not mention your name in connection with it – not for a while yet.'

'Because of Marius, you mean? Because people will say I bribed you to take him back?'

'Partly – though I think all that is well on the way to being forgotten. The real thing is, Stern, that your name is beginning to be associated with a series of extremely tough and offensive anti-Semitic articles . . . in the *Scrutator* and elsewhere. A good many of my parents are Jews.'

'So am I,' Gregory said.

'And the rumour is that there will soon come a whole book of the same . . . so violent in tone that even your own firm won't touch it.'

'I've found a printer that will. Salinger & Holbrook.'

'I dare say.' Glinter changed down into second gear and proceeded at a very prudent speed downhill past Dover Castle. 'Look here, Stern. I don't know you well –

only as a parent. But I've known some of your friends and authors – I was at school with Fielding Gray, though rather junior to him, and for some years after the war I played a bit of cricket with Canteloupe. So I think I am just entitled to say that I do not consider what you are doing to be decent. You understand the word as well as any man in the Kingdom. I do not say that this stuff of yours is Fascist or immoral or racialist or racist – none of the catchwords. I just say it isn't decent.'

'That's what Canteloupe said.'

'Well then, old chap: don't you think you'd better stop? Anyway, until you do, I shan't be putting up your name on the wall in the indoor rifle range.'

'Just as well you've already cashed the cheque,' said Gregory.

Glinter, who liked a blackish joke, laughed pleasantly.

'That blazer you're wearing,' Glinter said: 'Household Cavalry. Not a very fussy crowd, when it comes to what they say about Jews. But I don't see any of 'em putting his name to one of your articles.'

'They wouldn't know how to write them,' said Gregory complacently.

'Nor they don't need to. I'm just pointing out,' said Glinter Parkes as he turned into the forecourt of Dover Priory Station, 'that those chaps you've ridden with – you were on mounted duties? – '

'Oh yes – '

' – Well, those chaps you rode with, all those years ago, from Knightsbridge up the Mall to the Horse Guards, they don't think very much of what you're doing.'

'How can you know this?'

Glinter stopped the car under a ragged advertisement for Son et Lumière at Dover Castle the previous summer.

'We have a Riding Master in Birchington,' said Glinter,

'to whom we send boys, yours among them, twice a week. An ex-Corporal of Horse. He was one of those who rode with you, Stern. His wife reads the *Scrutator*, sometimes aloud. He doesn't care for all he hears. He tells me Marius has the same gentle hands with the reins that you once had. This used to give him great pleasure. Now, he says, it makes him sad.'

'Who is this man?'

'He is called Gordon Prince.'

'British Army Pentathlon Champion . . . soon after the war.'

'That's right. Remind me, Stern: the Pentathlon consists of running, pistol shooting, swimming, riding – and what's the other event?'

'The sabre.'

'Ah yes: the sabre. A distinct tang of *The Prisoner of Zenda* about the whole affair. Faintly absurd, but in the end coming down to one thing – honour. A good man, Gordon Prince, a good man to ride with from Knightsbridge up the Mall to the Horse Guards.'

'I remember.'

'So does he. "By God, sir," he said to me the other day, "I wouldn't ride with him now".'

Fielding Gray, not wanting to drive in the dark, took a train to Cambridge. Len, on Tom's behalf, had been definite: whatever it was, and he wasn't saying on the telephone, wouldn't wait. He promised Fielding a four-course dinner in the Provost's Lodging. Maisie had been very upset when Fielding said he would have to leave her alone with the steak and kidney pudding, which she had already ordered specially from the kitchens.

'Cambridge,' she said. 'I hope you're not going to see that bloody young Morrison. Is it him that's in trouble then?'

'I don't know anything about it at all,' said Fielding.

'Last time they rang you up from there it was about that boy from Venice, you said.'

'This time nobody's saying anything.'

'A message from God, you said just now when you rang off.'

'Yes. Exigent and mysterious. A divine summons.'

'Nothing divine about Tom Llewyllyn.'

'He's not so very far from it. As Provost of Lancaster, he speaks for the Blessed Henry the Sixth, the Founder. Or so it was held until within living memory. If the Blessed Henry the Sixth summons you to his own College, Maisie, you go.'

'What stuff they fill your heads with in those colleges.'

'Not mine, Maisie. I never went. They turned me down for Lancaster because I'd been a naughty boy.'

'And I suppose that explains,' said Maisie, 'why they've only got to whistle and you come running like a little dog now.'

'I wonder,' said Rosie at dinner, 'why Sir Thomas Llewellyn is so keen to see Mummy?'

'So do I,' said Gregory. The first course was Oeufs

Benedict. Gregory, about to complain that he'd already had poached eggs for tea, reflected that after all the cook (a new man, at that) could not possibly have known this. 'All I can tell you, my Rosie,' he said, 'is that Tom apparently asked for your mother as his "sister-in-law".'

'Which implies,' said Tessa, who was intimate in the household, 'that whatever has happened concerns *her* side of the family, or his and hers, but not just his.'

'Tom has nobody who is "just his",' said Gregory, 'or not that we know of. Speaking in terms of family, that is.'

'Which only supports my deduction,' said Tessa, who, like Gregory, inclined to a literal and pedantic mode of thought, 'that what has happened cannot concern just his side of the family, as this does not exist.'

'If you ask for your sister-in-law,' said Rosie, who was more imaginative than either of her companions but also given to spelling things out, 'it implies that the crisis is common to both sides of the family . . . which narrows the field pretty drastically. Auntie Patricia?' she suggested, naming her mother's sister and Tom's wife, who was retired from the world (almost certainly for ever) in St Bede's asylum.

'Please not, in all the names of Jahveh,' Gregory said.

'How many are there?' asked Tessa.

'Sixty-six or ninety-nine,' said Gregory, glumly guessing.

'I'm afraid you're going to be liverish, Daddy, with all these eggs. When I heard from you on the telephone that you'd had poached eggs at tea, I did ask the new cook to change the menu, thinking you might get costive, but he said, "What nonsense, duckie, she's much too big a girl to be bothered by four little eggies".'

Gregory looked puzzled.

'It's called "she-talk",' Tessa explained kindly; 'all the waiters at Aunt Maisie's hotel use it all the time. Aunt Maisie is "he", because she's a lady, and Major Gray is "she" or "the drum-majorette".'

'Ah,' said Rosie: 'we should have told Daddy that the drum-majorette has been summoned to Cambridge too.'

'By the Provost of Lancaster?' asked Gregory.

'We're not sure,' said Tessa. 'Aunt Maisie rang up to say that Major Gray had had to leave at a second's notice to go to Lancaster College. Lancaster College, she said: nothing about the Provost, and I didn't like to start asking questions because Aunt Maisie was very upset. She said that she'd have to eat a whole steak and kidney pudding which the Head Chef, who is called Stella, had made specially. Since Stella is so temperamental none of it must be left or he'd start crying. She also said that now Major Gray would not be able to come here and collect me, and would I ask you if I could spend the night?'

Gregory spread his arms in assent.

'She is sending my things over in a taxi,' said Tessa. 'What is rather puzzling, though, is why Aunt Maisie can't come in the taxi to collect me instead of just sending my things. I mean, even if she *has* got to eat a whole steak and kidney pudding – '

'She's being kind,' said Rosie, smoothing her long black hair. 'She knows you'll love sleeping here, and I shall love having you, and that we shall be able to walk to school together tomorrow morning.'

'I'll walk with you and Teresa,' said Gregory, 'if I may.' Gregory was one of the few people who habitually used Tessa's real name. 'It will be our last chance,' he said, 'for all of us to have a walk together, before I go abroad. I always like walking with you,' he said to Tessa, 'because you are so straight, so straight and neat . . .

while my Rosie,' he said, 'skims like a little bird. You know,' he said, looking rather vague and worried, as if uncertain whether the association of what he was about to say with what he had just said was not too loose for courtesy, 'you know, I heard a funny thing today, about Marius. His Riding Master remembers me from the days when we were soldiers in the same Regiment. He says that when Marius is on a horse he has the same touch, the same gentle hands as I once had.'

'Oh,' cried Rosie, clapping her hands, 'what a lovely thing to be told.'

'You must be very proud,' Tessa said.

'Yes, Teresa. It has made me . . . quite suddenly . . . very proud.'

In the event, Fielding beat Isobel to the Provost's Lodging in Lancaster by a short head. The door was opened to him by Len.

'Servants' night off,' Len said; 'we don't want anyone listening in on us this evening.'

'I hope that doesn't mean cold food for dinner.'

'No, duckie. Uncle Len will improvise with his portable electric oven and the char's gas ring. The only cold thing is the caviar. Any complaints?'

'As far as that goes, no. But why all this drama? And when do the explanations start?'

'As soon as Mistress Isobel Stern arrives.'

This Mistress Isobel Stern now did, whirling her Lagonda under the Annan Arch and into the Provost's

Court, executing a skid turn round the Rylands Fountain, and stopping neatly in line with the Lucas Columns which framed the Provost's door while Len and Fielding were still standing on the doorstep.

'Madame Sauce,' Len said.

'Pissing time,' announced Isobel, and galloped past them, through the open door, and down the hall towards the loo, nearly flattening Sir Thomas Llewyllyn as he emerged from it.

A few minutes later, just as Isobel finished her pissing, the party was joined by Messrs Ptolemaeos Tunne and Piero Caspar (his new surname), who had driven from the Fens in Ptolemaeos' Mini.

'Jo-Jo is looking after Baby,' Ptolemaeos began ominously, 'not that Baby will be much of a problem – for the time being, that is. Mrs Statch's Fenland Slumber Brew (made from *Papaver Paludis*) will have knocked her out for a good twelve hours. The question must be . . . what will happen when she wakes up?'

'First things first,' Isobel said. 'The question must be, as far as Fielding and myself are concerned, what happened before she went to sleep?'

'Nobody knows . . . for certain. Except perhaps one person, who disappeared too quickly to be asked any questions. Jeremy Morrison. It might be helpful,' Ptolemaeos said to Len, 'if you could send for him . . . *if* he's anywhere in the College. In Hall perhaps?'

'Dinner in Hall is over,' said Len. 'Not that Jeremy often condescended to dine there. I'll ask Wilfred on the Gate to send someone to look for him – and give him a message if he sees him coming in.'

'I do not think,' said Piero Caspar, 'that Girolamo – Jeremy Morrison – will be coming back here to the Lancaster College tonight.'

'And why not?'

Piero looked at Ptolemaeos.

'You begin,' Ptolemaeos said.

'Dinner?' said Fielding, looking very firmly at Len.

'Yes, dinner,' said Isobel; 'we'll never get anywhere on empty stomachs. I imagine you've got *me* down here to play the loving Auntie when Baby wakes up . . . as her loving Daddy' – she glared at Tom – 'is still hanging around here, a safe fifteen miles and more from his daughter's sickbed – or whatever it is – and the location, I presume, of the accident – or whatever it was. I also notice that no one appears to have sent for Canteloupe. So I deduce that both Baby's father and her husband, and possibly the male sex in general, are considered to be, for whatever reason, unsuitable for the task that is to hand. Auntie to the rescue, it has clearly been decided, and I respect your wisdom and shall do my best. But we still have a few hours' grace while *Papaver paludis* does its stuff, so can we please hear whatever there is to hear at our leisure and over dinner . . . for which I hunger like a lion, or should I say lioness?'

'Baby is not the only problem,' said Ptolemaeos, who was standing in the doorway and showing no interest in moving. 'Young Morrison, now. I agree with Piero. I do not think that he will return here tonight, if at all. All that, of course, will be Fielding Gray's department.'

'Why?' said Fielding.

'Because you've just spent a month alone with him in Greece and Italy, and presumably you will have excellent insights into his behaviour, past and future.'

'I shall exercise no insights into anything until I have been fed.' And then, when Ptolemaeos still showed no sign of moving, 'Why this reluctance to let us out to dine, Ptolemaeos? You are usually the first at the trough.'

'There is something about what has happened – such little of it as we actually know – that has put even me off my *assiette*,' Ptolemaeos said. 'However, I must allow that it would be discourteous in me to frustrate the rest of you, so by all means let us go and dine. And as we do, let Piero discourse . . .'

In Wiltshire, Canteloupe and Leonard Percival dined tête-à-tête in the Lancelot Room (named after a Derby winner owned by the third Lord Canteloupe). The dishes were kept warm on a hot-plate, from which they served themselves.

'The question is,' Canteloupe said to Percival, 'was the stolen Asolano sent here in its frame? Or had it been taken out? It's a very different thing storing a framed picture from storing a canvas. So what's the betting about that?'

'Impossible to say. Or is it? You see, it is much easier to take a framed picture off a wall – even a very big picture – and put another in its place, than it is for anyone other than an expert to cut a picture out of its frame and fit another into it. Remember that the chap who did this job – Lord Whatever-the-Eldest-Son-Was-Called-in-Those-Days – '

' – He was travelling under an assumed name, Mr fitzAvon with a small "f" – '

' – Remember, then, that Mr fitzAvon with a small "f", always assuming it *was* him who organized the theft, was an amateur who would have found it much easier to hire porters to carry a large wrapped or crated rectangle than to perform the delicate task of detaching the painting from the frame. But on the other hand he may have found someone else to do this at some stage – any stage – after the theft.'

'Let us, Leonard, consider the first possibility. The picture is stolen in its frame and sent home, still in its frame, under diplomatic seal, on the strength of fitz-Avon's diplomatic status. It then arrives down here. What does fitzAvon's father do about it?'

'Opens up the package and has a look.'

'He was a man of some taste. He would have realized that the painting was not only curious but valuable: he would very much have doubted whether fitzAvon could have had the money to pay for it . . . though this might not have been altogether out of the question, as very good bargains are to be had in times of disruption. So what does he do now?'

'Packs it up again and decides to postpone any action until he has heard fitzAvon's account of the matter.'

'But all he hears of fitzAvon, then or ever, is that he is dead. The accepted version,' said Canteloupe, 'was that he had been killed by "enemies", possibly French agents who suspected that he was using his diplomatic privileges as cover for spying or running messages.'

'Would they have known about the Asolano?'

'The circumstances and reports of fitzAvon's death are vague in the extreme. If you remember, Leonard,' said Canteloupe, looking Percival straight in the eye, 'there are excellent reasons why they should remain so.'*

'I remember, Detterling,' said Percival, returning Canteloupe's look, 'or rather, I remember to forget.'

---

* *The Survivors* by Simon Raven, (Blond and Briggs, 1976).

'Good. The only thing any of us know for certain about fitzAvon's death is where he is buried.'

'So,' said Leonard Percival: 'the Peer has received the parcel – and then the news, possibly not unwelcome, that his renegade son is dead . . .'

'. . . He marries a second wife, a few years later, and gets another and more satisfactory heir . . .'

'. . . But meanwhile, Detterling, what has he done with the parcelled painting? He will also have received and inspected the water-colours. Disreputable stuff, however acquired. He will have looked at the large painting in its frame . . . and realized it has a connection with the water-colour sequence. But the water-colours are signed "Canzoni", whereas the oil painting, which is a much larger version of the first water-colour, is signed "Asolano". *Asolano pinxit*. What does our noble lord, this man of taste, deduce?'

'That the whole thing is jolly fishy. He decides to hide the lot and make discreet enquiries. The Canzonis go into a locked cupboard in the library, inside a leather cover, secured with bronze clasp and padlock, which bears the title "The Little Flowers of St Francis de Sales". This was where I found them, inside a wrapping which bore fitzAvon's name and some sort of official insignia (no doubt an order for privileged carriage from the Chancery in Venice) when I was going over the place with Balbo Blakeney after my cousin's death. So much for the water-colours. Now for the framed canvas: where did he hide that?'

'Stop,' said Leonard. 'Balbo Blakeney, you just said. He was a close friend of your cousin's for the last four years of his life. He designed the new garden to help hide the growing enormity of Cant-Fun, he was intimate with the inside of the house, he was there when you discovered the Canzonis and became an expert on them. He even knew, before either of us did, that the Ragazzi della Peste in San Martino had gone for restoration. Why isn't he present at this discussion?'

'Balbo blabs. He gets arseholes drunk . . . though he's not as bad as he used to be. And then Baby doesn't like having him in the house.'

'Lady Canteloupe is away, Detterling.'

'Probably not for long.'

'Then get Balbo here quickly. Send the Cant-Fun helicopter to Lancaster. It can land on the rear lawn.'

'Odd,' said Len as he carried in the second course (a gratin of écrevisses). 'Canteloupe's man, Leonard Percival, has just been on the telephone. He wants permission for Canteloupe's helicopter to land on the rear lawn. Early tomorrow morning.'

'Jesus,' said Ptolemaeos Tunne, 'who's been telling Canteloupe already? We'd much better keep him out of this until Baby is fit to be sent home. His distress would be terrible – if he heard exactly how she acted.'

'Canteloupe's request has nothing to do with Baby. He simply wants to collect Balbo Blakeney in a hurry – he's got some antiquarian bee buzzing in his bonnet.'

'Did you give permission for the helicopter to land here?' said Tom.

'Subject to your approval, Provost. He's to assume it's all right unless I ring back within half an hour.'

'Let it land,' said Tom. 'It belongs to his corporation

but for some reason it flies the pennant of the Hereditary Commodore of the Severn Reaches. This will give the students and Junior Fellows something rather than myself on which to focus their resentment.'

'So *that's* all settled,' said Fielding. 'Now, where were we? Repeat, please, Piero. I want to make sure I've got it all straight.'

'I am with Miss Baby – with Lady Canteloupe – in my bedroom at about three o'clock this afternoon.' Tom sat shivering over his plate, looking miserable. 'We are playing chess. We do not wish to play downstairs, because Madame Guiscard's baby distracts us with its noises, and Madame Guiscard with her melancholy remarks.' Tom looked partly re-assured: since he has heard this once already (thought Isobel) there is really no need for these blow-by-blow reactions; but then he always was . . . well . . . funny about the idea of Baby's being alone with a man, even for a game of chess (and is this little wop, one may well ask, telling us the strict truth?).

'We are joined by Girolamo – by Jeremy Morrison,' Piero went on. 'I have left a message with Madame Guiscard to tell him to come up, and when he does I think we shall all play backgammon – Chouette – a game in which three players may take part, though one of them is only giving advice to another. So when Jeremy arrives, I topple my King to Lady Canteloupe – for she has a Castle to my Bishop and already one passed Pawn – and I go to fetch the backgammon set which I have foolishly left downstairs in the Gaming Room.' Piero paused and wetted his lips with his tongue. 'As I return up the stairs and along the landing,' he said in an even, neutral tone, 'I hear a sort of howling, of a man in pain.'

'In pain, Mr Caspar?' said Isobel, who had not met Piero before that evening.

'In pain, Mrs Stern. I go in. Miss Baby is crouched on the bed, fully dressed, as she was for our game of chess, in a tweed jacket and rough brown corduroy trousers. She is hissing, hissing with her mouth spread wide, almost, it seems, from ear to ear; and she is poised, as if to claw or to leap at Jeremy . . . who is standing at the end of the bed, fully dressed too, like Miss Baby, and crying and howling and saying, "I'm so sorry, if only you knew, oh please stop, I am so sorry." When he sees me, he howls again, and rushes past me out on to the landing, and he is gone.'

'And . . . and Tullia?' said Provost Llewyllyn.

'Tullia, Tom?' said Piero.

'Baby's proper name.'

'I had forgotten. She is there, hissing still. Not at me, but at the place where Girolamo had been standing. Her eyes are narrow, almost closed, and her cheeks bulging and knotted, and she hisses through her parted lips, showing her teeth very forward. It is horrible.'

'Does she . . . say nothing?'

'Nothing. I must have help, I think. The two women, Mrs Gurt and Mrs Statch, are having their afternoon off. I call for Madame Guiscard, down the stairs, but she does not come. Then Mr Tunne comes. He has been at the Horse Racing, at Newmarket, but he has returned early, thank God – '

' – Nardo Cumbria was there, making me quite ill with his new scheme for a cut-price equine sperm bank. So I came home,' said Ptolemaeos, 'to escape from Nardo and found Piero coming down the stairs and yelling for Jo-Jo . . . whereat I went upstairs and found Baby still crouched on the bed and hissing like a vampire. She wouldn't listen or talk or make any gesture of recognition; so I fetched a syringe and filled it with Mother Statch's knock-out lotion, and then, with Jo-Jo's help – she'd heard the rumpus at last and come into the house from the garden – Piero managed to hold Baby still enough, despite all her writhing and kicking and butting and gnashing, for me to inject her in one arm.'

Tom's face shrivelled.

'She's always hated injections,' he said.

'It had to be done.'

'And all this time she said nothing?' said Fielding.

'Nothing,' said Ptolemaeos. 'It's going to be very interesting to hear what she has to say when she wakes up at four this morning. I want you there, Isobel, as you've already guessed, to cope with her – you were always close to her, I believe – and I want you, Fielding, to hang about the place and latch on to any clues you can find about Jeremy – what he did or where he's gone.'

Tom, it was clear, was not invited, and was apparently relieved not to be.

'I'll just enquire if Wilfred has found Jeremy,' said Len . . . who returned, five minutes later and with the main course, to report, as all present had expected, that Jeremy Morrison was nowhere to be found in the precincts of Lancaster College.

When Leonard Percival rang up Balbo Blakeney, told him that a helicopter would pick him up on the rear lawn of Lancaster the following morning at nine of the clock, and then indicated what was going forward in the house in Wiltshire, Balbo was both flattered and amused, flattered by the attention and amused by the purpose assigned. He had heard, through Sir Jacquiz Helmutt and other of his art world informants, that the supposed Asolano had now been found, on thorough examination, to be a copy by Canzoni; and he had speculated as to the possible fate and present whereabouts of the original and genuine picture: but it had not occurred to him to connect its disappearance from Burano with the pseudonymous Mr fitzAvon, for the simple reason that he, Balbo, did not know, as Canteloupe did, just how ruthless, devious, cunning and determined a man Mr fitzAvon had been.

The picture which Balbo had been encouraged to form of fitzAvon was that of a debauched and pathetic fop, a public embarrassment to his father who was only too happy to pay for his absence. Mr fitzAvon, in the orthodox view promoted by the family, had been the kind of futile jackanapes who might well commission a series of naughty pastiches from an ingratiating hack, but not a man capable of planning and perpetrating a major crime of robbery and violation. And another thing, Balbo thought now: no one ever seemed to remember or to use fitzAvon's real name. He was always known by his alias, never by the family name or by the courtesy title in which he must, as the eldest son of a senior peer, have been addressed at the time. In short, thought Balbo gleefully, Canteloupe has been keeping quite a lot back about Mr fitzAvon. If he deserves, in Canteloupe's present view, to be considered capable of pulling off an affair like this, then he is a very different man from the one I have been hearing about all this time. True, I always knew he was murdered, a fact which implies that he moved in a fairly tough milieu; but I had put this down to a squalid barroom brawl in a season of anarchy, that kind of a thing.

Any number of more spectacular conjectures, both about the murder and the man, are now in order.

Why, thought Balbo, has Canteloupe been at such pains to conceal the true character of fitzAvon under an effigy of straw? And how much does Leonard know about it all? Well, these questions, though fascinating, could be put aside for the time. The immediate problem was, of course, what Mr fitzAvon's father, had made of, and then done with, the Asolano when it reached Wiltshire . . . if, that was, one was prepared to assume that it had ever done so, and one might just as well go along with the assumption for the sheer fun of the thing. Very well: if Mr fitzAvon, now promoted from philandering dandy to vicious rakehell, from a mere porn-fancier to a potential Vautrin, had sent a painting of that kind home from Venice under diplomatic seal, sometime around 1796, what should I, as his father, knowing what I did of him, have done on its arrival?

Presumably, thought Balbo, fitzAvon would have addressed the freight to himself. Therefore I, as his father, having regard to the conventions in the matter and perhaps fearing my son's violent displeasure, would *not* have opened the crate (or whatever) but would have had it stored away. And later, when I heard my son was dead? Hmm . . . careful now, I should have said to myself: who knows what that infernal brute may have been up to? So I'll send for two senior and reliable servants, tell them to bring crowbars and so on, and then, swearing them to secrecy just in case, have them open up that box or at least enough of it for me to have a cautious look inside . . .

Isobel and Jo-Jo were appointed to be at Baby Cante-loupe's bedside in Tunne Hall when she awoke from her drugged sleep, which she did at 4.20 A.M. She was bored, calm and hungry. Jo-Jo, knowing the household, was despatched for refreshment. 'None of your damned fen fishes,' said Baby; 'I crave the flesh of mammals,' and was shortly provided with a platter of thickly sliced red beef, mustard and cornichons.

'And so,' said Isobel when Baby had wolfed this refection, 'what happened?'

'When?' said Baby.

'Yesterday afternoon.'

'Nothing very much,' said Baby in a matter-of-fact manner. 'When that Morrison boy arrived up in Piero's room, Piero stomped out, waggling his bottom, to fetch the backgammon set. Then Master Morrison said how delighted he was to have been invited to join us – said it in a knowing sort of way, and started coming altogether too close – and I told him to get out of the room. I imagine he got out of the house as well?'

'Yes,' Isobel said. 'You don't know where he went? He seems to be lost, and we thought that Fielding . . . as his friend . . . might go to look for him.'

'He can stay lost for what I care,' said Baby. 'God knows what happened to him. He simply went . . . just as Piero came mincing back with the backgammon. Can you mince with a club foot? – anyway he does. Just as

163

Piero came mincing back, Morrison left at the double. Piero will tell you.'

'He has,' said Isobel. 'What happened after Morrison had gone?'

'I had hysterics. It all seemed more and more ludicrous, and I couldn't stop laughing. I suppose I must have sounded very odd going on and on . . .'

'You did,' said Jo-Jo.

'. . . So eventually Ptoly came and gave me stuff to quieten me down. And now I've woken up, but I think, if you don't mind, that I shall go to sleep again.'

Which she did.

Isobel looked at Jo-Jo carefully.

'For whatever reason,' Isobel said, 'she's taken against both of them – against Mr Caspar even more than Mr Morrison. She'd better go home to Wiltshire. In her present state she won't alarm Canteloupe – though she may depress him. So if nothing sensational happens within the next thirty-six hours, we'll send her home. Then I must go to my old Hebrew in London and get him ready to go off to Trieste. Shall you go with Baby? Just in case she needs looking after later?'

'I can't go back to Wiltshire. That's where I was betrayed by Alexandre . . . where Oenone was dumped on me instead.'

'I see,' said Isobel. 'So what shall you do?'

'Stay here . . . with Ptoly and Piero. One of them may think of something – something to be done about Oenone, I mean. I shall be contented, in a numb sort of way. I've remembered a place where I used to read, by a pool in the garden; so I shall take Oenone there every day, as long as this lovely autumn weather lasts, and read her poetry, about women who have been unhappy, to warn her what's waiting when she grows up.'

'A pool with a waterfall,' Isobel said.

'No. Just a pool among small fir-trees, with a little ring of grass round it.'

'A pool with a waterfall,' Isobel repeated. 'Every day, for many days, I was taken there by a girl who looked like you.'

'When you . . . you and Mr Stern . . . went missing last summer?'

'Yes. I loved that girl. My captor, that's how I thought of her, though really she was just my gaoler. I longed to kneel and bow my neck to her. You know what stopped me? She had begun to think of me as her queen. Although I was her prisoner, I was also her queen, a royal victim of conspiracy or civil war, princely as well as captive. So I did not kneel to her, on pain of destroying her love; and she, my beloved captor, could not kneel to me on pain of destroying mine.'

'Very soon my husband is going to Trieste,' Isobel went on, 'to treat with the people who detained us last summer. This time they do not want me. He will not be long in Trieste, but he has decided – so he told me on the telephone a few hours ago, when I rang up from Cambridge to make sure he was all right – he has decided to go on a tour, all by himself, when he has finished in Trieste, somewhere, he said, in the lands of legend. He was always a Romantic.'

Isobel paused, came round the bed, and knelt before Jo-Jo.

'I can serve you if you will let me, you and your child. While my husband is away, I can send my Rosie to stay with her friend Tessa, and take you to a place where I can serve you. I have always loved Baby, who loves you and whom you love, so let me take you and serve you in my way.'

'Stand up. Please stand up.'

'I cannot make you come with me. But think of this when you sit by your pool. Think of me, as I sat by another pool, where I wished to serve but was thwarted. When you have thought, make up your mind and prepare accordingly. My husband leaves after the week-end. On Tuesday morning I shall come here. If you are sitting by your pool – '

' – You do not know where it is, you could never find it – '

' – If you are sitting there, I shall find you and take you with me, you and your child. If I do not find you, I shall go away alone.'

'Very well,' said Jo-Jo. 'If you find us by our pool you can have us – for what we are worth.'

Some three hours after Isobel had knelt before Jo-Jo, Ptolemaeos woke Piero and told him to come down to his study. Since Ptolemaeos tended not to rise until ten or eleven, this did not bode well.

However, Ptolemaeos seemed quite mild when Piero came into his study fifteen minutes later. He had arranged all the coloured telephones on the desk in two ranks, as though he was about to review them, and it was to them rather than to Piero, at first, that he directed his voice.

'Isobel Stern tells me,' he said, 'that Baby has gone right off you. Good. Presumably she will want to return to Wiltshire, and this she will be fit to do tomorrow.

Again, good. But now tell me, Piero Caspar: what went wrong?'

'I don't know, sir. I wasn't there when it happened.'

Ptolemaeos lifted his gaze from the ranks of telephones and turned it on to Piero Caspar.

'No. You were fetching the backgammon set. What *should* have happened?'

'To be candid, sir, I should not have been fetching the backgammon set. It should have been there already, but I had forgotten it. I had told Lady Canteloupe, who does not like Jeremy, that Jeremy was coming over with your permission, and I begged her to be friendly to him, just for a little while, as he had been kind to me before she came here. She agreed. So what should then have happened was this: as soon as Jeremy appeared, we should have started to play backgammon – the three-cornered version, Chouette – and at some early stage I should have suggested a system of forfeits – that the loser of each game must take off one garment, which he might not replace. This would suggest to Lady Canteloupe that I was attracted to Jeremy as well as to her and desired to turn the game into an eventual orgy, when we were all nude or nearly. When she realized that this was my intention one of three things would happen. *Either* she would be angry or jealous or disgusted or humiliated – in which case she would go away from here, as you wished; *or* she might like the idea, despite her apparent coldness to Jeremy; *or* she might pretend to like the idea in order to please me. In either of the two latter cases, I had thought of means, probably more effective than mere oral suggestion, of disgusting or humiliating her, et cetera, et cetera, and thus compelling her to leave this house and not come back.'

'I see. A Sicilian machination. None the worse for that,

perhaps. But as it was, when Jeremy arrived as expected, you had to leave him alone with Baby Canteloupe while you fetched the set – and during your absence something quite appalling took place. What, Piero Caspar?'

'I do not know, sir.'

'But there must be an explanation of the state they both got into.'

'No doubt, sir. But I can't give it to you. When I left them, they were talking, uneasily but politely. When I returned – well – you know what I found – '

' – Baby hissing like a serpent in hell and Jeremy howling like a stuck hyena. Jeremy lit off, still howling, and hasn't been seen since. Baby went on hissing until she was sedated, a job which took all the strength of you and me and Jo-Jo combined.'

'It is a grief to me, sir. I have always . . . liked Miss Baby . . . and I would not have wished to cause her misery or distress. To make her jealous or angry and get her out of the way – that was one thing, a suitable thing, for she has a kind and noble husband and does not need me. Nor I her. True, she may have influence with her father, Provost of the Lancaster College, but if I am to be allowed into that College I think you are the one that will arrange it.'

'Thank you for your trust.'

'So to *annoy* Miss Baby, to drive her away from this house, this was certainly needed and I pardon myself for arranging it. But if I have made her *unbalanced* . . .'

'She seems all right now, Isobel tells me.'

'But she was not all right when you injected her yesterday. And another thing, perhaps worse: where has Girolamo – where has Jeremy gone to?'

'Major Gray will look for him.'

'Where?'

'It is not your responsibility, Caspar. You are to blame for none of this. However sound or otherwise your original plan, and whatever might or might not have come of it, *your* scenario was never put on and you bear no guilt at all for the one that was.'

'I brought them face to face, and then left them alone.'

'You could not possibly have anticipated what occurred. We don't even know what *did* occur.'

'I shall not mind all this badly, sir, if only Jeremy can be found and made all right. The little Canteloupe started this game herself, you might say, by coming here in the first place and seeking me out, and she has only herself to thank if the play turned sour on her. But Jeremy, he has been only kind – '

' – To you, perhaps. But he too may be playing games.'

'However that may be, sir, I wish that he may be delivered from harm. For he is of my heart, as nobody has been since I went to St Francis's Island.'

'Let us assume,' said Balbo to Canteloupe and Leonard Percival in Canteloupe's study, 'that both the packet which contained the Canzoni series and the much bulkier one that housed the Asolano had been addressed by Mr fitzAvon to himself. Perhaps the carrier brings them both on the same day, if they have come on the same ship; more probably not; in either case no matter. The water-colours, to judge from the writing on the wrapper, he sent to himself in the name of fitzAvon; the Asolano was probably addressed in the same way, though he might possibly have directed it to himself under his real name – which was what, Canteloupe?'

'He had one of the titles which disappeared when the Peerage went sideways at my cousin's death. We needn't bother with that now.'

'Can't you remember it?' said Balbo.

'I'm not sure which it was,' said Canteloupe crossly. 'His father, though later the first Marquess, was at that time only an Earl, so fitzAvon could have chosen any one of the three or four minor titles.'

'So never mind that just now,' said Leonard Percival gently. 'You were saying, Balbo . . . ?'

'I was saying that when the two packets arrived they would probably have been addressed to fitzAvon, under whatever denomination, and that his father would have thought it both polite and wise, knowing the man's temper, to leave them unopened and have them stored somewhere against his son's return. But then came the news of his son's death. So now, attention. My lord decides to open the packets . . . the smaller one first, I think. In this he finds the set of Canzonis, typical evidence, if any were needed, of his son's louche and blasphemous taste. In the second packet he finds the framed altar piece. Being something of a cognoscente, he has a rough idea of its provenance and value: something definitely fishy here. Shall he hang it? After all, he tells himself, even if it was procured in some . . . unorthodox . . . manner, no one from Burano is likely to walk this way just now, and the irregular mode of exporting this object from its own country is largely condoned by the British aristocratic tradition of "collecting" foreign art treasures without ceremony. On reflection, however, he decides against hanging the picture: it would probably offend the bourgeois canons of the Hanoverian monarch who is arriving shortly to be his guest and recuperate in the Wiltshire countryside from one of his recurrent bouts of mental disorder.'

'One can go on all day long working out what he didn't do with it,' said Leonard Percival: 'you're here to tell us what he did.'

'All right,' said Balbo. 'Once more, attention. He doesn't want the picture on display – not when the Royal family are present, or on any other reputable ocasion; furthermore, he knows that it must be kept in a suitable state of warmth and dryness. So he has it *masked*, by another painting, perhaps, or by a tapestry – anything which could be fitted over it and fairly easily detached at will. He also decides, being given to sardonic humour and at the same time respectful of justice, that the cover must in some sense act as a monument or memorial to the benefactor – Mr fitzAvon – who has donated the painting beneath it. Not a portrait of him – that, in all the circumstances, would be overdoing it – but just some little reminder.'

'And I suppose he forgot to tell anyone else he had done this,' grumbled Canteloupe, 'and having occasionally uncovered the picture for his own lonely delectation, carried the secret with him to the grave, remembering, first, in the Byzantine fashion, to extract the eyes and tongues of the craftsmen who made or fitted the covering, whatever it was.'

'He certainly measured the frame,' said Balbo patiently, 'before having it wrapped up again. He ordered the covering – I incline more and more to a tapestry – in London, brought it down here when it was complete, fitted it, perhaps himself, over the picture, and then had it hung, for his own convenience and private inspection, in his study. Where else?'

'This study?' said Leonard.

'No. In those days his lordship's study was what is now the First Night Nursery. Let us all pay a visit, therefore, to Lord Sarum of Old Sarum.'

'Any change in Baby?' said Ptolemaeos Tunne to Isobel Stern.

'None for the worse . . . or not as far as her health goes. She's playing backgammon with Jo-Jo, undismayed by any association of the set with the – er – incident. She is uninterested in whatever occurred and unembarrassed by it. She is unaffectionate to Jo-Jo, though condescending to gamble with her, uncivil to myself and utterly ungrateful to you for your hospitality.'

'But not unfit, I trust, to leave here tomorrow?'

'She can certainly leave here, she *should* leave here, tomorrow. But she should not, I think, drive herself, so I shall take her to Wiltshire in my Lagonda. Her own car can be driven back there by a hired driver.'

'Shouldn't you take her in her car? I mean . . . your Lagonda is rather uncomfy.'

'So she said, the little bitch. I'll tell you what it is: Canteloupe's spoilt her. She's only twenty. She should be making a living as a typist,' said Isobel, 'and heating up tinned soup for dinner on a gas-ring, and mending her own tights. Not wafting about on a cloud like a rococo goddess and being my Lady Wipe-my-arse. She can't even bother to take proper care of that little boy.'

'At least she'll be back with him tomorrow,' said

Ptolemaeos, 'though of course he's much better off with his nurse. Most children are if they're lucky enough to have one.'

Sarum's ginger nurse greeted the deputation to the nursery quarters with great charm and pleasure. Sarum, being already possessive of her, scowled.

When Canteloupe had explained that they wanted to examine the First Night Nursery, the Nurse gathered up Sarum and led them all along a corridor, past two bathrooms (one for Sarum and one for her) and into a tall panelled room which looked out over the park to the river and the bat-willows.

'You see why he liked it as his study?' said Balbo.

Opposite the window was a sensible iron bedstead for Nanny and by it Sarum's cot.

'Hullo, Tully,' said Canteloupe, in belated greeting to the infant, who responded by turning up his snub nose even further.

'Well?' said Leonard to Balbo. 'A monument or memorial to fitzAvon, you said. Probably on a tapestry. No tapestries that I can see.'

'Over the head of the cot,' said Balbo.

Over the head of the cot was a small, square alcove in the wall (Isobel, had she been there, might have compared it to an 'aumbry') at the back of which was a statuette, perhaps three inches high, of a naked boy or young man with crisp, short curls all over his scalp and his rump turned to the audience.

Balbo stretched his hand into the alcove.

'You can't move it; I've tried,' said the ginger Nurse, and gave a merry laugh.

'Very few people knew the secret,' said Balbo, nerving himself for a gamble: 'for although it did not quite die with the first Marquess, the transformation of the study into a nursery, during the alterations of 1805, made first for vagueness, then for carelessness and at last for obscurity about its contents. A cunning second Marquess, let us hazard, anticipating the prudishness which was to come with a young queen, knowing the value of the Asolano, knowing, too, that it was quite probably "hot" and that he lived in an age of increasing moral sensitivity about the appropriation of such objects – a cunning and prudent second Marquess decided it had best stay out of sight and out of mind. Out of everybody's mind,' said Balbo, 'after his own instantaneous death from a fall while steeplechasing.'

He grasped the statuette. As the Nurse said, it was secured in its place. On its invisible side was (what else, in memory of Mr fitzAvon?) a rampant phallus. Please God, Balbo prayed. He tried pressing the phallus up: it would not budge. All right; try pressing it down then . . . and two large panels slid back over the head of the brass bedstead, leaving a recess in the high wall some fifteen feet tall by six across by two in depth. From a canopy at the top of the recess hung a tapestry, queasy in sentiment but not inept in execution, of Christ surrounded by gambolling children.

'Now look underneath,' Balbo breathed.

Since no one else moved to do so, the ginger Nurse did. She found a dangling cord, hidden under the right edge of the tapestry. Balancing Sarum competently on one arm she pulled the cord with the hand of the other.

The tapestry swept away to the left. A throng of pretty boys lifted their dress and thrust their firm, white thighs towards a deprecatory yet eagerly observant Virgin, each boy pointing to a black bubo beneath a hint of black pubes.

'Asolano,' said Balbo.

'Arselano?' said the Nurse.

'Taso-tano, Taso-tano,' Lord Sarum crowed.

'What a flop,' said Baby to Piero as they walked towards Isobel's Lagonda. 'That first night was fun in a ghoulish sort of way . . . digging up the past . . . but after that, what a flop.'

'There was nothing there except a memory,' said Piero. 'Once that had been used up . . . nothing.'

'Once you had shown the woman how you would have corrupted the child,' Baby said.

'Once the woman had permitted and exulted in the child's corruption,' Piero rejoindered.

'With me, it was just a dirty little itch, like a mosquito bite which you scratch until the pus runs out,' said Baby.

'With me, I suppose, it was just a cringing anxiety to oblige a vain woman who might later be useful,' said Piero.

When they had thus succeeded in poisoning for each other even what they had had (which was not nothing), when they had finally turned their brief but quite genuine and joyous lust into a handful of damp garbage, Baby climbed into the Lagonda and was driven away by Isobel.

Jo-Jo had said a guarded good-bye to Baby in the hall before withdrawing to her pool. Ptolemaeos had merely waved from the Library window as Baby crossed the drive with Piero. Nobody cared about Baby's departure, herself least of all. All those who were left behind (Ptolemaeos, Piero and Jo-Jo, if one didn't yet count Oenone), remembered the hideous, grimacing thing that had crouched hissing on the bed; and one of them, Piero, remembered the terrible howl of pain and despair which Jeremy had given as he bolted from the room.

Fielding Gray, charged with the search for Jeremy Morrison, had taken a country train from Ely to his own home at Broughton Staithe, thinking that Jeremy might conceivably have gone there, and had drawn a blank. The next place to look for Jeremy was obviously Jeremy's own home. Having considered and rejected the idea of announcing his approach by telephone, he boarded a bus from Broughton (the same bus as he had taken many years ago when going from Broughton to visit Peter) to the Morrisons' house at Luffham by Whereham. Here a stately lunatic who styled himself the 'Chamberlain of the Household' (formerly Detterling's man-servant, Fielding remembered) reported that Master Jeremy had not been seen since the beginning of term at Lancaster. After this, Fielding took a train for London, to put his affairs in order, in so far as this was possible, and plan what he would do if Jeremy did not shortly reappear.

'I wonder,' said Theodosia Salinger, 'if they would ever let women play.'

The Salinger girls were seated in the spectators' gallery of the Tennis Court at Lord's, where Ivan Blessington had brought them after luncheon at the Ritz.

'I thought the game would interest you,' Ivan said. 'A big, strong lass like you would have no difficulty with the hard ball and the heavy racket . . . nor with the basic stroke. You cut down on the thing,' he said, chopping at the back of the padded bench in front with the edge of his hand and raising a fly which thought it was there for the winter.

'They wouldn't let a girl play at Lord's,' said Carmilla, 'because you can't belong to the MCC. But at Queen's . . . or Hampton Court . . . ?'

'Why not at Cambridge?' said Ivan. 'There's a Court there.'

'I'll enquire when I get back there,' said Theodosia. 'But I mustn't let it wreck my badminton.'

A bell rang.

'You win the point outright,' said Ivan, 'if you strike the ball from this end into the far gallery – and ring the bell. I wish all the rules were as simple. It'll take you a month to learn them.'

'Chase better than half a yard,' called the marker.

'I see what you mean,' Theodosia said, and gave a little shiver of excitement.

'We must be off back to Cambridge,' said Carmilla.

They stopped between the Pavilion and 'Q' Stand to look at the October green.

'Poor Da,' said Theodosia.

'Just to check up finally,' said Carmilla to Ivan Blessington: 'you *have* seen Ashley Dexterside, who knows exactly what to do about Gregory Stern's book?'

'Yes. Stern leaves for the continent today – Monday. He will deliver his text to Ashley, person to person, when he gets back. He now seems much vaguer than he was about when this will be – I gather he's prolonging his trip – but whenever it is Ashley will be ready at five minutes' warning.'

'Good,' said Carmilla. 'That's that taken care of. How are Betty and Jakki and Caroline?'

'Well, I thank you. All three of 'em loved it when you came to tea the other day. Come again, any time.'

'I'm glad you've taken on this nasty job for us,' said Theodosia. 'Funny; all those times Carm and I came here with Da, we never went into the Tennis Court.'

When Jeremy Morrison turned up at Oudenarde House that same Monday afternoon, Walter (Wally) St George, the assistant master was delighted to see him. Glinter Parkes, the Headmaster, was having an afternoon off playing golf, otherwise he would have been quite pleased to see Jeremy too. For after all, young Morrison had an important father, he himself had been an agreeable boy while at Oudenarde, apparently responsive to Glinter's homilies and appreciative of Wally's conjuring tricks and anecdotes; he had recently presented a seat, which not every Old Boy troubled to do; he had won the Kilmarnock Gold Medal for a Latin poem at Cambridge in June: he was, in short, a Credit to the School and what was more he looked it (with his big, round, friendly face, his brown wavy hair, his strong, soft, brown hands to match), and if he *had* once or twice been suspected of precocity, well, that was some years ago now and no one (as far as could be known) the worse for it.

As for the events at Tunne Hall (as Len liked to call it) Wally knew nothing of these. Glinter, had he been there, just might have remembered how Isobel had been urgently summoned by Provost Llewyllyn and then wondered what Jeremy was doing, four days later, so far away from Lancaster College; but since he would have known of no connection between Isobel and Jeremy, he would almost certainly have seen no connection between the two incidents, and in any case he was fussily four-putting on the eighth green of the Cinque Ports Golf Course when Jeremy appeared at Oudenarde House.

Monday afternoon was 'Odds and Ends'. Jeremy went politely round with Wally to watch carpentry, raffia work, gardening, shooting (in the indoor range which was being financed by Gregory Stern), and junior judo.

'In fact,' said Wally, 'we really concentrate on teaching 'em all to box, but judo's such a fad these days that we've decided to take it on as well.'

After all this, Jeremy said that he would like to have a bit of a walk on his own, and Wally, who knew how sentimental Old Boys could be and did not despise them for it, let him loose with his blessing, adjuring him only to be back in Minden Wing in time for School Tea at five.

'Tell me,' Jeremy said to the plainest boy he could find

179

(in case Wally were still watching him) among those who were messing about on the footer ground, 'where can I find Marius Stern?'

'He goes riding at Birchington on Mondays, so you can't,' the boy said, revelling in the opportunity to disoblige.

But Jeremy too, in his day, had gone riding at Birchington. The stables were in the woods, near the aerodrome: there was a small clearing, with elementary obstacles, in which the boys generally exercised, though sometimes they rode two by two through the woods and over what little still survived of the heath. Either way, Jeremy would find Marius. He must. He left a friendly note for Wally excusing himself from School Tea on the plea that a 'nasty knock' in the engine of his Morris 1000 needed a garage, set off past the Barbican for Lord of the Manor Corner, turned left there, and then, after another four miles odd, to the right, and approached the stables by the rough road which led past the Big Game Museum and on to the little gymkhana ground.

Ex-Corporal of Horse Gordon Prince remembered Jeremy as a passable if heavy rider and a cheerful pupil. He was flattered that this personable young man (whose father, he recalled, had at one time been in the Government) should have come to look up his old Riding Master on his way home from visiting his old school, particularly as Birchington was not really on the way anywhere. So when Jeremy asked after 'my friend, Mrs Stern's son Marius,' the Corporal of Horse said, 'Come this way, sir,' and led him off to the stable yard, opining to Jeremy as they went that Marius had the hands of a blooming little angel, sir.

In the stable yard, Marius was grooming his horse alongside Palairet, whom Jeremy did not know. Prince called Marius over to Jeremy ('Here's a friend of your ma's and an old friend of mine') and himself went to correct Palairet, who was doing something wrong.

'Hullo,' said Jeremy.

'Hullo,' said Marius, and shuffled.

'Long time since we met.'

'Yes, sir.'

'You called me "Jeremy" then.'

'Yes,' said Marius: 'Jeremy.'

'I have to say something important, Marius. Listen. I must go away. Later, you may hear nasty things about me. They are not true. Do you understand clearly? Any nasty thing you hear about me is not true. I thought I must tell you before I went, because . . . because of the way we liked each other last summer.'

'Yes, Jeremy,' said Marius, looking at the ground.

'Do you remember that afternoon at Newmarket?' Marius merely nodded. Palairet came and stood beside Marius. 'Good afternoon, sir,' he said objectively to Jeremy; and to Marius, 'The Corporal of Horse says it's time for the coach, Stern.'

Jeremy was being seen off, and knew it.

He shook hands with Marius, who smiled radiantly with relief, nodded to Palairet, crossed the yard, refused the Corporal of Horse's offer of 'Chai', badly hurt the man's feelings (though he had declined with the best grace he could muster), and found, as he drove back towards the main road, that his engine had developed a 'nasty knock' which certainly needed a garage.

It had been decided, some time ago, that Leonard Percival should 'be on hand' in Trieste in case Gregory wished to consult him at any stage during his meeting with Shamshuddin & Co., the people who had been responsible for kidnapping him and Isobel the previous summer and were now leaning on him in the matter of what Leonard called 'The Bumper Anti-Schonk Omnibus' and by other titles even more tasteless.

The original form had been that Gregory's talks with Shamshuddin would last three days, after which Gregory, having satisfied him that his preparations for the production of the Omnibus were up to the mark, would return to London and set the presses of Salinger & Holbrook to roll off his polemic. The programme was now changed, in that Gregory intended to 'make a little tour of Hellas' before he returned to London, having represented to Shamshuddin that his book would need some revision as a result of their conference, a task best undertaken in surroundings that would remind Gregory with every breath he took of the sane and *echt* un-Hewbrew customs and procedures of the classical Hellenes.

Leonard Percival was not at all sure that he approved the change in arrangements. True, these would entail his tracking and watching Gregory (at Gregory's request and by Canteloupe's assent) all through Yugoslavia and over much of Greece, at a time when the weather should be ideal for the excursion and most summer tourists would have vanished, leaving the scene to the discerning. True, also, that Leonard had often longed to look at the castles of the Southern Peloponnese, whither Gregory purported to be bound. He did not, he could not, mislike the prospect: he simply and roundly mistrusted it.

The whole thing, he told himself now, as he drove the car which he had hired in the Piazzale Roma at Venice through the autumn evening towards Trieste, the whole blessed *bunderbust*, seemed to him – what was that French phrase? – *pas honnête*. His professional nostrils smelt lies and evasions: worse, they smelt silliness. Gregory was getting some trick ready; he was having recourse to atavistic cunning; he was plotting, somehow or other, to 'Jew' his enemies. And then God help us all, Leonard Percival thought.

On Tuesday morning, Jo-Jo Guiscard remembered that Isobel was coming to the Fens that day. If she found her, she would take her. If not, not. I wonder, Jo-Jo thought. I could drive into Ely and just forget the whole thing. Do I want to forget the whole thing? What is that woman planning? Do I even want to know?

In the end, she decided to leave the matter to God (so to speak). She went to sit by the pool, taking Oenone and a volume of Browning ('The Confessional' – that'll teach her, Jo-Jo thought), but on the way she concealed the beginning of the narrow path (just behind the summer-house) by blocking it with bracken, small bushes and

briars which she dragged off an unlit bonfire and arranged
(as she thought) to look like undergrowth.

Then, not really caring whether Isobel found them or
not, she started to read 'The Confessional' to Oenone.

Rosie and Tessa had their mid-morning bun together.

'I've got all my things ready to come back with you tonight,' said Rosie. 'How odd of God to be so kind.'

'Has your mother left?'

'Early this morning. I only hope she stays away as long
as she thinks – about three weeks. She says Daddy won't
be back before then and she needs a change of life. What
can she mean?'

'It's a thing ladies have at a certain age,' said Tessa:
'Aunt Maisie told me.'

'And Mummy told me, ages ago. But I don't think
that's what she meant this time . . . though that's what
she said. Not a change of air or food or place, but a
change of life.'

'I think,' said Tessa, 'that your father too is looking for
a change of life. You know when he said good-bye to me,
after he walked with us to school last Friday?'

'He kissed you on your lips. He has never done that
before. Only to Mummy and me. I was almost jealous.
Then I wasn't. I was glad.'

'It wasn't only the kiss,' said Tessa: 'he gave me
something. A little parcel. He told me to open it later.
When I did, I found something wrapped in a note –'

' – A bank note? –'

' – A letter. Wrapped in the letter was a little metal tube with a tiny roll of India paper inside it. Your father's letter said the tube was called a mezuzah, a thing Jews put outside their front doors to bless their house. He said that the scroll inside had all the Names of God written on it – he'd only been joking, he said, the night before at dinner, when he'd told me there were sixty-six or ninety-nine. Now I could count them for myself and find out . . . and please would I always carry the mezuzah with me, to remind me of him.'

'How sweet of him,' said Rosie. 'But I still don't understand what you are saying . . . about his looking for a change of life.'

'One reason for giving people presents to remember you by is because you think that you may soon in some way become different. When people leave school they give their friends photographs – to remind them what they used to look like when they were all young together. I think . . . your father wishes me always to remember him as he was on that morning. So fine and tall and kind and funny.'

'He has given me nothing to remember him by,' Rosie said.

'You need nothing, you have known him so well for so long. Anyway, he has,' said Tessa. 'When I opened the little scroll to read the Names of God, there was only one: EROS, the God of Love.'

Tessa took a piece of tissue paper from her pocket, unwrapped a little metal tube, took the tiny scroll of rice paper from it, and opened it for her friend:

EROS

Underneath the name, stuck to the paper, was a deep red stone, uncut.

'Rubies for happiness, Aunt Maisie once told me,' Tessa said, 'for happiness and for love. And so for the God of Love, for Eros . . . the letters of which also make Rose. So take this gift . . . my Rose . . . from the hand that took it from your father's.'

The boring thing, Isobel Stern thought (as Mrs Statch let her in and said, no, she'd no idea where that Madame Guiscard had got to), was that if she didn't find Jo-Jo, which meant that Jo-Jo wouldn't come, then she'd have to disappear all by herself for the next three weeks, since Rosie would kill her if she turned up again this evening and carted her back from Buttock's Hotel to Chelsea. And yet she could hardly turn up again in London without doing this. Therefore she must not turn up again in London, therefore she must stay away, therefore she must have a clear and interesting purpose in staying away, therefore she must find Jo-Jo, which all ways round she very much wanted to do.

Mr Ptolemaeos, Mrs Statch had said, was still in bed. 'That Mr Caspar' was with him in his bedroom, taking dictation or some such. Fielding Gray, as Isobel well knew, had left to look for Jeremy on the morning after the rumpus. She, Isobel, was on her own.

She let herself out of the drawing room into the garden and walked down the lawn to the summer-house. 'I shall find you,' she had told Jo-Jo. 'If you are sitting by your pool, I shall find you, and take you.' Suppcse she found Jo-Jo but she was not sitting by the pool? Presumably

186

this too would mean assent. But the pool was important, Jo-Jo knew it was important, and if she was in the place at all she would certainly be sitting by the pool, the finding of which was to be Isobel's test.

What on earth is the matter with Baby? thought Isobel, parenthetically, as she paused by the summer-house. She's regressing. As a little girl she was a horror, as a bigger girl she was worse, but then suddenly, when Patricia was taken away, she bloomed. For some years she went on, in every sense, blooming. And now – this. Keep your mind on your job, Isobel, she admonished herself, which just now is Jo-Jo. A pool among fir-trees. These fir-trees, crowding up the lawn all the way between the house and the summer-house. But they are so close, interwoven, entwined, mingled together, like the bristles of a shaving brush, little enough space between them at the roots and none a little higher. A wall of woven branches, an impregnable phalanx behind it. Even if I knew where to go, I could not possibly get through. There must be a path. Where does it begin?

And then a voice came back to her from the summer: Marius's voice. 'There was a special place in that garden,' Marius had said. 'Not even Jeremy knew about it. I found it once by accident, when I was desperate to be by myself, the only time in all the time I was with Jeremy, but that time I *had* to, I found a hidden path behind the summer-house, and went along it, and came to a secret place.'

'No place which has a path leading to it is secret, darling.'

'The *path* was secret. Even its beginning was hidden by the summer-house, Mummy, and curtained off by thick branches. Only if you were lucky enough to pull at the right branch could you see where the path started.'

187

'And exactly where did it go to, this path?'

She had touched the lobe of his ear.

'To a little pool. So just that once I was by myself. Not again.'

Isobel went behind the summer-house. Jo-Jo's crude imitation of wilderness had drawn attention to the beginning of the path rather than concealed it . . . once one was in the know. Isobel scratched herself quite badly on the briars, but she did not mind that, because she knew that Jo-Jo (if only she was there) would honour her spoken word and come with her, when found, bringing the child. As she moved along the path, which would hardly allow her passage, so narrow it was, Isobel began to hear Jo-Jo's voice:

> '"You think Priests just and holy men!
> Before they put me in this den
> I was a human creature too,
> With flesh and blood like one of you,
> A girl that laughed in beauty's pride
> Like lilies in your world outside."'

Canteloupe had thought of several possible presents for Baby from the proceeds of the Canzoni sale. Recently and as a result of his tuition she had been showing some interest in racing, particularly National Hunt, so why not a high class steeplechaser? He had also thought of a house or flat in the South of France, an emerald parure (Baby loved green stones), or, just possibly, a Rolls Royce.

But Baby, after her return from the Fens, showed neither excitement nor even common gratitude at any of these suggestions. She merely sulked. When asked if anything was the matter, she sulked even worse. After some days of this, Canteloupe made two decisions: first, that he would drop the topic of Baby's present altogether, at least for the time being; and secondly, that if he should ever raise it again, the gifts on offer would be of a very much humbler kind, in order to teach Baby a lesson in manners.

After a little while longer, Canteloupe came to a third decision. When Balbo had discovered the Asolano in the First Night Nursery, Canteloupe had at first told himself that since this might later prove a substantial cash asset (he remembered the interest in the fate of the *real* Asolano, this one as it must surely be, that had been shown in Los Angeles) he could spend even more of the Canzoni money on his present to Baby than he had originally planned to. But now that Baby had come home in this horrible fit of the sullens, now that she apparently neither desired nor deserved a present and was not going to get one (or only one much smaller and much later), there would be a lot of loose money lying about. Well, thought Canteloupe, one could never have too much liquid cash and he was determined not to fritter away this lot (a mistake he had sometimes made in similar circumstances in the past); but he could, he thought, afford a gesture, particularly since the one he had in mind would not involve actual disbursement. He would do the big thing: as justice, honour, liberality and the good name of his house required of him, he would hand back the stolen Asolano to the Church of San Martino.

Not being quite sure how to go about this, he rang up Balbo (who had by now returned to Lancaster) and asked to be put in touch with Sir Jacquiz Helmutt, the Cambridge art mogul, who agreed to send experts to examine the painting in the First Night Nursery and, if it was indeed the missing Asolano (as to which Balbo's account had left Sir Jacquiz in little doubt), to undertake negotiations, with all the Civil, Excise and Ecclesiastical authorities that must necessarily be consulted, to expedite the picture's return. What kind of ceremony, Sir Jacquiz asked, would Lord Canteloupe wish for its reception back in Burano? The very simplest, replied Canteloupe, and preferably one which did not require his own presence. If one was to make such a gesture, Sir Jacquiz rejoindered, one must do the thing *en prince*; this should be no shifty little hole in the corner operation: if it were, everyone would say that Canteloupe had given the painting back out of sheer guilt. There must be an air of munificence and even of magnificence about Canteloupe's act, as if to say, 'We English command and bestow at our pleasure: both as acquisitors and as benefactors we come on the grandest scale.' Court Dress, prescribed Sir Jacquiz, his imagination soaring, or even a Marquess's robes; coronets, he allowed, would be overdoing it and were probably forbidden in Italy, but Lady Canteloupe could appear in the finest family tiara to pull the cord to unveil the picture (yes, by all means let the tapestry remain with it – the combination made a characteristic Venetian joke). Let there come a Cardinal Archbishop to bless it and the first choir in Europe to sing it back to rest in its rightful place (what a pity one could no longer find a few *castrati*); and let a flagship of the Italian Navy (if such a thing there still was) fire a twenty-four-gun salute in the lagoon.

Canteloupe, while deposing that he still felt that a certain modesty would befit the occasion, conceded that it would look well if he and his lady were present, though

190

he had a private doubt, unexpressed to Sir Jacquiz, whether Baby, in her present mood, would attend such a function or grace it if she did.

So there it was, Fielding thought: whatever I am now to do about Jeremy's disappearance (and this is not at all clear to me) at least I have set my house temporarily in order, as far as I can: so much, and so much only, can I spend.(and very little it seems) until the next injection of earned money; if I exceed that amount, I shall have to start cashing in (which Heaven forfend) the last of my reserves of stock.

As to the accusations of under-declaring his income, which had been made by the Inland Revenue, he had heard nothing further. When he had last telephoned his accountant, he had been brusquely recommended to cultivate patience, as if a possible liability of well into five figures, to say nothing of a prospect of prison, were matters indefinitely amenable to phlegm. The accountant had, however, so far relented as to say that he might ring back later that day – and here he was, it seemed, doing so.

But in fact the caller was the so called Chamberlain of the Household at Luffham-by-Whereham. When this venerable person had been soldier-servant to Canteloupe (Detterling) he had of course been, as had Detterling, of the 49th Earl Hamilton's Light Dragoons, which was Fielding's Regiment also. Although Fielding and Chamberlain had never met as serving soldiers, they had known each other after Detterling's retirement, into which his servant, then known as 'Corporal', had followed him; and the man had been well aware, in his lucid days, that they had both belonged to the same Corps – a fact which, Fielding thought, he has presumably remembered now, because,

'*Res Unius, Res Omnium*, Major Gray, sir,' the Chamberlain's voice boomed at him down the telephone.

The old motto of the old mob.

'"The affairs of one are the affairs of his comrades,"' the Chamberlain translated, inaccurately and unnecessarily. 'You are looking for Master Jeremy, sir. When you came the other day, I told you the lie which he instructed me – indeed made me swear – to tell to all who enquired: I told you he had not been here. I now think my loyalty was misplaced, and it is time for both of us, as Light Dragoons, to assist each other. I can tell you that Master Jeremy came here in his motor to collect clothes; so clearly he did not wish to avail himself of those at his College – *id est*, sir, he did not wish, for whatever reason, to show himself there. He took two full suitcases: enough gear for a fortnight, if he is unvaleted, and for several months, even years, if proper service is available to him. He said he must go away and that I was to believe no ill of him; otherwise he was imprecise, and named neither destination nor day of return.'

'When did he come?'

'Thursday evening, sir.'

Soon after . . . what had occurred.

'He stayed the night?'

'No, sir.'

So he had now been on the road, as one must suppose, for nearly a week.

'However, sir, he made a telephone call which I

chanced to overhear. He rang up Lancaster College, the Porters' Lodge, I should say, addressed a person called Wilfred, and asked for Miss Theodosia Salinger. "It's very urgent, Wilfred," he said: "please make her come to the telephone, I know you're a favourite of hers and Miss Carmilla's, please make her come." Then there was a very long interval, a very long interval indeed, Major Gray, sir, let me say twenty minutes, at the end of which the young lady in question did indeed seem to have come to the other end. And as I gathered, sir, Master Jeremy persuaded her to meet him at what he called "the old place" in Saffron Walden the next morning for luncheon.'

The old place in Saffron Walden? Well, never mind where that might be: what mattered now was what words had been spoken there.

'After which Master Jeremy, who would not stay for dinner here,' said the Chamberlain sadly, 'motored away into the dark.'

'Have you told his father any of this?'

'No, sir. As I say, Master Jeremy swore me to silence; and I think it better, at least for this time, to respect the oath in regard to his father although I have now broken it in regard to you. *Res Unius, Res Omnium*, Major Gray. You will find him for me, if you can? Now his brother has gone away, for ever as they tell me, this would be a sad place without Master Jeremy's visits . . . rare though they be.'

And so now, Fielding supposed, the hunt was on. Tom, Len, Isobel, Ptolemaeos, Jo-Jo and the Chamberlain – they all seemed to assume that it was his duty to search for Jeremy. He himself thought so too. If Jeremy was running (and it looked like it) he was running from something which must, in the last resort, be blamed on Fielding: for it was Jeremy's affection for Piero that had taken him to the Fens (where he had encountered whatever he was now fleeing), and it was through Fielding's doing, however indirectly, that Jeremy had first met Piero on Torcello. If you interfere in somebody's life, thought Fielding, if you take him on expeditions, then you are responsible for the results of that interference or those expeditions, however fortuitous, however impossible to foresee.

His good-byes to Maisie and Tessa could be deferred until he had made enquiries of Theodosia in Cambridge. While there he would check with Len in Lancaster and Ptoly in Tunne Hall, in case anything further had come to light since he had last been there.

Since the first person he saw on coming through the Great Gate of Lancaster was Len, he applied to him *instanter*. Len walked him in a wide circle round the statue of the Founder in the Great Court and talked in a circle as well. The truth was that for once Len knew no more than anyone else did, no more about Jeremy's whereabouts or what had caused him to vanish, and was taking refuge in speculation in order to disguise the

194

ignorance which he would not, in his vanity (his only vanity but a very exigent one), plainly confess.

'Hissing,' said Len. 'What does that suggest?'

'Almost anything you care to make it suggest.'

'Japanese audiences hiss in applause.'

'English audiences hiss in abuse. So what?'

'Split personality. She hissed through a mask-like face – according to all the accounts I've heard – suggesting Japanese theatre and therefore applause. But her posture made it plain she was doing so in fear and hatred. Like Catullus, she both hates and loves, but does not know why.'

And so on. The only hard and possibly useful fact which Len told Fielding was that the College (like the Chamberlain) had decided not to inform Peter Morrison of his son's departure from Cambridge.

'Although Jeremy is *in statu pupillari*,' said Len, 'he is also over eighteen and adult in the eyes of the Law. That the Law is "a fool and an ass" in this respect is another matter. As, being of age, Jeremy is entitled to judge for himself what to tell his father about all this and about anything else it is not for us to interfere or delate.'

Fielding, having spitefully decided not to tell Len about Jeremy's telephone call to Theodosia (who must have persuaded Wilfred the Porter to hold his peace if Jeremy had not) now went in search of her. She had rooms, the Head Porter told him, out of College, but was often to be found in her sister Carmilla's set in Sitwell's Building. As he went up the steps to the doorway of Carmilla's staircase, someone came scuffling along the path below.

'Major Gray.'

'Nicos.'

'I saw you from the sitting room of the *Kyrios* Barraclough. He has gone to bed for an afternoon nap. Where is Yeramy, Major Gray?'

'I am trying to find him. I am looking now for Theodosia Salinger, whom he spoke with, I think, after he disappeared. They tell me she may be with her sister.'

'I know where she is. Come with me. I saw her setting off along this path, and from what she was carrying I know where she has gone.'

'Then tell me and I will follow her,' said Fielding, who had neither inclination nor energy for Nicos just then.

'No. You are impatient and annoyed that you have met me, just that bloody Greek boy, you think, to pester you when you have much to think of. You want to be rid of me, but I shall not tell you where she is – I shall only take you there. And you must hear me as we go.'

'Why not? I'm sorry if I appeared irritable, but – '

' – But you do not care for "penniless foreigners". Yeramy told me that. It made him laugh. Come.'

Ivor Winstanley, the celebrated Ciceronian, was watching an unusual lesson which was in progress in the Cambridge University Tennis Court. In all his years of frequenting the Court, for many of them as a player, more recently as an onlooker and aficionado (President of the CU Tennis Club), in all the thousands of hours which Winstanley had spent umpiring by the Post or loitering in the spectators' gallery behind the Dedans (hours which should more properly have been dedicated to his promised edition of the Poems of Cicero, now ten years behindhand in its preparation for the Press), in all this time, never had he observed a scene so bizarre and disquieting as the present one.

The Professional was instructing a tall and well set up young pupil, who moved gracefully, had mastered the basic stroke, both forehand and backhand, served a powerful railroader, and was cleanly and sensibly dressed in white flannel (*real* flannel) trousers and a rather loose cricket shirt. Everything as it should be, one would have thought, very much so – except that on a split second's inspection the pupil turned out to be a woman: Miss Theodosia Salinger, of Ivor Winstanley's own College, famous in the University for her badminton (now there was a suitable game for girls) but now trespassing in a strictly masculine precinct, for no female in Cambridge (or elsewhere, as far as Ivor knew) had ever presumed to play Tennis. The fact that Theodosia promised to be, within weeks, a better player than any of the male contestants for a half-Blue next summer was naught for Ivor's comfort.

There was, of course, nothing in the Laws of the Game or the Regulations of the CU Tennis Club to forbid Theodosia from playing – if only because such an aberration had never been conceived of. To try to get up prohibitory rules at this stage would be discourteous to Theodosia (whom Ivor, on slight acquaintance, very much liked) and would in any case bring a swarm of feminist blow-flies round his ears. No; there was nothing to be done; the thing was *fait accompli*, thought Ivor, perverse but irreversible, as unseemly and now inexorable as that wretched affair of Joan of Arc. He only hoped that Theodosia would not come to a similarly disagreeable end.

The lesson concluded. The luscious movements of Theodosia's fesses ceased. Ivor Winstanley, a realist, one

197

who made the best of what was given and knew when it was good in its kind, looked at the list to see when Theodosia was due for her next lesson and the luscious movements (perhaps she would come in shorts?) would be resumed. As he was about to depart, thinking that with a bit of bustle he would have half an hour to spare on Cicero before going to drink sherry with Balbo Blakeney, he passed another member of his College, Nicos Pandouros, as he came into the Tennis Court Building with that one-eyed friend of the Provost, the novelist Fielding Gray. What did *they* want? Pandouros was far too poor to keep racquet here, while Fielding Gray, though a frequent visitor to Cambridge, had never before shown interest in the game . . . of which, in any case, there would be no more that day. Ivor Winstanley lingered long enough to watch this unlikely pair accost Theodosia in the corridor outside the Court, and then, being too well-bred to eavesdrop and realizing that already he had wasted nearly five minutes of the scanty period (the first since the day before yesterday) which he had allotted to Cicero, he shuffled and snuffled his way out and set his nose for the New Court of Clare and so to the Postern Gate of Lancaster and home.

In the corridor beside the Tennis Court Fielding Gray said to Theodosia Salinger:

'The servant at Luffham says that Jeremy Morrison arranged to have lunch with you in Saffron Walden, the day after he vanished.'

The Professional called from the end of the corridor:

'I'll start the shower up for you, Miss Theodosia. Give it three minutes to get warm.'

'Right you be,' called Theodosia to the Professional. To Fielding she said,

'Yes. I had lunch that day with Jeremy in Saffron Walden.'

'I've been asked to look for him.'

'By his father?'

'His father doesn't know yet. It's thought better that he shouldn't. I've been asked by his friends. Just what was the matter with him?'

'He didn't say. He said he had urgent personal reasons for going away. He had done nothing wrong, he said, but he had been present when something occurred . . .'

'. . . Go on, please . . .'

'. . . He had been present when something occurred which had deeply distressed him . . . in such a way that he could not remain at Lancaster – or not for the time being – and wished to leave England altogether.'

'To leave England and Lancaster altogether?' said Nicos. 'My friend, my new friend, gone. Why?'

'I just don't know,' Theodosia said. 'He kept repeating that although much might be imputed against him by those who knew roughly but not exactly what had happened, he had nothing whatever to be ashamed of. He was leaving, not to escape punishment, but because he could only come to an understanding of what had happened, and of the mysterious reasons or forces which must lie behind it, if he returned to a certain place where a similar mystery was lurking, or so it now seemed to him when he recalled his tour with you last summer.'

'So he is going back . . . to one of fifty places. He didn't say where it was?'

'No. He simply asked for the money to take him there. Since I love him,' said Theodosia, 'despite all the beastly things he's done and the slimy way in which he has already treated me . . . since I love him almost more than I can bear, I did exactly what he asked – though for all I know this may be just another of his confidence tricks – and wrote him out a very large cheque. I can afford it now, you see, as he well knows.'

'Was he telling the truth?' said Nicos. 'About this place to which he must return?'

'I should have given him the money anyway, because I can no longer bear to deny him anything. Not speaking to him this term has been horrible. I don't know how I endured it, but Carmilla said I must, as I did. Then came this telephone call, and I answered, although Carmilla begged me not to, and I went to Saffron Walden and gave him the cheque.'

'But was he telling the truth,' Fielding insisted, 'when he said he must return to this un-named place?'

'I think so.' The Professional waved down the corridor and Theodosia waved back. 'I must go before I get stiff. I think he was telling the truth. And so now, where shall you follow him?'

'Miss Theodosia,' the Professional called.

'To places which we visited together,' Fielding said, 'and which have something of the kind of mystery he seems to be hinting at.'

'But you say there are so many of them?'

'Miss Theodosia,' called the Professional in the shrewish voice of a trainer or a nanny who is being officious for his charge's 'own good'.

'But two or three are outstanding in their quality of mystery . . . of the numinous or the arcane. Or the retributive,' Fielding said. 'I shall try them first.'

'Miss Theodosia.'
'Coming,' she called, and went.

Nicos and Fielding took the same route as Ivor Winstanley had taken ten minutes before. They passed the University Library, suburban-cum-institutional-cum-phallic, and turned into the New Court of Clare College. As they did so, Nicos said:

'Take me with you. I know something of Yeramy and a lot about some of the places – those in Greece – which you must now visit. As for the expense, I do not mind discomfort.'

'I do,' said Fielding. 'Sleeping in comfort myself, I should be discomfited by your discomfort.'

And yet, he thought, and yet. Obviously this journey would make nonsense of all his recent resolutions of economy, to say nothing of wrecking progress on his next novel, vital source of fresh revenue. All of this meant that some of his reserve must now go in any case: why not a little more, enough to maintain Nicos in the same style as himself (which should not be too difficult if he sought out slightly, though not painfully, more modest quarters than usual) and thus procure a knowledgeable and personable companion. For Nicos was quite right: he knew something of 'Yeramy' and more of Greece, particularly the Southern Peloponnesus, which could turn out to be an important area in his search. Nicos could be useful; it was, in any case, 'more friendly with two'.

'I think,' Fielding said to Nicos as they walked down

the steps from the New Court of Clare and into the Queen's Road, 'that I might consider it after all. But what about your studies here?'

'What of them? I do not have time for them, as the *Kyrios* requires my constant attention. In any case I doubt whether I am fitted for them. For ancient Greek, perhaps, but what am I to make of Latin? My results in the examination last summer were very dreadful. It took all of the *Kyrios'* friendship with the Provost to prevail on him to let me stay.'

'What of the *Kyrios* then? You are bound to him by many ties, not least that of gratitude. Can you bring yourself to leave him?'

'If it will help Yeramy. You know the Jews have a law whereby all the other laws and obligations are suspended if one is engaged in saving human life?'

'So I have heard.'

'That is my feeling about Yeramy. All oaths, all other ties must now be as nothing, I feel because Yeramy, who offered me his friendship, Major Gray, and, I think, his love, who at any rate trusted me with his secrets – this Yeramy is in trouble. Do you not think he is in trouble?'

'Anyone who runs from a place like Lancaster is in trouble.'

'Well then.'

'You can drive?'

'Oh yes. I have driven the *Kyrios* on many journeys.'

'Then come with me on this one, if you will. I shall leave London for Dover tomorrow evening. Come to Buttock's Hotel in the Cromwell Road not later than – '

' – THERE you are,' said Greco Barraclough, who had emerged, unseen by Fielding and Nicos, from the Postern Gate of Lancaster and was now advancing on them along the Queen's Road. 'Tea at four-thirty, I told you. No sign of you or of it. Luckily, while I was going to the Senior Common Room, where the tea is very nasty, Nico, luckily I met Ivor Winstanley, who told me he had just seen you and where. So I have come to fetch you and demand of you how you *dare* leave me without my permission and neglect to attend me at teatime as ordered.'

'I am sorry. I had important business with Major Gray. We are going to Europe together.'

'Going where?'

'To Europe, *Kyrie*, to look for my friend Yeramy Morrison, who is lost. I had known him – properly – for only a few days, and now he is troubled and lost. Major Gray and I must find him.'

'What rubbish is this, Gray?'

'He wants to come and for what I care he is welcome.'

'So he will leave me? Desert his guardian and benefactor?'

'He has been blackmailed by that sort of talk long enough. I made your case to him – the gratitude he owes you – as well as I could. He thinks – though he did not say so in so many words – that the debt has been worked out. So do I.'

'His oath?'

'There is a stronger claim, a prior loyalty.'

'"Yeramy,"' mimicked Barraclough nastily: 'Jeremy Morrison. In so far as there is a bond between them, it is new. The prior loyalty must be to me.'

'Must it?' said Fielding. 'Can new loyalties never take precedence over the old?'

'In any case,' said Nicos to the Greco, 'I am going with Major Gray.'

'Then go. Break your oath and absolve me from mine. Gray will be generous – for as long as your excursion lasts. And when you return, he may even persuade the Provost, who is his friend as well as mine, to have you back in the College. But he will not keep you from starving there. He will have sworn no oath, as I have: he chooses to live his own life, a life of independence, that knows of no obligations to the likes of you.'

'I shall perhaps stay in Greece, when we have found Yeramy.'

'Your people in Greece will shun you, because they will know that you have broken your oath to me. "Yeramy", even if he is there and even if you find him, will not stay with you: he will return to this College and to his inheritance. You will have lost all this' – the Greco waved over the meadow towards Lancaster – 'you will have lost me, you will have found nothing – '

' – I shall have found Yeramy – '

' – Whom, as I have just explained, you will instantly lose again. So there will be nothing except shame and low employment for you in Greece, and nothing to which you could later return here.'

'I could return to Yeramy.'

'*If* he is ever found. *If* he is sane when found. *If* he still wants anything to do with you, the little Greek whom he once took up on a whim. He, like Major Gray, has sworn no oath.'

'But he is true.'

'Is he? Have you heard anything of him since he vanished? Has this sterling new comrade of yours sent you so much as half a sheet of paper to explain where he is going or why?'

Nicos turned to Fielding.

'The *Kyrios* is right,' he said bleakly. 'He is my bread and butter, as you say. He will see that I am all right, that I have decent work and am cared for, even when his

204

oath to me has long expired. He would never plead that there was a limit, that time had released him – although it would be true. As long as I obey him, I am his man and he will stand by me. He is what is given, Major Gray. Just for a moment I thought I might take for myself, take something else, a life with you, with Yeramy, for such a life would be different, more brilliant. But now I see that it is an illusion. I could never trust you or Yeramy as I trust the *Kyrios* – him who is given. You understand all this?'

Fielding nodded curtly.

'You see, I was not really acting out of loyalty to Yeramy,' Nicos said, 'or not entirely: it was more that I had a hankering for new things. It is as well the *Kyrios* has reminded me how foolish it is for poor boys from the Mani to hanker after what is not for them. Good evening . . . Major Gray.'

For whatever reason, Greco Barraclough did not turn back for Lancaster but continued along the Queen's Road towards the Backs of Trinity and St John's, followed by a despondent and submissive Nicos. Fielding was therefore spared the embarrassment of their company while walking, via the Postern Gate and the avenue of elms, towards the Provost's Lodging.

'What's the matter with the elms, Len?' he said when he arrived there.

'Well, what?'

'I noticed just now for the first time. They're sort of wilting.'

'Autumn, chum. Season of mists and mellow mouldiness.'

'No. Not just autumn.'

'All right. Since you've noticed, not just autumn. Blight. Dutch Elm Disease. We're trying to keep it quiet until the College Council have decided what to do.'

'You can't keep it quiet. If I can see something is wrong, anybody can. And there's only one thing you can do: destroy them.'

'Right. But then the place would look rather naked. We're thinking of replacing them.'

'With saplings? They'll take generations to cover your nakedness.'

'With full-size transplants. Tom's discussing the financial bit with the Bursars at this very moment.'

'That kind of operation will cost you thousands.'

'The University Chest will help. Our avenue is an essential part of the Backs.'

'All right. But why try to keep it quiet?'

'Superstition. Tom's superstition. Deep down he's a Welsh peasant. He is anxious, not so much that the public shouldn't know what's happening, but that the trees themselves, the spirits of the trees, should stay in ignorance.'

'And he thinks that they won't hear him talking to the Bursars?'

'Not if they all talk low enough. Indeed, the trees *must not* hear. If the spirits of the trees, the nymphs or deities or whatever, know that we're planning to uproot the elms and destroy them, then no matter how compelling our reasons, those nymphs will become angry and take vengeance on us.'

'Surely Tom does not put it quite like that?'

'No. But it's what he's thinking. Or something like it. He's worried that the nymphs of the elms may have some inkling of our plan already. He thinks . . . that what happened to Baby Canteloupe out at Tunne Hall . . . might have been a warning to him.'

'But Baby's all right now.'

'Yes. For as long as Tom heeds the tree-nymphs' warning.'

'But that would mean *not* replacing the elms. Letting them rot where they are.'

'Right. So Tom's split in half, Fielding. One half, the rational half, says raise the money and replace the elms. The other half says, "But don't let them know you're planning this. They've been here much longer than you have, and they may turn nasty. Catch 'em by surprise and kill 'em – before they can get at Baby again."'

'But can you . . . kill the nymphs, the deities? You can destroy the trees, certainly, but then the nymphs become homeless and more vengeful than ever.'

'That's one story. But wood-nymphs are not immortal. Some authorities give them a limit of 999 years, and the same lot says that if a tree dies or is destroyed, then the nymph associated with it dies too, regardless of her age.'

'Supposing a tree lives more than 999 years. Is the nymph's life prolonged?'

'Spare me, Fielding.'

'What you're saying, then, is that Tom hopes to murder those elms, and the nymphs with them, before they have a chance to turn malignant.'

'That's about it. You might call it a metaphor. That's what Tom would call it. Yet he will hear the nymphs, as they wail for mercy and scream for agony, all the while those trees are being destroyed.'

'But surely,' said Fielding lightly, 'Tom could represent to them that it was all being done for their own good – better a quick, clean death than months or even years of festering away with this disease?'

Len took this remark with surprising seriousness.

'Perhaps they think we ought to cure them, them and their trees,' he said. 'And perhaps we ought.'

'There is no cure.'

'But they don't know that, and we could at least try.'

'And when you fail they'll blame you and turn nastier than ever.'

'There must be *some* means of appeasing them,' said Len.

'Careful, Len,' said Fielding. 'Much more talk like this, and we too will be thinking like peasants. May I use the telephone? I want to raise Ptolemaeos Tunne.'

Fielding Gray took a taxi through the evening to dine, by arrangement, with Ptolemaeos and Piero at Tunne Hall. He would tell Ptoly what he had learned that afternoon and would enquire whether he had any final message or information for Fielding before he went on his search.

'So that girl Theodosia has given him money?' Ptolemaeos said, as Piero carried plates of crispy fried fenland frogs' legs from the range to the kitchen table.

'A lot of money, she said.'

'And she also said that he needs to go to some place, unspecified but which he has previously visited with you, where he thinks he has scented . . . some kind of mystery . . . which, if properly understood, may further enable him to understand . . . whatever it was that happened upstairs in that room with the four-poster bed?'

'My room,' Piero said.

'There is altogether too much movement, too much running about,' said Ptolemaeos, his voice rustling with irritation. 'There's Jo-Jo and her brat gone off with Isobel, and Isobel's husband, I'm told, gone to Trieste on some murky mission, and Jo-Jo's husband gone to Clermont-Ferrand, of all places on earth, to nurse his own father; and now here's you going off after Jeremy, who's gone off God knows why or where . . . If only people would sit still, they would sort themselves out much quicker and easier.'

'That's what I keep saying,' said Fielding. 'Everyone agrees on the excellence of the advice – and rejects it out of hand.'

'"*Video meliora proboque,*"' said Piero: '"*deteriora sequor.*" Ovid. I have been reading Latin in your Library, sir.' He took Ptolemaeos' plate to the sink with his own and Fielding's, then started to stir an enormous pot.

209

'A stew of eels, conies and freshwater crawfish,' he announced. 'Mrs Gurt said it must be stirred vigorously for five minutes before serving. *"Video meliora proboque,"*' he repeated, working with his wooden spoon; '"I see the better course and I approve it. *Deteriora sequor* – I follow the worse." The sensible, the better course for me,' he said, 'is clearly to stay here with my wise and munificent patron, for whom I have only gratitude and esteem, and who will almost certainly procure me a place in one of the most famous Colleges in Europe. The worse course, almost insane you may think it, is to accompany Major Gray on his search for Jeremy Morrison.'

'I have not invited you to come with me,' said Fielding.

'But you will, or so I pray, when you have heard me speak. There is love here, and there is guilt. Love for Jeremy, of which I choose to say no more just now: guilt for what I have done, either to him or to that girl, or to both.'

'Come, come,' said Ptolemaeos, 'I thought we'd been over that. You were in no way to blame for what happened.'

'I was and am to blame for what I intended.'

'You did not intend anything very terrible,' Ptolemaeos said.

'But it seems that I have done something very terrible. And I should have realized that I might before I did it. My plan, to make that girl angry or jealous, was rooted in malice. Not exactly in personal malice directed against her, but in thinking of a malicious kind. I should have known that once one deploys thoughts or forces of that kind, there is no limit to the evil which may result, even if the original intentions are strictly limited. Some great evil did indeed result, and I must bear my part in discovering what it was and how it may be quelled or cured – and in quelling and curing it myself if possible. And so,' said Piero, 'I beg you, Fielding, to take me with you and let me help you. And I beg you, sir' – he turned, still stirring, to Ptolemaeos – 'to let me go and give me money and tell me that I may return to your service when this matter is done.'

'Rather a long order,' said Ptolemaeos, 'just as I was getting used to you.'

'If you say to me, sir, that you will give me no money if I go and will not take me back when I return, I shall be sad but I shall still go. With Major Gray, if he will take me; alone, begging my way in my Friar's habit, if he will not. And then, when I have done whatever I can, I shall go back to my brothers in the Dead Lagoon – where else? – and throw myself on their mercy.'

'I shall give you money,' said Ptolemaeos, 'enough to go with Fielding, if he will have you, or alone and in comfort if he will not. I shall also give you something equally essential – this passport in the name of PIERO JOHANNES CASPAR.' He threw a new passport on the table. 'Passably quick work,' he said, 'but then I have friends who have friends, as I once told you. Just as well for you, Piero Johannes Caspar, or you could not have gone – or not in safety – for a good while yet.'

'Then you approve my going?' said Piero. '"*Deteriora probas?*"'

'I did not say that. I have said I shall give you money, because I have an idea that Fielding may need a friend with money just now. I said I should give you this passport, because it would be a pity that such pretty work should be wasted. What I did not say,' said Ptolemaeos, 'is that I shall necessarily take you back when you come. I may, but then again I may not. In fact, your absence

211

will give me a good chance to assess your probable value to me as weighed against the annoyance of such ellipsis in your function as this present. Only when you return shall I let you know which scale has kicked the beam. "But there, my blessing with thee . . ." A blessing given in farewell, which, pray remember, is no necessary guarantee of welcome home. The choice is yours: stay and be cherished; or go, well furnished, indeed, but possibly to be damned.'

'I shall go,' Piero said. And to Fielding, 'I may come with you?'

'If you wish. If we find Jeremy,' said Fielding, 'how are we to share him?'

'No doubt,' said Ptolemaeos with some amusement, 'he will make his own preference plain.'

And now, completing the last leg of a long day, Fielding Gray was riding to London in a night train from Ely. Tomorrow evening Piero (who was not to come to Buttock's, as Nicos would have done) would meet him at The White Cliffs in Dover, and the morning after they would take the Hovercraft to Boulogne. Why, thought Fielding, did I not wish Piero to meet Maisie – or vice versa? Difficult to answer the question precisely; the best I can do, he thought, is to reply, in a very general way, that Maisie somehow has to do with life and having it more abundantly, whereas Piero has to do with death and the Inferno.

Item, thought Fielding: Could Piero drive? He thought

not. Pity. It would have been convenient to have some-body to drive him, as Jeremy had driven him last summer and Nicos could have done now.

Item: At least Piero will be well provided, Fielding thought, with money. Ptolemaeos had later in the evening been specific and very generous here. This would mean that the inroads on his precious reserve need not be as damaging as he had thought, for Piero could obviously pay his share of the petrol, the Hover-ticket, garaging, et cetera, and perhaps the odd hotel bill for Fielding, in gratitude (why not?) for being driven all the weary day long.

Item: Other thoughts about money were less alleviative. What would his accountant do, Fielding wondered, if he finally convinced himself that the Inland Revenue's accusation, that Fielding had under-declared his income, was well founded? Fielding decided to send the man a note, that night from Buttock's, saying that he had been called away on urgent affairs and could be reached, at a need, c/o The American Express at Cannes, Venice, Dubrovnik, Corfu and Athens, through all of which he would probably pass, though not necessarily, in the case of the last three, in that order. Let the accountant telegraph the result of his investigation, and if money were urgently needed to pacify the tax-gatherers then he himself would telephone his publishers, Stern & Detter-ling, throw himself on his knees through the mouthpiece (so to speak) and clasp theirs as a petitioner in the approved Homeric fashion. Fielding now remembered that Gregory was away: presumably Canteloupe would have to authorize the payment: would he do so? Fielding was owed no money by Stern & Detterling except for a pittance on the current six-monthly account, and he would be asking Canteloupe to remit several thousands – many thousands – to the Inland Revenue on his behalf. Rather a long order, as Ptoly had said of something else earlier in the evening. But then again, *Res Unius, Res Omnium*, as the Chamberlain had remembered: the affair of one Light Dragoon was the affair of all, and since Captain Detterling/Canteloupe of all people, if half the rumours one heard were true, had received the full benefit of this maxim, he must surely be prepared to confer benefits in his turn.

Item: What did he really want of Jeremy, should he find him? His love? His salvation, from whatever powers were now gathering to harm, goad or undo him? Proof of his innocence? The opportunity to tend and comfort him in his guilt? A place by his (Jeremy's) hearth in his (Fielding's) dotage? Oh, bloody hell. Next question, please. Would Piero sleep with him if he asked him to? Yes; out of sheer kindness. Therefore he would not, must not ask. Luckily he did not very much want to ask. Funny, that he should credit Piero with such warmth and humanity when only a few minutes ago he had been associating him with death, the Inferno, with Cocytus and with Styx . . . Are you there, old boatman? Piero has been given many an obol to pay the passages of the dead, of those who cannot afford to pay their own, whose relatives did not place the last offering, the Ephodios, between their lips. No more can you refuse the pitiful voices (like the squeaking of bats) now that Piero will pay for the tickets; no more can you be a niggard of your barge: crowded as a Thames steamer on Whit Monday it will sway across the river, delivering the poor, wandering souls to the pastures of the legitimate dead. Are you there, ferryman? I come with Piero, that cunning whore of Sicily and Venice, to pursue the friend of his heart (and mine?) into whatever hell the Furies have appointed for his exile. Come, ply your oar in earnest, grey Gondolier, and Piero will pay you with the red gold of courtesans to bring us to the other bank; meanwhile let the black waters lap about the gunwales, bringing sweet sleep.

PART THREE
Avernus

Hos iuxta falso damnati crimine
mortis.

Near them were those condemned to
die on false charges.

VIRGIL: *Aeneid*, VI 430

'You could so easily do it here,' said Isobel to Jo-Jo. She looked up at the jagged mass of grey rock scattered with outposts of pine. 'Pagan country. Desolate. Caves, clefts, grottoes all over the place. They wouldn't find her in months. Years. Decades . . .'

'There was a time, before the child was born,' said Jo-Jo, 'when I determined that if it should be female, I'd do just that. Expose it in the ancient Greek fashion. I'd thought of the Peloponnese. Of Taygetus. Of this part of the world too. Pagan country, as you say. But as you well know, I no longer want to murder her, or even to reject her.'

'But you cannot accept her?'

'Nor she me. She does not want my breast. Although she listens when I read to her, it is only because she cannot remove herself out of earshot and cannot, even at her age, be forever asleep. So she is tolerant . . . perforce and politely tolerant. But she does not want to be encumbered with me any more than I wish to be encumbered with her.'

Isobel began to walk towards her Lagonda, which was parked in a corner of the dusty courtyard, near the foot of a stone stairway that led up to an arcaded loggia in which, when the summer came again, the guests at the inn would lunch and dine off the inferior specialities of the region.

'Tomorrow,' said Isobel, 'this place closes. They are most of them seasonal, you see. So today we must look

219

for somewhere else. Do you wish me to look alone, or will you and Oenone come too?'

'Oenone can go in the back, in her carry-cot.'

'No. The roof is torn. You must be with her to protect her against draughts.'

'Then I will take her on my lap in the front.'

'No. It is not safe for infants to ride in the front. Even now I should not let Marius or Rosie ride in the front.'

'Then I must sit in the back with Oenone?'

'Yes.'

'It has been like that all the time,' Jo-Jo said, 'except once, when you let me leave Oenone for an hour with an elderly maid, whom you trusted, and took me to a cathedral. Then, and then only, I sat in the front. It was almost unbearably exciting. The way you sat over the controls and mastered them . . . bestrode and rode them. Can this not happen again?'

'Not now. Not today.'

'Very well . . . though for someone who promised to serve you are very severe. Where are we going on this fair blue morning?'

'Over these hills. Pine and rock. Down the other side, to cypress and flat fields. Along a straight road on which the Romans marched. By castle and abbey to ramparts and towers, and thence to the Elysian Fields. Near these we shall find a new hotel, and then we shall return to this one, to have dinner for the last time before we pack.'

'Are you tired of driving?' said Piero Caspar to Fielding Gray.

'Rather. Beguile me.'

'I have an idea. A fairly obvious one, but I think I should state it. It is something I think we shall have to cling to.'

'Well?' said Fielding, and felt a quick, warm shiver as he saw the first Aleppo pine.

'Miss Baby, Lady Canteloupe – she is alone with Girolamo, with Jeremy, in my bedroom in the Fens. I go to fetch the backgammon set from downstairs. What can happen then? She looks at Jeremy, and says to herself – as I intend she should, sooner or later – "Piero likes this Morrison. Piero, who has just spent last night with me, likes this huge, round boy. Why?" She looks at Jeremy again. Just a big, shambling peasant. A yokel, you would say. "I see nothing in him," thinks Miss Baby. "But he is smiling at me. Shyly? In suggestion? In either case I detest him – that mound of flesh. What does Piero see in him? And what, for that matter, does Fielding Gray see in him, that he fancies him enough to take him all over Europe?" You see, she is jealous, Miss Baby, on your account too. During the night she told me how you have gotten the child on her for Lord Canteloupe – '

' – She should not have told you that – '

' – She has told me, Major Gray. She has told me how she excited you by asking about her mother: she has imitated you in your imitations of her mother. Although she has no more need of you, she remembers your

221

intimacy, not without pleasure, and she wonders why you now like Jeremy. She does not want this to be. She does not want you any more, but she does not want Jeremy to have you. She wonders also why I too like Jeremy, why two of her men like Jeremy, and she is very jealous.'

'Possibly. But jealous enough to put on the sort of show she did?'

'That hissing. While I was in the Fens, I read Milton in Mr Tunne's library. When the fallen angels came to themselves in Hell, Fielding, they started uncontrollably to hiss. Envy: jealousy.'

'Not quite the same things.'

'But with a base in common: wanting what somebody else has got. The fallen angels wanted what God had got. They started to hiss . . . and went on hissing until Lucifer himself took control of them. Miss Baby wanted what Jeremy had got – or at any rate wanted *him not to have it*. So she started to hiss, and went on until Mr Tunne himself came to deal with her.'

'What you say may be true, Piero. But in Baby's case the cause you assign is insufficient. The fallen angels, you remember, had good cause not only to envy but *to despair*. To account for Baby's behaviour mere jealousy will not do. To produce such formidable and relentless hysteria, something really radical is needed: desperation or despair. I cannot see that Baby was suffering from anything radical enough, deep enough, to drive her to such extremity.'

'Yet there she was *in extremis*, Major Gray. Can you better my explanation?'

'We are looking for Jeremy to do that.'

With great difficulty Jeremy found a place to park his Morris 1000 under the ramparts. Having carefully memorized the plan in the Green Michelin (for it was now some weeks since he had last been in this place, and then only for a brief first visit) he walked along the base of the ramparts, up some steps to his right, past the Roman Theatre (which was on his left), and turned left round the southern end of the amphitheatre. Then he skirted the northern side of the theatre enclosure, went down a narrow street, took a turn to his left, walked past the west door of the cathedral in the square, turned left again, and very shortly came to the entrance to the cloister.

Why am I hanging around here? he thought. There is nothing for me here. Why don't I journey on to where I am really going?

He paid for his ticket and went into the cloister.

'This place is named,' said Isobel to Jo-Jo and Oenone, 'either from the *Campi Elysii* of the old Romans or from a flower called the Alys which is supposed to grow here. Formerly the tombs covered a much larger area – where the railway now runs and the canal.'

'You sound like a guide book,' said Jo-Jo.

'A French poet warns us,' said Isobel, ignoring this ingratitude, 'that in this place we should beware of the *douceur de vivre*, of the sweetness of living, and that we should speak no word of love among the dead.'

'That will suit me and Oenone,' said Jo-Jo: 'we do not believe in words of love. We heard them from Alexandre, our Alexander, who spake us false.'

'But many of the sarcophagi,' said Isobel, 'bear inscriptions, sculptures, variously Pagan or Christian in subject and feeling, which are vibrant with the phrases and the shapes of love.'

'I do not see them here,' said Jo-Jo. 'These sarcophagi are plain, crude, uncarven.'

'That is because all the finest have been stolen or given away by the Mayor and Corporation to distinguished visitors. A very few remain, specially preserved in two museums near the cathedral and cloister, one devoted to coffins of the pre-Christian epochs, the other to coffins dated Anno Domini. Most of these are carved with scenes in low or medium relief,' said Isobel, 'scenes Christian or Pagan, as I have just remarked, and sometimes, on some of the later coffins, both. And so now, in order to see what the tombs here were once like, we shall go to see the tombs there.'

'In the days when we bathed in Mr Tunne's sarcophagus,' said Piero Caspar to Fielding Gray, 'Jeremy, Nicos and I, Nicos told us that the house in which he once lived with the *Kyrios* Barraclough (as he insists on calling him) was only a few miles from Cape Taenarus, which is one of the gateways to the kingdom of the dead. Did he believe in such a place? Jeremy asked Nicos, as Nicos lay (not quite naked) in the sarcophagus. He believed, Nicos told us, in some kind of after-life, but not in such a kingdom as one might enter through a gate at Cape Taenarus.'

'Why are you telling me this?' asked Fielding, almost dizzy from fatigue and the whirling ranks of cypress through which he was now driving.

'Because a little later, when Jeremy lay (totally naked) in the sarcophagus, Nicos and I asked him the same question as he had asked Nicos: did he believe in a world or a kingdom of the dead? His reply was curious. If there were such a place, he said, its entrance could not be at Taenarus because Taenarus was by the sea. He felt very strongly that an entrance to the underworld could not be on the edge of the sea because the sea was too wholesome and bracing and clean; it would sweep away and altogether dissolve the dead (whether crumbling bodies or wailing spirits) who sought passage in its vicinity. A suitable entrance to the kingdom of the dead, Jeremy told us, would be near a still lake, such as Nemi or Avernus or a slow and sluggardly river such as Styx or Acheron; or a brackish pool or marsh, such as the Fens around Tunne Hall; could show in abundance; or, best of all perhaps, the inner waters (well away from the sea itself) of a stagnant lagoon, such as the Laguna Morta round Venice. Torcello, he said, or any of the smaller islands in that lagoon: *there* would be a proper entrance, for corpse or wraith, to the kingdom of the dead. Torcello . . . in whose Cathedral the Madonna weeps a tear for the dead with one eye while she watches them pass with the other.'

'I think her tear is for the living,' Fielding said.

'For both, perhaps. He had also heard, he said, of another Madonna in that region, though he had not yet seen Her. The two together . . . presiding side by side over a gate to the kingdom of the dead . . . they might explain.'

'Explain what?'

'He did not say. In those days he did not require any particular explanation. But now, to judge from what you say this Salinger girl told you about his reason for vanishing, he wants, he needs, he is compelled to search for some explanation of what occurred in Mr Tunne's house . . . an explanation, he told her, which may possibly be found in one of the places you and he visited last autumn. So what about Torcello, where I myself met you both, an island which obviously made a great impression on him? Why not Torcello?'

'There are . . . other places we visited . . . where there are two Madonnas who could "explain" and where there is also perhaps an entrance to the kingdom of the dead – since he seems to set some store by that. We went to Avignon, for example, where there is a slow river, making it a fitting location, on his view, for a gate to Hades.'

'The River Rhône. Too powerful. He said that a river, to make a suitable gate to the underworld, must be slow *and* sluggardly. There is nothing sluggardly about the Rhône at Avignon.'

'But there are two Madonnas, by which he also set store, two extraordinary Madonnas, up at Villeneuve-les-Avignon, one coal black and the other all the colours of the spectrum – '

' – But he particularly specified Torcello, Major Gray, Torcello and the Madonna in the Cathedral who sheds a single tear. Why are you so anxious to divert us to Avignon?'

'Because it is on the way, and it could be the answer, and I am not wholly convinced by your advocacy of Torcello. Obviously, you see, he liked the idea of two

Madonnas – one on each side of the gate to Hell. He made this picture very clear to you – '

' – Yes indeed, and persistently connected it with *Torcello*.'

'But that is the whole point, Piero. The second Madonna he referred to in the area *simply is not there*. He must have been thinking of the weird Madonna with the Plague Children in the church on the neighbouring island, Burano. But she is not there, Piero, and he knows She is not there, because we went to see Her and found Her gone. So if he is heading for a place with *two* powerful Madonnas, it must be somewhere other than Torcello.'

'Rubbish, my dear Major. The second Madonna – he associates Her with the area; for all Her temporary absence She has been there a very long time; and in any case at all She may be back by now. Added to this, he named the place, almost obsessively, a great many times. Torcello, Torcello, Torcello.'

'But this was all *before* the incident with Baby.'

'And why should not his obsession be quite as powerful after the incident with Baby? Torcello was, and could very well have remained, predominant in his thoughts as a place of mystery and perhaps of oracle. It is surely the most likely place to find him. Why do you not wish to go there?'

'Why indeed?' Fielding suddenly felt too drained to resist any longer. He trembled, and turned up the heating in the car. Piero was impermeable, he thought: arguing with him was like trying to wriggle through a fence of barbed wire. 'Why indeed?' he repeated. 'You are quite right. If he spoke as you say he spoke, he may very well, when in grave trouble or doubt, have made for Torcello. I wish to find him very much. To Torcello we shall go. I shall not turn off for Avignon,' he said in a low, sing-song voice. 'It was foolish of me to chatter about Villeneuve. I shall drive south and east towards Cannes and the Italian border and keep on until it is dusk.'

'But you are tired?'

'Yes. But I wish, so much, to find Jeremy. I shall drive on towards Italy until it is dusk.'

In the cloister, as Jeremy remembered from his visit with Fielding on their way back to England in the autumn, were many carven capitals. As Jeremy moved slowly along the eastern gallery he spotted the drunken Noah with his two sons (who were holding their hands up in priggish reproof), Elijah and the Ravens, and the infant Moses, afloat in his little cradle on the Nile (looking rather like Oenone when Jeremy had seen her by the pool in her carry-cot), just about to be discovered by the Pharaoh's daughter. The capital which topped the next pillar was plain, but the one after was worked with a low relief version of (as it appeared) Abraham and Isaac. There was Abraham with his knife raised (Jeremy diagnosed) and there was the angel coming down to stop the proceedings in the nick of time. The only trouble was (it now occurred to Jeremy) that Isaac was looking terrified, whereas in the Old Testament he had surely been resigned. Once Jeremy had noticed that, other discrepancies were instantly evident. Abraham was not a sorrowing parent set to perform his melancholy duty but a snarling youth of much the same age as Isaac. And the angel was not descending in merciful intercession but lowering in grievous wrath. Not Abraham and Isaac, then: Cain and Abel.

Jeremy backed away from the pillar while his stomach turned in nausea. Don't be foolish, he told himself; it wasn't your fault: you didn't kill Nickie, who in any case is not dead. But still his belly ached and churned. Not dead, no, but worse: a shambling frame of flesh and bone. Not murdered by his brother, but written off by him, left to rot. And yet, thought Jeremy, I am not being fair to myself: I do go there, I went only the other day, just before term began; I asked questions of the nurses, and I went to see him. 'Hullo, Nickie,' I said, as he turned his empty eyes to me: 'hullo, old boy.' But he just turned away . . . to that woman he was with. 'I am Patricia,' she said, 'Patricia Llewyllyn. You are Nicholas's brother. I knew your father, long ago and in another world, though I never knew him as well as my husband, Tom. But I knew him, and now I shall take care of Nicholas.' As she cradled Nickie's head on her breast, her eyes became fierce. 'He is my son in the eyes of God,' she said: 'never seek to take him.'

Remembering the story about Patricia Llewyllyn, that some years back she had hideously savaged and maimed an adolescent boy (with her teeth, some said, though Jeremy was uncertain about that), had at any rate committed some atrocious assault which had been the cause of her confinement to St Bede's, Jeremy had sought out a Senior Superintendent and asked whether the relationship between Patricia and his brother was in order.

'They are company for one another,' said the Senior Superintendent. 'She will not harm him. When she is not with him, she is on her knees in sackcloth, repenting of what she was and what she did.' 'Nevertheless,' Jeremy had said, 'with someone so unstable . . . is it safe?' 'Safe?' said the Senior Superintendent. 'Nothing can hurt your brother now. He is as safe . . . as safe as a corpse, Mr Morrison. But there are just a few . . . basic responses . . . left in him, and these she rouses from time to time. She is all of life that is left to him.'

Jeremy had decided to question the affair no further. He did not tell his father, whom indeed he had not seen again before returning to Lancaster. He did not choose to discuss the matter with Tom Llewyllyn. ('I say, Mr Provost, your wife and my brother are getting together in St Bede's. What do you say to that?' No, that was a discussion, *de bas en haut*, which was better far in the breach and would for ever remain so.) He had, however, just begun to remark on this odd friendship to Patricia's daughter, Baby Canteloupe, by way of making conversation and riding over an awkward gap while Piero was fetching the backgammon set that afternoon in the Fens . . . 'I saw your mother the other day,' he had said diffidently: 'she was with my brother Nickie; they seem to be . . . contented . . . with each other.' This much he had said thinking to treat sympathetically of the topic, also to show that they had something (if only a sadness) in common, perhaps to please her by reporting that her mother had an interest. And at first it had seemed that he had succeeded. She had made some comment, about her mother's fondness for boys, to which he had replied that although Nickie was hardly a boy any more they seemed to suit each other well enough. An anodyne, harmless remark, he had thought: but this time Baby's response had been horrible, catastrophic. Oh, how could he have been such a fool as to start the subject in the first place? He might have known that such an area must be mined with dynamite. Yet how was he to have known that a brief mention of Patricia and Nickie would produce a reaction so fundamentally violent that it would wrench Baby right out of the present reality which they were sharing, that it would carry her away, in a split second and by the width of a galaxy, from the room, the house, the fens, the world, that it would transform her into an alien thing crouching and hissing on the bed? What had done *that*? Surely not just a reference, however tasteless and tactless (and indeed it had hardly been allowed to continue long enough to be either) to her mother and his brother in St Bede's?

But he had seen what he had seen, it had happened before his own eyes, and he could not return to England, to Lancaster, with a quiet mind until he knew what was at the bottom of this appalling phenomenon. He could not face Tom Llewyllyn until he had some explanation of his daughter's seizure, her worse than seizure, her dissolution. And of his own. As for Baby Canteloupe, he knew she had now recovered, for he had persuaded Theodosia (on the day they had had lunch at Saffron Walden) to institute tactful enquiries through Len, and a telegram from her, waiting at the Poste Restante at Pau, had informed him that all was apparently well. But the hideous transformation which he had witnessed, however brief its period, still required explanation; and his own vile reaction to it required even more: it required, it *necessitated*, expiation. There was a riddle here that must be read; a spectre that must be exorcized; above all, a personal abomination that must be cleansed.

He knew where he must go to ask and be answered. So why was he dallying here? Why had he already loitered many days along the road? Why had he deliberately and even before he left England elected a route that would take him right down to the Pyrenees before he turned east for his true destination? Why was he idling in this cloister now? Well, he had been punished with a nasty pain in his gut by the unexpected appearance of brother Abel . . . a pain which in his case often preceded nervous

231

diarrhoea. There was no public loo here, that he knew; but just over the square, above the crypt where the sarcophagi were, there was a nest of *cabinets* presided over by a beldam in black. Fielding had compared her to the old woman who kept the WCs in the Bois de Boulogne in Proust's novel, *Swann's Way*: for he had heard her greet a shuffling visitor as 'M'sieur le Marquis', just the kind of snobbery in which Proust's woman had excelled, bestowing titles on all her clients unless they were obviously of the lower orders, in which case they were not admitted. I really must get on with Proust, thought Jeremy. I really must get to that woman's loo.

'One matter for concern,' said the Chairman of the Board of Salinger & Holbrook: 'the proposed printing of this book by Gregory Stern. Not good for our reputation; could even get us in trouble with the Race Relations people for anti-Semitism. I gather that we are to print at the request of the Misses Carmilla and Theodosia Salinger. Colonel Blessington, you are their nominee and represent their interests here: what have you to say?'

'First, that they wish the book printed. Beyond any question whatever.'

'And if this Board should object? What action would you or they take?'

'We should go on one side and count their shares.'

There was an ugly silence.

'But I can report that there has been delay on the Gregory Stern front,' said Ivan Blessington. 'His book

232

will not be coming in for printing until much later than we had thought.'

'But it will still come in?'

'I imagine so.'

'And you cannot deter the Misses Salinger from wishing it upon us?'

'It is not up to me to deter the Misses Salinger,' said Ivan, 'but to speak for them. They wish the book printed as soon as Mr Stern hands the typescript over.'

'When will that be?'

'Soon after he gets back from Europe.'

'Yes, but *when*?'

'In his good time, Mr Chairman.'

'I find you offensive and unhelpful, *Mister* Blessington.'

'So be it, Mr Chairperson.'

'There you are,' said Isobel: 'Oedipus talking to the Sphinx on one side of the sarcophagus, and Androcles talking to the Lion on the other. A Pagan theme on the same coffin as a Christian one.'

'Uncle Ptoly says it was quite common,' said Jo-Jo, plonking Oenone down in the special seat of the Curator, who had for some reason disappeared up the spiral staircase to the entrance. 'A form of insurance, he says, to keep in with both sides, just in case. The sarcophagus in his library is one like that. Oughtn't we to be doing something about a hotel? I mean, if our place closes to-morrow . . .'

'Plenty of time,' said Isobel. 'Plenty of room at this

time of the year in the places that do stay open. Let's just see what turns up.'

'All right with me, but you seemed quite eager, earlier on, to find somewhere definite.'

'All these tombs have relaxed me. Still two bedrooms, I think?'

'Always two bedrooms, as long as Oenone's around. I'm sure she listens and peeps.'

'What nonsense. A perfectly nice, normal baby, minding her own business. Look at her now,' Isobel said, 'lying patiently on that hard seat.'

'Exactly. A nice, normal baby would be making a fuss about that. Oenone's keeping quiet so that she can overhear us. I cannot help thinking of her, you see, as somehow inquisitorial. Now, here's the real test. With this coffin, one end and one side are blank. On the other end is a man ingratiating himself with two other men, and a rather impertinent bird above them with its beak wide open – '

' – The cock crowing at Simon Peter – '

'That's the easy one,' Jo-Jo said. 'On the carved side is a naked young man with a bow, which he is offering to a horrid old beggar . . . while a rather bossing man in armour is trying to stop him.'

'Paris – your Alexander – was a great hand with a bow.'

'But he wouldn't be giving his away to anyone else, not him. Mean, he was. Ask Oenone.'

'There's a possible clue to one end. A corkscrew kind of snake, like an adder. Carved on a slant with its head down, pointing at the beggar's right ankle.'

'The young man is rather fetching, the shy way he's handing over the bow. Certainly not my Paris/Alexander . . . brash, boastful brute.'

'Handsome with it.'

234

'Handsome is as handsome does. What do you say, Oenone? I wish I knew more about him – the boy on the coffin, I mean.'

'Let us wait,' said Isobel, 'until the Curator comes down again, and then ask him. We're really in no hurry.'

Tessa Malcolm and Rosie Stern were walking home from Collingham's School. They had decided to make a diversion round the Round Pond before striking south for Cromwell Road and Buttock's.

'Most of those boats,' said Tessa, 'are controlled by wireless from the shore. It must have been much more fun when they weren't. In those days, Aunt Maisie told me, they ran on something called clockwork. You wound up the engine and shoved your boat off and just hoped it would get to the other side, which it sometimes didn't. No danger like that with all this modern apparatus: no excitement.'

'Daddy says they used to have aeroplanes which worked on elastic bands,' said Rosie. 'Sometimes they plunged into the ground, but sometimes the wind caught them, and they soared away over the Park, over the Albert Hall, and were lost for ever.'

'There has been a lot of soaring away just lately,' Tessa said. 'Your father . . . your mother . . . Major Gray.'

'Well, they all seem to enjoy it,' said Rosie, 'and so do we. I love Mummy and Daddy, of course, and I wouldn't want them to vanish for ever like those toy aeroplanes with elastic bands, but I shan't mind if they stay away for really quite a long time, as long as I can be with you.'

'It might be nice, though, to have Major Gray back. I can tell Aunt Maisie misses him.'

'What is he doing?'

'It is something to do with that Jeremy Morrison, who he went away with last September. Aunt Maisie doesn't approve at all. Waste of time and money, she says, when he ought to be getting on with his book.'

'When Marius rang up yesterday, he said Jeremy Morrison had been to Oudenarde House to say good-bye, because he was going away somewhere. Jeremy Morrison told Marius not to believe anything bad which he heard about him.'

'If it's not anything bad, it must be something pretty important,' said Tessa, 'to make him leave Cambridge in the middle of the term.'

'So it looks as if Major Gray must have gone after him. I expect your Aunt Maisie is jealous.'

'I only said she misses him,' said Tessa with testy loyalty.

'He likes you, did you know,' said Rosie.

'Of course I did. And I like him.'

'I mean, he fancies you. I saw him looking at your knees. A short look, but very intent.'

'And I saw him looking the same way at your hair. I don't think it means anything.'

'Marius says that old men just like looking,' Rosie said.

'But sometimes they like touching too,' said Tessa. 'Aunt Maisie warned me. If you once let them start touching, she said, you'll never get them to stop.'

'Was she talking about Major Gray?'

'She didn't say so. In fact she said she wasn't. Of course it's all right for gentlemen you know like Major Gray to kiss you sometimes or hold your hand, she said. But I thought she put rather a lot of emphasis on the word "hand", so I did slightly wonder.'

'Do you suppose Major Gray fancies Jeremy Morrison? After all . . . that holiday last autumn and now chasing after him like this . . .'

'Aunt Maisie says he is infatuated. Then she looked cross that she'd said it and told me she hadn't meant it.'

'"Infatuated" means fancying.'

'Men, Aunt Maisie said, get infatuated with God knows what when they have the male menopause – the change of life.'

'Is that the same in men as in women?'

'I don't know. It was all part of what I was told to forget,' Tessa said, 'so I didn't like to ask questions.'

'Mummy said she wanted a change of life when she went away.'

'So you said. I think she just meant a change, full stop.'

'I only hope it suits her,' Rosie said; 'then she might put off coming home. But I suppose Daddy will turn up again soon if she doesn't.'

'He wouldn't make you go back to Chelsea if you didn't want to,' said Tessa: 'it's only a woman who'd do that. Men are far less possessive.'

'Not all of them,' said Rosie; 'you should see Marius with Mummy.'

'Chilly,' said Tessa, as the Round Pond rippled in the breeze. 'Home now, do you think?'

'Yes. Home.'

When Isobel and Jo-Jo heard footsteps on the spiral stairway down from the entrance, Jo-Jo moved Oenone from the Curator's seat, thinking that this must be the Curator and he might be offended if he found a baby in his chair. But when a figure came fully into sight after the last twist of the stairs, it turned out to be Jeremy Morrison.

'I thought you were the Curator,' said Jo-Jo inanely, and put Oenone back.

'The Curator's upstairs in the loo,' said Jeremy. 'At least, a man in uniform came bursting in just as I was leaving and went crashing into one of the *cabinets* without paying the crocodile.'

'The crocodile?'

'The old hag that runs the place.'

'What are you doing here?' said Isobel.

'Passing through,' said Jeremy as he joined them by the sarcophagus. 'Philoctetes,' he said examining the side. 'My favourite story.'

'Tell,' said Jo-Jo.

'Philoctetes was the finest archer who embarked for Troy with Agamemnon's expedition. But on the way he was bitten in the foot by a snake. The wound stank so horribly that they left him behind on an uninhabited island in the Aegean, where he just managed to survive by shooting game with his special bow. Then the Greeks were told by an oracle that they would never take Troy unless they had Philoctetes' bow: so they sent Odysseus

238

and the boy Neoptolemos, Achilles' son, to get it. Naturally Philoctetes, who was still all alone on his miserable island, refused to part with it, despite all their wheedling, and said that if they wanted it they must take him too; but his stink and his fits were so ghastly they couldn't agree to this.'

'Stalemate?'

'Yes,' said Jeremy, looking steadily at the coffin as if he might have been wondering who was once inside it, 'until, that is, Odysseus and Neoptolemos take advantage of one of Philoctetes' fits to steal the bow. When Philoctetes wakes up and realizes what has happened, he starts crying desperately, not only because his source of livelihood has gone, but also because he has grown fond of Neoptolemos, who seemed to return his affection, or at least to feel sorry for him, and now that friendship has been betrayed. Just as his grief becomes unbearable, he looks up to see Neoptolemos hurrying back with the bow to return it, unable to endure the thought of his own treachery. But of course Odysseus follows him – that officious brute in the armour – and sets about getting hold of the bow once more . . . because it is absolutely vital to the Greek war effort. A story of expedience versus friendship, you see.'

'Like this one,' said Jo-Jo, going round to the end of the coffin, 'in which Peter disowns his Friend. How was it all settled – in the case of Neoptolemos and Philoctetes?'

'A god came down and commanded Odysseus to let Philoctetes come to Troy – stench and all – and handle his own bow.'

'Yes,' said Isobel. 'Only the intervention of a god can settle that sort of muddle. Much the same could be said of the story of Peter. Both tales show expedience winning in the short term and friendship loyal and victorious at the last. Wishful thinking if you ask me. It is usually the other way round. Whatever,' she said to Jeremy, 'did you do to my niece in Ptolemaeos' house in the Fens?'

'Nothing. I just mentioned that I had seen her mother in St Bede's with my brother Nickie.'

'A sensitive subject,' said Isobel, 'for all of us: but hardly enough to call up what came.'

'That's what I thought. I gather Lady Canteloupe is now all right?'

'In a sullen way, yes. She seems – or pretends – to have forgotten exactly what happened.'

'I shan't forget. It was so foul – I'm sorry, I know you both love her – but it was so foul that I must have it . . . explained. More than that, I must have it purified.'

'You think that is possible?' said Isobel.

'I am going to a place where I think there may be at least . . . exoneration. Something I once saw there, something I heard there, makes me hope this. I cannot go back whence I came until I have been – well – eased, and also assured that there will be comfort, more, salvation, for your niece.'

'Have you far to go to reach this place of easement?' Isobel asked.

'No. But I am afraid to arrive there in case I am wrong and there is no consolation. I am snatching at excuses to loiter. I feel dreadful.'

'You don't look it. You appear calm and confident.'

'That is how I was brought up to appear. But I am afraid, Mrs Stern.'

'"Isobel", I think, from now on. For we shall render you a friendly service, if you will return it. You have a car?'

'Yes.'

'Then you should leave it here. I will show you where to park it safely. I shall then drive you in my own car to wherever you are going, and shall see to it that you loiter

240

no more . . . though since Oenone will be with us there can be no undue haste. Also I shall try to help you find what you are looking for, if only in order to understand what happened to Baby, my niece.'

'I shall be glad of company. I have been alone. And as for us,' said Jeremy to Jo-Jo, 'we have agreed to agree? Or at least not to differ openly? Despite your curt dismissal we agreed to a truce that afternoon by the pond?'

'I shall be civil, Mr Morrison.'

'And what service,' said Jeremy to Isobel, 'are you asking in return?'

'You must ride in the back of my car with the baby. My friend likes to sit by me in the co-driver's seat, you see, but she cannot leave the child unattended in the back nor carry it with her, as this is unsafe, in the front. Now she can have her way and you can nurse Oenone. She will love your big round face.'

Jeremy went and stood over Oenone, who bubbled slightly.

'There you are,' said Isobel to Jo-Jo: 'I told you something would turn up. We shall take Jeremy – for Jeremy he is to be to all three of us from now on – back to our inn for the night, leave tomorrow betimes, and stage in whatever hostelries are to be found each day at dusk.'

In the early autumn evening Tom Llewyllyn and Len walked down the avenue of trees, which led from Lancaster Bridge to the Postern Gate on the Queen's Road, for the last time. Tomorrow the destruction of the diseased elms would begin.

The grandiose scheme, whereby the trees should be replaced by fully grown transplants, had been abandoned on grounds of expense. For although Lancaster might, on application, have been awarded assistance from the University Chest, it would take months of debate and lobbying before the money would be available (if ever it were) and it was the view of the College Council that if action there must be, it must be immediate and consonant in cost with immediate means. The trees must be down before the avenue became a nightmare of skeletal decay. As Balbo Blakeney had reminded the Council, the difference between an elm that was stripped by autumn and one that was defoliated by disease was plain for all to see, and in a double rank of elms over a hundred yards long the spectacle would be horrible. 'Flanders Fields without benefit of poppies,' Balbo said. All this, along with a declaration by the left-wing College philistines that even if a grant were to be made by the University they would oppose its acceptance for this purpose ('In this day and age there is no money to be spared for fancy landscape gardening'), had decided the Council simply to clear the ground at once and to postpone any discussion of further operations until the soil had settled.

And so now the Provost and his Private Secretary walked under limbs that would be lopped tomorrow and between trunks that would all be toppled before the week was out.

'When I was a young man,' Tom Llewyllyn said to Len, 'I spent the last few weeks before I was married on a walking tour of the West Country. One day I came to a plateau in the Quantocks, a place of most exquisite beauty, scattered with groves of willow and lady-birch. But already the bulldozers were busy; and a strident

242

notice proclaiming that the area had recently been acquired by some Ministry which was going to develop it into a new kind of holiday or recreation camp, to be called Westward Ho!

'Later on, much later on, I heard that the place had duly been butchered by the bulldozers and then smothered in caravans and Nissen huts. There had been a Royal and Ministerial opening. On the day of the opening it started to rain. It did not stop. Even when the rain let up elsewhere, it did not stop falling on Westward Ho! The site turned into a marsh. The caravans sank and the Nissen huts rotted and the kitchens swam in garbage and the ablutions became a midden. All sog and rust and mire and turd. One by one the holiday-makers slunk away, demanding but not receiving their money back. The people in the village below said that the genius of the groves, who had fashioned them as shelters and bowers of sweet love, was angry at their desecration and was taking his revenge on all who had come to exploit them in their ruin and shame. And indeed the only people known to have been happy there were a pair of lovers on the run, who were effectively hidden and comfortably sheltered in one of the sounder caravans. So perhaps the genius, who had dedicated his former groves to the uses of love, made an exception in their case; but if so, it was brief, for one of them was killed in a car accident. But then again perhaps the genius was not responsible for this death (which took place some miles away from his precinct) and was even grieved by it; for he gave the survivor a splendid marriage, with a stranger met by chance among what remained of his willow and lady-birch: a goodly husband and a rich house did he give her, and oneness of heart, which is the best gift of all.'

'How do you know all this, Provost?'

'Because the one who survived the accident was my

243

sister-in-law, Isobel Stern. Her dead lover was called Lewson, a man who was in any case damned, whatever the genius of the groves may have made of him. But I tell you this tale, Len, to warn you that the genius of this place – of our College, our Lancaster – may be angry with us for what we are doing, and so may the wood nymphs, the Dryads of his rule.'

'So you have said, my dear, or at least suggested, several times before today. But in your story the *genius loci* was angry that his groves had been denied to the local lovers whom he favoured. We are denying nothing to anybody.'

'We are destroying beauty, murdering trees.'

'We have no choice, Tom.'

'Better beauty in decay than mere scorched earth.'

'No. Corpses must be buried or burnt.'

'These trees are not yet dead.'

'Oh Tom, Tom. The thing has been decided as it had to be decided, by the College Council duly assembled.'

'I am the first of the Council. I stand and speak for the Founder. I am the murderer. Already the nymphs have possessed my daughter, and may do again.'

'The nymphs may go into the Fens,' said Len, adopting the Provost's level of reasoning, 'for they were reared very close to them, but they cannot cross the salt sea. As you know very well, Baby and Canteloupe left this afternoon for Venice.'

'For Venice . . . and its marshes. Do you think that nymphs bred by the Fens cannot communicate with those of the lagoons and marshes?'

'Baby and Canteloupe will be under the protection of the Blessed Virgin, Tom. They are going to Venice to restore one of her pictures to a church in Burano. Jacquiz Helmutt is going to be there as artistic adviser and English liaison officer. There will be no improprieties practised by tree nymphs or marsh nymphs or any other kind of nymphs as long as Sir Jacquiz Helmutt is there on the rostrum.'

'Of course you are right,' said Sir Thomas, suddenly calm. 'I am being thoroughly foolish. But, oh Len, I am so sad for our trees.'

Leonard Percival first knew there was something wrong when Gregory Stern did not come out to his car, which was waiting outside the hotel. Gregory had planned to set out from Trieste in a hired and chauffeured car during the early afternoon of the day after the conclusion of his conference with Shamshuddin and his minions about his forthcoming book. The conference had been due to end the previous day; there was the hired Renault and its chauffeur waiting, as arranged, outside the Albergo d'Annunzio; there was he, Leonard, waiting as agreed in his Fiat at a discreet distance, ready to follow Gregory into Yugoslavia and along the first leg of his journey towards Dubrovnik and Greece: and where was Gregory?

At three P.M. Leonard went into the Hotel and asked to speak with Signor Gregory Stern, who, he presumed, was still in his suite . . . possibly ill or waiting for a telephone call from some tardy correspondent, business or personal. But no. The Signor had vacated his suite, the clerk told Leonard Percival; on his instruction his luggage had been put in his car outside, while he himself had left the Hotel by the rear entrance, having first asked the clerk to tell the chauffeur that he would be back in about ten minutes.

What possible purpose could the Signor have had in visiting the Post Office when every conceivable postal or telephonic service was provided, far more swiftly, quietly and efficiently, by the Hotel?

The clerk did not know.

The chauffeur had seen nothing of the Signor in the one hour and fifteen minutes since he had had his message from the clerk.

None of the employees at the counter of the Post Office recalled a tall, dark Englishman.

Gregory had not returned to the Hotel during the fifteen minutes which it took Leonard to make these enquiries.

In short, thought Leonard, I've lost him. I've boobed. Not my fault. But of course this is just the sort of thing which I came to prevent. But *why* has this happened? Well, I had a feeling, on my way here, that he was getting ready to play silly tricks; so perhaps he's played one and wound up skidding into a crap-heap, which is what happens to people that play silly tricks with other people like Shamshuddin. On the other hand, all must have been well at the conference, which must have ended yesterday, thought Leonard, as planned. In any other case Leonard would have had an alert, for there was a simple signal (a red volume of the Leob Library to be left by Gregory in the pigeon-hole under his key behind the Porter's desk) by which they had arranged for Gregory to summon Leonard at the least sign of the conference's dragging on beyond its time or starting, for whatever reason, to turn sour. No red volume equalled a green light for Yugoslavia and Greece. This afternoon, now. The absence of Gregory, more than an hour after the wheels were ready to roll, equalled heap big mingi fuck-up, thought Leonard, reverting in his uneasiness to the nig-nog lingo he had used many years ago on a rather similar mission (*mutatis*

246

mutandis) in Kenya, when it was still a proper country properly ruled by proper people . . . who would not have appreciated the way he had just mashed up his balls here and now. Cunty, cunty, loosy Monkey. What the shit did big-dick Percival do now? Attend to his duodenal ulcer, that's what, before it blew a hole in his belly.

And so, a few minutes after Len and Tom had gone from under the elm trees in Lancaster, Leonard Percival went once more into the Hotel d'Annunzio, negotiated a sweaty passage through a jabbering mob of charabanc-borne Japs, and reached the bar. Here he asked for a glass of milk and, on impulse, for the English Signor Gregory Stern, who was staying in the Hotel.

'*Giornalista?*' said the barman.

'Friend.'

'I know Signor Stern. Suite Number Three. 'E come in here. I take things up there, when doing Number Two in this bar, late night. So. Friend, not journalist? Your milk will cost you fifty thousand.'

'Here.' Percival handed it over.

'Tough little girl in black. She talk to 'im as 'e leave the lift. As I come down to go on duty, thirteen-forty-five, a quarter to two, you say. She talk to 'im near lift. Then he go to the clerk and say something and leave with 'er by the back. Fifty more thousand for tip please.'

'Here.'

'She pretend to be bad girl, *putana*, feeling herself to excite 'im, as if she pick 'im up for quick jig-jig. But I see she do it wrong, not liking. Whyever he go with her, not jig-jig. Is all.'

Artemis. The tough girl in black whom Isobel had fancied, the girl of whom she had told Gregory and Gregory, before leaving England, had told Leonard. Artemis: so named by Isobel for her purity. At the last minute Artemis had somehow hi-jacked Gregory, or

247

persuaded him that he must go with her. How? Why? *Where?* They would make a recognizable pair: strong, tight-faced, spare, chaste Artemis in black, unskilfully pretending to be a *putana*, and huge, shambling, doubtless unhappy Gregory. Recognizable, yes: but how did he set about finding them? 'Excuse me, sir or madam, but have you seen a couple answering to this description? If so, which way were they going?'

Talk about boobs and fuck-ups. Sweet Jesus Christ.

'Talk about the Pied Piper,' said Len. 'There's Fielding Gray and Piero Caspar already chasing after him. Why do you two want to get in on the act?'

'I, for one, do not,' said Carmilla. 'But Theodosia says she is in love with him and won't rest till she knows what's become of him. I cannot let her set out alone.'

'Why not?' said Len.

'Because I should worry about her.'

'But you don't even know which way he went.'

'He went,' said Theodosia, 'to one or more of the places to which he went with Major Gray last September.'

'That's a lot of places.'

'Starting with Pau,' Theodosia went on, 'because he asked me to send him a telegram there to tell him how Lady Canteloupe was getting on. But I don't think Pau's his real destination. He just fancies a long ride to soothe himself.'

'I dare say,' said Len; 'but exactly where are you going to look for him?'

'I think,' said Theodosia, 'that some useful hints are to

248

be had from Nicos Pandouros. He was getting very friendly with Jeremy just before . . . just before he left.'

'Look,' said Len, trying to be patient. 'If you girls want to go off into the blue to look for Jeremy Morrison, no one's going to stop you. I can vouch for it that it'll be all right with the Provost, and that you'll be welcomed back with open arms when you choose to come. But we're all going to miss you. Jesus Christ, I'll miss you like I'd miss my own head, even if it's only for a week or two. You're . . . you're special,' said Len, 'they don't come like you very often, and I just hate to think of all your time and talent being wasted on trying to find that inflated Cherubino.'

'A good description,' said Theodosia. 'He's also a thumping crook. But I think that now he is in real trouble and not just pretending. Anyway, I can't be doing without him any more, Len, and that's the nub of it.'

'Right,' said Len. 'I shall procure you leave of absence, in the first instance until the first day of Full Term next, though I shall hope you'll be back before the end of this. Starting tomorrow, I take it?'

'No,' said Carmilla: 'not till Monday.'

'Monday? But I thought Theodosia just couldn't wait.'

'I've got to wait,' said Theodosia. 'I am to play Second String for the University Tennis team against Hampton Court on Saturday. Tough opposition, whom we are keen to beat for the sheer prestige of the thing, as University Tennis has been at very low tide lately. Our Captain, Myles Glastonbury, is relying on me, and I cannot let him down.'

'Sweet*heart*,' said Len, not knowing whether to laugh or cry, 'you sound like something straight out of the *Boys' Own Paper*.'

'The *Girls' Own Paper*,' said Theodosia, 'if you don't mind.'

'So that's settled,' she said to her sister as they left the Provost's Lodging; 'not that I ever thought there'd be any difficulty. "Special", as Len calls us, we may or may not be, but we're certainly *privileged* right up to the ears. Two big rich girls. So: off on Monday . . . after a word with Nicos.'

'Irritating news in the second post,' said Carmilla: 'Ivan Blessington says that the Board of Salinger & Holbrook are making a fuss about printing Gregory Stern's book.'

'But we've given our word.'

'I don't think we need worry. Come up to my place and read his letter. He says that a little hint about our shareholding nearly stopped the show, and he's confident that all will go as we would wish. Two big rich girls, like you said.'

'Nice, having someone like Ivan to leave things with when we're going away for a bit. What is it about him? You couldn't call him clever or shrewd or quick. He has no particular gifts of intelligence or intuition. And yet I have a feeling that he is utterly and absolutely reliable.'

'He's a gentleman,' said Carmilla. 'That's all about it, and that's what it's all about.'

'You're beginning to sound,' said Theodosia, 'like something out of the *Boys' Own Paper.*'

'I'm glad we're going to be in Venice for a few days before the ceremony,' said the Marquess Canteloupe.

'So I suppose, or we wouldn't be going,' his wife said.

'We can visit some of the places we went to when we

250

were here last time. With your father and Daniel Mond. Remember?'

'I remember.'

'The Gritti is always agreeable; and Tullius will be quite all right with Nanny for a week or two.'

'No doubt of that.'

'Balbo Blakeney will be coming just before the ceremony.'

'He can't come too late for me.'

'After all, he did find the bloody picture . . . But don't worry. He'll be with Sir Jacquiz Helmutt and his wife at the Danieli. Helmutt has to make a last minute check of the arrangements in the Church of San Martino. You may have to take a small part.'

'Do a strip show?'

'Look,' said Canteloupe: 'you don't have to stay with me in Venice if you don't want to. You can turn right round and go home the minute this aeroplane lands. In fact, with Leonard away it would be quite convenient if you did go home. You could keep an eye on all the things which Leonard usually looks after. We can't expect Nanny to do *that*.'

'I thought the Corporation had lent you a man to sub for Leonard.'

'Not much of a man.'

'I expect he'll do for a week or two. Since I've got nothing else on,' said Baby Canteloupe, 'I may just as well be with you in Venice. The Gritti will serve as well as anywhere, as that's what you've arranged. Daisy and Sarum will be blissfully happy without either of us. Since I've got that little rat, Piero, out of my hair, nothing worse can come of Venetian memories than harmless boredom. And I can even put up with the food so long as I don't have to eat it at the same table as Balbo Blakeney.'

'Both dead,' said Jean-Marie Guiscard, who had telephoned from Clermont-Ferrand, to Ptolemaeos Tunne. 'My father died within an hour or two of hearing about my mother. I'd better talk to Jo-Jo. She'll have to bring Oenone and come for the funeral.'

'She isn't here,' said Ptolemaeos.

'Where is she? With Baby Canteloupe?'

'No. She's gone off with Isobel Stern.'

'Gone off? With Isobel Stern? For how long?'

'God knows. It was all rather sudden. But I suppose they'll have to be back in three weeks or so, when Gregory is due home from *his* trip . . . unless Isobel has decided to chuck him.'

Ptolemaeos was deliberately telling less than he knew and implying more, to get his own back on Jean-Marie for having married and removed Jo-Jo. Not that he disliked Jean-Marie, or had ever thought that Jo-Jo would stay in Tunne Hall and the Fens for ever; he rather enjoyed, however, making Jo-Jo's husband smart a bit.

'But why didn't Jo-Jo let me know that she was going away . . . and where?'

'I expect you'll get a post-card in due course,' said Ptolemaeos, knowing that Jo-Jo, who had funked ringing up Jean-Marie had nevertheless posted a card to Clermont-Ferrand before leaving with Isobel.

'But I can't postpone the funeral while I wait for a post-card.'

'Don't,' said Ptoly. 'She hates funerals. Her mother and father and two brothers were all buried at the same time after their motor smash, so she got enough then to last her for life.'

'But in France it is expected that a daughter-in-law should – '

' – Come, come,' said Ptolemaeos. 'You're not married to a French *bourgeoise*.'

'Indeed not,' said Jean-Marie, remembering his aspiration to resemble an upper class Englishman and telling himself that he must not let the shock of his parents' death cause him to revert to type. 'Of course she can't be bothered with all that silly rot about family funerals.'

'That's the spirit,' said Ptoly, warming to Jean-Marie, whom indeed he had always liked. 'I'll tell you what to do. Plant your parents, then come back here and sit it out with me. I don't think Jo will be gone long, it's just that she's been a bit off level by this business of having Oenone. Childbirth often turns 'em funny for a bit. I dare say Isobel will sort her out and bring her back as good as new. But if she don't, we'll see what's to be done, you and I.'

'Good egg, Ptoly,' said Jean-Marie bravely: 'I'll be along by Tuesday.' But to himself he said, as he put down the receiver, that the little bitch needed her face slapping: all that money, of course – it made her independent; but money could not excuse – he was about to use the phrase 'disobedience to one's lawful and wedded husband,' but just in time he substituted 'sheer bad manners'. However, he told himself, he must go on trying to see the thing from the point of view of the upper class Englishman, whose attitudes were more sensible and elegant than any other in the whole world. In this role, then, the best course was to pay no attention whatever, to pretend, when she got back, that he had hardly noticed her absence, and to display, for as long as she did not return, total indifference.

Leonard Percival had decided to go south. From what he remembered of Gregory's account of being kidnapped by Shamshuddin & Co. the previous summer, Gregory had reckoned (though he was far from being certain) that he and Isobel had been taken to a small island off the Dalmatian Coast. It could be reasonably presumed, therefore (and if it couldn't nothing else could) that he would now be taken (by the same people) to the same place.

However, since it was already late in the afternoon when Leonard finally realized that Gregory had been abducted, and since his ulcer, despite his expensive glass of milk, was playing up something shocking, Leonard had (guiltily) deferred his departure until the next morning and booked himself a room for the night in the Hotel d'Annunzio. What he needed, he told himself, was a quiet, plain, wholesome Italian dinner, followed by a good rest. And in the end it had turned out that he had done absolutely the right thing, however wrong and self-indulgent his reason. For while he was dining in the hotel restaurant a young woman dressed in black had calmly seated herself at his table, named herself to him as 'Artemis from Shamshuddin', and presented him with a note from Gregory. Discussion would have to be resumed, Gregory wrote, as Shamshuddin had become uneasy about the attitude of Salinger & Holbrook towards printing his book. Recent enquiries in that direction had revealed that objection had now been raised by the Chairman of the Board and others. Until confidence had been restored in this matter, Shamshuddin had invited him to be his 'guest'. Although Shamshuddin had not told Gregory where he was to be held, he was quite willing that Gregory should have a friend and adviser in the neighbourhood, who might be of use in case of further awkwardness or uncertainty, and was therefore permitting Gregory to notify Leonard that if he cared to spend the next few days at the Albergo Garibaldi in Mestre he would be promptly informed when and if his services should be required. It appeared that Shamshuddin and his friends had for some time been aware of Leonard's 'attendance' on Gregory (Christ, thought Leonard, I really am getting past it) and would have no difficulty, Gregory wrote, in finding him to deliver this note.

Having read this through and sighed deeply, at thoughts of his own demonstrable past incompetence and evident future impotence in this whole affair, Leonard had signified to Artemis in basic Italian, the only language in which she appeared able to communicate with him, that he would remove to the Garibaldi in Mestre the following day. Here he had found that a room overlooking the Railway Station had thoughtfully been reserved for him.

'Venice,' said Fielding Gray, 'is a great city for unexpected revelations.'

'Let us hope,' said Piero Caspar, 'that nothing too tiresome is revealed this time.'

'We had better stay at the Gabrielli, I think. About my mark, these days. And about yours, with that money of Ptoly's. *Something*, I hope will be revealed, or else our journey and Ptoly's money will have been wasted.'

'Jeremy, in one piece, offering a rational explanation of his behaviour . . . I'll settle,' said Piero, 'for that. No nasty shocks. You remember the revelation we had last time we were both in Venice?'

Fielding nodded.

'I ought to. I used it, albeit very discreetly, as material for a long novel . . . which was published while you were still withdrawn from the world.'

'But if you had been less discreet or less loyal, things could have turned very nasty for Lord Canteloupe.'

'I don't know. To prove, to the satisfaction of a Court of Law, that some idiot boy in the marshes near Oriago is the legitimate descendant of a spy called fitzAvon, who was in fact the eldest son of the man who subsequently became the 1st Lord Canteloupe, and that therefore the said idiot boy is now the rightful Marquess – even if it could be done it would cost a fortune, and *cui bono*? Who is even going to try?'

'Still, it must have made Canteloupe uneasy . . . the knowledge that he now possessed a huge fortune and a magnificent title to neither of which he had any claim whatever . . . he can't have cared to have that on his conscience.'

'Canteloupe's conscience is as tough and malleable as chewing gum. If he's prepared to pass Sarum off before the world as the true heir of his body, why should he bother about masquerading as Canteloupe? He isn't the first, after all. Every single so-called Canteloupe who has reigned as Marquess *after* the birth of fitzAvon's son – Nicolo he was called if I remember right, born in true wedlock to a peasant girl called Cara in the village of Samuele near Oriago in 1979 – that is every single Marquess Canteloupe except for fitzAvon's father who was the first – has been phony.'

'And little Sarum, when and if he inherits, will be doubly phony,' Piero remarked.

'What odds does it make?' said Fielding. '*Vanitas vanitatum, omnia vanitas*. If the coronet fits why not wear it?'

'In the first place,' said Shamshuddin to Gregory, 'I was uneasy at the leisurely manner in which you proposed to carry out the revisions to your work. To say that you could do them while drifting round Greece hardly showed a proper sense of urgency.'

'There is plenty of time. The articles I have written are quite enough for your purpose for the time being. Let them sink in before we weigh in with the book . . . for the printing of which, as you know, very responsible arrangements have been made.'

'Ah,' said Shamshuddin: 'that, as I have already told you, was the second matter to bother us. Come and stand by the window and let me show you the view.'

As Gregory rose, Shamshuddin's henchman Pontos (a jowly youth in a dark suit and a blue tie) and the girl Artemis rose with him. God knows, thought Gregory, as they crossed with him, one on either side, to the window, what they think I might be planning. To strangle Shamshuddin, who carries a dirk sheathed in the leather lining of his coat? To leap through the window and swim to safety through that marsh?

'This is an abandoned farmhouse which we have partly refurbished,' said Shamshuddin, 'on an islet near San Francesco del Deserto in the Lagoon of Venice. If you look to the right you will see the Campanile on Torcello: if you look to the left you will see the Church of San Martino on Burano.'

'So,' said Gregory, 'this time you are telling me where I am.'

'Oh yes. This time we are old friends. We want you to feel trusted and confident. Let me remind you that your friend, Mr Percival, is not many miles away. You have nothing to fear; you need expect nothing except kindness . . . Artemis, if instructed, can be very kind indeed . . . provided only that you sit down and write your revisions, here in this farmhouse, in the substance and style we have required of you during our recent conference, taking, let us say, one week.'

'But what is this sudden rush, Shamshuddin? Salinger & Holbrook will not be expecting the finished typescript for nearly a month. And there is nothing to be gained by such hurry, even if the printers agree to turn it off early.'

'There is our problem, Mr Stern . . . the second thing that brought uneasiness to us. As I have told you, enquiries in London now reveal that there is, after all, uncertainty about Salinger & Holbrook. The firm may not be prepared to print your work. The Chairman of the Board is being obstructive.'

'I have the promise of the two principal shareholders. The Chairman is a puppet.'

'Even so, there is now doubt . . . so much doubt that when I heard the news – just before you were to leave Trieste – I at once decided that it would be better, after all, if you remained with us . . . so that if the arrangements should go wrong, we could all discuss what was to be done, immediately and together. And meanwhile I have provided, as you see, a peaceful and comfortable place for you to do your work undistracted from the world but with such occasional recreation as Artemis will provide on request.'

'She doesn't look the kind to frolic to order.'

'She knows her duty.'

'In any case,' said Gregory mildly, 'I shall not need to trouble her. I have something to tell you, Shamshuddin. I should have preferred to leave it until later, until after I had done my tour of Greece, but I always reckoned that matters might take this kind of a turn, and so I am fully prepared to tell you now.'

Gregory smiled at Shamshuddin, nodded to Pontos, and bowed very slightly to Artemis.

'Everything, as I have explained, has been responsibly arranged,' Gregory said, 'for the revision, the printing and later on the dissemination of my book. This spot of bother at Salinger & Holbrook can only be temporary, in view of the undertakings I have received; the book, when printed and bound, will be distributed by a small private agency which specializes in operations of this kind; the contents of the book, along with my name on the cover, will guarantee a success of scandal and the consequent projection of virulent anti-Jewish propaganda.

'Yet I have to tell you,' Gregory continued gently, 'that the book will not now be finished or delivered, that it will never be either printed or distributed. The arrangements I have made are contingent on my personal word to the printer and distributor; this word will never now be given; and neither printer nor distributor will accept the word of anyone else.'

'What exactly are you telling me, Mr Stern?'

'That unless I deliver the typescript to the printer with my own hands, and instruct him to proceed in my own voice, the book will never be printed. I have to tell you now that I shall neither revise nor deliver the typescript, and that in consequence, no matter what anybody else may do or try to do, the book can never appear under the respectable auspices you require for it.'

'We have a copy of the existing text. Even unrevised it could do much for us.'

'If you print that text, my agents have instructions to disown it on my behalf. The world would then realize more or less what has been happening, and your imposture would merely work you discredit and contempt.'

'Mr Stern,' said Shamshuddin politely, 'you must know very well what we might do if you make of yourself a nuisance like this.'

'Yes,' said Gregory, 'and I no longer care. You do what you wish, Shamshuddin. The point is, as far as I am concerned, that I must do what I consider to be decent, what my friends consider to be decent, or at any rate *not do* what they and I consider to be indecent. If it would interest you to know, I despise the Jews every bit as much as I despise you and your organization and the Arabs whom (for whatever reason) you support. Between you all you have ruined Lebanon, the land that flows with milk and honey, and bored the civilized world stupid with your mindless and fanatical quarrels. "A plague on both your houses" is the only comment proper in the mouth of any man of understanding. The fact remains that I am a Jew and it is therefore not decent that I should propagate festering lies about the Israelis. If you had only been content with a reasoned and moderate case against them, I should happily have made one out for you, for God knows that would have been easy enough. But you wanted lies, you insisted on factitious hatred, rabble-rousing hysteria. You shall not have them from me, for this simple reason: the men with whom I have grown up in England, the men with whom I have served my country and pursued my profession and passed my leisure, consider what I have been doing to be indecent, to be distasteful and shameful, Shamshuddin, and since I love them I shall do it no more.'

'Oh dear me, Mr Stern,' said Shamshuddin, 'you mustn't go looking for kudos of that kind. It could make you so very annoying.'

'I am not looking for kudos of any kind. I am simply behaving as my friends would expect me to behave . . . as I should expect them to expect me to behave.'

'Put it how you like, Mr Stern, you know very well that we cannot allow . . . disaffection . . . of this nature. So why don't you decide to be sensible and helpful again? Get on with your revisions, take a little time off with Artemis now and then, and deliver the text for printing when you are ready, giving your personal go-ahead which you say is required. There is, as you observe, no particular hurry: but delivered in the proper form it must still be.'

'It shall not be delivered by me; and without such delivery it is disowned.'

'Oh dear. I hardly think that you have considered the consequences. For dereliction such as this, you know, we must exact very spectacular punishments indeed. We cannot have it said that we are mocked.'

'Anything you may do to me, Shamshuddin, will only confirm the impression of all decent men – that you and yours are the lowest kind of scum. Yet not perhaps the lowest of all; for the Jews, or at least the Israelis, are equally low – and sometimes, I must admit, I wonder why I should go to the trouble of refusing you on their behalf.'

Sir Jacquiz and Lady Helmutt (Marigold) flew to Venice in a privately hired jet, paid for by some Trust or other on which Sir Jacquiz was prominent. The choir of Lancaster College came too, as did Balbo Blakeney who had, after all, found the bloody picture, in Canteloupe's phrase, and was therefore very properly being carried free to the ceremony at which it would be returned to its rightful place and owners.

The form of this ceremony Sir Jacquiz was now outlining for the benefit of Lady Helmutt and Balbo.

'There will be a Service of Thanksgiving to start with, to be said and sung in Latin. We have brought our own choir' – he gestured to the rear of the jet, where twenty little boys in gowns and Eton jackets were romping spitefully and being sick in each other's top hats – 'since the Italians are quite incapable of raising anything suitable in that line.'

'How did you persuade them to let it be done in Latin?' asked Balbo. 'They usually insist on the vernacular these days . . . sucking up to the proles.'

'Quite easy. Rather a large tip to the Archbishop of Chioggia, who will be taking the service. A pity we couldn't have one of our own College priests, who would have sung much better, but San Martino, when all is said, is a Catholic Church, and we must make some concessions to our hosts.

'After the sung Epilogue to the Service of Thanksgiving (*In copia et divitiis, Domine, nos in aeternum maneamus* – let us dwell for ever, O Lord, amidst riches and plenty)

Lady Canteloupe will unveil the Asolano, which will be hanging in its original place, over the side altar third from the west door in the south aisle, concealed beneath a curtain of tapestry designed for it, as I surmise, by the 1st Marquess Canteloupe.'

'I told you that,' said Balbo; 'you did no surmising.'

'Let him go on,' said Marigold. 'We shall have no peace until he's finished.'

'As her Ladyship pulls the cord,' intoned Sir Jacquiz, 'the choir will break into an anthem, the music for which was composed by the Bulgarian Jeremiah Burphus – *Ut Romulum Remumque nutrivit lupus/Ita Virgo illuminationem spargit* – "As the she-wolf gave suck to Romulus and Remus, so the Virgin spreads light upon us," a very neat pun (*lupus*, Cante*loupe*), a graceful compliment to the Marchioness, and an elegant reference to the subject matter of Asolano's picture.'

'How long is all this going to take?' asked Marigold. 'Balbo and I want to know whether a single flask will go the distance.'

'There will be ample refreshments *after* the ceremony in the Locanda Cipriani, five minutes away by boat on Torcello. There is no need to take your own.'

'Says you,' said Marigold.

'Now, after the unveiling – '

' – There you are, you see, I knew the bloody thing was going on even longer – '

' – After the unveiling, and by special dispensation of His Holiness the Pope, the Anglican Bishop of Glastonbury will utter a special blessing. He insists, I'm sorry to say, on speaking it in English, as he and his wife are enthusiastic members of the Religion for the People group, whose avowed aim is to eliminate what they call superfluous decoration or obscurity from all liturgies. Mungo Avallon, as the Bishop is allowed to style himself, will be totally out of place at an occasion of this kind, but he is an old war-time friend of Canteloupe, who insists on his taking part. After he has blessed the picture, there will be a final anthem – '

' – Sweet Jesus Christ – '

' – No, Marigold, not "Sweet Jesus Christ" but a new one for which I have written the words to accompany the dulcet tones of Psthyst – *Domine, tibi gratiam agamus/ Cum pro pictis tabulis/Tum pro egregiis et fidelibus custodibus eorum* – "Lord, let us give thanks for works of painting and their dedicated and distinguished curators."'

'I.e. for you and your gang. Not a word about the painters themselves, I notice.'

'Their reward is in their vocation. Anyway, most of them are men of dissolute habit, quite unfit to be mentioned in a sacred building.'

'Was this true of Asolano?' Marigold asked.

'We don't know much about him,' said Balbo. 'He is reputed to have abducted and married a Jewess.'

'There you are, darling,' said Marigold to Jacquiz: 'Asolano liked Jews. So won't you squeeze him into your anthem after all? He's rather sensitive about all that just now,' she confided in Balbo, 'as he's been reading Gregory Stern's anti-Jewish pieces in the *Scrutator*, and keeps carrying on as if the whole thing were personal and Stern were running a one-man pogrom to turn him, Jacquiz Helmutt, into scrubbing soap. Paranoia isn't in it. Do you suppose that wop Archbishop will mind having him in the Church of San Martino when he sees he's a Jew?'

'I can't imagine so. Anyway he can always say he isn't.'

'That's the trouble. He hates being one but he'll never deny that he is one. He's even talking about having our boy bar-mitzvahed when the time comes.'

'How is your boy? And his twin sister?'

'Healthy. Otherwise impossible to say. Do you remember a science fiction novel,' said Marigold, 'called *The Midwich Cuckoos*? I think they made a film of it, with George Sanders.'

'I remember it vividly. It was about children begotten on human females by some agent from outer space. They all have identical faces and absolutely blank eyes.'

'Well that,' said Marigold, 'is what's growing up in my house. Only two of them, but two too many if you ask me. It'll be interesting to see what the Rabbi makes of him when he's being prepared for his bar-mitzvah . . . though of course there's another ten years to go till then, and anything could happen in the meantime.'

'His children are well guarded,' said Shamshuddin: 'he saw to that quietly and efficiently before he left. In any case, to retaliate through the children is inappropriate here and would not convey to the world the message that we wish to convey.'

'His wife?' said Pontos.

'No,' said Artemis: 'if possible, please not.'

Shamshuddin raised his eyebrows. 'So she went beneath your skin?' he said. 'You need not worry. No one knows, just now, where his wife is, and in any case she too would be an inappropriate target.'

'Then what?' said Pontos.

'Something must be done . . . not unworthy of the man himself (whom we must in a fashion respect, despite and indeed because of the nuisance he is causing us) and at the same time carrying suitable retribution for his disobedience and broken word. We must make an example to all those that may be tempted to think or act like him, and in particular to those friends of his whose attitudes, as he says, have persuaded him to defy and disoblige us. So this is what we shall do,' Shamshuddin said, crossing to the window from which he could see the Campaniles both on Torcello and on Burano; and looking steadily out of it he told them.

'Dartford Tunnel,' said Carmilla to Theodosia, as they got out of their taxi at the garage in Milton where they kept their Volkswagen during Full Term; 'Dover this evening, White Cliffs Hotel for the night, leave at dawn tomorrow, Monday.'

'Right,' said Theodosia, as she paid off the taxi driver. 'If it wasn't for the reason, I'd be looking forward to this trip.'

'What will you do with Jeremy if you find him?'

'Love him.'

'In every way?'

'In every way I can.'

'Amen,' said Carmilla warmly, at the same time detecting dubieties in her sister's phrasing which might not promise well for the future. 'Off at dawn, then, charge down the *auto-route*. Venice by Tuesday night, forty-eight hours from now. And let's just hope Nicos Pandouros was right to steer us towards Torcello.'

'He was basing what he said on what Jeremy said while immersed in that sarcophagus of Ptoly Tunne's,' said Theodosia taking the wheel. 'Now I've been in that sarcophagus, last summer if you remember, and you have not: so let me assure you that when you're floating in there, hull down in warm water, totally relaxed and almost weightless, you tell the truth. Now then. I know, because he told me, that Jeremy is looking for an explanation, perhaps a justification, of something horrible which happened to him. We know, because Nicos has told us, that Jeremy is obsessed by a place, possibly a marsh or a lake, where he believes there could be an entrance to the underworld . . . a place which is presided over by two powerful Madonnas. He has mentioned the Venetian Lagoon in this connection, and in particular Torcello . . . where we know that there is at least one very remarkable Madonna – and why not another, as there is a second Church on the island, to say nothing of other Churches on other islands very near to it? So what do we infer from all this? That Jeremy will look for his explanation precisely in this place of his obsession, where there is an entrance to the kingdom of the dead flanked by two Mothers of God, and that this place is almost certainly Torcello. Nicos is surely right, *cara mia*. It must be odds on that Jeremy will sooner or later fetch up in Torcello, if only because he has spoken so much about it.'

'Sooner, if he is so hot for certainty. We may already be too late.'

'If so, there will still be some trace of him that we can follow.'

'If he gets his answer, what will he do with it?'

'Act in accordance with it, I suppose.'

'And if he doesn't?'

'I expect he'll go on looking. Keep a sharp eye open,' said Theodosia, 'for the road to Chelmsford; I want to be through the tunnel and on to the A2 before dusk.'

267

Leonard Percival, bored sick by his hotel by the Station at Mestre but hardly daring to leave it for five minutes in case the girl in black should come to him with a message, at last received an unstamped envelope (presumably delivered by hand, though later on no one remembered seeing the hand that had delivered it) which contained a complimentary ticket to the Ceremony of Unveiling, by the Most Honourable Marchioness Canteloupe, of Asolano's Celebrated Painting of the MADONNA CON I RAGAZZI DELLE PESTE, now to be restored to its rightful situation in the Church of San Martino in Burano, by the Generous Donation of Captain the Most Honourable Marquess Canteloupe of the Aestuary of the Severn. The ceremony would take place, it appeared, at noon on the coming Wednesday (the day after next) and would be followed by a Collation in the Locanda Cipriani on Torcello, to which Leonard was also invited and to which guests would be conveyed by Special Launch from Burano to Torcello.

For a minute or two Leonard thought that this invitation must have been sent to him on the instructions of his employer; but then he realized that Lord Canteloupe had not the faintest idea that he was in the Hotel Garibaldi in Mestre, must indeed imagine that he was by now hundreds of miles south and probably in Greece.

'I tell you,' said Canteloupe to Baby, 'that the Hotel on Torcello is closed.'

'The Hotel on Torcello,' said Baby, 'is the Locanda Cipriani. The Locanda Cipriani is opening to provide luncheon on Wednesday after the Ceremony. There is therefore no reason on earth why it should not also open some of its upstairs rooms to receive you and me for the two nights, of today and Tuesday, before the ceremony.'

'They won't like it.'

'*Make them do it.*'

'But why? Aren't you comfortable here in the Gritti?'

'*I want to be* on Torcello. I want to sleep two nights on Torcello. I can't explain why, or not very easily, but that is what *I yearn to do*,' Baby said, 'and since you promised me a present, some time ago, and I have not yet had it, please let this be my present – tonight and tomorrow night on Torcello and perhaps Wednesday night after the Ceremony as well. If anyone on earth can arrange this, it must surely be you, if only because of your immense prestige in the Tourist business as High and Mighty Mikado of Cant-Fun.'

The reference was not tactful, as Canteloupe did not care for his connection with Cant-Fun and never ceased to wish to himself that his money and his 'immense prestige' came from some other source (though from what?). But while he was annoyed by Baby's apostrophe of him as a sort of Super Circus Master, he was aware how important it was to keep her in a good humour until after the unveiling, and indeed he was pleased that she was at last showing some sign of being interested in something (though precisely what or why was obscure to him). He therefore engaged in three hours negotiation with the management of the Cipriani Hotel, who finally agreed to open up the residential accommodation in the Locanda for the following week (as a shorter period would be uneconomic) provided Lord Canteloupe undertook to pay in full, over the entire period, not only for his own rooms, but also for any others which might not be occupied – i.e. for the whole lot, as Canteloupe thought at the time, though in this, as he was later to find, he was mistaken.

Money, Fielding thought; everything, when I get back to England, will turn on money.

Piero and Fielding sat silently in the cabin of a water taxi as it emerged from the mouth of the Grand Canal and started to make the wide arc across the Lagoon that would bring it round and down to the Gabrielli Hotel.

So far, thought Fielding, I have comforted myself by insisting that I have not used as much of my reserve as I expected to and that something nice may have happened by the time I return to England. But why should it? The plain fact is that my reserve is down to its lowest level since the early sixties, and that I may well have to face a crippling bill for taxes on undeclared income. Furthermore, my car has gone badly wrong, thus causing delay and extra expense on the journey here; it will have to stay in the Garage in the Piazzale Roma indefinitely and until some arrangement (God knows what) is made for it;

Piero and I will have to fly home; and once there I shall at once need a new car. *Money*. It is no good just drifting on and hoping that things will come right: I must absolutely premise that everything will go wrong, and take the necessary action – which is to obtain money. 'Put money in thy purse.' No, not in my purse, but in my bank: lots of lovely money in my bank.

Stern & Detterling. Detterling. Canteloupe. Tell Canteloupe that he must now make himself ready to find anything up to £20,000 to be paid to me, Fielding Gray, either from Stern & Detterling's resources or from his own. Tell him that the two secrets, the ancestry of the idiot boy in the marshes near Oriago, and the paternity of the male infant in the pram in the Wiltshire rose garden, must, together, be worth this sum. Tell him to arrange payment in the form of an advance from the firm on a new series of novels, or of a loan by the firm against my expectations from rights and royalties, or of the private purchase by himself of a share in my future profits; tell him to set it up or trick it out as and how he will, but that there must be, by such and such a (pretty near) date now to be agreed, the sum of £20,000 available for immediate transfer, in part or whole, to my, Fielding Gray's, account in my, Fielding Gray's, bank.

When they came to Asolo, Isobel, Jo-Jo, Oenone and Jeremy put up at the Villa Cipriani, where they engaged two double rooms, one for Isobel and Jo-Jo and one for Jeremy and Oenone, who much preferred sharing a room with Jeremy providing that her mother or Isobel (preferably the latter) popped in from time to time. During their journey Oenone had been quiet and contented in the back of the Lagonda with Jeremy, beside him in her carry-cot; and on the fairly frequent occasions when he took her on his knee or in his lap she had glowed with bliss. To Isobel too she responded warmly, while to her mother she was merely polite. For all her adoration of the man of the party, however, she appeared well aware that certain offices were best performed by the females, and in the matter (for example) of nappy-changing she preferred even Jo-Jo to Jeremy.

Jo-Jo too had been happy on the journey, sitting with Isobel in the front and watching her limbs flex over the controls. When it was time to retire for the night Jo-Jo would start glowing (rather like Oenone in Jeremy's lap) but would drag her feet like a bashful child until Isobel took her firmly by the hand and led her away to the room which they now shared. For after the first day, during which Jeremy had scored his initial success with Oenone in the back of the Lagonda, Jo-Jo had asked him outright if he would have Oenone with him in his room, as she herself wished to be in the same room as Isobel but could not be if Oenone were there too, because she (Oenone) made her (Jo-Jo) feel guilty. Jeremy consented to take on Oenone and for the first time a double room was engaged for Isobel and Jo-Jo. That evening, when bed-time came, Jo-Jo made her début in the role of foot-dragging *ingénue* and even proposed to linger for another drink (though the bar had closed and it would have been difficult to obtain one); but Isobel settled her nonsense by saying that she did not like girls who 'sozzled', and that in any case she had her 'travelling bottle' of whisky in their bedroom should Jo-Jo be overcome by alcoholic craving during the night.

This ritual was performed on each night that followed.

As Isobel had laid down at the start, they neither loitered nor hastened on their road, keeping a schedule that took careful account of the needs, appetites and vulnerabilities of Oenone. They said nothing to each other of the object of their journey, nor of how they would set about attaining this at journey's end.

But now, during dinner at Asolo, Jeremy said to Isobel and Jo-Jo:

'There is a notice in the foyer. The Locanda Cipriani will be open as a hotel for one week as from last Monday, yesterday, and everyone staying there will receive free tickets for a ceremony on Burano tomorrow followed by a celebratory luncheon in the Locanda itself.'

'A ceremony on Burano?'

'It seems that Canteloupe is handing back some picture to the Church of San Martino. Lady Canteloupe is going to unveil it. I propose to be . . . discreetly . . . present. You see, the picture is one which I very much need to see . . . and which I missed last time I was there because it had gone away to be restored. I do not understand,' Jeremy said, 'why they say that Canteloupe is responsible for its return, but that will no doubt be explained later and is in any case a question of little importance. What is important is that I should see that picture.'

'Why not wait until after the ceremony?' said Isobel. 'If Baby sees you, you might set her off again.'

'Don't worry. I shall be in the shadows, in the best Venetian manner. I particularly want to see the actual unveiling. The Madonna with the Children of the Plague. And thence to Torcello, to see the other Madonna.'

In the end it was all very easily arranged. Bookings for the next two nights (Wednesday and Thursday) at the Locanda Cipriani were readily made and at a pleasing discount, since the Villa Cipriani, where they now were was of course in the same chain. They would leave at nine the following morning and be at the Piazzale Roma on the outskirts of Venice by ten-thirty. The Cipriani organization would have arranged a boat to take them all on to Burano for the ceremony at San Martino (for which they were given tickets on the spot) and another boat to carry their luggage out to the Locanda on Torcello. It was felt that the ceremony might be rather an ordeal for Oenone, who would not have her favourite Jeremy to comfort her since he would be lurking behind pillars out of sight of Baby Canteloupe; but as Isobel observed, Oenone might as well learn now as later that everything could not always be arranged to her entire convenience. With such occupation and deployment determined for the morrow they retired to bed early, Jo-Jo making only the barest pretence of wishing to linger.

At nearly the same time as Jeremy & Co rose from their dinner in Asolo, Fielding and Piero sat down to theirs in Venice.

'Tomorrow,' said Fielding, 'we shall take the nine-fifty-five boat from the Fondamente Nuove to Massorbo, walk over the meadows to Burano, and find out whether that picture Jeremy wanted to see – and presumably still does – has been put back in San Martino. After that we can go on to Torcello.'

Piero, who had seen in the foyer of the Gabrielli an advertisement of the ceremony in San Martino along with an announcement that tickets for it and/or luncheon which would follow it were on sale at the Head Porter's desk, nevertheless said nothing about this. For if Fielding got to know about the ceremony now, he would insist on taking tickets and going to it; and after what had happened at Ptoly Tunne's house in the Fens Piero was not anxious to be present and in view when Baby Canteloupe unveiled the Asolano, lest sight of him should again provoke her to make some ghastly hysterical scene. On the other hand, while Piero did not wish to be seen by Baby, he was very keen to accompany Fielding to Burano and Torcello, being certain that it was this area for which Jeremy would be heading and being eager to get sight of him again as soon as possible.

Piero's two intentions were, then, at variance: in order to be prompt in apprehending Jeremy he must linger in an area infested by the inflammatory Baby. By keeping Fielding and himself away from the actual ceremony, however, he would lessen the risk of being spotted by her; and for the rest he must reconcile his conflicting aims as best he might.

Carmilla and Theodosia Salinger arrived at the Piazzale Roma on Tuesday night, more or less to plan but rather later. It took some time to buy a parking ticket in the high rise car park as the man at the desk was talking on the telephone. It seemed to Carmilla, who had some little Italian, that the man was receiving instructions to transfer the luggage, from a car which would arrive the following morning, out of the car park and on to a boat which would take it to the Locanda Cipriani at Torcello. The man was obstinately insisting that the Locanda Cipriani was closed at that time of the year but was being resolutely informed that an exception was being made for one week, intelligence which he eventually accepted. When, therefore, they had made arrangements for berthing the car, Carmilla proposed to her sister that they should telephone the Locanda for rooms and go straight out to Torcello. She had always wanted to sleep on the island, she said, and they would be right on the spot in case of any sight or sign of Jeremy there.

Fifteen minutes later they had already passed the Island of San Michele, where the dead sleep in banks of drawers, and were skirting the crumbling warehouses of Murano, where the living blow tasteless articles of glass, well on their way to their night's lodging.

'I'm so glad we came out here,' said Baby to Canteloupe at dinner on Torcello. 'Thank you for arranging it.'

'I've hardly seen you all day.'

'When I left you in the cathedral this morning, I walked up the canal, not the one that goes from here to the public landing stage, but a wider one, a channel really, which divides the island east to west. I walked with the water on one side of me and what Ruskin calls "meadows" on the other, only they're not meadows, they're just flat stretches with a kind of reed growing out of them. But they set me thinking of Ruskin, so I decided I'd go back to the cathedral and climb to the top of the Campanile, as he did: "for there is none to hinder," he wrote. But there is these days, Canty. There's a fence to keep you away from it, until you find a gap, and then a huge padlock on the door, which Ruskin says was swinging loose when he came. Somehow I had forgotten how long ago that must have been, I was expecting to find everything just as he described it, so I was angry and disappointed when I found that door padlocked, I felt that Ruskin must have been telling deliberate lies, making the whole thing up for the sake of a purple patch. But then, "Someone must have a key," I thought. So I knocked on the door of one of those little houses behind the other Church, the round one. No one answered, but a man a sort of peasant in an apron, came up from behind me and showed me a key. "I expect he's watched me trying to get in," I thought. Anyway, he led me back to the Campanile and unlocked the padlock and pulled back the bolt, and led me up the stairs, such a lot of stairs, Canty, but oh how it was worth it. There was the whole Lagoon spread out beneath, just as Ruskin said, so he hadn't been lying after all. There were the wild sea banks to the north and the Dolomites far beyond them, and there too the cities and factories and furnaces, which came after Ruskin and are murdering his Venice, all down the coast as far as the Brenta canal, and south of that the dunes and pines and salt-marshes, which Ruskin loved. And there were all the islands, Venice itself and the Giudecca and Murano, the small islands with prisons and hospitals, and near Torcello was San Francesco and a tiny island beside it, on which I saw a black figure moving towards a house.

'And then I started thinking, Canty. For hour after hour I stood there – '

' – I sent someone to look for you at lunch-time – '

' – But of course he couldn't find me as I was at the top of the forbidden Campanile, looking out over the Lagoon, having my thoughts.'

'A lira for them.'

'*Cui bono?* That's what I thought, Canty. To what

conceivable good for what possible person? None. Nobody. There are only negatives – misery, pain, disease and death. This is what the Madonna in the cathedral is weeping for. But somewhere, I thought, there must be another message, some kind of consolation, even perhaps a reason, but if not that at least a rule or a lesson, by which we can live in contentment.'

'But you have always lived in contentment.'

'Excitement, not often contentment. *Never* in contentment now.'

'But still in excitement?'

'No. That too has gone. It left me one afternoon in the Fens, when I saw what I saw. I thought it might come back but it didn't. Now I do not think it will ever come again.'

'So no excitement any more . . . and no contentment. Then why are you so happy now?'

'Though I may appear happy, I am only resigned.'

'And therefore contented, surely.'

'No. Resigned to the negative message which I had today. Contentment can only come with the second message, the message of consolation, the lesson or the rule. I feel that this is near, therefore I appear happy.'

'What makes you think it is near?'

'That little black figure, perhaps, by the house on the tiny island. An illustration, in miniature, of God's design: a being with a house to live in and just enough land to live off, in the middle of a desolate and polluted lagoon: man on his pathetic ball of earth in the middle of an arid and poisonous universe.'

'A lesson in itself?'

'No. It compares but does not explain or instruct. The message which I am expecting must do at least one of those two things. As it happens, I do not think it will explain.'

'Why should it not?'

'Because the explanation is already evident and is hardly worth the trouble of stating. The explanation, the only possible explanation of the world before us, is the malignancy of God. His Mother in the cathedral knows of this malignancy and pities the creation that both stems and suffers from it. But neither She nor anyone else is going to admit all this openly. Although it is evident, as I say, it is unwise to talk of the Ruler of the Universe in this fashion.'

'You are talking of Him in this fashion.'

'I should not do so if He were *my* Son.'

'If He is Her Son, can she not intercede with him?'

'Perhaps She does, but She has achieved nothing. In the two millennia since She bore Him, His creation has merely got fouler and fouler. So what is needed is *instruction:* we must be told how we are to bear ourselves in these hideous circumstances, and what we are to do. The Madonna in the cathedral offers no lesson of that kind, nor does the black figure by the house on the island. But both offer hope, in a way: hope that there *will be* instruction if only we long for it enough; and since that afternoon in the Fens I have yearned for it, Canty, and now, after a day at the top of that Campanile, I yearn even more.'

'Can you take me up there? Tomorrow morning, before the ceremony on Burano?'

'I don't know.'

'But it shouldn't be difficult to find your man with the key. A simple enquiry . . .'

'He left me in the gallery at the top,' Baby said, 'then came again at dusk, held up the key, and signed to me to follow him down. When we got to the bottom, he held the door open for me, then slammed and bolted and padlocked it. He raised his right hand to the crown of his head by way of saluting me – he didn't have a hat – pointed to the gap in the fence, in case I should miss it in the twilight, and moved off round the Campanile . . . in the rough direction of the backs of those little houses. Ah, I thought, he's making for his back door. When I was nearly at the Locanda, I remembered I hadn't tipped him; I went back to the house I'd gone to this morning, knocked on the front door, explained to a woman who answered just what I wanted, and tried to peer inside for my peasant. But she blocked my view, so I assumed he was having his tea or in the loo or something, and I offered her a ten thousand lire note . . . which she shoved back at me and slammed the door.'

'She was cross because he'd shown you the way up there. It isn't allowed and he might have got the sack . . . from whatever job he does here.'

'I expect that's it.'

'And of course the money would have made things worse if anyone ever found out that she'd accepted it for him.'

'Yes,' said Baby. 'I don't think it would be sensible to look for him again, do you?'

Carmilla and Theodosia Salinger clumped wearily into the dining room.

'Donald's girls,' said Canteloupe.

He rose and went to them. Carmilla presented her cheek for a kiss: Theodosia offered her lips.

'What luck you're here,' said Canteloupe, at the same time wondering what on earth they could be doing on Torcello in the middle of the Michaelmas Term: 'you must come to the unveiling tomorrow.'

'The unveiling of what?' asked Carmilla, greedily seizing the menu as she sat down.

Canteloupe told them.

'We've only got trousers to wear,' said Theodosia, who

280

was not as tired as Carmilla (although she had done most of the driving) and remained standing.

'You look marvellous in your trousers. Please come.'

'Yes, please come,' said Baby, who had joined the group. 'I've a feeling it could be rather a relevant occasion.'

'Relevant to what?' said Carmilla, and reeled off a very long list of things to eat to the hovering waiter.

'I hope you haven't ordered too much for me,' said Theodosia.

'Thea has to think of her training,' explained Carmilla to the Canteloupes: 'she plays second string in the Cambridge Royal Tennis team.'

'That's my girl,' Canteloupe said, and helped himself once more, uninvited but unhindered, to Theodosia's lips.

Meanwhile Carmilla, who was much disordered by hunger, was saying to Baby:

'A relevant occasion, you said, Lady Canteloupe. Let me ask again: relevant to what?'

'I think,' said Baby, 'that Asolano's picture will give up its true meaning only when it is back in its proper place.'

'Do you know?' said Carmilla, who thought this was a pretentious remark and in any case now dropped the subject flat, because the waiter had just beckoned her over to the Buffet of Hors d'Oeuvres to make her choice.

'Lord and Lady Canteloupe will come from Torcello to the quayside at Burano in a special barge,' Sir Jacquiz Helmutt said to Marigold and Balbo in the restaurant of the Danieli.

'The Bucentaur?' said Balbo.

'They will arrive at eleven-fifty-five precisely,' said Sir Jacquiz, ignoring this silly sarcasm, 'and by then everyone must be in his place. No one will be admitted after eleven-fifty.'

'Goodness, how severe,' Marigold said.

'They will be greeted by a Captain's Guard of the Bersaglieri, who will run before them into the Church playing a fanfare on their bugles. At this point, just as the service begins, I have decided that we should, after all, do honour to the name of Asolano.'

'Jacquiz loves the idea of his marrying with a Jewess,' Marigold said to Balbo.

'Since it is too late,' said Sir Jacquiz, 'to insert his name in the final anthem or the epilogue, it will be proclaimed in a special prologue.'

'Proclaimed by whom?'

'You'll see,' Sir Jacquiz said: 'we're really doing the old boy rather proud.'

'Can you not hear them?' said Tom Llewyllyn over the port in the Senior Common Room of Lancaster College.

'Candidly, no,' said Len.

'Hear what?' said Jean-Marie Guiscard.

'Shush,' went Ptolemaeos: 'don't encourage him.'

Ptolemaeos had brought Jean-Marie in from the Fens to dine at High Table, and now they were having dessert. Ivor Winstanley, the Latinist and Ciceronian, was at the head of the table with Jean-Marie on his left and Ptolemaeos on his right. Next to them were Len and

Provost Llewyllyn. Then came a Sociologist and Metallurgist (his guest), of both of whom the less said the better. So far it had been quite a jolly evening, the feature of which had been a description by Ivor of Theodosia Salinger on the one occasion he had managed to get sight of her while she was wearing her badminton shorts (her flannel slacks being presumably at the cleaners) in the Tennis Court. Ivor had been inspired, almost like Betjeman, Ptolemaeos reflected: just what Jean-Marie needed to cheer him up. It would be a pity if Tom was going to throw one of his glooms and spoil everyone's fun. Jean-Marie must not be allowed to encourage him by asking the wrong sort of question.

But Tom had heard Jean-Marie's query and was prompt to answer. 'The Dryads,' he said, 'mourning for their trees, which we have destroyed.'

'If the trees die,' said Ivor Winstanley firmly, 'the Dryads die also and do not live long enough to mourn. See Pausanias' account of the grove which was cut down to make way for an Imperial Villa at Lerna.'

'There are other views,' said the Metallurgist, to everyone's surprise. 'See Valerius Flaccus' account of the dispossessed but surviving tree-nymphs whom Medea sheltered and then employed as messengers.'

'The passage is suspect and excised from most editions,' said Ptolemaeos, hoping to kill the subject.

'Surely,' said Jean-Marie, who appeared after all (thought Ptolemaeos), to be enjoying this morbid discussion, 'we know, on the authority of Periphrastes the Mage, that tree-nymphs do indeed die when their trees have been destroyed but take quite a long time expiring.'

Now that, thought Ptolemaeos, is really going to set Tom off. What in fact happened was that Tom rose, bowed to his assembled Fellows, and went quietly out.

'What will he do?' said Ptolemaeos to Len.

'He will go down into the Avenue,' said Len, 'and ask the tree-nymphs to do what they like with him but not to harm his daughter, Tullia.'

'Extraordinary,' said Ptoly. 'For years Tom has been a pillar of logic and reason. And now this.'

'Change of life,' Ivor Winstanley said. 'Male menopause. It makes for some very peculiar behaviour.'

'I suppose so,' said Ptoly. 'There's a lot of it about in our set just now. Fielding Gray, chasing that ridiculous truant boy, Morrison, as though he were Sexton Blake with Piero as Tinker, and Gregory Stern, Jew-baiting and -bashing, verbally at least, like the very daemon of Himmler.'

'Lord, what fools these mortals be,' said Ivor Winstanley, somehow contriving to fill, drain, re-fill and pass between the beginning and the end of the quotation.

The morning after they had arrived in Venice, both Piero and Fielding overslept.

'Never mind,' said Fielding, 'we can take a later boat to Massorbo. The eleven-fifty-five. Which gives us plenty of time to see if there's any mail for me at the American Express.'

There was, as it happened, a letter waiting for him at the American Express, from his accountant. This he could tell, first from the cover, and secondly from the circumstances that his accountant was the only person to whom he had given this address, for use, he had said, in emergencies. He was about to open the envelope and find out just what emergency had arisen (presumably, he thought with a sinking heart, the man had written to confirm that he had under-declared his income and to tell him that he must now immediately etc., etc., etc.) when he saw a notice which announced a ceremony on Burano for the unveiling of some picture which Canteloupe, of all people, was giving back to the Church of San Martino. A limited number of tickets, it appeared, were available at the Information Desk.

'What luck,' he said to Piero; 'we might never have known.'

At the Information Desk was a long queue of elderly Americans asking cretinous questions. When it was finally Fielding's turn, he was told that the tickets (a limited number) had run out.

'Perhaps your hotel may still have some, Signore?'

The Gabrielli hadn't but the Head Porter thought that perhaps the Gritti had, and it did.

'But we shall never get there by eleven-fifty when it says the doors close,' Piero said, wishing to subvert the expedition before he was swept off into the presence of Baby, 'and besides, I don't feel very well.'

'Don't be so feeble,' said Fielding, guessing the reason for Piero's reluctance; 'you invited yourself on this trip and you can bloody well see the thing out.'

'But this ceremony has nothing to do with Jeremy, and Jeremy is why we are here.'

'If he is in the area, he may well be there. He's very keen – or was – to see that picture. Anyway, it's quite obvious that God intends us to attend, otherwise I should never have spotted that notice in the American Express. I see there's one in here too – which must have been staring us in the face when we booked in last night. Christ, I am getting slow. Why didn't you see it? You've got two eyes.'

At this stage the speedboat which the Head Porter had

summoned for them arrived at the hotel jetty. The driver had collected the tickets from the Gritti on the way, having been intelligently briefed by the Head Porter, and to Piero's dismay they were able to head straight off for Burano. Fielding too was displeased, despite the saving of time, as the driver was making a surcharge on the tickets of 50 per cent for his trouble in picking them up at the Gritti, and had also announced that he would not go to Burano unless he was paid to wait and bring his passengers back. Since Fielding intended to visit Torcello before returning, the trip would now be very expensive indeed. Was there no end to the drain on his resources? This thought prompted Fielding to take his accountant's as yet unopened letter from his pocket – to which he had to return it instantly as Piero was being sick all over the cabin.

'I told you I wasn't well,' he gasped between splatters: 'we must go back.'

'Nonsense. Get out into the stern.'

The stern, to the immediate rear of the cabin, was in the open air. Piero did as he was told. The driver seemed not to have noticed what had happened, and in fact a careful inspection showed Fielding that virtually nothing had happened: the whole eruption must have been wind and spit and a little spare bile, carefully coaxed. Fielding looked at his watch: 11.30: they were just going to make it. He joined Piero in the stern.

'Why the performance?' he said.

'I was afraid of being seen by Miss Baby. She has a devil, and the sight of me may rouse it.'

'Good. Anything odd in her behaviour may help us to understand what happened between her and Jeremy.'

'There will be a horrible public scene.'

'The bigger the better. Particularly if Jeremy too is there.'

'If there is violence and I am conspicuous, there may be enquiry. Then someone may remember me from my time in Venice and say that I am not whom my passport says I am.'

'Too late to worry about that now. Anyway, *Res Unius, Res Omnium*.'

'What is that?'

'It means . . . that in our set . . . mine and Canteloupe's . . . we see each other through. One way and another, you now belong in our set. Only on the edge, but in it.'

'And so you and Canteloupe will see me through if anything goes wrong?'

'Yes.'

'I should like that. I hope no trouble will happen, but I should like . . . being seen through it . . . by you and Canteloupe.'

They returned to the cabin. 11.30. *Res Unius, Res Omnium*, thought Fielding bitterly: and here he was getting ready to blackmail Canteloupe . . . into seeing him through. But of course Canteloupe, if deftly and tactfully approached, might consent to help Fielding, or ensure that Stern & Detterling helped him, without any pressure other than Fielding's plea of need. £20,000 without pressure? Tell me another one, do, darling, *Res Unius* and all. Anyhow, whatever was to be done 'twere best 'twere quickly done, so what a bit of luck that Canteloupe was here in Venice. When should Fielding approach him? This afternoon after the ceremony? Tomorrow? Or should he, after all, leave it till they were both back in England, where financial arrangements would be much more easily and accurately contemplated? Whatever else, timing was important. He must catch Canteloupe when he was likely to be euphoric. Immediately after the ceremony, then, when he was still glowing

with his own generosity and the importance it had conferred on him? Or would he be suffering from let-down,
from a kind of *Tristitia post Gloriam*? Well, thought
Fielding, a lot must depend on how urgent the matter
actually was. 11.37: just time: once more he took his
accountant's letter from his pocket.

The first person to arrive in the Church of San Martino
was Leonard Percival. He wanted to have a good look
round. However, the usher who had taken his ticket and
shown him to a place on the right near the front of the
nave became fretful when Leonard started to go walkabout, and then officious. It was made plain to Leonard
that he had been given his seat in order that he should sit
in it, so sit (as a good-mannered guest) he now did.

At first he had been flattered at being placed so near
the front; but then he realized that of course the climax
of the ceremony would occur when the picture was
unveiled, that the picture would be unveiled where it was
hanging, and that it must surely be hanging over the
closely guarded and highly decorated side altar behind
him in the south wall, in order to see which he would be
compelled to turn. In fact he had been given one of the
very worst seats . . . as he now confirmed by trying to
look at the side altar in question. This he could do by
turning, as he had surmised, but the turn was one of
nearly 180 degrees, and it was also necessary, if he were
to get any sort of view at all, that he should crane
agonizingly to the right. What he saw when he did so was
a curtain of tapestry which was embroidered with Gentle

Jesus and a crowd of drippy children, many of them maimed. This hung under a canopy which protruded perhaps a yard from the wall, and from the right hand end of which a cord was dangling. This, Leonard imagined, would be pulled by Lady Canteloupe at the moment designated. On either flank of the side altar beneath the tapestry were sentinels, cloaked, booted and spurred policemen (an order of dress which he had thought to be obsolete) who were leaning on drawn and dirty sabres. A strong whiff of the Green Room here, thought Leonard, God, these wops.

A party of German tourists now arrived and were seated in two rows on the left hand side of the nave, on the level of the side altar, the third on the right, where it was all going to happen. Excellent view for bloody thrusting Krauts, thought Leonard, they should have built a wall a mile high all round Germany after the war and locked the whole lot inside it for ever. Beelzebub, this ulcer. Now three obviously English people: a statuesque woman, a boyish girl carrying a baby, and a large furtive young man, who looked around warily and seemed relieved when parked, by the usher, behind a column. The girl with the infant was also parked behind it: quite right, Leonard thought, babies have no business at public ceremonies or anywhere else except in the nursery and in their prams in the municipal gardens. Much the same applied to women when you came down to it. He remembered a story of Canteloupe's, about the organizer of a cricket match who had set up a barrier round the pavilion with a notice that read NO DOGS WOMEN OR CHILDREN BEYOND THIS POINT which was manned by an ex-Drill Serjeant of the Coldstream. One female had nagged to be let through to her husband ('One of the players, you know'), exactly the sort of woman whom the arrangement was designed to exclude. Having endured ten minutes of bitching and clacking, the Drill Serjeant, who had brought his flask with him, had said, 'Madam, you can come through if you show me your prick.' That had shut her up all right. But it wouldn't, Leonard thought, have shut up the cruiser weight (with the youth and the young mother), who was now showing herself more than a match for the usher and had chosen her own seat, not right under the veiled picture (for she was not arrogant or presumptuous, only firm) but with a very fair and gently angled view of it. This woman, he now realized, was Gregory Stern's wife, Isobel, whom he had occasionally met, over the years, when the Sterns visited Detterling's house in Wiltshire. What the bloody hell's she doing here, thought Leonard, and then: should I tell her I've mislaid her husband? or should I report the matter to Detterling first? Wait and see how he's placed after the show's over . . . at this crush on Torcello perhaps?

Meanwhile, a lot more people had been arriving, priests and monks, officials and politicians (by the look of them), some arty types with long hair and loud shirts but respectable suits, two more parties of tourists, a delegation of Gondoliers in their straw hats with ribands, a flurry of nuns with a platoon of poorly but neatly dressed children (orphans?), and a group of heavily moustached men, one of whom carried a banner which suggested they were a society or guild of fishermen. Then came two braw and bonny girls in trousers, from the look of them as English as two Beefeaters at the Tower, and a minute or two later Balbo Blakeney, looking scruffy, and a tall, dark, superior Yid in a frock coat, holding by the elbow a girl (well, a bit past that, but as pretty as paint so give her the benefit) who looked up at the tapestry, beneath which the trio were taking their seats with some of the senior officials, and had a fit of giggling which the superior Yid (one of Balbo's art barons?) imperiously checked.

Suddenly there was a loud bang as the South Door, through which everyone had entered, was slammed to – though not before Fielding Gray (for Christ's sake) had leapt through it like the demon king arriving on a panto-mime stage, side by side with a lissom faun with a limp – probably that Eyetie boy of whom Detterling had told him, thought Leonard, the one who had once lived in Venice and went AWOL, a few weeks back, from a monastery in the Lagoon. But there was little time to think about this precious pair, because now the West Door swung open and the sound of bugles playing a Double March came soaring through, followed by two files of Bersaglieri, all black hats and green feathers, who came ramping up the nave and formed three deep on each side of the High Altar. After a brief pause they blew an Olympian Fanfare, which was succeeded by a blast of thunder from the organ. Up the nave now came a choir of surpliced boys followed by a prelate with crozier and gorgeous purple vestments, followed in turn by Detterling in tails and the Marchioness Canteloupe, who looked like the young Victoria when they came to tell her she was Queen (please God, thought Leonard, don't let me blub). And now the choir and the organ and the bugles really let rip, the 'Hallelujah Chorus,' only instead of 'Hallelujah' they were singing 'Asolano . . . Asolano . . . Asolano, Asoooolaaano, Asooolaaano' . . . while Detterling and his consort took their places under the veiled picture; the sentinels executed an operatic sword salute, and the prelate mounted a spiral stairway to a pulpit from which, it appeared to Leonard, he was going to conduct the service.

Asoolaano
Aasolano Aasolano

291

Aasolano Aasolano
Asooolano Asoolaano,
Asooooolaaaaano

As the Chorus concluded, a second prelate, whom Leonard recognized, from a photograph in Detterling's study in Wiltshire, as the Bishop of Glastonbury, Mungo Avallon, moved into a smaller pulpit (a lectern, perhaps?) opposite the main one. His vestments (of a distasteful mauve) were inferior to those of the principal prelate (the Archbishop of Chioggia, Leonard now gathered from a programme in front of him) but his crozier of gold and rubies well and truly trumped that of the Archbishop, which was ornamented with pieces of obvious paste. The Archbishop, as if conscious of this deficiency, parked the offending staff crossly behind him and began fiddling with a battery of microphones, to the evident contempt of Mungo Avallon, who would manage without any such frippery when his turn came, thought Leonard, good old C. of E. Todgers can do it, down with weedy foreigners.

'*Cari, qui coivitis in nomine Domini,*' began the Archbishop with a noticeably shifty air; and no wonder, thought Leonard, they're meant to do it all in the vernacular these days, somebody's bought the old bugger, that Jew chum of Balbo's, he looks as if he could buy the Virgin Mary, or at any rate would have the nerve to try . . .

. . . Why can't he put more guts into it, thought Marigold Helmutt, as the Archbishop drivelled on, after all Jacquiz (or some fund he knows about) is paying him a stack of ready money to do it, what rotten value they give round here, the Danieli's just a rip-off with bedrooms no bigger than the loos used to be . . .

. . . My word, I wish they'd get all this done with, thought Balbo Blakeney, I'm longing to see that painting again, there'll be another bloody anthem and then more natter from His Sanctity or whatever they call him and *then* a sung Epilogue before they let Baby pull the string (little bitch, but she really looks edible this morning, this afternoon, it's 12.15 already), roll on the unveiling . . .

. . . So, thought Fielding Gray in his place beside Piero at the back of the church, the gang's all here and no mistake. Canteloupe, Baby, Leonard Percival, that crook Helmutt and his fuck-box of a wife, that prize piss-artist, Blakeney . . . and Isobel Stern, by God – I suppose Gregory's still off on that trip of his – and those two huge, smooth Salinger girls, and Jo-Jo with her child and Jeremy, *Jeremy*, JEREMY, lurking, yes, obviously lurking, in the lee of that column, concealed from most of the congregation, but clearly visible to me here at the back . . .

. . . What's Girolamo doing with Madame Guiscard and her brat, thought Piero Caspar, I thought they didn't get on together, but they seem friendly enough and the baby adores Jeremy – it's as good as asking him to take it from its mother, stretching its arms out, and by Heavens he's taken it, taken it into his bosom with the ease and confidence of a trained nurse, with love too, you can see that, who would ever have thought that Girolamo would get keen about a baby . . .

. . . If only he'd keep her for ever, thought Jo-Jo, as she handed over Oenone, but I suppose that's too much to ask. I wonder how my Jean-Marie is getting on in Clermont-Ferrand, I shan't half have some explaining to do when I see him . . .

. . . And now an anthem, thought Isobel, high time that old cadaver stopped drizzling away like a cystitic pee. *Nos in oculis tuis sumus faeces, Domine* – 'we are turds in Thy sight, O Lord' – *sed per te magna et pulchra facimus surgere de terra* – 'but with Thee to aid we make

293

great and beautiful things to arise from the earth.' God have mercy on two particular turds in His sight, Isobel Stern and Jo-Jo Guiscard, who may, mustn't be, may be parted when this little outing is over. O my hot girl, Jo-Jo, I must have you, I've never wanted a girl before except Artemis, I suppose that started me off, latent is what I was and now I've come out, as faggots say, but Jesus Christ I want you, Jo-Jo, with your throbbing crutch, you and your stiff little clitoris, God knows what I'll tell my old Jew boy when he gets back, I think Jo-Jo will be able to manage that dripping wet frog of hers, but my old Jew is another matter . . .

. . . It's taking too long, thought Jacquiz Helmutt, let's hope His Grace has the common sense to cut his next piece of palaver . . .

. . . I might have known this would happen, thought Baby Canteloupe: why didn't I go before we left Torcello? I thought there'd be a lav on that barge, but not a bit of it and of course I should have known there wouldn't be. I'll just have to bottle it, that's all. Well, here we go into the Epilogue of the Service of Thanksgiving, then I pull the cord and we have the special anthem for the unveiled picture, then that buffoon Mungo Avallon has to say something, then there's a final anthem, I should just make it – provided there's somewhere to go before we embark again on that barge . . .

. . . She seems a bit restless, thought Canteloupe as he glanced at Baby, but she looks absolutely super, like that day I took her out from that poisonous progressive school, and she waved the jam spoon in the air and said she wanted to go to a proper school with work and games and marks and competitions, so that she could be the best and know it, she'd keep on until she was. I wonder what's been wrong with her. Whatever it is, Torcello has made her a lot better, and today she's looking fine, just fine, just fine . . .

. . . Now, thought Leonard Percival, this must be nearly it. 'As the Epilogue ends (*"Divitias aeternas da nobis, Domine"*)' he read from his programme, 'Her Ladyship will unveil the MADONNA WITH THE CHILDREN OF THE PLAGUE, while the Quiristers chant the anthem (especially arranged for the occasion by Sir Jacquiz Helmutt, knt) *"Ut Romulum Remumque nutrivit lupus".*' I wonder, thought Leonard, what it's like sucking at a wolf's tit . . .

. . . My turn after that absurd anthem, thought Mungo Avallon, I'll tell 'em all right, tell 'em what I think, what every true Christian thinks, about all this money being spent on jamborees like this one while the children all over the world starve . . . the real Children of the Plague . . .

. . . God, I'm longing to see that picture, Balbo thought, that flap of the Madonna's wrist, the flexing of those white thighs . . .

. . . Any minute now, thought Sir Jacquiz, thank God Chioggia *did* cut down on the Collects . . .

. . . I wonder whether the cord will stick, Marigold thought, it's happened before. My God, Helmutt will get into a wax . . .

Jeremy nudged Jo-Jo; 'I think we should take a look at the unveiling,' he whispered. Holding up Oenone to disguise his face, he peered round the pillar. I'm looking forward, he thought, to those thighs which Fielding was on about when we were here before . . .

. . . Jeremy, Jeremy, Jeremy, thought Theodosia Salinger, please be here somewhere so that I can find you. I'll try to let you fuck me if I find you. But can I do that, even for you? Open my legs for you to put that thing into me? Carmilla had fun with Jeremy, but didn't

295

do that with him. So perhaps we could just do what he and Carmilla did. I'll ask her what it was when this is over. Oh dear, tennis and badminton are much more fun than love, but love just comes whether you want it or not, it buttonholes you like the Wedding Guest and goes on nagging at you, on and on and on . . .

. . . It would really be a very good thing, Carmilla thought, if Jeremy dropped dead. Then Thea could get on with her life and her games in peace . . .

. . . Baby looks splendid, Isobel thought. Just a bit nervous, but who wouldn't be in her place . . .

. . . *Dignitatem et Honorem et Gratiam funde in animas nostras* . . .

. . . Well, at least Miss Baby hasn't noticed me, Piero thought, and even if she should, she doesn't look as if she's in the mood for a scene. Rather marvellous, she looks, like when I first met her at the dinner in Lykiarki's Palazzo . . .

. . . That letter, thought Fielding: I hardly had time to read it. I must look at it *very carefully* as soon as we're out of here, even before . . .

. . . *Reges nostros exalta, et Divitias aeternas da nobis, Domine* . . .

. . . Here we go, thought Baby.

As she rose the sentinels once more saluted with their sabres. The bugles blew. Mungo Avallon, who could never resist a theatrical gesture, raised his crozier in triumph (much as he despised the whole affair), and Alessandro Chioggia lifted both hands and clasped them above his head. Baby tugged on the cord. The tapestry swept back.

Very poor view of those thighs, thought Jeremy, something's in the way.

Well at least the machinery worked, thought Marigold, even if there has been another kind of hitch.

There was dead silence except for the sound of Baby's piddle, which rattled on to the marble between her feet.

Jacquiz contemplated Christ Crucified, a wooden statue (as he supposed) nailed to a cross, which hung in front of the scarcely visible Asolano.

'I always thought,' said Jo-Jo loud and clear as Baby's cascade subsided, 'that circumcision was an aesthetic blunder. Don't you agree, Jeremy? That carving of Christ would look all right with a foreskin: as it is, He's just ridiculous.'

Provoking, thought Balbo: we'll have to wait till they take this damned crucifix thing down. Some sort of protest, I suppose: Christianity before Art, that kind of thing.

Mungo Avallon waved his crozier like a Morse flag in approval. 'The pure message,' he shouted, 'the pure message.'

Baby stood absolutely still, legs apart, looking up at the Christ, while the pool of piss flooded down the steps of the side altar towards Canteloupe.

Isobel moved down her row, stamping on feet and bashing past bosoms. As she came closer, she could have no doubt of it: though the congealed blood of the Christ disguised His hands, torso, legs and feet, though the clotted hair masked His eyes and forehead, and though sweat and filth caked His navel, she'd know that body anywhere, if only from the nick on the bulb of the penis where the Rabbi's knife had slipped; for many years she'd loved it and she'd know it anywhere:

'My old Jew boy,' she sang out; 'it's my old Jew.'

While the cloaked and booted policemen carried Gregory crucified to the Water Ambulance at the quay, Fielding Gray re-read his accountant's letter.

The whole thing was risible. Stern & Detterling, asked to state what monies they had received or credited on his behalf during the last three years, had given the gross figures: they had neglected to say that from any money which came from outside they deducted ten per cent as commission before passing it on to Fielding; they had failed to point out that much of the money received and paid on was in any case VAT and therefore irrelevant from the point of view of the Inland Revenue. Once the ten per cents and the VAT payments had been summed the whole of Fielding's apparent 'under-declaration' was accounted for. So simple and stupid was the error that had caused him weeks of anxiety.

Still, the news was good in its kind; and the second item in the accountant's letter was even better: he understood, the accountant wrote, from an acquaintance in the publishing world, that Stern & Detterling had recently received a payment of £20,000 for the right to film two of Fielding's earlier novels. The accountant was passing on this information (guaranteed exact) as he understood that Fielding had left London in a hurry and might not have told Stern & Detterling where they should send this pleasing information. When Fielding next saw one or other of them the accountant concluded, would he please instruct Stern and/or Detterling (Canteloupe) not to be so careless (indeed imbecilic) when they, or their employees, returned figures in future.

Well, thought Fielding, Gregory Stern I can never more instruct; *Ergo Quintilium perpetuus sopor Urget?* he thought. Never more? Gregory who was so generous when I was maimed, unknown, untried. Gregory who gave me, one morning long ago, gave me what? – that Jewish thing – a mezuzah, yes, mezuzah, that was it, a tiny cylinder which contained a tiny scroll with the names of God written on it – gave me this for a charm and blessing – *Ergo Quintilium*, oh Gregory, Gregory – gave me this for my safety and his love, as I set out on a long journey. Gregory who – stop this. It can do no good. Orpheus himself could do no good nor all his music. So where was I? 'Gregory Stern I can never more instruct, that's where I was; and as for Detterling (Canteloupe) I think perhaps that I shall let him off, at any rate for this afternoon. He has had a difficult day so far. And again, I might so easily have been going to him, if this letter hadn't reached me just in time, to grovel or to threaten, in either case to lower myself and roll in filth. I am not worthy to instruct Detterling (Canteloupe) or anyone else on any topic: I am a turd in the eyes of the Lord. For the time at least let me keep silence . . . and since they've taken Gregory away, I'd better grab the chance of seeing that Asolano.

'You mean . . . you're not going with him?' Jo-Jo said.

'No,' said Isobel. 'Gregory is dead, probably murdered, and they're taking him wherever they take murdered

299

people in this country. I am going with you and Oenone, on that boat, to have some much needed luncheon on Torcello.'

'But they're bound to need you . . . for enquiries.'

'I've told them where they can find me. In the Locanda Cipriani on Torcello, where I propose to spend the next two or three nights. But there's nothing much, nothing helpful I can tell them – except his identity, which I've done already. He went away on such a date, I can tell them, to keep (as he said) an appointment with the leader of the anti-Israeli organization who was called Shamshuddin; and he wound up, as you have seen for yourselves, hanging on the South Wall of the Church of San Martino. So where do you go from there?'

She stepped from the quayside on to a launch labelled 'Cipriani'. Jo-Jo followed with Oenone.

'I suppose,' said Jo-Jo, 'that in the end he wouldn't . . . after all . . . do what they wanted, and that was their way of punishing him.'

'Something of the kind, and good for Gregory. I always knew my old Jew boy had guts. A grand man – and now a dead one. So if you don't mind, we'll say no more about him and discuss the future instead. I claim you and Oenone, Jo-Jo. I need a mate,' Isobel said, 'and Oenone needs a mother. I shall be her mother and you shall be my mate.'

'And what shall Jean-Marie be?'

'Whatever he's told to be. It's your money, as they say. He's already made a huge thing of being upper class and eschewing and despising jealousy; now his sincerity will be put to the test. As for me, I don't mind sharing you with him.'

'That's very generous of you.'

'Whatever else, he'll be glad of someone to take proper care of Oenone.'

'Jeremy's the one she really likes.'

'Well she can't have him,' said Isobel, 'except now and then, when we'll ask him to stay. Marius will like that too . . . only I rather think Marius has grown out of him. Where *is* Jeremy?'

'He stayed behind to look at the Asolano.'

'Ah. This Asolano. What the day is really about. Jeremy has a very proper sense of priorities.'

Jeremy, examining the now unencumbered Asolano as it hung over its side altar, was joined by Fielding Gray.

'So there you are,' said Fielding. 'Piero and I have been looking for you.'

'You shouldn't have troubled. Where is Piero?'

'He disappeared during the confusion.'

'Funny,' said Jeremy: 'I should have thought he would have stayed to take a look at this painting. Like us.'

'Piero is shrewd but not intelligent. At bottom,' said Fielding, 'he has a gutter mentality. He does not understand, as you and I do, that art is important, or why.'

'Well, why?'

'Because it comforts and it explains. It purges and it absolves.'

'Has giving pleasure no place among its functions?'

'Pleasure is too loose a word. What do you make of this effort?'

Jeremy considered the Asolano.

'It makes my cock twitch,' he said at length, 'and it fills me with disgust and a sense of waste. Those beautiful thighs – already diseased and very soon to rot. It explains nothing, but it does suggest a course of action and therefore a possible means of absolution. I hope Baby Canteloupe got the message.'

'And what is that?'

'I am now going to Torcello, to have lunch and make sure. To check up, Fielding. Earlier on, I didn't want Baby to see me . . . because she might have associated me with whatever private horror set her off on that afternoon in the Fens. But now I don't think it will matter if she does see me, I even think that she may want to see me.'

'Shall I come too? I can give you a lift in my speedboat.'

'Thank you very much. You know,' said Jeremy as they walked together down the nave, 'although it was a horrid business about Gregory Stern, it has helped to make the thing clearer.'

'A message of sacrifice? A re-enactment of God's dying for our sins?'

'No. A re-enactment of God's dying in repentance for His own sins. A re-enactment of the penance of God for His abominable cruelty to His creatures, which is illustrated rather neatly by the picture beneath today's crucifixion.'

'God's cruelty illustrated by Asolano . . . but not explained, you say?'

'How can it be explained?'

'Very simply,' Fielding said. 'God commits cruel acts because God is cruel. However, whatever that picture omits by way of explanation, you indicated just now that it gave you hope – it suggested a course of action, you said, and therefore a possible means of absolution. What action? What absolution?'

'That, as I also said, is what I am going to Torcello to find out – or rather to confirm. The absolution I refer to is, of course, personal – for you and for me. There can be no possible absolution for God.'

'Not even though He had Himself crucified to show His repentance?'

'No. Too little and too late. The agony on the cross was insufficient to pay for a whole eternal Universe of waste and suffering. So no absolution for God, Fielding, but perhaps for humanity . . . in the way suggested by His Mother in that picture.'

'All she is doing is flapping her hands about.'

'You have not understood. Perhaps, when we get to Torcello, you will.'

As Fielding and Jeremy left the Church, Balbo Blakeney came out from behind the High Altar, walked down to the Asolano, and stood in front of it. The usher approached and tugged his sleeve.

'Church is closing now,' the usher said.

'Very well. I shall stay here until it is open again.'

'Is not allowed.'

Balbo turned and looked at the usher. 'This is my picture,' he said: 'I found it. But for me it would never have been given back.'

'You deposit fifty thousand lire with me in case you do damage. Then you stay.'

'Very well.' Balbo handed over the money. 'By the way,' he said, 'can you tell me what they're going to do with the forged Asolano . . . the one that hung here before?'

The usher giggled maliciously.

'When they finish mending it, it come back here. *This* one . . . *real* one . . . too valuable to hang in damp old church for long. So we sell 'im and put up fake again, just like before. Nobody notice. If notice can do nothing. Our picture now.'

The man spat on the floor.

'Bloody damn English. You still want stay? Church open again at sixteen 'undred.'

'Very well,' Balbo said. 'But tell me this before you go: what shall you do with the money you get for this picture? Will the Archbishop of Chioggia decide? Or the Patriarch of Venice?'

The man laughed outright.

'Bloody damn English mind bloody damn business,' he chuckled. 'Me go for *pranzo*.'

For a long time Balbo stood in front of 'La Madonna con i Raggazzi della Peste'.

After a discreet interval, he thought, that little swine and his friends, including the Parocco, who will have to have his cut, will turn this picture into money for the purchase of the pleasures of the flesh; the pleasures that will, if only temporarily, console them for being the filth they are. Well, and why not? thought Balbo. That, in the end, is what the picture is about: the miseries, the filth, and the consolations of the flesh; the miseries inflicted by God on creatures he made from filth; and the consolations about to be administered by His Mother.

'I must say,' said Marigold Helmutt to Sir Jacquiz as they disembarked from one of the Cipriani launches on to a private jetty near the Cathedral on Torcello, 'you got us away from all *that* fast enough. You might have waited for poor old Balbo.'

'He wanted to stay behind. He hadn't had a proper look at the picture in its new situation.'

'A pleasure which you forwent readily enough.'

'Little boys' thighs,' said Jacquiz: 'not my thing.'

'I saw some of the Madonna's face at the top right hand. It was about on a level with Gregory Stern's. She looked rather intriguing. Silly, but intriguing. Then, just as I was getting interested, that poor woman started to bawl out who it was on the cross and you whisked me away. Won't they want to ask you any questions?'

'*I* shall certainly want to ask *them* questions when the sweat has cooled. It was all their fault that the ceremony was ruined – the usual Italian negligence. How did that thing get under the tapestry? Why didn't they look there to make sure that everything was in order before the ceremony began?'

'Obviously they had no idea, at any stage, that anything was there. Why should they have had?'

'How did it get there without their knowing?'

'I suppose . . . someone took it into the empty Church last night . . . and hung it up behind the tapestry.'

'Precisely. There should have been better security.'

'The sort of security we have in England? You know, Burgess and Maclean and that little bugger in the Admiralty and booze lovers like Philby and Philip Toynbee croaking away about how noble they all are.'

'This is a different kind of thing on a different level.'

'Like the Great Train Robbery? That level? How well did you know Gregory Stern?'

'We've had dealings.'

'Did you recognize him when that curtain opened?'

'No. Nobody did, until his wife piped up. I thought it was a carving.'

Jacquiz paid a man at a table and they went into the Cathedral.

'Why have we come in here?' Marigold asked.

'Because luncheon won't be ready yet.'

'I don't think much of that Madonna under the apse.

Cold fish. When did you realize that he wasn't a carving – Gregory Stern, I mean?'

'When Mrs Stern started up.'

'I think I'd realized just before. Who on earth could have done it?'

'He's been writing a lot of very nasty things about Jews and Israelis. Perhaps the Israelis did it . . . to stop him from writing any more.'

'What did you think about the stuff he wrote? You're a Jew.'

'A lot of it was true – certainly when he said that the Israelis have no title to Israel. The trouble was that he was hysterical.'

'So now the Jews have punished him for his hysteria?'

'No. For the bits that made sense,' said Jacquiz. 'The truth is what they don't care for.'

Leonard Percival, who had just come in and was loitering under the ambo, had heard the end of this conversation and wondered whether he should set these people right. Then he realized that everyone would make his own interpretation of the apparition in San Martino and that he couldn't go round putting right all those millions, who, like this couple, were going to get it wrong. Gregory would just have to take his chance.

'There are those two enormous girls who were there,' Marigold was saying. 'I wonder whether Baby Canteloupe has been able to change her knickers yet? I used to carry a spare pair in my handbag, but that was for another reason. What are those birds on that screen?'

'Peacocks. They symbolize wisdom.'

'I thought it was vanity they symbolized. What a lovely little wop that is who's just come in. Pity about his club foot. What do you actually look like, club feet? Do you think he'd show me his? Hullo there,' she called to Piero, who was looking at the Last Judgment on the West Wall, '*Ciao.*'

'For Christ's sake,' said Sir Jacquiz, 'let's see if we can find a drink.'

'God, you are being dreary. I only wanted – Ouch,' Marigold screeched, 'you're hurting,' as Jacquiz hustled her out of the Cathedral, 'you filthy *pig*.'

Piero, Leonard Percival, Theodosia and Carmilla all turned towards the noises of altercation, saw Jacquiz and Marigold disappear through the South Door into the portico and then, a few seconds later and just as they were all about to turn back, saw Fielding Gray and Jeremy Morrison enter from the portico through the South Door. Percival left the cover of the ambo, Theodosia and Carmilla came marching down the steps from the throne, and Piero forgot the torments of the damned, as all four converged on the new arrivals.

After Fielding Gray, the only person present who knew who everybody else was, had explained to the Salingers about Leonard Percival and Piero Caspar, and to Jeremy and Piero about Leonard Percival, and so on and so forth, the business of the congregation by the South Door in the Cathedral on Torcello was summed up by Piero in one word to Jeremy:

'Why?'

'If you mean, why am I here,' Jeremy replied, 'the answer is that something happened to me which required an explanation – and indeed rather more than that. In any case I could not return to Lancaster until I'd had some sort of enlightenment.'

'So you looked for it here?' said Theodosia.

'And did you find it?' said Carmilla.

'That remains to be seen.'

'First things first,' said Fielding Gray. 'What exactly happened, that afternoon in the Fens? Baby Canteloupe, we know, had some kind of seizure, and you were so horrified that you took off there and then. But what happened to bring all this on?'

'Piero left me alone with Lady Canteloupe while he went to fetch the backgammon set. In order to make conversation, I . . . I . . .'

'. . . Yes . . . ?'

'I told her that last time I had gone to visit my brother Nicholas at St Bede's, I saw her mother with – '

' – I see,' said Fielding; 'a really cosy topic for a few minutes' casual conversation.'

' – Don't interrupt me, God damn your eyes,' said Jeremy. 'What I was going to say, the whole point of it all, was that I saw her mother *with* Nickie, and that she seemed to be taking care of him, and that he seemed to be responding, in so far as he has anything left to respond with.'

'You see?' said Theodosia hotly to Fielding.

'I see,' said Fielding. And then, doing his best to make up for his brashness: 'You felt that it gave you something in common . . . that Baby would be glad to know that her mother had a useful and affectionate connection . . . with a relation of somebody whom she knew.'

'That's it, more or less,' Jeremy said. 'And at first it looked as if I had got the thing right. She went rather quiet and thoughtful, and said that her mother had always liked boys, having never had a son of her own. So I said that Nickie wasn't exactly a boy any more, but that

308

she seemed to be treating him as one and that in the circumstances it was rather a happy arrangement, I thought. "Oh did you," she said, and started shaking all over, "well, did you know what had happened to the last boy she had fancied, before she went into St Bede's?"

"No, I didn't know," I said, which wasn't true as I'd heard rumours, but I thought this was the best reply, so, "No," I said, "I didn't know, I'm sorry," but by then she was no longer hearing, she was crouching on the bed, hissing. Hissing. "I'm sorry," I said. "I didn't know," and by this time what I meant was that I didn't know this conversation could possibly bring about such ghastliness or why; but as I say, she was way past hearing or understanding, just crouching there hissing like some devil in a hell by Bosch.'

'But why *hissing*?' Carmilla Salinger said.

'A very good question,' said Baby Canteloupe's voice.

The congregation turned towards it. Baby was standing under the Last Judgment, where Piero had been a few minutes before.

'Come over here,' said Baby, 'and we shall have judgment. On ourselves – and on God.'

'Ah,' said Jeremy, as if he had long been waiting for something of the kind.

'But first,' said Baby, 'there is a message for Leonard Percival. Canteloupe is looking for you to say that on no account should you reveal that you were watching over Gregory Stern.'

'I lost him,' said Leonard pathetically, 'some days ago. I can't tell them anything . . . except that he was taken off by a woman from the organization with which he was treating. I don't know whether that would help them.'

'Whether it would or not,' said Baby, 'you're to tell them nothing, Canteloupe says. Gregory's dead and there's nothing more to be done about it. If you try to help them, they'll simply keep you here and ask you silly questions for ever. Forget it. And don't think any of it was your fault. Obviously Gregory turned obstinate at last and finally dug his toes in, and he must have known what was coming to him.'

'The trouble is,' said Leonard, 'that a lot of people are going to think that the Israelis did it, to shut his mouth and give warning to others. It would be nice if the truth could be generally known – that it was he himself who shut his mouth, that he refused to go on betraying his own people.'

Carmilla and Theodosia exchanged looks.

'I think we can take care of that,' Theodosia said.

'How?'

'We know an honest man,' said Carmilla, 'whose evidence will be believed.'

'What evidence?' said Percival.

'Simple and conclusive,' said Theodosia: 'please just leave it at that.' And to Baby: 'We shall have judgment, you said.'

'But first,' said Baby, 'you shall have a little history. My mother had no son. I was a surrogate. She told me things . . . taught me things . . . showed me things . . . which, she said, she would have told, taught and shown to me if I'd been a boy. She used to make me lie on her bed, then she'd crouch over me, fully dressed and covering much of me with her skirt, showing me what she would have shown her son, though neither of us could actually *see* what she was doing because it happened under her skirt. I always told my father, who suspected that something of the kind was going on, that she only told me things and *did* nothing. But all the time she was showing me things about my anatomy – or rather, the anatomy which I would have had if only I'd been a boy. I had a little toy snake. She used this for her demonstrations. A little toy snake of rubber. She used to put it into me, very gently, and then she caressed it – all this unseen, under her skirt – saying that this was how I must ease myself if I got tense, rid myself of any tension or strain that might trouble me. As she caressed and fondled the snake, the snake caressed and fondled me. And it disgusted me, too, this great woman crouching over me on the bed, with her sweaty, flabby thighs, unseen but so close to me. Yes, it disgusted me. And yet the excitement was so great that I longed for it. One day, while she was playing with the snake, she began to talk of a young lover she'd had. He'd compared her breasts, which were long and sagging and droopy, to snakes, slipping and sliding snakes. After she told me this, she began to hiss, not for the first time, because she often hissed gently as she rubbed the snake, but this time she hissed more fiercely, and I realized . . . from the movement of her arm where it disappeared under her skirt . . . that she was putting the snake into herself, so that now it was in both of us. Her eyes had gone absolutely blank: she hissed more and more violently, then trembled and heaved and shuddered. After this had stopped, she got off the bed, saying nothing but taking the snake with her, and went away, leaving me there alone with legs still spread on the eiderdown.

'Soon after she went away for good. She'd been going to London more and more often, and now she stayed there and didn't come back, stayed there searching for a more satisfactory son than I could be to her, and in the end found one . . . with disastrous results, because her passion, her lust, whatever it was, unhinged her totally.

'That afternoon in the Fens, when Jeremy Morrison said she was taking care of his brother, I knew, I thought I knew, what she must be doing to him. Crouching over him and covering him with her skirt, hissing. I remembered the sweating, flabby thighs, the movement of the arm as it went beneath the skirt. And then I thought, Piero is playing some game, he wants to make me be with Jeremy, make me be with him like my mother is with his brother Nicholas. Jeremy has the same horrible soft flesh as my mother, his flesh with mine, her flesh with his brother's, my mother crouching over his brother, hissing, crouching over Jeremy, hissing, hissing like my mother hissed that day she lost control, the first time she lost control, and put that snake into herself, and shook and trembled and heaved and hissed. So I too crouched on the bed and hissed, to show him how horrible it was, and I couldn't stop, I just had to go on, remembering my mother crouching and hissing, so disgusting, exciting me with the snake while pretending it was a boy's cock, exciting me and revolting me with her foul flesh, Jeremy's flesh.

'Sorry,' she said to Jeremy: 'I dare say some people like your flesh. They liked my mother's didn't they, Fielding? But it is not for me. Do you understand, Jeremy?'

'I think so.'

'What I do not understand,' said Piero, 'is why this outburst upset Jeremy so much that he had to disappear. I see that it might have unnerved him a bit; but why should he have fled?'

'Yes, why?' Baby said.

'I did not know, then, what had caused her to behave like this,' Jeremy said. 'I could not return to Lancaster and live there with her father, seeing him daily and remembering how his daughter had looked and behaved because of something I had said. I needed explanation – '

' – Yes,' conceded Piero; 'you needed explanation. It wasn't at all nice, what you'd seen. But surely you didn't have to sneak away like Judas – to desert your friends and your College, to snub and to shame us all and worry us half to death, to wander over half Europe – you didn't have to do all *this* simply to find an explanation of what you'd seen on that bed.'

'It wasn't just what I saw on the bed that needed explanation,' Jeremy said, 'though that was very horrible. There was another twist to it all: the way I reacted to it myself. That was far worse. Understand this, all of you: I enjoyed what I was seeing; it gave me . . . delight. It was disgusting, it was atrocious – and I loved and relished it. This little girl who was also Lady Canteloupe, crouching and shuddering and hissing, oh, I didn't know why, not then, but I got the general message, especially the revulsion for myself, and this made me so wild with frustration and suspicion and curiosity and fear and excitement that in three seconds my prick was as hard as a cannon and in ten I'd had the most furious, volcanic orgasm I'd ever experienced. I was revelling in *her* misery and hate and humiliation – that's what it comes down to. *That* was what needed explanation at any cost. Not the incident in itself, ugly as it was, but my demoniac joy of it.'

'You said just now,' said Carmilla, 'that you might find it here. The explanation.'

'Possibly. But I need more than a mere account of cause and association. I need to be told how such horrible things – this demented girl heaving and hissing, and myself taking an almost insane pleasure in the foulness of it all – I need to be told how such things can be *permitted* . . . and what can be done by way of cure or remedy or absolution – or purification.'

'I need to be told too,' Baby said. 'Well, now – now – after this morning on Burano and after *this*' – she pointed to the Madonna at the east end – '*now* both of us have been.'

'Yes. I came here after Burano,' Jeremy said, 'to

confirm that the Madonna, the Madonna under the apse, is weeping.'

'And she is,' said Baby. 'She is weeping a single tear for the misery and agony and impurity permitted – more than permitted, caused and created – by the Malignity of God, Her Son. She is not going to do anything about it. She is far too cold and haughty for that. But she is, at least, moved to weep.'

'And in Burano we saw what is to be done – by way of remedy,' said Jeremy, 'even if the Madonna *here* is too grand and cold to do it.'

'In Burano we saw a sacrifice,' said Leonard Percival: 'a man had sacrificed himself rather than commit shameful acts.'

'Noble but futile. An act, largely, of repentance. Curing nothing. Absolving nothing. Even when God sacrificed Himself,' said Baby, 'it changed nothing. Not one single jot of misery, past or to come, was abated. Gregory's action will help nobody.'

'So Gregory, though he tried hard, got it wrong. But nevertheless we know what action *can* be taken,' said Jeremy, 'to cure and to absolve, to purify impurity. We look to the Mother of God in that other picture on Burano, as I have just been doing . . .'

'. . . And as I did,' said Baby, 'peering through the crucifixion while I stood there pissing myself with the shock.'

'. . . And we tell ourselves,' said Jeremy, 'that we must do what *that* Madonna is about to do. The only thing She can do, offering the only comfort She can offer, probably the only comfort which those diseased boys could understand.'

'She will offer the comfort which my mother is offering your brother,' said Baby Canteloupe. 'I understand now, and it is no longer horrible; her flesh is no longer horrible because it brings comfort, the only comfort she can give or he can receive.'

'And I also understand,' said Jeremy, 'why you appeared to me to be so horrible that afternoon in the Fens, and why the horror filled me with violent lust. It was because neither of us had yet understood what we both understand now, the Malignity and Impurity of God, which His Mother deplores yet cannot prevent, but amid which She can, as Asolano suggests, administer solace.'

'When I was first disfigured by that bomb in Cyprus,' said Fielding Gray, 'I thought my new ugliness was truly horrible. So horrible that I was excited by it, as Jeremy was excited by Baby's fit. I used to stand in front of a glass and masturbate – fast and hard and painfully – in the horror and excitement of my new deformity. The cruelties and impurities which God inflicts can be alleviated only by crude physical pleasure, by more impurities. Later on I found someone else to take pity on me and pleasure me. She understood that the only cure for my hideous condition was the provocation, the satisfaction, the renewal of lust. You weren't so much taking pleasure in Baby's beastly predicament,' he said to Jeremy, 'as consoling yourself for it, as defying God by exhibiting physical tumescence and joy in presence of and in despite of this enormity of His creating.'

'That pornographer,' said Leonard: 'Canzoni. The one who did the water-colours that Detterling sold in California, the pictures of the orgy which followed after the Madonna had seen and pitied the diseased boys . . . Canzoni had the right idea, you think?'

'You might say,' said Baby, 'that Canzoni translates into crude action what Asolano only contemplated as a distant and indefinite possibility. Nevertheless, it is all there in the Asolano Madonna's face and gesture: here is a kindly, decent, rather silly woman, outraged by the suffering she sees, determined to do what she can to comfort those boys, who are diseased and almost certainly doomed, and realizing, or just about to realize, that there is only one thing she can do.'

'Does She like the idea?' Fielding asked.

'According to Canzoni,' said Percival, 'She can hardly wait to begin.'

'Remember that neither I nor my sister have seen Canzoni's pictures,' said Carmilla Salinger.

'Nor I,' said Fielding, 'nor Jeremy. All we've got to go on is the Asolano.'

'According to Asolano, she is resolved but nervous,' said Baby Canteloupe, 'less afraid of contamination, which is a terrible risk, than of failure or rejection. Of her own pleasure she has not yet begun to think, but most of it will probably come from the pleasure and gratitude of those whom she wishes to console. I think that is right,' she said, and then added, rather oddly, 'I may be able to tell you more about this later on, should I again be with you.'

'It is very important,' said Theodosia Salinger to Ivan Blessington a few days later, 'that the Press should get it absolutely clear. So can we please go over your statement once more?'

'Right,' said Ivan. 'I shall tell them that two days after he left England Gregory Stern rang me up from Trieste. He had decided that in no circumstances would he now allow his anti-Jewish book to appear before the public, and would I therefore cancel any arrangements I had made for printing and binding it. Would I also reject any application I might receive from any agency that might subsequently produce a text, allege it to be Stern's and request that it be printed.'

'*That* should make the matter clear enough,' said Carmilla.

'Is the lie substantially true?' said Ivan.

'Substantially,' said Carmilla. 'Lord Canteloupe's Secretary, Leonard Pervical, the person who knows most about what Gregory Stern was doing during the last days before he died, says there is no doubt that Gregory was kidnapped by the anti-Israeli group with whom he had just been holding talks. Gregory, he says, had obviously been getting ready to reject the demands of the group. This is clear from some of the things he had been saying to Mr Percival, things which were obscure when he said them but can now be seen, with benefit of hindsight, to refer to this intention. It is, then, as plain as anything can be that Gregory was murdered, as a punishment and an example, by this anti-Israeli group and not by some Jewish faction. Your statement to the Press should finally silence those who are spreading the latter version.'

'Is it really worth all this trouble?' said Ivan. 'His friends know the truth. Does it really matter that some of the world may have got it wrong?'

'He was trying to make a gesture or a statement,' said Theodosia, 'something to do with the importance of being loyal to one's own people even if one doesn't think very much of them. His death was the result of a positive and voluntary act of self-assertion. We don't want him presented as a mere passive victim of Jewish spite.'

'Amen to that,' said Ivan. 'I have some chums in Fleet Street who'll help me put the word round, and I'll cue off straight away. You two go and have a word with Betty and the girls – they're longing to see you again.'

317

'So you see, sir,' said Jeremy Morrison to his father over luncheon in the Infantry Club, 'I now understand rather more than I did, and I should let you know straight away that I am willing – happy – to fall in with whatever plans you have for me in regard to the estate.'

'What do you now understand that you did not understand before?'

'The importance of taking things as they come and doing one's best, for oneself and others, in the circumstances that obtain. It is a favourite theme of Fielding Gray's and has been emphasized by recent occurrence.'

'Are you still seeing Fielding Gray?'

'We are going to France together in the New Year. If I am to do your will over the estate, sir, you will kindly allow me my own choice of friends.'

'Very well,' said Peter Morrison. 'This generalization you have just made, about taking things as they come, et cetera: please interpret it in particular and practical terms appropriate to your own situation.'

'One: they are taking me back at Lancaster, despite my recent excursion, without making any trouble or conditions – or not so's you'd notice. Two: although I must read hard to make up for lost time, I can nevertheless devote *some* of each vacation to receiving training and instruction in estate management and so forth. Three: very few people on the estate, I now realize, will give a damn, these days, that I am being true to my inheritance and taking on what I regard as a trust; but those few that do understand this – the Chamberlain, Nanny, Mummy's old maid, Sukie – these few, I promise you, will have no cause to be ashamed of me if I can help it.'

'I do not think I can find much fault with any of that,' said Peter. 'You should go to our man in Lincoln's Inn early in the Christmas Vacation, by which time he will have been instructed what arrangements to make about the estate and the money and be able to explain them to you. You will do me the honour of entertaining me in your house at Christmas, Jerry?'

'My house, sir?'

'By Christmas it will be so. You will invite me to stay for a few days before you go away with Fielding?'

'Of course, father. Whatever the legal arrangements, it goes without saying that Luffham is your home whenever you wish until . . . until . . .'

'. . . Until I am dead. Thank you. One more thing I should tell you now, as a decision will be required of you. The likelihood is that a General Election will be held next summer. I shan't stand again; instead I shall be raised to the Peerage in the rank of Life Baron in the Dissolution Honours.'

'And what decision, my dear father, do I have to make about that?'

'Whether or not to style yourself "Honourable". Although you can never inherit the title, you may call yourself "Honourable" just like the son of a proper hereditary peer. On the other hand you may consider, as many do, that it would be inappropriate. I make no objection to either course.'

'But you must have a preference?'

'None, I assure you. I consider all styles and titles to be merely childish toys.'

'Then why will you accept this Barony?'

'Because I have a weakness for childish toys. Like your

319

Provost and my old friend, Sir Thomas Llewyllyn, I hanker after the balls of tinsel that dangle from the tree.'

'You will go into residence immediately,' said Ptolemaeos Tunne to Piero Caspar. 'You will read for the History Tripos. Your fees will be paid by me. You will receive, in addition, a personal allowance of four thousand pounds a year. You will be at my absolute disposal during your vacations, which I shall interpret as beginning one week after the end of Full Term and as ending one week before the beginning of the next Full Term.'

'This is generous, sir.'

'Don't thank me. I had virtually decided to turn you off. Sir Tom Llewyllyn persuaded me otherwise.'

'Why?'

'As for myself, I do not like people to act on whim or impulse, and it seemed to me that you were doing just that when you went with Major Gray. But Sir Tom persuaded me to regard it as an act of genuine loyalty . . . and later pointed out that you had played an important part in reclaiming Jeremy Morrison and assisting his own daughter. He also pointed out that your intimacy with Jeremy – which is to continue, Caspar, at all cost – could be very useful to me in a certain project I have in mind – a project which will require the co-operation of a respected member of the Lower House. Jeremy's father will serve.'

'So I shall get round Girolamo to get round his father . . . to do what you want?'

'Yes. But that will be some time away. Meanwhile, I

repeat, keep close to Jeremy Morrison. Thus and thus. You should present yourself at Lancaster tomorrow. Buy what you need in the shops at Cambridge – here is a letter authorizing you to use my accounts. You will not have your own set of rooms until after the New Year, but for the rest of this term you will be housed in Greco Barraclough's guest room – which will be ample for all your purposes. Do you get on all right with that Greek boy of his?'

'He despises me as a catamite and a whore. I despise him as a prude and a peasant. Nevertheless, we contrive to enjoy each other's company without mention of these little defects.'

'One more thing. Tom thinks that as a Sicilian and a natural adherent of the old gods you may be able to help him with his Dryads.'

'His Dryads, sir?'

Ptolemaeos explained about the nymphs of the avenue.

'A service of exorcism should get rid of them,' Piero said.

'That's the Catholic answer. Tom wants the Pagan. He doesn't want to get rid of them but to propitiate them.'

'Sicilian gutter-boys are not acquainted with the procedures of pre-Christian bucolics.'

'Sicilian gutter-boys are shrewd enough to give pleasure to their patrons by making something plausible up.'

'Of course, sir. But I need say nothing until he consults me?'

'You will have to wait on him tomorrow when you go into residence. He'll probably ask you then.'

In Isobel Stern's house in Chelsea, Jean-Marie Guiscard was giving Oenone her feed. Jo-Jo Guiscard and Isobel were out at some film which Jean-Marie hadn't wanted to see. If he had, Oenone would have been left with the cook, whom she adored almost as much as she adored Jeremy, and who adored her. Since looking after Oenone wasn't the cook's job, he had been offered extra money; but he said he would be quite content without that if only they would all call him 'Beryl'. A day or two later he had appeared in woman's clothing, looking rather like Old Mother Riley, and no one had seen any reason to object, the less so as Rosie was away from home for the time being (not that Rosie would have minded in the least) staying with Tessa Malcolm in Buttock's because Tessa was the only person who could comfort her for her father's death.

All ways round, things might have turned out a lot worse, Jean-Marie Guiscard thought. The house was comfortable, Beryl's food quite excellent, Oenone contented, and Jo-Jo blissfully happy being married to Isobel. Who was he to complain and spoil everyone else's pleasure? He had his own source of satisfaction: his book, *La Demoiselle d'Arques*, was to appear both in French and English early in the New Year. Canteloupe said Stern & Detterling had already had good offers for the English version from Penguin and a leading house in New York. Meanwhile, Jean-Marie had now started research on a new book – Cathar practices in the Pyrenees – and there would be plenty of money and no hindrance from Jo-Jo

322

when he went off to Pau to do field-work in the Spring. To crown his blessings, he could reflect that his parents, who would not have approved of this state of affairs, were safely dead. Happy the man, he thought, whose parents are dead before he is forty and do not hang about to be a bloody boring nuisance.

'I've had an invitation,' said Sir Jacquiz Helmutt to Lady Helmutt (Marigold), 'to attend a Memorial Luncheon that's being got up for Gregory Stern.'

'A Memorial Luncheon? I don't think I've ever heard of one of those before.'

'No more have I. But they've got to do something for the old boy pretty soon. They can't have a Memorial *Service* because they haven't even buried him.'

'Why not?' said Marigold. 'Why not before they bury him?'

'Because it just isn't done. The form is that you bury Caesar before you praise him . . . otherwise there might be a nasty row, as there was in the play, if not necessarily for the same reasons.'

'You mean, the corpse might get up and hit people if they didn't say the right things.'

'Something of the kind. There is a deep and atavistic fear which dictates the conventional procedure . . . which is, in any case,' said Sir Jacquiz wearily, 'to have a funeral before you have a Memorial Service. Now, a funeral they *cannot* have, because the body is being kept on ice by the Italian Police to assist in their investigations. Since it is the only thing that they have to assist them they'll probably hang on to it for months.'

'Do you mean . . . that of all the people at that service at Burano, no one can tell them anything?'

'I mean exactly that. That's why everyone was allowed to leave Italy without any fuss. Even the Italians were capable of seeing that none of us could have anything to tell them. We went to see a picture unveiled, and when the curtain opened there was a corpse on a cross. What more could anyone conceivably tell them? Even those who knew Gregory can't add anything . . . except that after a time they recognized the body as his, and were rather taken aback as he was supposed to be touring round Greece. The whole thing was obviously the work of some organization which he had displeased . . . the PLO or something similar, the papers say now, but I still think it may have been Jews or Israelis . . . and in either case the police are going to get nowhere. The people who did it left no clue and no message (rather odd that – these days terrorists are usually very keen to claim their crimes) and were no doubt hundreds of miles away before the ceremony even started. So the Italians, though impotent, are hanging on to the body as an earnest of their futile good intentions; any interment will have to wait till God knows when; and Canteloupe and the widow are arranging a Memorial Luncheon straight away instead. Do you want to come?'

'When?'

'Thursday.'

'I'm taking the twins to the psychiatrist. The new man – very booked up, so I can't change it.'

'Do you think he'll be able to get through to them?'

'No. But we must try everything.'

'I suppose so. Very well. I'll accept for myself alone,' Sir Jacquiz said, 'though I very much dislike Memorial

324

Functions. When somebody's dead the best thing you can do, for their sake and yours, is forget about them.'

'Oh, come, come. "Let us now praise famous men," and all that.'

'By all means, while they're still alive. Why bother when they can no longer hear you?'

Rosie Stern and Tessa Malcolm were doing their homework in Buttock's Hotel. Fielding Gray came in to see if they needed any help, and Maisie Malcolm came in a few moments later to fetch him out again as she wanted his advice (or so she said) about the rather striking shade of crimson proposed by the decorators for the new curtains in the Dining Room.

'Your Aunt Maisie,' said Rosie to Tessa, 'does not like it when Major Gray pays you attention.'

'She never used to mind.'

'She does now. That's why she's so pleased to have me staying – because I'm always with you and he can't get at you alone. But even as it is, even though I *am* with you, she still comes and takes him away again . . . as she did just now.'

'Major Gray,' said Tessa, 'never so much as touches me. He used to kiss me and occasionally pat me on my shoulder; these days he doesn't even do that. So if Aunt Maisie thinks . . . anything funny about him and me . . . it's all in her imagination.'

'Perhaps he's tempted. Perhaps that's why he doesn't pat you or kiss you any longer – because he thinks that if he did he'd be tempted even more. Perhaps your Aunt realizes this and is determined to keep him away from temptation.'

'If you go on talking like this,' said Tessa in her husky little voice (huskier than usual since she was annoyed), 'I shan't be quite so glad that you're staying here.'

'If I went, you wouldn't have me as chaperon,' said Rosie, 'and think what might happen then.'

'I told you, Rosie Stern: nothing has happened and nothing ever will. Major Gray is like my father.'

'But you still fancy him, don't you?'

Tessa went as crimson as the new curtains proposed for the Dining Room.

'If your father hadn't been murdered – '

' – I'm sorry. I mustn't take advantage. Darling Tessa, I'm sorry. I promise I'll never talk about you and Major Gray again.'

'All right. I'll forgive you – on one condition.'

'What?'

'That you stop making a fuss about going to your father's Memorial Luncheon.'

'I don't want to go – but I'll go if you'll come with me.'

'I haven't been asked.'

'You should have been. We both know how much he loved you.'

'I haven't been asked,' Tessa said. 'And if you want me to forgive you for what you said, you'll go with Marius and your mother and behave as nicely as you know how.'

'I wonder whether that woman friend of Mummy's is coming?'

'Of course she is. She is the wife of Jean-Marie Guiscard, whose first book is being published by your father's firm. So he will attend, and Madame Guiscard, as his wife, will come with him.'

Rosie smirked in an ugly manner.

'Your Aunt Maisie isn't the only one who's glad I'm staying on here,' she said.

'Of course she's not. I am too . . . if only you won't say silly things.'

'I've promised not to – about you.'

'Silly things about *anybody*, Rosie. About Madame Guiscard, for example.'

'I've said nothing about her, except to wonder if she'd come to the Memorial thing.'

Tessa sighed.

'You said it in a certain way . . . and with a certain kind of look.'

'All right,' said Rosie. 'I won't say anything like that, ever again. I've just been imagining things, like your Aunt Maisie must have been imagining them about you and Major Gray.'

'Lord Canteloupe has written to me,' said Theodosia Salinger to her sister.

They were standing side by side, looking out over the Great Lawn of Lancaster from a window in Carmilla's set in Sitwell's Building.

'First of all,' said Theodosia, 'he is inviting us to the Memorial Luncheon for Gregory Stern.'

'Need we go? We never really knew Gregory Stern, and I've got such a lot of work to do. That trip to Venice has put me right behind.'

'And I've got a Tennis Match that day anyhow. No. We won't go to the lunch. But there's another invitation in Canteloupe's letter. He wants you and me to go to him in Wiltshire for Christmas. Not just Christmas, but the whole of the vacation. And to come for other vacations too.'

'He likes you,' said Carmilla. 'Lady Canteloupe has gone off to work in that leper colony and there's going to be a divorce, the papers say. Lord Canteloupe likes you.'

'I hope so. I like him.'

'What about Jeremy?'

'That's over, Carm. Strictly no good for either of us. The night after the ceremony he came to my room in that Locanda on Torcello. Because I loved him and we'd come a long way to find him I tried to do what he asked. I couldn't. That horrible great *club* of his. I don't want that inside me or anywhere near me. I never shall. Or any other man's. So when he couldn't get it into me, Jeremy insisted on . . . making stuff all over me instead. I hated that too. Now . . . Canteloupe would never want to do anything like that.'

'How do you know?'

'He hinted . . . ever so delicately . . . in his letter.'

'Perhaps he wants you as a mother for Sarum.'

'Tullius, he always calls him.'

'A mother for Tullius then. Should you take that on?'

'If I could finish this last year here first, and still go on playing tennis and badminton later.'

'I can't imagine Canteloupe stopping you – him of all people . . . You . . . parted friends . . . with Jeremy?'

'Oh yes. And he's been to see me, since we've been back here, to say he'll return all that money he had. He'll give it back to me in January, he says. His father's making some new settlement.'

'So that won't cost him much trouble – repaying you, I mean.'

'No. But it's nice to have things straight – even though neither of us now needs the money.'

'Balancing the account?'

'That's it,' said Theodosia. 'Balance the account, draw a couple of lines to indicate finality, and close that particular book.'

'Lonely,' said Canteloupe. 'Do you find it lonely, Leonard? Baby gone, Jo-Jo gone, Jean-Marie gone. This morning I went into that room where Jean-Marie did his typing . . . and looked out on that copse where Jo-Jo and Baby used to play backgammon and read to each other. Now that winter is here the trees are bare, and you can see the pond in the middle. Jo-Jo always used to tell us how much Jean-Marie would enjoy looking out on that copse when the autumn came and the winter. But now they're all gone. Nobody left to sit in it or look at it.'

'Sarum is here.'

'Tullius.'

'Tullius and Daisy.'

'Daisy is only a Nanny when all is said.'

'You say the Salinger girls have accepted for Christmas?'

'Yes.'

'For the whole of their vacation?'

'Almost. They need two days in London to talk business with Ivan Blessington. Then they'll have till term begins again.'

'Well then,' said Leonard, 'you've got that to look forward to.'

'But will they come back at Easter?' said Canteloupe.

'That's up to you, Detterling.'

329

Daisy brought Sarum in to say good-night. The two men rose and looked at him as he snuggled happily in Daisy's arm.

'Baby agreed with Max de Freville,' said Canteloupe at length, 'that he has Piero's eyes.'

'He has his own eyes, my Lord,' said Daisy.

'Then let's hope they are as sharp as Piero's.'

'Who is Piero, my Lord?'

'An old friend of her Ladyship. Now an undergraduate at Cambridge.'

'An old friend of her Ladyship, my Lord? When he's still a boy at College?'

'He first met my wife when they were both very young. But even then he wasn't exactly a boy . . . or not at heart. I can't really explain, my dear, except by saying that some people are born old. I wonder whether that is the case with Tullius?'

In the end Fielding Gray took Rosie to Gregory's Memorial Luncheon, at which they sat with Marius and Isobel at the end of one table. Marius had special leave from school to attend, which he had not wanted to do as there was an important football match that day at Oudenarde House; but Glinter Parkes had insisted (though Isobel might have given way if pressed in the matter). 'There are certain pieties which have to be observed,' Glinter had said to Marius, 'and this is one of them. It is tremendously boring and annoying for you, I know, but since boredom and annoyance make up ninety per cent of life, you must learn to put up with them.'

Marius quoted this remark to Fielding, and was overheard by Jo-Jo Guiscard, who had come separately with her husband and had stopped, on the way to her seat, for a quick word with Isobel.

'That is a very negative remark,' Jo-Jo said. 'There are times when life is ninety per cent happiness.'

'I wish I could remember a few,' Fielding said.

'Have you never been in love?' said Jo-Jo.

'The first person with whom I was in love shot himself,' said Fielding, 'and the next, as I later discovered, was being paid to deceive and decoy me.'

'How interesting,' said Rosie. 'Is it only other men you fall in love with?'

'No,' said Fielding. 'I was just giving Madame Guiscard some examples of love affairs which have made my life rather less than ninety per cent happy.'

'All very negative,' said Jo-Jo, and went on her way to sit by Leonard Percival.

'What news of Baby?' she said to Leonard.

'Nothing much, apart from what you can read in the papers. Detterling has had a wire to say that she has been accepted as a probationer and is very happy.'

'What on earth is she going to do there?'

'You know what St Francis is supposed to have done with lepers?'

'Yes.'

'That, or something of the kind, is what she will do ... if I am to judge from her conversation in the Cathedral on Torcello.'

Much to everyone's surprise, Maisie Malcolm, who had not been invited (since no one except Fielding, who was sworn to silence, knew of any good reason for inviting her) turned up in time for the big speech, which was to be made by Gregory's old partner, Canteloupe. At a sign from Fielding, she was given a seat and a glass between

Jean-Marie Guiscard and Jeremy Morrison, who had accompanied his father to the Luncheon, and not very far from Tom Llewyllyn, who had been compelled to come by Len on the ground that Gregory had been Tom's first publisher. Maisie arrived just as Ptolemaeos Tunne was concluding a preliminary speech, which had some witty jokes in it made up by his secretary elect, Piero Caspar. Piero, like Jeremy, had come up for the day from Lancaster and now sat between Len and the Literary Editor of *The Scrutator*, who made a peculiar braying noise when Canteloupe rose to make his speech and propose the toast to Gregory.

Since Canteloupe was a bad speaker, and had indeed taken on this task only because it was an absolute duty ('piety' as Glinter might have said), his speech, which he read in a low monotone, fell pretty flat . . . or rather, it would have done, had it not been for the spectacular behaviour of Mrs Maisie Malcolm, who, as all raised their glasses at Canteloupe's feeble behest, climbed on to the table and,

'"A was a man,"' she proclaimed, remembering one of Tessa's holiday books, '"Take him for all in all, thou shalt not look upon his like again."' She drained her glass in a bumper, and then, remembering (though less precisely this time) another of Tessa's holiday books, 'Let his sword go to him that can get it,' she cried and flung her glass over her shoulder, thus quite seriously wounding the Literary Editor of *The Scrutator* on the crown of his bald head.

After the luncheon, while the Literary Editor of *The Scrutator* was being carted off by self-important ambulance men and everyone else was milling about between the tables, Jeremy came over to talk to Fielding about the trip they were planning to France for the New Year.

When they had been talking for a few minutes, Marius tugged at Jeremy's sleeve.

'I'm sorry I was unfriendly when you came to Birchington that day,' he said. 'You took me by surprise. And I didn't want Palairet to be jealous.'

'Do you like Palairet?'

'Yes. But he is very stupid. I need to be with intelligent people. Ask Major Gray to take me with you over the New Year.'

'But your mother – '

' – Will be delighted to have me out of the way. She doesn't need me in the way she used to. I could tell when I came up last night. She'll happily pay to have me off her hands for most of the holidays.'

'No need for that. I can pay for you,' said Jeremy grandly.

'But she'll want to pay, so that she won't feel guilty. Rosie told me at lunch that she insists on paying Mrs Malcolm more than ever to keep Rosie at Buttock's. Rather splendid what Mrs Malcolm said, didn't you think? I intend that my father's sword shall come to me.'

'Then you must get it.'

'I know. Can I come with you and Fielding?'

'Yes,' said Fielding, who had been pretending to listen

to Isobel's very boring talk about her affair with Jo-Jo but had really been overhearing the exchange between Marius and Jeremy, of which he much approved. 'Yes,' he said. 'Of course you can come. We'll leave the day after Boxing Day,' he said to Jeremy. 'You owe it to your father to spend Christmas with him, otherwise we'd go even earlier.'

'But you too will be engaged for Christmas,' said Jeremy. 'At Buttock's with Mrs Malcolm.'

'I don't think Mrs Malcolm will mind much when I leave.'

'But Tessa – '

' – We'll leave the day after Boxing Day,' said Fielding, abruptly settling the matter; and to Marius, 'I should be very surprised, from what I've been hearing, if your mother makes any objection, but you must get her formal permission.'

'I'll tell her I want to talk with men like you to make me do well in my scholarship exam next summer.'

'She won't need to be told that. Just go and ask her now.'

Isobel had moved off to talk with Piero and Len.

'Did Tom really ask you that,' she was saying to Piero: 'what to do about the Dryads in his avenue?'

'Really and very seriously,' Piero said.

'What did you tell him?'

'That wood-nymphs like attractive young men. Now, there had been some talk about turning Jeremy Morrison out of his nice rooms by the river as a punishment for his absence without leave. That would make the nymphs very angry, I said, as his present rooms are very near their avenue and they like boys like him to be near them.'

'The thing was,' said Len, 'that some of the left-wing gang wanted Jeremy punished to spite his father and show that there was no longer any privilege in Lancaster.

Although Tom stands up to the left pretty well, he felt that he might have to yield over this – after all, Jeremy was badly in the wrong, just taking off without a word – but Piero's advice about the wood-nymphs carried the day.'

'Lucky Jeremy,' said Isobel as Marius came up and took her hand. 'Yes, my darling?'

'Can I go with lucky Jeremy and Major Gray to France the day after Boxing Day?'

'Do they want you?'

'They say they do.'

'Well, I suppose so. But why do you want to go?'

'If I am to get my father's sword,' said Marius, 'I must learn from men like them and not hang around with a lot of women.'

'Even Achilles lingered a while among women,' remarked Len.

'Only until someone showed him a sword,' said Isobel; 'and then he was off. "The Minstrel Boy to the war is gone",' she quoted, '"In the ranks of death you'll find him. His father's sword he has girded on" – or that's what he aspires to do – "And his wild harp slung behind him." All right, my little minstrel boy,' she said to Marius, touching the lobe of his ear. 'It is high time you left your Mummy in the women's quarters and went to the war. In another and better age we could have sent you to sea with the Royal Letter or purchased a pair of colours for you in a regiment on foreign campaign. As it is, we will send you to the vasty fields of France as Ensign to Fielding Gray and Jeremy Morrison, with a comfortable wad of Travellers' Cheques. And one thing more.'

She felt in her handbag and produced a gold ring which held a cornelian incised with a dolphin.

'Kneel, Marius,' she said.

Marius knelt on one knee before his mother.

'This was your father's ring,' she said. 'He gave it to me before he left on his last journey, so that I knew, although he did not tell me, much of what might happen. I now commit it into your keeping.' She placed it in the palm of Marius' right hand. 'Wear it with honour.'